Praise for Beth Williamson's
Devils on Horseback: Zeke

Rating: 4 Stars "Williamson successfully captures the flavor of a traditional Old West town in her third entry in the Devils on Horseback series. Her characters leap off the pages as they wage the traditional battle of good versus evil."

~ *Romantic Times Book Reviews*

Nymph Rating: 4.5 Nymphs "I love this series and Devils on Horseback - Zeke has cemented that fondness! ...If you're a fan of the series, you truly won't be disappointed."

~ *Scandalous Minx, Literary Nymphs Reviews*

Rating: 5 Angels "Beth Williamson is firmly stamped on my must buy list. Devils on Horseback: Zeke held me in its grip from the minute I opened it. Zeke is so wounded, so raw, and so appealing that I just couldn't put the book down. ...pick up the Devils on Horseback series by Beth Williamson today."

~ *Rachel C., Fallen Angel Reviews*

"Grab the tissues ladies and indulge yourself with this wonderful Western romance. No one can write a western like Beth Williamson and Devils on Horseback – Zeke is just an amazing read. I hated to finish it."

~ *Talia Ricci, Joyfully Reviewed*

Rating: 5 Hearts   "This third offering in the Devils on Horseback series has maintained, if not surpassed, the expectations of Williamson's fans. The book is certainly worth waiting for, as I am awaiting her next book. I guarantee that you will be thrilled that you took the time to read this and then you will anxiously await, as do I, her next rendition."

~ Brenda Talley, The Romance Studio

Blue Ribbon Rating: 5 "DEVILS ON HORSEBACK: ZEKE is a highly entertaining, historical erotica romance. ...Brimming with humor, an entertaining plot, a feisty heroine and a vulnerable, yet strong hero, this is a fun story that is sure to be a winner. I recommend DEVILS ON HORSEBACK: ZEKE to those looking for a truly delightful erotica romance."

~ Dottie, Romance Junkies

Look for these titles by *Beth Williamson*

Now Available:

Devils on Horseback: Zeke

Beth Williamson

A Samhain Publishing, Ltd. publication.

Samhain Publishing, Ltd.
577 Mulberry Street, Suite 1520
Macon, GA 31201
www.samhainpublishing.com

Devils on Horseback: Zeke
Copyright © 2009 by Beth Williamson
Print ISBN: 978-1-60504-424-8
Digital ISBN: 978-1-60504-238-1

Editing by Sasha Knight
Cover by Scott Carpenter

First Samhain Publishing, Ltd. electronic publication: December 2008
First Samhain Publishing, Ltd. print publication: October 2009

Dedication

To every person out there, man or woman, who has endured suffering in silence, who does not speak of their pain for fear of the unknown, and who has survived that which might have broken others. You are not alone, know that there are others like you who stand beside you.

Live life knowing you are loved.

Prologue

March, 1866

Tanger, Texas

"What the hell is that smell?"

Zeke Blackwood opened one eye against the bright light streaming in the window. When a thousand pain pricks shot through his head, he groaned and rolled over.

"Get out, Lee." His voice sounded like a broken violin string.

His younger brother, as usual, didn't listen. "It fucking stinks in here. Did something die?"

"Shut up and *get out.*" Zeke rubbed his hands down his face, the scrape of whiskers loud in the quiet room. Agony shot through his fingers and he blearily tried to focus on them. Were they broken?

"You know it's almost noon. Gid and I have been working like dogs to get the damn restaurant rebuilt and you lay in here like you ain't got nothing to do." Lee pushed at his shoulder. "I'm sick of it."

Zeke barked out a laugh. "Me too. Sick of life, sick of nothing but old ladies and bad food. Sick of never sleeping more than an hour or two at a time."

Six months of darkness, each day even worse than the last,

had pushed him so far down into a whiskey bottle he didn't think he'd make it out. The only person who still talked to him was Lucy Michaelson, the saloon owner. The red-haired beauty had accepted him as he was without pretense, thereby becoming the recipient of Zeke's drunken rants. He wanted nothing more than to forget all the bloody memories dancing around in his mind. However, whiskey had only served to make them dance faster.

He made it to the edge of the bed and rolled until he reached the floor. The world shifted beneath his feet as he finally made it upright, at least until his gut decided to heave the opposite direction. Zeke dropped to his knees and groped blindly for the chamber pot. After he emptied the contents of his stomach—about half a bottle of cheap whiskey—he leaned his head against the side of the bed and closed his eyes. The silence in the room was only broken by his heavy breathing. Lee must have given up.

A damp cloth was shoved in his hand. "I ain't gonna clean up your leavings." Lee hadn't left after all. He'd just gone to get a rag.

Zeke was infinitely glad his brother had only lost an arm in the war instead of his life. He didn't know what he'd do without him.

As Zeke brought the rag to his mouth, his hand shook so bad, it looked like it belonged to an old man, instead of a twenty-five-year-old. A sob almost erupted from his throat and he slammed his lips shut to keep it from escaping. He'd never been as miserable or pitiful, even during the unending days in the Yankee prison camp. He closed his eyes against the prick of tears when Lee's hand landed on his shoulder.

"The whiskey's gonna kill you, Zeke. You gotta stop." Lee was usually caustic and could be counted on for always telling the truth no matter how brutal. This time his tone didn't match his words, in fact, he sounded almost gentle.

Zeke's throat tightened as he struggled to speak. "I...I can't. Jesus, Lee, I... The nightmares get so bad. I need the whiskey to forget, to have peace." He fisted his right hand, the nails biting into the clammy skin of his palm. The left hand was unable to make a fist since two of the fingers hurt like hell.

He didn't want his friends to know how bad his drinking was, but there was no hiding it from Lee. Zeke was a mess, inside and out. He had no purpose anymore, nothing to look forward to. His nightmares about what happened six months earlier replayed themselves over and over. Whiskey helped dull the sharpness of the pain.

Too many mornings he'd woken with a pounding head, a taste in his mouth like old shoes, and no memory of how he ended up in his bed. The sheets smelled like old sweat, vomit and desperation. Zeke knew one day he wouldn't wake up in his bed. Perhaps he wouldn't wake up at all.

"Yes you can. Don't be such a baby, just quit." Lee sat down heavily on the mattress, pushing rancid air past Zeke's nose.

His stomach heaved against the stench, but he swallowed back the bile. "I can't. For once in my fucking life, I just *can't.*"

Lee put his palm on Zeke's head, the comforting warmth seeping down through his matted hair. "Then for once in your life, let *me* help *you.*"

Zeke closed his eyes as the tears rolled down his face. He reached out for his brother, reached out for the lifeline he needed to survive.

Chapter One

June 1866

"Yes, you have to wash the damn dishes." Lee threw his arm in the air. "How do you expect me to do it?"

Zeke scowled at the piles of dirty tin plates in the wooden sink. "It wasn't my idea to rebuild this place and I don't know shit about running a restaurant. Gideon needs to hire somebody who does."

Lee narrowed his gaze. "Washing dishes don't require nothing but water, soap and two hands."

"That's not what I'm talking about and you know it." Zeke picked up the bucket of hot water from the stove and poured it on the dishes. "We're lucky nobody has taste buds in this town or Gideon's cooking would've killed them. You can't be a waitress worth shit and I'm damn sick and tired of doing dishes." He added a bucket of cold water to the mix. "We need a woman."

"Speak for yourself. I don't need a woman." Lee harrumphed. "The ladies in this town are crazy anyway."

It had been a long three months since he'd sworn off booze, made even longer by Zeke's constant thirst for whiskey, as well as the battle against his dark memories. He'd fought hard and long, with the help of his brother, cousin Gideon and friend Jake, to conquer the demon that had taken over his soul. He'd likely always have to fight that particular demon, but Zeke was waking up in the morning clearheaded again. The thought of being with a woman, however, made the demon dig its claws in deep. Because then he remembered Allison, and the other woman who had taken him on a ride into hell, Veronica Marchison. He just wanted to forget.

It took great effort to ignore the pain and think about what had to be done for the business. D.H. Enterprises had gone from being gunslingers to restaurant owners.

They'd been in Tanger for almost a year and had become true citizens. Their friend Jake had married the miller's daughter, Gabby, and been voted onto the town council. Gideon, Lee and Zeke had rebuilt the restaurant that had burned last year, contributing to the rebirth of a town almost laid to waste by raiders.

New folks were even starting to move into town every day. Gideon had been smart enough to suggest rebuilding the burned-out structure for half of the business from the owner, Cindy Cooley. She had been the victim of the raiders, and now spent her days at the mill recovering from the experiences that scarred her, both physically and emotionally.

With Cindy's approval, the Devils had worked to get the restaurant rebuilt. It gave Zeke something to focus on, at least for a short while. Now, however, the problem was three single men having no experience with restaurants—other than eating in them on occasion—had no idea what they were doing.

"What about Cindy? Is she coming out of her bedroom anytime soon?" Lee looked towards the mill.

"Probably not. She suffered two months of God knows what at the hands of those raiders. I wouldn't want to come out either and face this place without her granddaddy." Zeke still missed the old codger and even sometimes missed the coffee he brewed that a spoon could stand up in.

"Then we need to hire somebody else and soon." Lee tossed a towel at Zeke.

He caught the towel before it hit him in the face. "Talk to Jake, he'll know who to ask. The man knows every person in town." Their friend Jake was the most comfortable with the people of Tanger, as well as being the most social. With he and his wife running the flour mill, Jake had many opportunities to use those skills.

"Good idea. I'll go see him now." Lee headed out the back door after shooting a smirk at his brother, leaving Zeke to finish the dishes alone.

With a snort at the indignity of doing such a menial chore, Zeke plunged his hands into the soapy water and got busy.

Gideon walked into the kitchen a short time later and grinned when he saw what Zeke was doing. "He left you again, didn't he? Lee's getting too big for his britches. We're gonna have to put a stop to that."

"Tells me he can't do dishes with one arm." Zeke dipped the clean plate into the bucket of cool water. "He went to talk to Jake. See if we can figure out who can work here, 'cause, Gid, your cooking is gonna kill us."

Gideon laughed, a huge gut-busting guffaw that came from somewhere near his toes. Zeke's smile was genuine at the sound of his cousin's mirth.

"That's the gospel truth and I won't deny it. But right now I have something to talk to you about." Gideon picked up the towel and started drying the clean plates. "With so many new folks arriving, Tanger needs a lawman. You have a mind to be sheriff?"

Shock rippled through him at the suggestion. Zeke dropped the plate in his hand into the sink, splashing his shirt and the front of his trousers. Cursing softly, he took the towel back from Gideon and tried to save some of his dignity.

"Who the hell suggested that? And had they been drinking, 'cause only a drunk would suggest a drunk for a sheriff."

Gideon pointed at Zeke's wet shirt. "Even with your obvious clumsiness, the town council talked about it just this morning and voted to give you thirty days to prove you could do the job."

Zeke had spent six months showing the town exactly how useless he was and what an ass he could be while drinking. It was unlikely the citizens of Tanger would choose the drunkest, most reticent man who'd settled in town less than a year earlier.

"They want *me* to be sheriff?" Zeke frowned at his cousin. "Are you sure you heard them right? And what do you mean thirty days?"

Gideon ran his fingers through his curly brown hair and shrugged. "That's what the town council voted on, and now that Jake is one of the members, he knows what they talk about. You see, some of them ain't convinced you're the right man, some are, so they want to give you thirty days to prove you are. Then you get the job permanently."

Zeke had never heard of such a thing. "I ain't no lawman, Gid." He was an experienced strategist, a planner, a soldier. Upholding the law was marginal at best during a war, and this job would force him to be very exacting in that regard. There were rules, strict rules he would have to follow.

"You've never been a lawman, but that doesn't mean you can't be. You were a good soldier, no, you were a *great* soldier. You can do it. I think you should do it." Gideon seemed to be convinced.

God knew Zeke needed to do something, anything to remember what being a man felt like. He'd been floating along with no direction, nothing to hold onto, to be proud of. Being a lawman would likely make his battle against whiskey that much harder. However, it would also bring structure to a meaningless existence.

"What happens during the thirty days?" Zeke found himself wanting to know more about the job, *needing* to know more.

"Well, I guess you need to be a good citizen, help folks when they need it, keep the peace as best you can. I'm sure the council will give you the particulars."

Zeke looked out the window, considering what he'd be agreeing to. He'd be judged by what he did, or didn't do, expected to behave, no doubt that included no whiskey or women. What would all that get him? A respectable job, something to grab onto. A purpose.

If the town council really wanted him as sheriff, Zeke Blackwood was up for the challenge. God help them all.

"Okay, I'll do it."

Gideon smiled and smacked him on the shoulder. "I knew you would. Doing dishes would drive any man loco."

Zeke swallowed back the urge to celebrate with a shot of booze. He tried to grin back, but settled for a small smile. "I can't wait to tell Lee."

The town council was made up of an odd assortment of people, including old women, even older men, Jake and Gabby. The red-haired Devil and his raven-haired wife had to be at least thirty years younger than anyone else at the table.

Zeke wasn't sure what to feel, other than nervous, which he refused to allow himself to be. He said his polite hellos, grateful for the presence of Gideon and Lee in the chairs beside him.

"Mr. Blackwood has told you about our offer?" Oliver Johnston, the man who ran the livery in town, peered at Zeke through his thick spectacles.

"Yes, sir, he has. I've considered it and decided to accept." That sounded plain enough.

Hettie Cranston, the widow of the former hotel owner, cleared her throat. She had taken her late husband's seat in the council when he passed two years ago. Nobody had the balls to tell her to leave, although she hadn't been asked or elected to sit on the council. "We do expect you to cease frequenting Lucy's saloon, its, ah, women, as well as drinking altogether. Your habits have become well known, and some of us aren't certain you are the right choice. So, for thirty days you are to be a model citizen, help those who need it, keep the peace, and demonstrate the best judgment possible. That's a requirement for becoming the sheriff permanently."

Her partner in crime, seamstress Edith White, was the most caustic of the group, which seemed unlikely considering Hettie's sharp tongue. "We didn't all vote to hire you, but the majority had their say." Her beady eyes pinned Zeke to the chair. That old woman made him nervous, reminded him of the horrible nanny Gideon had for two years as a child, the one who would give him the strap for even the slightest infractions.

"I appreciate the confidence the majority had in me." Zeke felt like telling the old biddy to go to hell, but figured it wasn't a very good idea. He decided to change the subject instead. "Did you all pick a new mayor yet?"

Oliver tapped his fingers on the table. "As you know, we've been running the town since Phineas Wolcott's perfidy was discovered." The former mayor had made off with most of the town's money. Although some of it was recovered in Kansas City, he was never caught. For nine months, Tanger had limped along with a small population and a rigid town council making decisions. Oliver glanced in Gideon's direction. "However, the

17

man we asked to replace Phineas said no."

Zeke looked at his cousin in surprise. "They asked you to be mayor? Why the hell didn't you tell me?"

Gideon nodded. "I'm not the right man for the job. They need someone who's spent more time in Tanger."

"But I'm good enough to be sheriff?"

"I think you're perfect to be sheriff." Gideon looked at Jake. "I'm obviously not the only one, either."

Zeke was confused by the faith these folks had in him considering his drunken binges and the amount of time he'd spent at Lucy's. He didn't know if he could do it himself, but he sure as hell would try his damnedest. What made them so sure it was the right choice?

Jake finally spoke up. "Zeke, at least give it a try."

"Was it you? Were you the one who suggested me?"

"No, it wasn't me." Jake turned to his wife, the black-haired Gabby, who had kept her distance from Zeke since the moment they met, except for one extraordinary day when she'd joined him to fight to regain Tanger, the only time they'd been united in purpose.

However, it was a day for surprises. Gabby had always treated Zeke politely, never giving him any of the effusive hugs that were her habit since becoming deliriously happy with Jake. Not that he'd cared who she gave them to, but Gid certainly got his share. Her dark gaze met his and she smiled. Unbelievably, he felt the corners of his mouth twitch in response. It appeared Gabby had been the one to nominate him for sheriff.

"If I'm going to be the sheriff, the town needs a mayor. I can't be reporting to seven people." Zeke folded his arms across his chest. "I do better when there's a chain of command."

Gideon pointed at Zeke. "He's right. I nominated a good

candidate, but so far, the council can't agree on the nomination."

"Who?" Zeke frowned. If someone was willing to step into the position, why the hell couldn't they agree?

"We've told you, Mr. Blackwood, a woman in the position of mayor is highly irregular." Mr. Johnston pushed up his glasses.

"She's run the mill for years, she's a good businesswoman, a loyal citizen of Tanger, and she's young enough to handle the job." Gideon stood and challenged the rest of the council with his steady gaze. "I don't think it should matter one whit that Gabby's female."

Gabby? Gideon had nominated *Gabby* to be the mayor? Oliver was right, it was highly irregular. Women were so emotional, completely driven by what they felt. What made any man think she'd be good at running an entire town?

However, everything Gideon said was true. On paper, Gabby was the perfect choice. Too bad she had tits.

"At least let Gabby try, just like Zeke." Jake's normally relaxed expression had hardened. "Give them both a thirty-day trial and see how they do. What's the worst that can happen? Tanger has had its fair share of disasters already."

The love shining from Gabby's eyes as she looked at Jake made Zeke turn away. Jesus, it was more than he could stomach. He wondered if he'd ever experience such pure happiness. It sure as hell seemed unlikely, considering he never planned to marry.

Some murmurs sounded as the town council considered Jake's proposal. Zeke was hard-pressed to believe they hadn't flat out said no already. Female mayors just weren't normal, no matter how much he respected her. If the town council said no, he couldn't take the offer of a thirty-day trial as sheriff. Although he wanted the job, he'd gone and put himself in that

19

corner by insisting on having a mayor.

"Let's take a vote, everyone." Oliver raised his hand. "All in favor of Zeke Blackwood as sheriff and Mrs. Sheridan as mayor say aye."

Jake, Gabby and Edith said "Aye" immediately. After an evil-eyed look from Edith, Hettie grudgingly said, "Aye."

"All opposed?"

The other three men on the council said "Nay" but it was a formality. With four of seven voting for Gabby to be mayor, she had already secured the position.

"Well I'll be damned," popped out of Zeke's mouth.

Not only did Tanger have a new *female* mayor, but now it had a new sheriff too, at least for the next thirty days. Gideon grinned, Jake kissed Gabby, Edith and Hettie speared Zeke with their evil old-lady look, and Zeke cursed under his breath. He knew they'd be watching him as if they were hawks and he the mouse.

He had a new job. God help him.

"There's no jail." Zeke walked down the wood-planked sidewalk beside Gideon. "Where the hell am I supposed to put people I arrest?"

"We'll make a jail, maybe in that piece-of-shit house we lived in down at the end of Main Street. Just need some strong wood and steel bars. I'm sure Martin would be willing to help." The blacksmith might be fifty, but he was still good at what he did and he'd become friends with Zeke.

"Yeah, he will." Zeke resisted the urge to scuff his boots in the dirt like a little boy. The thing he was worried about, well there was more than one thing, but the biggest thing was that he knew nothing about being a lawman.

No, he knew less than nothing, and that bothered him. What if he messed up real bad and someone got hurt? Zeke didn't want to be responsible for hurting the citizens of Tanger any more than they'd already been hurt. It angered him that he didn't know what he was doing or have any confidence as sheriff. He wanted a purpose, but what if he failed at it?

Anger was better than self-pity, but it didn't make the cramping in his stomach go away. Zeke hated being off-balance and having no idea how to overcome the odds. From the time he was a young man, he was used to being in charge. After his father had been stricken with a palsy, Zeke had taken over as head of the household, shouldering a burden too heavy for a twelve-year-old boy. It had shortened his childhood and forced him to be as serious as the situation.

The new sheriff's job was more than serious, it was the town putting their trust and their lives in his hands. It wasn't the first time he'd been given a huge responsibility, but it was the first time he had no idea how to accomplish the job. He'd need to step lightly and follow every rule to the letter.

"Don't worry, Zeke, the raiders are gone. The only thing that's happened in the last nine months is a runaway pig and a stolen pie." Gideon squeezed his shoulder. "It's not as if you're going to be alone. We'll be right here, ready to help if you need it, but I don't think you will."

Zeke nodded. "I wouldn't count on that. I don't have a fucking clue how to be a sheriff." He managed a chuckle. "I don't plan on failing though."

"And you won't." Gideon shook his head. "You were a top-rate soldier, the best I ever saw. It's not such a big change from the army to a lawman."

"I sure as hell hope you're right." Zeke wanted to succeed more than anything. Thinking about what would happen if he failed made his stomach hurt. Failure was something he didn't tolerate, ever. He didn't plan on starting with this job.

Lee walked out of the restaurant, silhouetted in the lamplight from the door. "Where have you two been? You ran off without finishing the dishes, don't think I didn't notice."

The appearance of his brother reminded Zeke he had some news to share. God knew how Lee would take it.

"We were at the town council meeting. Let's put some coffee on so I can tell you what happened." Gideon sounded relaxed, a feeling Zeke wouldn't share until he was the sheriff in earnest.

Lee narrowed his gaze. "You'd better tell me now."

"You're looking at the new sheriff of Tanger." Gideon smiled broadly and pointed at Zeke.

The expression on Lee's face was comical—shock, disbelief and then he burst out laughing. Gut-busting, knee-slapping guffaws exploded from the normally snide blond. Tears leaked from the corners of his eyes as he held up his hand at them, apparently trying to regain control of himself.

Zeke didn't think it was funny at all and brushed past his little brother into the restaurant. At nine in the evening, there were no customers left except Martin, who was nursing a cup of coffee. The silver-haired giant nodded at Zeke in greeting.

"You might as well know too. I'm the sheriff now, even if my ass of a brother doesn't believe it."

Lee stepped in behind him, still laughing. Zeke resisted the urge to punch him until he shut up. "It ain't funny."

After wiping his eyes, Lee was able to look Zeke in the face. "You're serious about this. The town council made you sheriff?"

"Damn serious. Hell, Gabby's the mayor too." Zeke's tongue stuck to the roof of his mouth as the responsibility began to sink down into his bones. God, he needed a drink.

Control, Zeke, control.

"Hell, Zeke, why didn't you tell them no...or maybe you didn't want to say no?" Lee leaned against the doorframe, his brown gaze too sharp.

"I didn't want to say no. I've been drunk and stupid, with nothing to do other than breathe, sleep, eat and shit." Zeke held out his hands, unnerved to see a tremor in them. "This is gonna give me what I can't seem to find in Tanger. A purpose."

"You really want this job?" Lee frowned.

Zeke searched way down deep and thought about what he needed, and what he didn't have. He didn't have much of anything besides his friends. Perhaps if he worked as sheriff he might finally feel as though he'd found a new home, and a reason to live.

"Yeah, I think I do."

Lee nodded, his eyes reflecting nothing. "Then take it. One of us might as well be respectable."

Zeke turned to Martin. "I'm going to need your help building a jail cell starting tomorrow morning."

"Sure thing, Zeke. I'd be happy to." Martin could always be counted on to help, thank God.

Zeke's stomach cramped and he took hold of his runaway thirst for whiskey with both hands. Being sheriff wouldn't be an easy job by any means—it'd be hard as hell no doubt, especially knowing he had thirty days to prove himself worthy. After talking to Lee, the urge to find a bottle of whiskey began to ease and in its place, a bit of excitement. It was the first step to get Zeke out of the hole he was in.

Tanger had a new sheriff and he could only hope he'd be the best sheriff the town had ever seen.

Chapter Two

Naomi Tucker squeezed her sweaty palms together under the table and focused on Lucy Michaelson. The older woman scrutinized her as if she was looking for a job as a doctor or a lawman instead of a saloon girl. It didn't matter what the job was, Naomi had to take it. It had been about two days since she'd had a halfway decent meal and her money had run out twenty miles outside of Tanger.

The one thing she wouldn't do was beg. If Lucy didn't hire her, Naomi would look elsewhere in town even if it meant less money. The war had cost her more than she ever imagined, but it would not take her dignity.

"You done this kind of work before?" Lucy tapped her fingers on the scarred tabletop.

Naomi forced herself to ignore the noise and tried to hide the tattered edges of her sleeve. "Yes, ma'am, I have."

"Ever worked on your back?"

She expected the question, but it still stung like a slap. "It's not what I'm here for." She had made a promise to herself to never sink that low again, and she planned on keeping it. "If that's what you're looking for, I don't think I can do it." Brave words for a girl who'd survived on bread crusts and water. She barely resisted the urge to ask for whatever was cooking in the kitchen.

Lucy held up her palms, evidence of calluses clearly written in the roughened skin. "I ain't insisting on nothing. My girls do what they want, when they want. I was just gonna say if you bring anybody upstairs, the house gets half."

Naomi shuddered at the very idea she'd have to let strange men touch her again. She swallowed the bile that had crept up her throat.

"I don't intend on servicing men that way, ma'am." Naomi was a lot of things, but stupid wasn't one of them. She learned from her mistakes, past and present.

"I can respect that. It ain't all that fun, most times, is it?" Lucy sighed, a stray red curl bobbing up and down on her forehead.

Naomi didn't know how to answer the question or even if she should so she just kept her mouth shut.

"I hired on two other girls a few weeks ago. I expect the three of you to pull your weight around here. Finally got enough business going to have two nickels to rub together. Job includes a room upstairs—linens and things are up to you. Meals from the kitchen are served three times a day only. It ain't great, but it's food and if you miss it, you go hungry." Lucy pointed at the stairs. "There's but one bathing room up there and we all have to use the hot water. Twice a week on Tuesdays and Saturdays. Don't steal, don't cheat and treat the customers nice."

Naomi couldn't stop the grin from sneaking across her lips. She had a job!

"I think that's about it. If you have any questions, ask Joe, he's that ancient-looking man behind the bar." Lucy stood, the bright blue velvet dress straining against her ample bosom. "I'm guessing you'll take the job."

"Yes, ma'am, I surely will and thank you for giving me a chance."

Lucy scrutinized Naomi up and down, pausing to look at the not-so-impressive cleavage beneath the faded yellow dress. "Can you sing?"

Naomi didn't expect the question or the almost sexual way Lucy had examined her bosom. Not that anything would surprise her, but it still made her feel odd. "Well, I guess so a little. I used to sing in the choir back before the war."

The blackness of the past roared in her ears, blocking out whatever Lucy said. The sight of the church burning, of her father screaming as he lost his life in the inferno trying to save members of his congregation. Her heart hammered so hard it almost broke a rib. Through it all, Naomi kept a smile on her face, nodding to her new boss.

"Like I said, you don't have to, but Joe can play the piano some. You think about it."

Naomi kept her hands clenched, trying to keep her focus on the here and now instead of the long-ago memories.

Lucy walked towards the bar. "I've got a dinner date with a friend, so you head on upstairs and introduce yourself to Louisa and Carmen." Lucy flapped her hand towards the stairs. "Since you're the last one, you get the smallest room at the end of the hall."

The sun streaming in through the batwing doors was suddenly cut off. A blinding halo of light surrounded whoever it was, like an angel come down from heaven.

Naomi forgot her discomfort, her hunger, even her desperation as she stared at the figure walking in the saloon.

"Zeke, honey, I told you I'd meet you down at Elmer's. You didn't have to come all the way up here to escort me down." Lucy sounded like a young woman flirting, and with the angel no less.

"Ain't no bother, Lucy. It's a beautiful day." The figure

moved into the saloon and Naomi blinked, trying to focus on who it was. "You hire another new girl?"

"Yep, just now. This here's Nammy."

"Naomi." Ignoring Lucy's mispronunciation of her name, she stepped forward and focused on his face. "Naomi Tucker."

They were the last words she'd probably be able to get out of her mouth for a while. The angel was beautiful with soft, wavy blond hair, chocolate brown eyes tipped with the thickest eyelashes she'd seen, wide shoulders, the hint of whiskers on his narrow cheeks and a mouth curved into a sardonic grin. The pistols hanging low on his hips were lethal looking.

Holy Mary.

"Where did you find her? She's a mite skinny." He spoke about Naomi as if she wasn't standing five feet from him.

"Came in with the supply wagon. There ain't much to her, but I'm willing to give her a chance. Besides, it's not as if there's a line of girls at my door begging for a job." Lucy walked towards her office. "I've got to get my shawl. Be right back." Her departure left Naomi alone with the stranger.

She clenched her teeth together to keep the angry retorts from escaping. The two of them had spoken about her like she was the runt of a sow's litter at market and all the rest of the piglets had been purchased.

"And you are?" She finally found her voice and instead of shaking from nervousness, it shook with anger.

The man tipped back his hat and pierced her with a cool gaze. "Zeke Blackwood, Miss Tucker. It is Miss, isn't it?"

"Yes, it is." She struggled with the urge to show him how sharp her tongue could be, knowing Lucy was friends or perhaps more with him. It could cost her the first job she'd had in a month if she didn't keep a leash on her temper. "How do you do?"

"I do right fine most days." He stared a moment too long at Naomi, sending a shiver straight up her spine. The cold-eyed stare told her nothing about the man other than he liked to intimidate people, but she wasn't dancing to that tune. "Where are you from, Miss Tucker?"

Naomi pasted a smile on her face. "All over."

One blond eyebrow went up. "That's an interesting answer." He crossed his arms over his chest. "You on the run from the law?"

Naomi couldn't help it, she laughed. "Not hardly. I never took the easy way out, Mr. Blackwood. I've worked to stay alive."

"Zeke, call me Zeke."

Naomi swallowed hard. "I don't know you well enough to use your Christian name."

"Fair enough." His gaze never strayed from hers and it seemed he was interrogating her. "You fixin' to stay on permanently in Tanger?"

"I don't see how that's your business." In actuality, Naomi had no idea where she'd live from one week to the next. Home was literally where she hung her proverbial hat.

"Well, you see I'm the sheriff." He seemed to be uncomfortable with the title, strangely enough. "We've had lots of folks, ah, leave town, and Tanger needs new citizens." Did the man ever blink?

"I didn't realize you were the sheriff. How nice for Tanger." Her temper was bound to land her in hot water sooner than later.

"No need to get snippy with me, Miss Tucker. I'm looking out for the welfare of the town."

"I'm not being snippy. I'm just keeping my private life to myself." A lie, of course, she was being a smart-mouthed brat.

He stepped towards her, and the loose-hipped swagger only accentuated his appeal, dammit. When he stood a mere foot from her he stopped. Up close, his brown eyes were more like whiskey in a crystal-cut glass, a myriad of colors changing at every angle.

"Are you trying to intimidate me?" she blurted, angry and embarrassed at her reaction to the man.

The corner of his mouth lifted ever so slightly. "Is it working?"

Naomi didn't know how to answer him. If she told the truth, he'd likely use that against her, but if she lied, he might very well try harder. The moment stretched out until she could hear her own heartbeat rushing past her ears. Thankfully Lucy broke the spell by coming back into the room before Naomi did something stupid.

"Let's get on over to Elmer's then. I heard Gideon hired Margaret to cook. A good choice, I think. She's been so odd since her husband passed." Lucy tucked her arm into the sheriff's and led him to the door. He turned back and looked at Naomi, a warning, a threat or a promise in his eyes, she wasn't sure which.

As soon as the couple left her sight, Naomi sat back down at the table and released the breath she'd been holding. As she pressed a hand to her stomach, Naomi reminded herself of what she did have—a job, a place to live and three meals a day, exactly what she needed to live. Her experience in Passman had taught her to be cautious of accepting folks, to be wary and distrustful, with her survival instincts running at full speed. That's all she'd been doing for so long, surviving one day to the next. No time to think too hard, so why was she feeling all stupid because of the sheriff's behavior? He meant nothing to her and she had no intention of being in his jail anytime soon.

The logic of the situation didn't mean anything since she was shaking so hard, she had to put her head between her knees. It was lack of food making her off-balance, not Sheriff Blackwood. After a few minutes, she felt more in control of herself and sat up to find an old white-haired man in front of her with a steaming bowl of something in his hand.

His muddy brown eyes regarded her with something like pity. "You hungry?"

"Yes, sir, I am." Her stomach moaned in agony at the sight of food.

A small grin kicked up the corner of his mouth as he set the bowl and a spoon on the table beside her. "I'm Joe, the cook and bartender. It ain't nothing but stew, but it'll fill your belly."

"Hello, Joe, my name is Naomi." She smelled the concoction and her mouth filled with sweet relief at the thought of real food.

"Lucy hire you?"

"She did." Couldn't he go back to the kitchen and let her eat? Pretty soon she'd have to start gnawing on her tongue.

Joe nodded. "Been a dog's age since a pretty blonde came through that door, I expect she snapped you up for the color of your hair, but you need some meat on your bones, girl. A little thing like you ain't gonna last in a saloon long." He tsked as if he was describing a tragedy about to happen.

Hunger forgotten momentarily, Naomi sat up straight, her spine snapping into place. "I've had my fair share of tough jobs, Joe, including working in saloons, a pig farm and as a dance hall girl. I assure you, this job will *not* break me."

Too late, Naomi realized her pride had gotten hold of her

again and made her sound like a raving bitch to someone she needed to befriend.

Joe's white eyebrows rose almost to his hairline. "That so?"

"I'm sorry, sometimes I let my mouth loose before my head realizes what's happening." She held out her hand to him. "It's a pleasure to meet you, Joe, and I thank you kindly for the stew."

After a brief hesitation, the tall man leaned over to shake her hand. His grip was brief but firm. She appreciated the fact he didn't continue to treat her like a delicate flower.

"You're welcome, Miss Naomi. I think you'll do right fine."

Naomi smiled, a genuine grin she hadn't felt the urge to do in a very long time. Joe grinned back.

He sat beside her and gestured to the bowl. "Go on and eat, girl, afore you get the vapors."

Naomi wanted to roll her eyes at the thought of her getting vapors, but she controlled herself this time. Instead she dug into the stew with gusto, the salty taste of the meat and potatoes heavenly. She chewed the mouthful so fast, a loud burp came sliding up her throat, surprising both of them.

"Excuse me." Her cheeks heated, but she was so hungry she didn't care.

"It don't bother me none. I like a woman with an appetite." Joe settled back against the chair. "Lucy gone to dinner?"

Naomi nodded. "Yes, she left with Sheriff Blackwood."

The feelings and thoughts about Zeke Blackwood came rushing back at her. He'd turned her topsy-turvy in just two minutes.

Joe looked a bit surprised. "Sheriff Blackwood?"

"Yes, he said his name was Zeke Blackwood and he was the sheriff. Is that not true?" She continued to fill her mouth between sentences.

"I expect it is true. Tanger's been needing a lawman for a good spell. Zeke's a good man, but he needs to keep away from Lucy. She's the one who kept him dr—" Stopping in mid-sentence, Joe grinned sheepishly. "I ain't no gossip, Miss Naomi, but sometimes my mouth runs too." He stood. "I've got to clean up the kitchen now. You finish that up and bring the bowl in when you're done."

With a grateful smile, Naomi turned back to her dinner and watched Joe shuffle back to the kitchen. He had a hitch in his step and walked as only an old man could. She had a feeling she'd just made her first friend in Tanger.

Zeke listened to Lucy chatter as they walked to the restaurant, but he didn't hear what she said. At first he was trying to think of a way to tell Lucy this was the last time they'd have dinner together for a while, given the town council's edict. However, his mind wandered back to the saloon, back to the doe-eyed blonde. The sight of her in that yellow dress had almost sent him back out into the street. It was a strange moment, as if he'd stepped into the past when he'd first seen Allison Delmont.

The woman he could have loved. The woman who'd captured his attention and nearly his heart. The woman who'd been murdered in front of his eyes.

He took a deep breath to pure the memory of the bloody day when she died. Was there anything in town that didn't have bad memories for him? Naomi had reminded him of Allison in appearance, but as soon as she opened her mouth, he knew she was quite different. Sassy, opinionated and unafraid, Miss

Tucker had risen to the bait he'd tossed at her. Her brown eyes had thrown sparks at him.

Zeke had no idea why he was even thinking about her. She was too skinny, her tits were too small and for sure, her mouth was a detriment. Woman looked like she hadn't eaten in weeks and that dress was picked from the rag bag at the church.

So, what was it about her that grabbed his interest? He didn't need or want a woman in his life, especially not one who aggravated him with one sentence. The last few days had been hard enough to get used to being the sheriff, get the jail together and keep his hands off the damn whiskey. A woman would foul everything up even worse.

"Zeke, you're not listening to me." Lucy pinched his arm. "A lady doesn't like to be ignored while she's with a gentleman."

She knew she wasn't a lady and he sure as hell wasn't a gentleman, but he didn't correct her. Lucy was a true friend and that's all that mattered.

"Don't pester me, Lucy." Zeke tugged his hat lower on his forehead. "I ain't in the mood."

"That little blonde got your tail in a twist?" Lucy was too keen by half. "She reminds you of Allison, don't she?"

A surge of anger and hurt ripped through him. "I'm done talking." Zeke pulled his arm out of hers. "You want to have dinner with me, you'd best stop now."

"No need to get all sore with me." She pouted, tugging at his sleeve. "She told me she don't work on her back anyway."

The admission shouldn't have surprised him, but it did. Naomi worked in a saloon, and many girls who did worked as whores too. It didn't matter one way or the other since he'd been ordered to stay away from the saloon and its women, which included Naomi. "It's no never mind to me as long as she stays out of my way." Zeke would be sure to stay out of hers.

He ate dinner mechanically, without even tasting the meatloaf and mashed potatoes. It wasn't until he has halfway through the meal he realized it was good. Actually it was more than good, it was delicious. He stopped in mid-chew and looked up at a smirking Lee in the doorway to the kitchen.

"Told ya Margaret would be perfect." He nodded in greeting at Lucy. "What do you think?"

Zeke swallowed the meatloaf. "I haven't had food this good in years, since before—"

Lee's eyes clouded with the same grief that slid through Zeke. "Yeah, before."

It seemed like a lifetime ago they'd sat at the dinner table at Blackwood Plantation back in Georgia and enjoyed long dinners with their family. Zeke hadn't allowed himself to think of all they'd had, all they'd lost, very often. He closed his eyes for a second to beat back the dark feelings before they could grab hold of him.

"Margaret settling in to stay then?" Lucy popped a bite of mashed potatoes in her mouth.

Lee nodded. "Gabby brought her over and although she's quiet as a grave, the woman can cook like an angel."

"Amen to that." Zeke tried the green beans. "Damn, even these are good and I normally don't like 'em." He waved his fork at the kitchen. "She making desserts too?"

His brother simply raised his eyebrows. "Finish your dinner and you'll find out."

Zeke threw a green bean at Lee, but he sidestepped it and went back into the kitchen.

"You know, I always thought your brother was just a mean bastard," Lucy mused.

"That's not very nice." Zeke felt his earlier annoyance at her returning. "You don't know what we've done, or been through. Don't judge him."

"And you don't know what I've been through." Lucy's eyes hardened.

"Are we gonna fight now?" Zeke frowned at the sudden hostility between them.

Lucy sighed. "No, I think I just got my back up at the way you looked at Naomi."

Zeke didn't know what to make of that. Was Lucy jealous? It wasn't as if he'd ever made any promises to her aside from the ones he'd made to pay his tab at the saloon. They'd never even been intimate, at least not that he remembered anyway.

"You ain't got a reason to get your back up. You and I are friends and that's all it'll ever be." Zeke used the last of his meatloaf to clean up the mashed potatoes. Lucy stayed silent, moving her food around her plate. He screwed up his courage to tell her what needed telling. "I don't know if you heard or not, but I'm the new sheriff in Tanger." Her eyebrows flew toward her hairline, but he held up his hand to stop her from speaking. "I got thirty days to prove I can do the job before it's permanent. And part of the town council's requirements include no drinking, no whoring, no saloon at all."

It took a moment for it to sink in, then she swallowed hard. "You can't come by to see me, and we can't have meals together either, can we?"

He shook his head, uncomfortable with her distress. It's not like he was leaving town or wouldn't ever speak to her again.

"I had hopes, Zeke, you must know that." She looked at him from beneath her lashes, a sheen of tears in her eyes.

Zeke couldn't have been more shocked. Lucy had hopes about him? She'd never said anything or even hinted about it.

Granted, she'd held a bucket under him while he'd puked, but that wasn't exactly a marriage proposal. Jesus, he didn't know what to say.

Fortunately Lee saved him the indignity of looking like an ass.

"She made pie, Zeke." He sounded like a kid at Christmas. "Lookee here." He set a plate with a beautiful slice of peach pie on the table. "I already had three pieces. Zeke, you ain't never had something so sweet before."

His appetite for dessert had fled with Lucy's distress and her admission. He didn't want to disappoint Lee, so he took the plate.

"Looks mighty tasty." He shoveled a forkful into his mouth and the explosion of sweetness almost made him want dessert. "It's wonderful."

He pushed back his chair and nodded to Lucy. "I'm gonna go say howdy to Margaret and let her know how good dinner was. Be right back."

Before Lucy could say anything, Zeke walked into the kitchen, relieved to be away from her for at least a few minutes. Lucy was a good friend, but she could be too much at times. Margaret Summers stood at the huge stove—they'd had to order it special for the restaurant—with four pots and pans cooking at once. Her light brown hair was in a bun at the nape of her neck and her dark eyes watched him warily. He took off his hat and held it before him.

"Afternoon, Mrs. Summers. I had to come in and let you know that dinner was right wonderful. Best I've had in five years. Gideon and Lee did right by hiring you." Fortunately, Zeke didn't have to eat Gideon's cooking anymore either.

Margaret brushed a stray hair off her cheek. "Thank you, Mr. Blackwood."

"Zeke, please. You're part of the family now. I think it'd be all right if you called me Zeke." He smiled, trying to make her feel more comfortable.

She wiped her hands down the white apron that emphasized the curves she'd been blessed with. If Margaret stopped hiding in dark corners, she'd likely catch herself a new husband.

"Then please call me Margaret." She offered a tremulous smile.

"I will do that, Margaret. Thank you for a great meal." He slid his hat back on his head. "We really do appreciate you taking this job on. The three of us, well, we're as stupid as a bag of doorknobs about cooking and such. And now that I'm going to be the sheriff, well, we needed you more than ever. So thank you."

"No thanks are necessary, Mr. Bla—I mean Zeke. I was needing a change and a steady income anyway. It's been some time since I lost Ben." Her eyes clouded with grief, which was Zeke's queue to skedaddle. He didn't think he could handle anyone else's grief besides his own.

"You let me know if you need anything." With that, Zeke quit the kitchen and went back into the dining area.

Lee sat in the corner alone, surveying the four tables that had customers eating dinner, pointedly ignoring Lucy. The two of them had never gotten along and all during Zeke's drunk phase, the hostility had only grown.

Lucy smiled like a sunrise when she saw him, and that's when the truth hit Zeke square between the eyes. She was in love with him. Damn, how had that happened? He'd never so much as kissed her hand.

Zeke didn't know what to do about Lucy—women were not his specialty. He sat down heavily and shoveled in the remaining pie. Might as well at least fill his belly if he had to deal with females all day.

✳

The next day dawned cloudy and a little cool. Zeke gulped the last of his coffee, still amazed at how clearheaded he felt in the mornings when he hadn't been drinking the night before. With a salute to Gideon, he left the restaurant and headed down the street.

The town council asked him to walk the streets during the day, and several times in the evening. He'd been doing just that, and actually enjoying it, which was a surprise. Folks were a bit suspicious the first day he'd walked through with the badge on his vest, then they began to warm up to him.

This was his third morning as sheriff as he made the rounds through town. Aphrodite's was quiet, as it usually was in the mornings, yet coming out the door was the blonde, Naomi.

She was dressed in a plain green frock, with no lace or anything frilly on it. In fact, it looked like a work dress. She held a sheet-wrapped bundle in her hands. Stopping dead in her tracks, she looked at him with surprise clearly written on her face.

"Mr. Blackwood." Her gaze dropped to the badge. "Or should I say Sheriff Blackwood."

He tipped his hat, recognizing too late his pulse had sped up at the sight of her. She was as beautiful as he remembered, with large doe eyes and lashes that could probably double as dusters.

"Either one is fine, ma'am. You see I'm still trying out the badge for size. The town council was looking for a lawman, and, well, I'm an ex-soldier so they thought I might be a good choice. Anyway, reckon it'll be another month before it's official." He almost babbled at her for Chrissakes. "You headed out for a walk?"

She nodded. "Lucy told me there's a lake just outside town. I thought I'd do my laundry and perhaps go for a swim."

The thought of her wet and maybe even naked sent a shiver up his spine. His body reacted, even though he told it not to, and he shifted to ease the discomfort of a sudden burst of blood to his dick.

"Would you like an escort?"

She looked as surprised as he felt by the invitation.

"I mean, there's lots of men who would take advantage of a female alone. So, I could, ah, protect you." Zeke had never felt like such a complete idiot before. Why didn't his tongue work right?

"That's very kind of you, Sheriff. I expect you're right about strangers, but I carry a small pistol with me at all times. Thank you for the offer." She tied on a straw bonnet with daisies and did a little curtsey before she walked away.

A curtsey?

What the hell was that? Zeke remembered the last time he'd seen any woman curtsey and it was before the war, before the death and destruction. It was during the last dance at Blackwood Plantation, when hearts were light and the booze was plentiful. Miss Naomi just put herself into his memories with her little curtsey.

He only hoped he could dislodge her, or she might take up residence in his mind permanently. And there was no way in hell he wanted that to happen.

After watching Naomi walk away, Zeke pulled his head out of his ass and continued his rounds. The town council had informed him a new bank was opening finally. It'd been almost a year since the last banker, the ex-mayor Phineas Wolcott, had pulled up stakes and left town. Tanger's residents were wary of anyone handling their money, with good reason, so it was up to Zeke to do some reconnaissance and find out what he could about the owner.

The door to the bank stood open, although even if it hadn't been, he probably would've walked in anyway. Zeke stepped inside and noted a dark-haired man standing behind the teller station. In a split second, he knew the stranger had been a soldier—the damned knew one of their own when they saw one.

"Morning." Zeke pushed up the brim of his hat as he walked towards the man. "I'm Sheriff Zeke Blackwood."

The stranger stepped around the side of the teller station with a hitch in his gait and Zeke noted the black cane with the silver handle. A wounded soldier for certain.

"Good morning, Sheriff, I'm Richard Newman." He held out his hand and Zeke shook it, pleased to note calluses. An ex-soldier turned banker was a welcome surprise.

"Pleased to meet you." Zeke gestured with his arm. "You fixing to open up shop soon?"

"That I am." Richard walked back around the teller station. "I'm trying to make sense of the mess left behind by the former, ah, owner of the bank. Apparently when he left, there were a number of papers left in a jumble, including the deed to this property." He peered at a piece of paper. "Owned by a Veronica Marchison and leased to a Phineas Wolcott."

"Veronica owned the building?" That was certainly news to Zeke. The cold-hearted bitch had done her best to destroy Tanger, including selling its residents as slaves to Mexican whorehouses. She deserved more than the bullets that killed her and he hoped she was currently rotting in the darkest pit of hell.

"Apparently so. I understand she's deceased?" The man had a lilt to his speech, but Zeke couldn't pin down what kind.

"Oh she's dead for certain. Too bad I wasn't the one to kill her." The snarl was unexpectedly harsh and made Richard start a bit.

"Not a popular woman in town then?"

"You could say that. Her husband owns the general store right next to this building. He's the man to talk to if you've a question." Zeke reined back the fury currently spinning around his guts. No need to scare the new banker in town with the horrors of what occurred the year before.

"I'll do that." He set down the paper and regarded Zeke with a thoughtful stare. "Confederate Army?"

"Yes, sir." Zeke tapped his forehead with two fingers in a small salute. "You too?"

Richard nodded. "Yes, Colonel of the Third Virginia Infantry."

A myriad of images rushed through Zeke's head, memories and nightmares mixed together. He saw the same reflected in the banker's eyes. He'd been right—Richard was a fellow veteran, a man who'd traveled to the worst place on Earth and survived.

"Welcome to Tanger, Richard." Zeke felt a weight lift off his shoulders. The new banker would be good for the town.

"Thank you, Sheriff. I'm glad to be here." The two men shook hands again, this time as new friends.

Chapter Three

Naomi brought the dirty glasses to the bar, glancing behind her as she did to be certain *he* wasn't there. She hadn't seen Zeke since his invitation to escort her to the lake that morning. She'd half-expected him to follow her despite her refusal, considering the hostility he'd initially thrown her direction. He almost outright accused her of being on the run from the law. The man had made assumptions about her that were not only completely unfounded, they were insulting. Then his behavior had been almost chivalrous, which confused her.

Granted, she'd done things she wasn't proud of in the last three years, but Naomi prided herself on staying within the law and maintaining her honor. Not that a man like Zeke would expect a woman to have honor, but she did.

She'd tried working an honest job, or at least what folks thought of as an honest job, back in Passman three months ago. It had brought her humiliation, heartache and more nightmares to contend with. She hadn't, however, broken any laws except perhaps those in her heart and soul.

Naomi had to shake off the bad memories as they crept up her spine. No need to dwell on Passman or its mayor when she had good fortune right in front of her at the saloon.

Both nights at the saloon had gone smoothly, without anyone bothering her or making her feel unwelcome. Well, at least not the customers anyway.

She'd settled in her small room upstairs, which smelled a bit of mothballs and sweat, but she tried to make the place her own. Louisa was very friendly, even offered to help her sweep the room to get out the year's worth of dust. The redhead had moved to town from Alabama somewhere and was bright and bubbly like champagne. Carmen, on the other hand, was a tight-lipped Mexican woman who did her best to be as difficult as possible. She was barely civil to Louisa and outright sneered at Naomi.

The men seemed to love both of them, and on more than one occasion in the last couple of days she'd seen them go upstairs with customers. Naomi wasn't going to judge them for their choices. She was thankful Lucy didn't force her to entertain men upstairs.

Since she'd started on a Wednesday, the saloon hadn't been very busy, giving her a chance to get comfortable before the weekend. If she was right, come Friday night the local cowboys would descend on the saloon and the real work would begin.

"Tomorrow will be busy. You watch yourself, Miss Naomi." Joe's expression was grave enough to send a skitter of goose bumps up her spine.

"You make it sound like an Indian raid, Joe." She set the empty glasses on the bar. "How bad can it be?"

"You just watch yourself, y'hear?" Joe had been more sweet and cordial than anyone else in Tanger. If only he were forty years younger, he'd be a perfect man.

Naomi grew to taste the bitterness of her naive words twenty-four hours later. Dozens and dozens of men had descended on the saloon, most of them under thirty, but many old geezers joined in as well. Smelly, sweaty, dirty and even some dolled up like fancy men—there were representations of all kinds of males squeezed into the newly renamed Aphrodite's Saloon. Apparently when Lucy reopened it eight months earlier, she decided to name it after the Greek goddess Zeke had told her about. At least that's what Louisa had told Naomi.

Her bottom was black and blue from all the pinches, slaps and gropes. She couldn't count how many times she'd knocked away a meandering hand only to hear a laugh in response. Many of them had asked if she was Aphrodite with her golden hair.

It had only been three hours since the horde had come and already she was close to exhaustion. She needed a short break, just ten minutes to herself before she smashed someone's nose or beat them with a beer glass. Joe had warned her, but she hadn't listened closely enough.

Louisa was flirting with two young cowboys hardly old enough to shave. Naomi made her way through the crowd, barely missing a hairy hand grabbing for her right breast. She snarled at the man, earning another obnoxious chuckle.

"Louisa," she hissed. "I need ten minutes. Can you cover for me?"

Louisa's eyebrows shot towards her hair. "You taking a man upstairs, Naomi? I thought you didn't do that kinda thing."

Naomi rolled her eyes. "No, I'm not taking a man upstairs. I need to visit the privy."

"Oh, okay." Louisa winked. "Have fun now. I'll take care of things for you."

"Thanks." Without correcting her new friend's assumption, Naomi headed for the back door, more than eager to leave the cacophony of the bar behind for a brief respite.

She almost made it.

Too late Naomi realized the men in the saloon wanted her to look at, to touch, nearly as much as they wanted the liquor she served them.

"Now where you going, darlin'?" A large hand closed around her upper arm, stopping her in her tracks. "It ain't gonna be no fun without you here to look at, angel."

Naomi tried to pull free, but the stranger tightened his grip. "Let me go."

He yanked her back until she landed square on his lap. Her temper flared as she struggled to get up. It wasn't as if he smelled bad or that he was ugly, because he had pretty blue eyes and sandy brown hair and had the pleasant odor of soap about him. He was holding her there against her will and she'd made a promise to herself to never let that happen again.

She twisted and tried to scratch his face. "Let me go. *Now.*"

"You are a feisty filly, ain't ya? Whaddya say, angel, will you take me upstairs and make this godforsaken saloon worth more than stale beer?" He smiled and waggled his eyebrows.

Naomi saw nothing but red as she picked up the heavy mug of beer and brought it crashing down on his head. Then all hell broke loose.

Zeke thumbed through the stack of wanted posters in the makeshift jail, trying to remember which ones he'd already looked at. The small shack didn't have much, but Martin had been building a cage in the corner that'd keep a prisoner overnight. It was all Tanger could afford to do until more folks moved into town.

One particular new person in town kept sneaking into his mind. Naomi had been haunting his thoughts since they'd met, and he just couldn't seem to shake her.

The door flung open, startling Zeke. Joe ran in breathing like a racehorse. The white-haired bartender was a bit quirky, but he was a good man who'd stuck by Lucy through the worst of times. The older man's face was flushed red and he wheezed with each breath.

"Fight...at the...saloon." He held up one finger and put his hands on his knees.

Zeke was already on his feet heading for the door. "Who started it this time?"

He didn't give Joe a chance to answer. Zeke was out the door and halfway down the street in moments. There had been too many fights at Aphrodite's since it reopened. Hell, he'd been in dozens of them himself when he was drunk. Sometimes he'd even been the instigator.

As sheriff, he had to keep the peace in town, which meant in the saloon in particular. He knew each broken chair and bottle cost Lucy hard-earned money. Many a nights she'd told him how much of a struggle it had been to get the saloon going again and how angry fights made her. In the wee hours one morning, before he became sheriff, Zeke had made a drunken promise to her to stop the fights. Now he could arrest anyone who started one.

His boots slammed into the hard-packed dirt as he ran down the street. On more than one occasion, he'd ended up with black eyes, stitches and sore knuckles after a saloon brawl. Lucy had cleaned him up. This time, he didn't have any intention of coming away with a scratch.

By the time he made it to the saloon, he'd built up a good head of steam to go with his rising temper. Whoever was responsible would be the first guest in the new jail. Sounds of breaking glasses, grunts, a few screeches and Lucy shouting spilled out into the darkness of the street. A chair slammed into the bar just as Zeke burst through the doors. Splinters flew every which way, some of them grazing his cheek.

He threw up his hand to protect his eyes as he tried to see what was going on. Louisa and Carmen hid behind the bar—the two watched the brawl like it was a damn circus show. Lucy stood in front of the bar, waving what was left of the chair she'd just smashed into bits. She looked angrier than he'd ever seen her.

About fifty men pummeled each other around the room. Some were even rolling on the floor picking up tobacco spit and dirt on their clothes. Zeke kicked at them but they ignored him. Lucy saw him and mouthed, "Do something."

He pushed his way through the fights, yanking men by the collars, pushing others into chairs, hell he even pulled hair to get them to break apart. By the time he made it to the center of the disturbance, he was panting and thinking the job might not be worth this much trouble. He knew he'd found the instigator when the knot of men grew thicker.

Patience was something he might have on a good day, but this definitely didn't count as one. He started punching men and they went down fast. The zip of battle lust coursed through him as he made his way through the idiots. That's when he realized who stood on the table in the middle of the fight.

Naomi Tucker.

Her green dress was ripped at the shoulder, exposing smooth alabaster skin. Her hair was sticking up every which way and her mouth curled into a snarl. In her hands, she held two thick glass mugs, each bearing the bloody marks of a few hits, more than likely on someone's head.

His heart hammered at the sight of this wisp of a woman fiercely battling fifty men. Like a Valkyrie from Norse mythology, she was a warrior goddess come to life.

Someone poked two fingers into his back.

"Get on with it, Zeke, while I've still got a saloon left," Lucy yelled in his ear.

He knew he had to do something, but Naomi had shocked him. Not many women were able to do that, however he'd already come to the conclusion she wasn't like any woman he'd ever met. She confused him, dammit. That thought energized him into action. With a few grunts and curses, he made it through the men and to her feet. When she glanced down, her eyes widened with surprise and a smidge of fear. Good thing too. She needed to be afraid because she was in trouble.

He took out his pistol and fired a shot into the ceiling, with silent apologies to Lucy for the damage. The loud bang echoed through the saloon and everyone stopped as if frozen. Naomi watched him with wary eyes.

"This fight is officially over. If you don't want to end up in jail, then get your hands off the man you're punching now. Y'all owe Lucy for the damage, so leave an extra dollar for her trouble." He took a deep breath and surveyed the bloody faces in the room. "Who started it?"

Fifty men pointed at Naomi. She gasped and scowled at Jeb, the big stupid cowboy who stood next to her with a gash on his cheek and a goose egg on his forehead.

Without a word of warning, Zeke grabbed her and threw her stomach down on his shoulder. It didn't take her but a second to start beating on his back and struggling to break his hold. Nothing doing. Zeke had his prisoner and he wasn't about to give into her wailing.

Naomi was stronger than she looked. In fact, she almost got away twice, but Zeke held fast, tightening his grip until he could feel every bone, muscle and, dammit to hell, curve in her body. By the time they got to the house the Devils had dubbed the "shit shack", which now served as the jail, she had inflicted at least a half dozen bruises. For certain, his thighs would never be the same from her shoes.

"Keep still, Miss Tucker," he said for the tenth time. "You're under arrest for starting the saloon fight. You're going to spend the night in jail no matter how many times you kick me."

She grunted and kicked him harder. Little witch.

"Put me down."

That's exactly what he wanted to do, but until the cell was in front of him, she was stuck on his shoulder. He kicked the door open and cursed when he realized it was dark as hell. The moon hadn't risen yet and the lamp had gone out.

"I'm going to drop you on your head if you don't stop wiggling." Then Zeke did something he never expected to do. He smacked her on the ass.

That not only shut her up but she stopped moving. Satisfied he'd gotten the best of her, he stepped into the gloomy interior of the new Tanger jail.

Naomi was caught between being angry and being scared. This big, threatening man with a badge had her in his power and could do whatever he wanted in the darkness. Unwilling to let him take advantage of her, she was prepared to do anything to protect herself. The hard form of the knife in her shoe provided a bit of comfort. If only her hands were closer to her feet, dammit.

Her behind smarted from his hand. The fact that he'd even dared to do it made her pride smart just as much. Men thought they had the right to do whatever they wanted to a woman without consequences. This particular man had a surprise in store if he assumed Naomi would allow him any liberties.

Beth Williamson

"Please put me down," she said through gritted teeth. "I'm getting a headache."

"We can't have that, can we?"

As she slid down the front of him, Naomi was struck with the realization of just how hard he was—*exceptionally* hard. There wasn't an ounce of give on the man. When she landed on her feet, she put her plan into action.

She let out a cry of pain. "Oh, my ankle." She bent over and reached for the knife.

A strong hand closed around her wrist. Enough to stop her movement, but not enough to cause injury.

"I'm an ex-soldier, darlin'. That move wouldn't work on a five-year-old." His deep voice caressed her ears in the inky shadows.

Before she could utter a word of protest, he'd captured both her wrists into one hand and pulled her across the floor. He must know his way around the building because they didn't run into one piece of furniture.

"You're going to have to help." He let her right wrist go and guided her hand to a lantern. "Lift the glass so I can light the wick."

"Do it yourself." She pulled her free hand away. "Better yet, let me go so I can go back to the saloon."

He snorted. "That's not going to happen. There's a new rule. Anybody who starts a fight in Lucy's saloon spends the night in jail. You're lucky I don't make you pay for all the damage."

"You couldn't, only a judge could." She didn't have any money left to give and the threat of going into debt because of a randy cowboy made her fists clench.

"This ain't civilization. The town council and me, we make

the decisions for Tanger." The firm belief in his voice told her what he said was true. "A little saloon girl like you can be held responsible if we say you are."

Oh, she knew it wasn't civilization. These small towns in Texas were their own kingdom, taking anything they wanted, when they wanted, and damn any consequences. The bitter taste of anger and betrayal burned on her tongue. She had to remind herself this was Tanger, not Passman.

"I can't pay for my breakfast, much less broken chairs. That fool decided he was going to force me to—well, you know— and I'm not for sale, at any price." Her voice shook with fury. "Don't threaten me anymore, Sheriff, I'm done with it."

A thick silence sat between them, pulsing with a life of its own. Naomi figured Zeke hadn't run across many women who stood up to his fierceness. Not to say she wasn't afraid, but her need for survival overcame that fear. Once upon a time, the opposite was true and Naomi had been afraid of her own shadow, but no more.

"Lift up the glass so I can light the wick." His tone had changed from impatient to barely contained anger. Naomi was satisfied to know she affected him too.

"What if I won't?" She wanted to see just how far she could push the good sheriff.

"I throw you on the chair and sit on you so I can have two hands free."

Naomi had no doubt he'd do it. Zeke appeared to be just as driven as she was, even if they were on opposite sides of the fence. A small, grudging respect for him bubbled up. The thought of him sitting on her wasn't pleasant at all—he was a big man and would likely smash her into bits.

"Fine. Where's the lamp?" she snapped, ready to confront whatever the sheriff was planning.

He took her wrist and guided her hand to the cool glass of the lamp. A shiver raced up her skin at his touch, making her heart thump hard. His skin was callused and firm, the fingers long, the palm wide. Normally men had dirty, clammy hands that made her shudder in disgust, yet her reaction to Zeke was far from normal. She wasn't going to call what she felt desire, yet, but it was damn close.

A hiss sounded from her right as he struck a match. Her eyes watered against the bright intrusion. His face was half-hidden in the meager light, a myriad of shadows disguising the real man who existed behind the badge. The cold-eyed stranger gazed at her, and to her credit, she held his stare until he gestured to the lamp.

"The match is gonna burn out before you lift the damn thing."

Naomi felt a splash of heat in her cheeks as she lifted the glass. The wick lit quickly and she let the globe slide back into place. His gaze found hers and the coolness she'd expected had been replaced by heat. The shadows of the flames danced on the wall behind him, making Zeke appear as though he stood on the verge of hell itself, calling her to join him. Her mouth went dry at the thought.

"I know it ain't much of a jail, but it'll do." He was back to being a gruff sheriff again, the visual lover he'd been disappearing in a blink.

Naomi glanced around at the small building. It had obviously seen better days, judging by the tired appearance of the wooden walls. The cookstove in the corner appeared to be the only source of heat. Atop it sat a battered tin coffeepot. A rickety desk stood in front of her, holding the lamp as well as piles of paper stacked neatly atop. Behind it sat an even worse-looking chair.

It was the object in the far corner that caught her attention. A cage.

Oh, hell no.

The bars were obviously put together by hand, uneven yet thick as her wrist. The entire thing couldn't have been more than five feet wide by six feet long with a sorry-looking tiny cot inside it. The cage looked to be built for an animal rather than human.

"You are not putting me in that thing." She cursed the quiver in her voice and her gut.

He raised one blond eyebrow. "Since you broke the law, Miss Tucker, that's exactly what I'm going to do."

She tried to pull her wrist free, but it was like tugging on the steel cage. There was no give to the man whatsoever. "I'm not a dog to be put in a cage."

"It wasn't built for a dog. You'll be safe in there for the night." He started walking over but Naomi dug in her heels.

"You're going to have to knock me out because I will *not* let you put me in there." Naomi wasn't about to tell Zeke why she wouldn't get in the cage. It certainly wasn't his business to know she'd been kept captive by a crazy man back in Louisiana six months ago. The memory of the four days was enough to make bile crawl up her throat. Her captor had forced her into a cage likely meant for a dog. Before he could do anything besides entertain himself by making her jump, she got free. It was only through the grace of God and a piece of good luck she'd been able to escape.

He frowned as his eyes flashed fire, the first emotion she'd seen from the cold man. "You have no choice."

Zeke tugged harder and Naomi leaned back, putting all her weight into staying put. Her feet started to slide on the loose dirt littering the wood-planked floor. She tried her best to resist, but he was too strong. No matter how hard she yanked, he was like an oak tree, completely unbendable.

"Don't make me hurt you, Miss Tucker. I'm just doing my job." He stopped to glare at her. "I have to do my job."

"Your job is not to put me in a cage." She leaned forward and tried to bite his hand, desperate like a fox caught in a trap to free herself.

He moved so fast, quick as a blink, and she was back to chest with him as he held her captive with one big arm. The door to the cell creaked open and the sound scratched her ears until she was sure she was bleeding. Zeke got her near the damn cage so fast, there was no way she could have stopped him.

She punched the steel bars. "Dammit, you son of a bitch. Let me go."

Zeke put his lips near her ear. "I'm surprised at your language."

Her temper flared even brighter. Much as she wanted to control her emotions, they ran wild. "Oh shut up, Sheriff. You don't need to be so pompous."

Then he did the last thing she expected, he threw back his head and laughed, a hearty gut-busting one that sounded rusty from disuse.

"I'm glad this is so funny to you." She tried again to move. "It's not so funny from where I'm standing."

Zeke got his laughter under control and with a final swipe of his eyes, he met her gaze. The merriment had transformed the sober, staid sheriff into a different man, more handsome and appealing, which surprised and unnerved her. It made him much more dangerous to her equilibrium.

"You are a spicy one, aren't you, little one?" He smiled then, a beautiful wide grin that knocked her for a loop.

Naomi honestly hadn't any idea what lurked beneath the hard shell of the man. He showed the world such a cold, distant, albeit striking exterior. She'd certainly believed that façade to be the truth of who he was, but now she saw it was the lie, and this smiling man was the truth.

"You have no idea." She frowned, willing him to hear what she couldn't say. "Don't put me in the cage."

"Truth is, it's not quite ready for a prisoner, so we'll have to make do." He gestured to the cell door. "It's not attached yet. The blacksmith is waiting on parts for the hinges."

She choked on a laugh. "Half a jail for half a sheriff?"

"Not very nice, Miss Tucker." Taking the rope dangling from the bars, he looped it around her wrists, and she found herself tied up instead.

As she gaped at the rope, he acted as if nothing odd had happened. "I'm going to get us some supper. You hungry?"

"No, I'm not. My stomach is tied up in a knot so tight I doubt I'll be able to eat for a week." She bared her teeth at him.

"I know the feeling. Sit tight and I'll be back in a few minutes."

Regardless of how she felt, or how much she protested, the obnoxious sheriff just walked out of the jail and left her to rot tied to the cage.

Rat bastard.

Chapter Four

As Zeke walked towards Elmer's, he took a deep breath, then he took another. Naomi Tucker had him twisted into knots and he needed to clear his head, desperately. From her temper to her passion to her fire, the saloon girl was everything he didn't like in a woman. He shouldn't want her, or desire her at all. Merely thinking about being with her could put his new job in jeopardy.

He didn't want to believe the attraction had anything to do with her blonde hair and the resemblance to Allison. She'd been the person to remind him there was still good in the world after the war. Her death haunted his heart and his dreams. He didn't want to believe someone as annoying as Naomi Tucker would remind him of the sweet, gentle beauty.

Then why the hell was he fascinated by her?

It irked him that Naomi was the one person who'd made him laugh in years, and dammit, he'd *smiled* for Christ's sake! Something about her sharp tongue, her fighting spirit, called to him at a base level. Life just sparkled off her like one of those exploding fireworks on the fourth of July. Hot, bright and loud. Getting tangled up with Naomi was the last thing he needed. What he really needed was to keep this job and get hold of a purpose, namely being a lawman in Tanger.

His boots echoed on the fresh wood planks as he entered

the restaurant. Lee raised his eyebrows from his seat at the table by the kitchen.

"Late supper?"

"Something like that. You got any beef stew left?" Zeke took off his hat and ran his fingers through his hair, dismayed to realize he was sweating because of *her*.

"Nope, but I've got some cornbread. Damn, Margaret can cook it every day and I'd never leave." Lee's attitude had changed from angry all the time to angry only half the time. Within the year they'd lived in Tanger, he sometimes even seemed happy, which was a miracle in itself. Zeke hadn't been able to bring happiness to his brother for quite some time. Since Lee had lost his arm, there had been very few of those light moments. He made a mental note to introduce Lee to Richard Newman—as wounded veterans, they might be able to help each other heal.

"Give me some of that and something to drink. Cider, milk, water, whatever." Zeke sat down heavily.

"Yes, sir." Lee stood and snapped a salute. "What put the bee up your ass?" he said as he walked towards the back.

"A fight down at the saloon. Had to arrest the person who started it and I need to spend the night at the jail." Zeke didn't know why he didn't tell Lee his prisoner was a woman. It was as if Naomi was his little secret, his hot, sexy secret with the razor-sharp tongue.

"I didn't think Martin had finished the cell."

Zeke grimaced. "He didn't. I'm making do with rope."

"I thought the fights had gotten better. Didn't Lucy hire some new girls to keep the men distracted?" Lee called from the kitchen.

Zeke couldn't help the tingle of awareness for exactly who

Lucy had hired. He'd never expected she'd be sitting in the jail making his life difficult only days after meeting her.

"Sometimes womenfolk mess it up worse than men." Zeke firmly believed that. Females tended to make men all crazy and situations hazy.

"That's the gospel truth." Lee came in carrying a small basket. He held it out to Zeke. "If we didn't need them for food and babies, I don't think we'd put up with as much as we do."

A soft "harrumph" sounded from behind him. Lee whipped around to find Margaret standing there, and he hadn't even heard her enter the room. Her light brown hair was a frizzy cloud from a long day's work in the kitchen. She glared so hard at Lee, Zeke thought perhaps she'd burn a hole in him. To her credit, Lee glanced away first, a bit of embarrassment on his face.

Zeke hid a smile in his hand by pretending to cough. "Thanks for the vittles, Margaret." He took the basket and saluted Lee. "Back to the jail."

As he walked out of the restaurant, he heard Lee tell Margaret she shouldn't eavesdrop. When another "harrumph" sounded, Zeke closed the door and left. It was time to get back to his prisoner, like it or not.

Naomi had acted as if she was afraid of the jail, truly afraid he would do something to her while she was his prisoner. It wasn't unheard of during the war, and even after, for men to not treat women properly, but for God's sake, Zeke was a lawman. As such, he would never intentionally hurt anyone he arrested and only used force when necessary, or when ducking a punch.

It bothered him that she'd even think he'd hurt her. The war was over, and society was no longer running wild. Zeke had taken the job to not only find a purpose, but also to bring order to Tanger, not to cause disorder.

His hand dug into the handle of the basket as he walked, his irritation with Naomi growing. She'd been nothing but trouble even when she wasn't in his presence. Zeke might have to talk to Lucy about giving Naomi the boot.

That saloon girl needed to get out of his life.

Naomi leaned her forehead against the cool steel bars and forced herself to pray. It had been a long time since she'd spoken to God and doing so went against her vow never to do it. This situation called for some pride swallowing and praying. Both of which she was prepared to do.

The weak lantern barely lit the corners of the cage. There had to be more in there than a straw mattress on a wooden cot frame. No doubt critters of the four-legged variety as well as the multiple-legged ones. A shudder ripped through her as her gorge rose. She hated spiders worse than anything.

The thought of anything crawling on her as she slept, or pretended to sleep, forced a small whimper from her throat. When she was in the cage in Louisiana, it was situated in a root cellar, where too many insects made their presence known. Jesus, did she have any happy memories to dwell on? Why was her every thought so dark?

"Stop it," she whispered. "It's nothing but a cage, not your first, likely not your last."

Hearing her own voice had a calming effect on her rising panic. Nothing like talking to herself in a jail cell so everyone could believe she was crazy.

She snorted at the thought.

"And here I thought you were unhappy in that cell." Zeke closed the door behind him, his face a mask of cold indifference again. Gone was the laughing, smiling man and in his place, the bastard sheriff with nothing to do but throw her in a cage.

"I am unhappy. The thought of kicking your ass made me laugh."

He pursed his lips together and swallowed, then glanced down so the brim of his black hat hid his face. She couldn't tell if he was angry or not. The man masked his emotions really well.

"I brought some food." He held up a basket and the smell of cornbread wafted past her.

Her stomach rolled. "I told you I wasn't hungry. There's no way in hell I'm going to be able to eat while I'm tied up like an animal." She stepped back away from the bars as far as she could, two feet at most. Perhaps reining in her temper would be a good idea. Zeke didn't strike her as the kind of man who reacted well to outbursts of anger. "P-please let me out." It was the please that made her stutter. She didn't want to ask anything of him, especially after the way he'd treated her.

Damn the man. Instead of answering, he went over to the desk and picked up the chair. She watched with interest as he carried it over to the cell and set the chair down just outside the cage. When he sat and reached into the basket, Naomi should have been angry he chose her incarceration to have a picnic.

But she wasn't.

She felt absurdly comforted to have another human being near her, even if he was the person who tied her up in the first place. He bit into the cornbread then pulled out a jar of what appeared to be milk. Against her will, her mouth watered at the memory of how sweet, fresh milk tasted back home. She swallowed the urge to ask him for a drink.

Acting the gentleman, Zeke pulled his neckerchief off and set it on his leg to perch the cornbread on while he opened the milk. As he took a long gulp, she watched his throat move, fascinated with the symphony of muscles and bone in his neck. When he finished, a milk mustache remained on his strong upper lip.

Naomi burst into laughter, she couldn't help it. The image of Zeke Blackwood, the big, bad lawman, with milk on his lip sent howls through her. He started eating the cornbread again, observing her as she tried to control her mirth.

A stitch stabbed at her side, finally breaking her laughter down. She leaned over and took several deep breaths, still chuckling now and again. Until she glanced up and saw the milk. After a few minutes, she was able to look at him without laughing like a hyena. The cornbread must have wiped some of it off, but each time he took a swallow, the white mustache reappeared.

"I'm glad my supper makes you laugh." He chewed on a bite of cornbread. "Never had that happen before."

She pointed at the milk. "Never saw a lawman drink milk like a kid before."

Zeke's eyes widened ever so slightly when he understood what she was saying. He used his thumb to wipe off his lip, then stuck the digit in his mouth. Tingles spread through her as he licked the milk off his calloused thumb and she wanted to tell him to stop. There was no reason for the attraction between them to happen, yet it did. Without rhyme or reason, her body seemed to take over at moments, reacting to him as she'd never done with a man before.

Naomi looked away towards the lantern. "That wick is lousy. I can barely see my hand in front of my face."

She was thankful her voice didn't shake, but various parts of her still thrummed with arousal from seeing the sheriff lick his own finger. Wasn't she in a pickle? In jail for a saloon fight, attracted to the sheriff who put her in there, and ready to mount him because he liked milk.

"Tanger doesn't have a lot of money. The town almost died out last year and it's just getting back on its feet." He held up the last bite of cornbread. "The restaurant's been open a month but only serving good food for a week." He popped the bite in his mouth and thankfully wiped his hands with the neckerchief. She didn't need to see another tongue show, thank you very much.

"Lots of towns are dying. There ain't much money anywhere since the war. Folks do what they can to get by. I can show you how to make better wicks." Naomi didn't know what possessed her to say that. What would the sheriff care about making lantern wicks?

He tipped his hat back and regarded her. "You have skills other than serving drinks then?"

Naomi swallowed back a sharp retort, annoyed with him for ruining her fun. "You'd be surprised how many skills I've had to learn, by necessity mostly." She shrugged. "I found that most of them didn't put food in my belly for long."

Zeke's expression softened. "I know what you mean."

Their gazes locked and the moment hung in the air. A connection between them, a common bond, blossomed against Naomi's will. She didn't want to be anything like him, or to soften her opinion of the hard-nosed lawman, yet she was helpless to stop it.

"I think you mean that."

He shook his head. "You sure are cynical, Miss Tucker."

"Pot calling the kettle black. You might just as well call me Naomi, seeing as how I've ridden your shoulder already."

Zeke rubbed his chin with two fingers. "That you did. Okay

then, you can call me Sheriff."

He said it with such seriousness, Naomi at first didn't react, but then the corner of his mouth lifted.

"I never would have guessed you were funny." She smiled.

"I have many hidden talents." He dropped the empty milk bottle into the basket.

Against her will, she felt a chuckle rumble in her throat. "Is Zeke your real first name?"

He frowned and didn't answer for a moment or two. "No, my real name is Ezekiel, my brother's is Cornelius." Zeke's face twisted in a grimace of distaste, as if he'd gulped down sour milk.

"Very old Biblical names, hm? You don't hear that much anymore." She reached through the opening and snatched a piece of cornbread.

"You figured that out?" Zeke plucked the cornbread from her fingers so fast she barely saw him move. "Most folks miss that. You study the Bible much?"

A rush of bitterness filled her mouth. "Something like that." She tried to take the cornbread back in an effort to forget her own personal ghosts. No need to dredge up memories of her father and his Bible teachings—they certainly didn't save his life.

He pulled back far enough she couldn't reach him or the bread. "That's not very nice, you know," she huffed.

"You said you weren't hungry." He balanced the cornbread on his palm. "Change your mind?"

She scowled. "I don't play that game very well." The one thing Naomi refused to do, had vowed *never* to do, was beg.

Without a word, he handed her the half-eaten cornbread. "Neither do I."

"Appreciate it." She took normal-sized bites, resisting the urge to scarf down the most wonderful cornbread she'd had in three years. No need for the sheriff to think she was a heathen. When she finished, she licked the crumbs from her fingers, savoring the flavor.

"Good, hm?" Zeke's voice had a husky tinge to it.

She glanced up to find him watching her like a great mountain lion. Naomi ignored the tingles of awareness running through her. "Very good. Who's the cook?"

He cleared his throat and waved his hand at whatever spell was in the air between them. "Lady by the name of Margaret. She works down at the restaurant."

Naomi jumped on the topic, eager to keep her mind off her crazy, uncomfortable situation. "That's where you took Lucy for dinner."

"Um-hm. Me, my cousin and my brother rebuilt it, named it after the old man who used to run it." He looked into the distance as if remembering, a deep pain in his gaze. "It burned down last year."

"Who's Margaret?"

Zeke shook himself, once again the unreadable man on the other side of the bars. "A widow who needed a job as badly as we needed someone who could cook."

"You fixing on marrying her?" Naomi didn't know how she let that question pop out of her mouth, but it did anyway.

Both blond eyebrows shot up. "Marry her? Hell no. I ain't never marrying. No sense in getting tangled up like that."

Naomi didn't know if she was surprised or relieved, perhaps both. It was none of her business who the sheriff spent his time with. "Then Lucy is just your friend?"

Zeke chuckled without humor. "Lucy is the only townsfolk

who still talked to me when I was at the bottom of a whiskey bottle."

That bit of information gave her a glimpse into the elusive sheriff's life, if only a tiny part of it. "She's given me a chance and I'm grateful for it."

"Too bad you had to spoil it by starting a saloon brawl. Never thought the first person in this jail would be a woman."

"What? The first person in the jail? I mean, I realize the cell isn't finished." Naomi forgot all of her discomfort. This was a *new* jail?

"Yep, the blacksmith put it together a few days ago and, well, we had to use what we could get so it ain't as pretty as it should be." He grabbed one bar. "It's strong though, or will be when the door gets finished."

"I can agree with that," Naomi said dryly. "Too bad you felt the need to test it out."

"Are you going to start that again? You know you did wrong, so just accept the night in jail." He stood and walked over to the desk, annoyance clear in the cadence of his steps.

"I did nothing wrong. That fool Jeb put his hands on me and when I said no, he didn't stop. I smashed a mug on his head and, well, that's when everything went wrong." She gripped the rough metal bars with her hands. "I only defended myself. Can't you understand that?"

He slapped the desk with one hand, then put his hands on his hips, his back to her. "I understanding defending yourself, but you have to understand that as the new sheriff of Tanger, I have to uphold the law or I'll be booted out on my ass."

"New sheriff? So the jail and its keeper are both new? Just my luck to be the first prisoner." Her journey to Texas had been riddled with one unfortunate event after another. She'd hoped to leave the bad luck behind, but apparently it had stuck to her like a leech. "I've only been in town a week, for pity's sake."

Zeke walked back over and stared down at her. Their gazes locked and the moment hung in the air, timeless and breathless. He reached out and one finger touched her cheek. Naomi didn't pull away because she couldn't. This time it wasn't out of fear, but wonder and longing.

"Give it time, little one."

Naomi felt the ground beneath her feet shift and knew she'd just stepped into uncharted territory.

She was scared. Zeke expected her to be tough, used to jail cells. Naomi was a saloon girl, yet he saw the fear and sadness in her eyes. Much as he wanted to treat her like just another prisoner, she wasn't.

In his experience, women were two types—regular females or ones like Lucy. He hadn't met many who didn't fall into those categories. Naomi happened to be one of them, although he was loathe to admit it, since she didn't make money on her back. She'd started the brawl, after all, but damned if she didn't hold her own, like a tiny warrior. Zeke didn't want to respect her, or do anything else with her, and he definitely didn't want to jeopardize his future as sheriff over her.

However, he found himself sitting on the cot, and in the dim light of the jail, he started talking. "I'm from Georgia, little town called Briar Creek. Wasn't much left of it after the war, so me and my friends came west."

Although she looked wary, Naomi reached for a piece of cornbread. "I'm from North Carolina."

He'd been right then, a displaced southern belle. "I don't rightly know what we expected when we came out here. It sure as hell wasn't this place."

"Tanger's not so bad." She nibbled on the cornbread. "Folks seem pretty nice, well, most of them anyway. Believe me, there's worse towns than this one, and far worse people."

He wanted to ask if she'd been referring to the bar patrons or him, but didn't want to know the answer. "I suppose they are, but this town's covered in blood too."

She looked saddened by what he said. "Sometimes there's nothing but life and death. I'll take life anytime, even if it's messy and out of control. Too many people I know don't have that choice anymore. I'll fight to survive, no matter what I have to do."

His stomach cramped because she spoke the truth, but that didn't mean he was going to admit it. At times, Texas seemed to be just as bad as the battlefields he'd escaped, but Tanger seemed to be where the Devils had finally stopped roaming. It sure as hell wasn't perfect, but they were trying to make it a home.

"How did you end up in Tanger?" He offered her milk, as if they were sitting on the riverbank with a picnic basket.

Naomi took a swig of milk from the bottle as well as any man. "Thank you." She wiped the residue with her fingers, and Zeke happened to notice they were long and slender. Foolish man had to pull his gaze away from her hands so he could focus on what she was saying. "I've been in Texas about three months, lived in a few towns, but moved around a lot. The supply wagon stopped here and I didn't have any more money to pay the driver." She shrugged. "I've been in some rough places, but Tanger really is one of the better ones."

"You always work in a saloon?" He took a drink of milk himself, more than aware her mouth had been on the same glass moments before. It sent a tingle of awareness through him.

She shook her head. "No, done lots of things, whatever I had to survive." This time when she met his gaze, a pulse beat between them.

Zeke had done many things to survive, and in this tiny woman he'd found a kindred soul. His friends never quite understood how Zeke felt about things, and truth be told, he didn't talk much about it either. Yet in that split second, it seemed Naomi understood completely. It was a bond he didn't want or need, dammit, but he couldn't deny it.

"If I untie you, you promise not to run away?" What the hell was he doing? She was his prisoner for God's sake, and he just offered to free her.

She narrowed her gaze. "I won't run, but I don't know why you'd free me so quickly."

He shrugged. "Now that we talked, well, I know you didn't start the brawl on purpose." Of course, she could have been lying, but he didn't think so. "If you stay here tonight, I'll release you in the morning."

As she finished the piece of cornbread in her hands, she chewed slowly, watching him with bulging cheeks. It would've been comical in any other situation, but there he was, giving his trust to a woman he barely knew.

When she nodded, he stood and untied her hands. She rubbed her wrists and whispered a thank you.

Zeke didn't want her to be afraid of him since he wasn't about to hurt her. "Let's get out of this cell."

Naomi hadn't lost her suspicious expression, and after she carefully walked out of the cell and let out a huge sigh when she reached the other side of the room.

He gestured to the desk. "Have a seat. We've got a long night ahead of us."

She scooted up on the desk, her feet swinging like a kid's would. "You know I lost a night's wages because of this."

Zeke hadn't thought about that, but she knew there would be consequences for starting a brawl. "You got a free dinner."

She chuckled softly. "Can I have more?"

Zeke gave her more cornbread and sat beside her. They stayed there for the next three hours. Although he didn't want to admit it, he'd never felt as comfortable with a woman before, not even Lucy. Amazingly enough, the urge to drink hadn't appeared once. They polished off the cornbread and the second bottle of milk. It was the oddest, yet most memorable meal he could remember.

In fact, he wanted more than a meal, he wanted to find out what her lips tasted like. Naomi was smart, funny and damn sexy. Zeke's attraction to her roared through him, making him break out in a sweat as he tried to stop thinking about how attractive she was. He hadn't been with a woman in nearly a year, and he wasn't sure what would happen if he gave into his baser urges with Naomi.

When the grey light of dawn crept into the building, Naomi looked up at the small windows. "I can't believe it's almost tomorrow already."

Zeke felt a pinch of regret that the new day had appeared, ending an almost perfect six hours with a woman.

"Me neither."

"Do you think Lucy will be mad at me?" Naomi stood up and stretched, the fabric of her dress pulling against the apple-sized breasts, hard nipples pointing straight at him.

"Nah, not for long. She knows how those cowpokes get. My guess is she got twice as much money for the damage and kept them all happy by arresting the person they thought started it." He raised one brow. "So you made her business even better."

69

"Well, it wasn't on purpose. All I want is to live and work in peace." The underlying pain in her simple statement hit Zeke square between the eyes.

He took her hand in his, the first voluntary contact they'd shared. She looked down at their joined fingers, then back up at him, her brown eyes clouded with confusion.

"I don't understand what's happening."

"Neither do I." His voice sounded hoarse and shaky.

Fear mixed with the most powerful arousal he could remember. Instead of giving into the fear he'd been living with, he did what he'd been aching to do since he'd seen Naomi. He took her in his arms and kissed her. Sweet, sweet heavenly saints, she tasted like cornbread, woman and home. Once he'd had one kiss, he took another, then another until he lost count of the hot, melting sensations. Tingles raced down his spine and straight to his dick.

Not one to miss a party, his staff stood at attention, straining against his trousers, knocking to be let out. Zeke's rush of blood from the rest of his body had his head spinning.

He took a breath and leaned his forehead against hers, feeling her shudder beneath his touch. Her sharp fingernails dug into his arms and he knew she must feel as out of control as he did.

"Please don't stop."

Her whispered plea was not what he expected, but he welcomed it.

"I do like to please a lady," he murmured just before he captured her mouth again. Reining in his snarling urges, he forced himself to savor each second with her. Slowly, he nibbled on her lips, alternately licking and nipping at the plump, delicate skin. A kittenish mewl burst from her mouth and he swallowed it.

Zeke scooped her up and set her on the desk, spreading her legs wide enough to step between them. He smelled her arousal and his nostrils flared with the musky, delicious scent.

"Naomi, I—"

She put her hand over his mouth, her gaze dark and guarded in the gray light of dawn. "Don't open your mouth and ruin it, Sheriff. I might change my mind if you do. Let's just feel good."

Sounded good to him. A woman who didn't want to talk before getting busy was a novelty, but who was he to look a gift horse in the mouth? Especially one who fit so nicely in his arms.

"Tell me what you like then."

"Mmmm..." she breathed into his ear as he nibbled on her neck. "I like that."

He outlined the shell of her ear, sending puffs of air with each lick. She shivered and tugged on his hair, which he took as a sign he was doing something right. As he suckled her earlobe, something resembling a moan came from her throat.

"Jesus, yes."

Well, Jesus had nothing to do with it, but Zeke could accept she mixed up her Biblical names. Her round breasts pushed against his chest, delightfully rubbing and teasing him, whether intentionally or not. He wanted to touch them, weigh them and roll the nipples on his tongue.

As he worked the row of tiny buttons on the front of her dress, he cursed whatever seamstress had made the particular garment. He needed skin, not frustrated fingers. She chuckled softly and brushed his hands away.

"I'll help."

Thank God for that. Zeke was surprised to see his hands

shaking, unwilling to believe he was acting like a randy young buck with his first woman. She knew what she was doing, judging by the seductive way she unbuttoned her dress, a sultry smile on her moist, reddened lips.

"You too, Ezekiel."

Somehow his first name wasn't as annoying coming from her luscious mouth. In fact, it was like a caress, a lover's whisper in the semi-darkness of the room. He could barely believe it actually made his dick harder.

When he unbuttoned his shirt, she leaned forward and kissed the exposed skin. The touch of her lips sent goose bumps down his body. She spread the shirt wide, tangling her fingers in the hair, causing pleasure and pain to mix together. When her fingernails scraped his nipples, he literally jumped.

"We'd better get these damn clothes off or I'll be done before we get started." His voice sounded so strained, he didn't recognize it.

She chuckled and tugged at his shirt. "Get busy then."

Zeke couldn't remember the next two minutes, but then he was nude and she was shimmying off her dress in front of him. A threadbare chemise was the only thing between him and her soft, golden skin. He ran his fingers down her arm, the small hairs standing on end beneath his touch. God, it had been so long since he'd touched a woman's skin.

When he cupped her perfect breast, she hissed in a breath even as the nipple tightened beneath his palm. How could he have ever thought they were too small? They were the perfect size, not too big or too small. He rubbed his thumb back and forth against the nipple, earning another moan from her.

"Mmm, more please."

To his surprise, she pulled off the chemise in the blink of an eye and suddenly they were both nude. Deliciously, amazingly nude. She laid her dress on the desk and climbed back up, spreading her legs for him. Crooking a finger, Naomi was more alluring than any siren who'd enticed a man to her.

Zeke couldn't resist. He stepped forward and nestled between her thighs, the soft curls of her pussy tickling the end of his dick. He smiled and spread her nether lips until he touched the moist folds hidden within. She was slick with her own juices and he slid easily into her entrance.

When his dick was just an inch or two into her pussy, he stopped and leaned his forehead against hers. Their breaths mingled.

"Look at me," he whispered.

She met his gaze, her pupils dilated in the dim light of the jail. He felt himself surrounded by her arousal. As he leaned down to kiss her, he thrust forward and embedded himself within Naomi's body.

A perfect, perfect moment that stole his breath.

She opened her mouth for his searching tongue and sucked him deep inside her mouth and her pussy. Sweet wet heat drove him to pound into her again and again.

Naomi spread her legs wider, scratching at his back even as her nipples pressed against his chest. Faster, deeper, harder they flew together. It could have been hours, it could have been minutes.

The orgasm began somewhere near his toes and it rose up through his legs, heading towards his balls. She shuddered in his arms and pulled him even closer until he touched her womb. The force of his orgasm roared through him like a prairie fire, consuming him, burning him until he forgot his name.

He felt her heart slamming against his, their breath coming in gusts like racehorses. The smell of sex, sweat and pleasure mingled around them. Zeke's knees shook with the force of it all even as she trembled in his arms.

"Holy hell."

✳

Naomi woke slowly, pulling herself from the deepest depths of dreams. She shifted against the rough fabric beneath her, trying to remember where she was. One eye popped open and when she spotted the steel bars, the entire night came back to her in a whoosh.

Zeke, the arrest, the incredible sex. Every second of it replayed in her mind with startling detail. Had she really been arrested, then tied up by the sheriff? And then experienced the most amazing intimate moments of her life in the blond man's arms?

One look at her wrist revealed some slight scratch marks from the rope, but nothing else. He'd brought her to the cot at some point while she slept. Hard to believe she would even be able to fall asleep in the jail considering how much the idea of being held against her will made her crazy. Yet she had, and slept hard too.

The bright sunlight streamed in through the openings in the wall, which on a good day might be called windows. She spotted Zeke in front of the right window, arms folded across his chest, fully dressed.

By the set of his muscles stretched taut against the blue chambray shirt, he wasn't relaxed at all. More than likely the man hadn't slept at all, which meant he'd watched her as she slept. That bothered her more than anything. Naomi hated feeling helpless, at someone else's whim or mercy.

He turned, as if sensing her perusal, and Naomi slammed

her eyes shut. Of course, pretending to sleep made her pulse race and her heart want to jump out of her body. She focused on taking slow, measured breaths, keenly listening for the scrape of his shoes on the floor.

"I reckon Lucy is waiting on you." His voice startled her so badly because he was now two feet away from her without ever making a whisper of sound.

Naomi's eyes flew open and she sat up, realizing too late the only thing covering her naked body was the thin blanket that now sat puddled on her lap. Zeke's nostrils flared as his gaze latched onto her already-hard nipples.

She fumbled for the edge of the wool and yanked it up so fast, she almost punched herself in the chin. Naomi met his gaze steadily, unwilling to lose more of her dignity, even if her cheeks burned hot under his stare.

"I expect she is. Hopefully I still have a job." The last thing she wanted to do was talk to Lucy, particularly if it meant losing her job so soon after getting it.

"Don't worry, she won't fire you." Zeke walked over to the desk and leaned against it.

"What makes you say that?" She glanced around, anxious to find her dress and put them on even playing ground. Naomi's state of undress gave Zeke a serious advantage.

"Lucy's got a good heart. She gives everybody at least two chances." He gestured to the cot. "Your dress is under there."

Damn him.

She didn't want to ask him to turn around because that would imply she was embarrassed to be naked in front of him. That, of course, would be stupid since he'd seen her inside and out. However, she hoped he'd be a gentleman and stop staring at her.

Zeke didn't live up to that expectation. If anything, he doubled his efforts to make her uncomfortable by ignoring her discomfort completely. What an ass.

Well, she'd give him something to look at. Without a bit of shame, Naomi threw the blanket off, enjoying the shock on his ruggedly handsome face.

"I should get dressed then." She struggled to keep a grin contained. Power surged through her as she stood proudly nude in the jail. It should have occurred to her to be worried someone might enter the building without warning. After all, it was a public building. Yet she didn't worry and she didn't care.

This was a battle she was determined to win with the enigmatic sheriff. She was fighting fire with fire.

She bent over, giving him the full view of her derriere, as she picked up the dress from the dirty floor. A slight gasp was the only indication he'd noticed. With a tsk, she rose with the clothing in her hand.

"It's filthy in here, Zeke. You really should sweep more often." Naomi brushed off bits of dirt and pebbles, very aware of the quiet man watching her so intently she might just catch on fire. She glanced up at him and smiled. "Hope I'm not embarrassing you."

Zeke's gaze burned into hers. "I don't embarrass easy." His voice was smoky, as if he'd been around cigars for hours.

Naomi smiled inwardly. "Good." She slipped on her dress, putting on as much of a show as she could. By the time she had her arms in the sleeves, he'd apparently had enough.

"For God's sake, you need to get this done today before somebody walks in." He turned her toward him and started buttoning up her dress, much more quickly than she thought possible with his big fingers.

"I thought you said it didn't bother you." Was he

embarrassed to have a naked woman in the jail or embarrassed that it was a scrawny blonde saloon girl?

"It don't." He shrugged. "We're grownups and it ain't nobody's business if we, ah, enjoyed each other's company."

The slightest tremble in his voice told her much more than any of his staring or blustering ever would. He was affected by her, which was damn good. Naomi couldn't ever remember anyone affecting her as deeply as he did. It was only fair she return the favor.

"Interesting way to put it," she murmured.

"Nobody needs to be in our business." He cupped her cheeks and kissed her so softly it felt like a hummingbird's wing. "You're new in town, and it's an awful small town. God forbid one of those biddies on the town council get it in her head to get rid of you for sparking with me and run you off."

Sparking? Felt more like a full-on bonfire to Naomi.

"Would you miss me?"

The corners of his mouth kicked up a bit. "You don't play fair, Naomi."

"No I don't." She wrapped her arms around his neck and kissed him hard. "Playing fair never got me anything but woe."

"We can't have that, can we?" He kissed her again, this one a long, deep kiss with hot, wet tongues sliding together.

She broke the kiss and stepped away, running her fingers through her tangled hair.

"I'll see you around, Sheriff." With a wink and a trembling belly, she left the jail, feeling the burn of his gaze on her back.

Oh yes, Naomi had won that battle. She had a feeling the war would be a hell of a conflict.

She couldn't wait.

Zeke trembled so hard after Naomi left he slid down on the floor behind the desk where no one could see him. He focused on breathing in and out, desperately trying to get control of himself.

What the hell had he just done?

He'd fucked Naomi like a common whore on his desk for Chrissakes. Not only that, but he'd enjoyed it without running like a goddamn chicken from her.

It was the first time he'd been with a woman in almost a year, since he'd been with that bitch who'd stolen too much from him. Even thinking about Veronica Marchison made his stomach roil. She'd been responsible for every second of misery he'd endured since then.

Zeke was torn between raw fury and a jolt of pain so harsh it made his eyes prick with tears. He wanted to turn back time, before he was shot in the shoulder and incapacitated by laudanum. He'd been at her mercy, or in her nasty clutches. Even thinking about Veronica so soon after being in Naomi's arms seemed sacrilegious.

The urge for whiskey, just one shot, burned in his gut. He needed something, anything to yank back the panic that threatened to overwhelm him.

He stared at the drawer beside him. When Martin had brought the desk in, he said it had been left by a family who didn't have room in their wagon when they left town. It was a battered, scratched up piece of shit, but it was free. In the middle drawer was a flask with more dents and scratches than the desk. Zeke hadn't touched it, hadn't dared to.

Yet now all he could think of was what might be in the flask.

He licked his lips, already tasting the smoky flavor of the imaginary whiskey. Before he even realized what he was doing, the flask was in his hand. He pressed the dented tin to his forehead, the metal cool against his flushed skin.

Zeke cupped the flask, staring at it until he felt a tear roll down his cheek.

"It's so fucking hard," he whispered. "I just need a sip."

He unscrewed the top.

By the time Naomi arrived at the saloon, her confident steps faltered. She knew what was coming, or at least suspected what was coming, and wasn't looking forward to it. Lucy didn't seem like the most patient person in the world or even remotely forgiving.

Done was done, however, and Naomi couldn't change it. She'd always stepped up and taken her medicine first, eager to get it over with. Might as well keep with that tradition.

She pushed open the doors and peeked inside. The broken tables and chairs were stacked neatly by the bar, the floor had been swept and a crate held all the broken glass. Someone had cleaned up, more than likely Joe. Naomi winced at the thought she'd caused the older man extra work.

"You might as well get on in here." Lucy's voice startled Naomi, and she stumbled as she entered the saloon.

Thankfully, the floor was just dusty and not littered with the shards of glass from the night before. Naomi straightened and wiped her hands on her already dirty dress. She turned to face Lucy with a straight spine and the courage that had helped her to survive the last few years.

Lucy sat at the table in the left corner, her feet propped up on a chair, a mug of coffee in front of her. The steam rose from the hot brew, as if she was a witch and her kettle bubbled with potions.

Shaking off the strange thoughts, she walked towards her boss, quaking with the urge to beg Lucy not to fire her, unwilling to allow it to burst forth. The one sin Naomi was completely guilty of was pride. Lord above, it had gotten her into way too much trouble already.

"Morning, Lucy."

The older woman let her breath out in one long, disapproving sigh as Naomi sat across from her.

"I ought to fire your skinny ass and put you on the next freight wagon moving through here." Lucy didn't sound angry as much as annoyed.

"I figured you might just do that." Naomi tried to swallow, but the dryness made her tongue stick to the roof of her mouth.

"Tell me why I shouldn't. I've tossed plenty of girls out on their ears for doing stupid things, but your stunt, well, that one took the prize for the stupidest." Lucy leaned forward, her eyes sparkling with some dark emotion. "What the hell were you thinking starting a saloon brawl? Are you touched in the head or something?"

Naomi had expected to have a shoe print on her fanny already so the fact that Lucy was even still speaking to her was a miracle. She intended to nurture that miracle and keep hold of her job.

"I've told you I don't work on my back. It's a dangerous job for your body and your mind. Can't do it, no way, no how." Naomi swallowed the dry spit and forged on, her stomach residing somewhere near her throat. "Jeb tried to force me to break that rule of mine and wouldn't take no for an answer. I couldn't let that happen, *wouldn't* let that happen again."

Lucy pursed her lips together. "He's a bit of an idiot when he's drunk. Pawed me plenty of times until I cuffed him on the ear with my rings on. He ain't bothered me since."

"Then you understand what I mean? He's big as a tree and I knew if I didn't do something drastic, he would've carried me upstairs no matter what I said. There was so much noise and ruckus going on already, no one would've even noticed me screaming." Naomi's eyes burned, yet she would not shed a tear, not for that idiot or what he tried to do to her.

"You rescued yourself." Lucy nodded, finally taking a sip of her coffee and giving Naomi a small rest from the woman's fierce expression.

"Sometimes there's not a gentleman around to rescue a lady, so she has to do it herself." Naomi had forgotten much about being a lady, but she held her tongue when it came to telling Lucy her entire clientele had the manners of a goat. "I'm sorry your saloon was busted up."

"Me too, but the boys all left enough money to fix it up." She set the mug down. "Apparently Zeke can put the fear of God in anyone."

Naomi nodded, unwilling to tell Lucy exactly what Zeke was capable of. "I'm glad the men listened to him."

"Carmen was practically drooling for me to fire you. Not sure why that gal has a bee in her bonnet about you." Lucy gestured to the stairs. "Louisa cried and begged me not to fire you."

That not only surprised Naomi, but it made her throat tighten. No one had cared if she lived or died for so long. To have someone she hardly knew cry for her, well, that was amazing.

"Louisa is a sweet girl." Although only a few years between them, Naomi felt much older.

"She's dumb as a stump, but she's cute and the gal can smile through a shit storm." Lucy stood and frowned down at Naomi. "I believe in giving everyone a second chance, so this here's yours. You're going to finish what Joe started last night and get the saloon ready for tonight."

Naomi wanted to smile, but nodded instead, absurdly grateful for Lucy's generosity. "Thank you."

"Don't thank me yet. You have no idea what they did to the outhouse." Lucy shook her finger at Naomi. "Watch yourself, girl. Ain't no more chances for you here."

Lee sipped the delicious coffee Margaret had made and gazed out at the early morning streets of Tanger. The restaurant had no patrons yet. It was his favorite time of day, when he could simply be at peace. Or at least the closest he could come to it anyway.

As he brought the mug to his mouth, he heard whistling from outside, a familiar sound he hadn't heard in quite some time. Zeke must've had a good night with his prisoner, whoever he was. Lee half-expected his brother to be in a lousy mood.

"Of course it's not too early, come on in, Richard." Zeke's voice boomed loud and clear, and to Lee's disappointment, slurred.

"Goddammit." He stood, intent on kicking Zeke's ass six ways to Sunday for drinking after three months of staying sober.

Zeke came in with a stranger behind him. The man walked with a cane and a limp. By the look on his face, he wanted to be anywhere but there. When his gaze met Lee's, he looked apologetic. Lee decided he liked this man already.

"Lee! There you are. This here is my friend Richard A-a-and— What was your name again? Oh, never mind." Zeke laughed.

"You're drunk, you idiot," Lee snarled.

"Now, Lee, remember your manners. Say hello to Richard." Zeke nearly lost his balance, stumbling into the stair banister.

Lee couldn't help but be angry with his big brother. They'd both worked so damn hard to keep him away from the booze. "What the hell happened? Did you fall into a whiskey barrel or did that bitch Lucy give you some?"

"Hey now, don't talk bad about Lucy. She didn't do nothing." He finally focused on Lee's face. "I'm sorry, Lee, I just couldn't help it." Naked agony shone deep in his brown gaze.

Lee's anger deflated a bit. "Let's get your ass upstairs so you can sleep it off." He turned to the stranger. "I'm sorry about this."

Richard held up one hand. "It's okay, Mr. Blackwood. There's no need for you to apologize."

The brothers Blackwood stumbled up the stairs leaning on each other as Lee struggled to get Zeke to his room. When he sobered up, Zeke was going to have questions to answer. When they made it to the bed, Zeke was laughing so hard, he fell face first into the mattress.

"What the hell were you thinking? It's been almost three months." Lee rolled Zeke over, shocked to see tears in his brother's eyes.

Zeke pressed his fist to his chest. "I just wanted to dull the pain and get hold of myself again. It's still just so damn hard."

Lee had no idea what he was talking about, but he was disheartened to realize Zeke was still struggling to control the urge to drink.

"Sleep it off." Lee pulled off Zeke's boots and put a blanket over him before he left the room. He wished he knew how to cure his brother, anything to stop the hell he lived through every day.

Richard was downstairs nursing a mug of coffee, looking very much at home in the restaurant. At that moment, Lee knew two things about the man. He'd been a soldier, and he wouldn't shy away from talking about it.

Most days, the Devils avoided the topic of the war with Lee, guessing the idea of dredging up how he'd lost his arm would be painful. They were wrong. Each day he wished he could talk about it with someone. Perhaps this stranger would be that person.

"Hope you don't mind, I helped myself to some coffee."

"No, you're welcome to it. Margaret went to get eggs from the mercantile so she ain't around to serve you." Lee gestured to the table. "Can I join you?"

"Of course, please do." Richard managed a small smile. "Your brother told me about you."

Lee's automatic defenses slammed into place. "With or without being drunk?"

Richard's eyebrows went up. "Without actually. He told me you were the bravest man he knew."

Lee let that sink in before he felt his cheeks heat with embarrassment. "Zeke is a bit biased. I think anyone who fought for what they believe in is brave."

Richard nodded. "And I believe I'll have some more of this coffee. Perhaps when Margaret gets back, eggs to go with it, and if you're free, some conversation too."

Lee smiled, and to his surprise, it was genuine. "I'd be happy to." Just like that, he'd finally found a friend.

Chapter Five

When Zeke woke in the afternoon, the familiar taste of pity and misery coated his tongue. He rolled over and tried to sit up, but his head roared in protest, followed quickly by his stomach.

What the hell had he done? He gave up three months of no liquor in a single instant, and over a woman. Jesus, he could also lose the new job as sheriff because of it. Hettie had been quite clear about the council's expectations, and they sure didn't include getting drunk in the morning less than a week after becoming sheriff.

God, he was a complete idiot.

If he were lucky, nobody saw him. He had a sudden flash of Richard Newman and Lee. So he wasn't safe yet, since obviously at least two people saw him.

Zeke pressed his hands to his forehead and sucked in a deep, calming breath.

"What you ought to be doing is praying to God you don't get fired." Lee's voice permeated the silence of the room.

"It ain't gonna help." Zeke rolled to his side and sat up, opening one eye to look at his brother. "I'm likely already fired."

"Me and Richard talked for a couple hours. He ain't gonna tell anyone. I sure as hell ain't." Lee scowled. "But you're gonna tell me what the hell you were doing drinking at six in the morning."

Zeke let loose a rusty snort. "I lost control, Lee. I was doing okay until sh— Well, I was doing okay until this week."

"Who is she?"

The question hit Zeke square between the eyes. "I don't know what you're talking about."

Liar.

"You can tell yourself anything you want, but don't you dare lie to me." Lee shook his head. "Whoever it is, you'd best leave her be and concentrate on being a sheriff. If you want this job that bad, you'd better."

With that, Lee left Zeke to his misery. He didn't blame his younger brother for being disappointed or angry. Hell, he was mad at himself. Stupid, stupid, stupid.

With a groan, he rose to his feet and readied himself for a new day as sheriff of Tanger, praying Lee was right and no one had seen him acting like the town drunk.

Zeke could hardly concentrate for days after the encounter with Naomi. For God's sake, he was even dreaming about her. Lee was looking at him as if he'd lost his mind while Gideon watched with his too-knowing gaze. Zeke still couldn't shake the itch that had settled on his entire body no matter what he did.

Perhaps he hadn't tried hard enough to stop thinking about her. Nothing like diving into his job with a bit more effort to keep his mind off a certain blonde. Jesus, he certainly hadn't meant to get involved with her, or any woman for that matter. It was the last thing he wanted or could handle.

As he did his normal morning walk through the streets of Tanger, folks nodded and said howdy to him. No one seemed to know what he'd done or what he'd wanted to do again and again ever since. Lucy likely suspected, but she hadn't said anything. He wondered what she had said to Naomi about the saloon fight, but he didn't want to ask.

It wasn't his business after all. *She* wasn't his business.

The door to the hotel stood open, stopping Zeke in his tracks and his mental meanderings. According to Lucy, the hotel had closed two years earlier when the owner picked up and left town, completely bankrupt.

His hand landed on the pistol riding his thigh as he stepped through the door. Sunlight brightened the lobby, highlighting the dust coating every surface and floating in the air like a storm of miniature creatures. He waved his hand, scattering them aside.

The sound of his boot heels echoed through the empty lobby. Someone had walked through recently, leaving impressions on the floor. Definitely not boots, but men's shoes for certain. Too big to be female in origin. Zeke slowed down to a snail's pace, keeping his ear cocked for any noise aside from his own.

He controlled his breathing, which kept his heart rate at a steady tattoo. When someone cleared their throat in the office behind the front desk, Zeke crouched down, gun solid in his hand. A sniff and a shuffle followed, making him believe whoever was back there wasn't worried about being stealthy.

He walked on his toes, keeping the heavy heels off the wood floor. As he approached, the reality of the situation hit him square between the eyes. This was the first time he felt like the sheriff, excluding the drunks and idiots he'd dealt with. Certainly his night with Naomi didn't count considering the end result.

The taste of excitement coated his tongue and his stomach

tingled with anticipation. He hadn't felt much about anything for quite some time, which told him Gideon had been right, this was the right job for him.

Zeke crept around the front desk, the unfinished wood offering a splinter or two to his hands. He didn't expect the intruder to come waltzing out of the office as if he owned the place, but that's exactly what the man did. Rising from his crouch, Zeke pointed both pistols at the man's heart and widened his stance.

"Mister, you'd better have a good reason for breaking in."

The stranger was perhaps a few years older than Zeke, with thick brown hair and a matching mustache. He was thin, but not overly so, with a suit made of some fine material. The gold chain from a pocket watch hung straight down from the green vest beneath the brown suit jacket.

"I could say the same thing to you." He shook a sheaf of papers at Zeke. "You're trespassing."

Zeke narrowed his gaze. "So are you."

"No, I'm not. I'm not sure why you think you have the right to enter my property without permission, but if you don't leave immediately I will find whatever or whoever passes for the law in this town and have you arrested." The crisp syllables, the nasally whine and the authoritative attitude told Zeke much more than he wanted to know. The man was a Yankee.

The hairs on the back of his neck stood up and the tingles in his stomach turned to lumps of hot ash. It hadn't ever left, that urge to do battle with his enemy, even if the war were over. Zeke holstered the guns before he shot the son of a bitch.

"I am the law." The words dropped from his mouth like sharp icicles. "If you own this place, I expect to see proof."

"Where is *your* proof you're the law?" The stranger glanced at Zeke's clothes as if they were shit on his shoes. "You certainly don't look like it."

"Out here in the west, ain't no call for fancy duds or manners. I'm the sheriff of Tanger whether or not you believe me." He pointed to the star on his shirt. "This here's your clue."

"That could have been taken from anywhere. What does it prove?" The stranger had the balls to cross his arms and tap his foot.

That just set Zeke off like someone had lit a fire under him. The man had the audacity to question his authority, insult him and the star on his chest. No goddamn way he'd accept that.

"It proves I can throw your scrawny ass in jail." He took the man by the arm, surprised to feel solid muscle beneath the fabric of his jacket. "For trespassing."

No matter how much the stranger blustered and went on and on about what a big mistake Zeke was making, they kept marching towards the jail. Fortunately, Mike had finally gotten the hinge pins in to complete the jail cell the day before so he could put the pompous fool behind bars. The thought gave him a certain grim satisfaction.

"Whatcha got there, Zeke?" Jake leaned against the side of the shit shack, his hat tipped back and an expression of unabashed curiosity on his freckled face.

"A trespasser in the hotel."

"I am *not* a trespasser. My name is Byron Ackerman and I own the establishment." He tried once again to yank his arm free, unsuccessfully of course. Zeke had the muscles and build of a man used to working hard labor from sunup to sundown. "Ask Mr. Marchison at the store. He was kind enough to sell me some supplies this morning."

"Wait, did you say Ackerman?" Jake straightened and looked apologetically at Zeke. "Gabby told me somebody had bought the hotel. I meant to tell you last week but she

89

distracted me and then... Oh hell, I don't know. I guess I forgot."

"You see. Whoever this man is, he understands reason and listens when other people speak." Ackerman stumbled when Zeke let him go, almost falling on his perfectly groomed head.

"Thanks a lot, Jake. You're supposed to give me the information from the town council right away, not a week after your dick takes over your brain." He wasn't angry with his friend, but annoyed that he couldn't lock up the fancy-pants Yankee.

"Sorry, I just forgot." Jake wiped his hand on his flour-coated pants and held it out to the fussing Mr. Ackerman. "Jacob Sheridan, pleased to meet you."

The stranger looked at Jake's hand, a second too long in Zeke's opinion, before he shook it. "The pleasure is mine, ah, Mr. Sheridan." He glanced down at the flour residue on his hand before pulling out a handkerchief to wipe it off with methodical thoroughness.

"Mr. Sheridan here is the mayor's husband and a town council member." Zeke couldn't help but feel vindicated when shock flashed across the stranger's face.

No matter how much the Yankee bothered him personally, Zeke wasn't mistaken about Ackerman. As he smiled, his expression turned much friendlier. What lurked behind his blue eyes remained carefully blank.

"A female mayor? I heard Tanger was different and I'm pleased to see that's true. I'd love to meet Mrs. Sheridan soon." Ackerman turned a cold gaze onto Zeke. "Sheriff, I'll be returning to my hotel now, provided I have your permission."

Zeke's expression was as deadly as the gun beneath his itchy palm. "By all means. I'm sure I'll be seeing you soon."

"Hello gentlemen." Naomi's voice was not only unexpected,

it made Zeke's entire body clench.

Good thing he could control himself, because she wore the same pretty yellow dress again, looking fresh faced and absolutely beautiful. His first impulse was to grab her and kiss her, the second was to yank her out of Ackerman's line of sight. What he should really do is turn and walk away. He needed to keep away from her.

The Yankee looked like a hungry wolf spotting a juicy sheep. He slicked back his hair with his left hand and straightened his lapels.

"Good morning, madam." He bowed slightly. "My name is Byron Ackerman. I'm new to town and pleased to meet you."

Naomi, to her credit, didn't stammer or blush. She stared at the man, her lips compressed tightly.

"Good day, sir." Her only response.

"And you are?" He held out his hand, yet Naomi didn't take it.

"None of your damn business, Ackerman."

Her hazel eyes widened at Zeke's snarl. "My name is Miss Naomi Tucker. It's a pleasure to meet you, Mr. Ackerman."

Zeke stared hard at her, his blood rushing through him. "Are you getting pleasure meeting this Yankee?"

"Shut your mouth, Sheriff. You're being contrary and rude." Her cheeks flared pink.

"I could put you back in jail faster than you can blink, *Miss Tucker*."

"Just try it." She pointed her chin toward him, daring him.

The argument made Zeke's body heat and damned if he didn't have the urge to fuck her up against the wall of the building in front of him, as well as to paddle her ass.

"Ahem, much as I'm enjoying this, I'm going to have to

91

interrupt." Ackerman sounded as if he really was enjoying it, stupid son of a bitch.

Naomi shot an icy glare at Zeke, then took a deep breath, pushing her delicious breasts against the yellow fabric. His teeth ground together when she finally held out her hand to Ackerman.

"I was just on my way to have breakfast at Elmer's Restaurant if you'd care to join me."

Zeke sucked in a breath at her brazenness. Inviting a man to eat with her? What the hell was she thinking?

Ackerman didn't need any more encouragement. "I'd be happy to join you."

"I'm sure Sheriff Blackwood and his friend have duties to attend to. There must be small children to scare and puppies to kick." She tucked her arm in the man's and turned him down the street. "What brings you to Tanger?"

Their conversation faded as the pair wandered away, leaving Zeke ready to bite nails in half. He'd obviously handled that completely wrong. Hell, he hadn't even had a chance to talk to her since, well, since the night he arrested her, the night he'd discovered she was more potent than any whiskey. Maybe he ought to talk to Lucy first and get an idea of how things went at the saloon.

Then he could paddle Naomi's ass.

"She's got you all tied up in knots, doesn't she?" Jake's comment made Zeke start a bit. He'd forgotten his friend was standing there witnessing everything.

"What makes you say that?" Zeke snarled.

Jake, as usual, laughed. "I guess that answers my question."

"Shut up, you fool."

That only make Jake laugh harder. Zeke walked away, heading for the saloon, his gut churning.

Lucy glanced up from the game of solitaire as Zeke slammed into the saloon. Her dark eyebrows rose when she saw the expression on his face, and perhaps in surprise that he was in the saloon at all.

"Sheriff Blackwood. What happened to bring you into the *saloon*?"

He let the jab fly past him. "I just met the new owner of the hotel." He sat down heavily across from her. "The man is an ass."

"Ackerman? Yep, met him last night." She laid a card down. "You don't like him? He's handsome."

Zeke snorted, ignoring the bait Lucy flung at him. "He's a goddamn Yankee, and a pompous windbag."

"So you don't like him." Lucy shook her head. "A shame, too. Louisa said he's very polite and mannerly."

Zeke's jaw tightened to the point that he heard teeth crack. "He's already visited a whore?"

"I didn't say he went upstairs with her, just that he'd been nice to her. There's no call to insult Louisa." Lucy threw a disgusted look at him. "You always expect the worst of folks."

"They usually don't disappoint me either." Zeke didn't want to fight with Lucy about what her girls did upstairs. Actually that made him think about what Naomi did or didn't do up there, no matter what she said. He cleared his throat and shook off the image of Naomi naked with another man.

"You're too cynical by half, Zeke." She laid her hand on his. "You need a good woman." When she squeezed his hand, he pulled it away.

"What did you do to Naomi for starting the saloon brawl?" he blurted, uncomfortable with the implication Lucy wanted to be that woman in his life. He felt nothing but friendship for her.

"Do to her? I didn't do anything to her." Lucy stood and threw the rest of the cards at him. "You don't care a thing about anyone but yourself." Lucy stomped away, cursing him to hell and back. She stopped at the bottom of the stairs and came back, hands on hips. "What did *you* do to her?"

Leave it to Lucy to turn the tables on him. Zeke kept his expression blank. "I arrested her for starting the brawl."

"I'm not sure that's all you did." Lucy might show the world one face, but she was extremely smart, maybe even as smart as Gideon. She had the ability to figure out things she shouldn't. "She came back looking mighty worn out."

"I only gave her something to eat, cornbread from the restaurant." Zeke waved his hand in dismissal. "Just now she sashayed up to Ackerman and walked away like she was a working girl on the *street*. I want to know what you said or did to her. I can't have that happening in Tanger." That ought to make the town council happy with him.

"What Naomi does is her business." Lucy clamped her mouth closed, a stubborn tilt to her pointy chin. "You're trying to bully me."

"I am not." *Liar.*

"Zeke, when you get your head out of your ass, you come back and talk to me. For now, get the hell out." Lucy pointed at the door and Zeke obeyed like a whipped dog.

He stepped back out into the morning air and took a deep breath, but it didn't help. His gaze wandered back up the street to where Naomi had disappeared with Ackerman. Against his will, his feet turned and followed the woman who had taken up residence in his mind.

Naomi regretted taking Ackerman's arm the second she touched him. He was cold and stiff like a frozen fish, which sent a shiver up her spine. Of course, the look on Zeke's handsome face was almost worth it. He'd been angry, annoyed and confused at the same time.

Served him right. Pompous, arrogant ass that he was, he practically called her a whore right there on the street. Naomi was hurt and embarrassed by the whole thing and now she'd set herself up for breakfast with a total stranger.

By the time they arrived at Elmer's, Ackerman had been talking nonstop about the hotel and how he hoped to make it a successful business by year's end. To be honest, she heard every third word. The man sure did think highly of himself.

"How long have you lived in Tanger, Miss Tucker?" Ackerman asked as he held the door open for her.

"Just a week, Mr. Ackerman." She walked in, half expecting Zeke to arrive any minute to berate her again.

Instead, a one-armed man gave her a disgusted look before he disappeared into the kitchen, shaking his head. She wondered who he was, and why he had been so openly hostile.

Ackerman led her to a table by the window, which suited her because her back was to the kitchen and the stranger's assessing gaze.

"Have you eaten here?" Ackerman smiled, one that did not reach his eyes.

"Not really. Although the cornbread is delicious." A memory of being with Zeke in the sweet shadows of the night, the taste and smell of all that was him, washed over her. A shudder ripped through her, leaving goose bumps and achingly hard nipples in its wake.

Ackerman didn't even try to hide his interest. In fact, his gaze snapped straight to her breasts, lust evident on his pale face. Naomi was used to men disrespecting her, and this just confirmed her opinion the man was not worth her time.

Too bad she'd invited him for breakfast.

"What will you have?" A woman appeared beside the table. Her light brown hair was back in a bun and she watched them warily. If Naomi had to hazard a guess, this was Margaret, the cook who'd been recently hired. She had ghosts behind her dark eyes, ones that called out to Naomi's own, creating an instant bond between them. A slight nod of the other woman's head was the only acknowledgement of what Naomi felt.

"What do you have for breakfast in this establishment, madam?" Ackerman must not realize he sounded like a pompous fool.

"Eggs, bacon, biscuits, grits and coffee." Margaret was definitely not one to be wordy.

"Eggs and a biscuit, please." Naomi pointed to the thick white mug on the table. "And coffee too if you wouldn't mind."

"Ah, yes, I'll have the same, but with bacon. I don't suppose you have butter for the biscuits, do you?" He brought out a handkerchief and wiped at the wood table, brushing imaginary dirt and crumbs to the floor.

Naomi didn't know how to react to such behavior, but Margaret did. She whipped a towel out from her apron and slapped it on the table hard, twice. Ackerman jumped a few inches off his chair while Naomi had trouble keeping a chuckle contained.

"There you go. Clean as a whistle." Margaret tucked the towel away. "I'll go get the coffee and butter."

"She certainly needs better manners." Ackerman tugged at his vest as he settled back into the chair. "I expect it's going to

96

take time to get used to Tanger and its residents."

Naomi nodded. "I'm sure you're right. Tanger is a mixture of all kinds of folks and we've all got something, er, different about us." She wanted to point out he was already fitting in nicely, what with his weird habits and all.

"I can see that." Ackerman met her gaze. "You, for example. Working at the saloon must be challenging for a beautiful woman such as yourself. You must be a busy girl."

What he didn't say was what Naomi heard. He thought her beauty led her right up the stairs to the bedroom, where she likely earned money on her back. She held onto her temper by a thread although it was a mighty thin thread.

"I work hard serving drinks and cleaning up. Lucy doesn't expect anything else and I don't provide it." Her hands fisted in her lap.

"That's good, very good. I'm glad to hear you are proud of your work. Women who enter the working world of men must always work hard to make up for their lack of strength and abilities."

It was a good thing Margaret arrived with the coffeepot and a crock of butter because Naomi was ready to crack one of the mugs over Ackerman's head. She'd spent her life fighting the prejudices against women, which had been heaped on her head by arrogant men.

"Ah, good, thank you, my good woman." Ackerman pointed to his empty mug, proving once again he had no idea how to treat people.

After Margaret filled his mug, she offered a ghost of a grin to Naomi before filling hers. She decided to come back without the hotel man to get to know the older woman. A true friend would be welcome in Naomi's lonely world.

By the time their eggs arrived, Ackerman still hadn't run

out of things to say about himself. Naomi considered poking herself in the eye with a fork to escape, but didn't want to ruin the eggs or biscuit. They were absolutely delicious, even if the company wasn't welcome.

"Naomi, my girl, you are a little distracted. Is everything all right?" He pointed at her plate. "You seem to be focused on your food and aren't even looking up to speak."

"I was quite hungry, Mr. Ackerman." She glanced at his plate. "And you've done your fair share of eating and talking at once."

The surprise in his eyes was followed by a wicked grin. "You've got an interesting sense of humor. I like it."

"Thank you, I think." Naomi shoved the last of the biscuit in her mouth. "I've got to be going."

"Of course, of course." He gestured to the table. "I hope you'll allow me to pay for your meal."

She stared into his eyes, trying to read what lurked behind them. Naomi had been the one to invite him to breakfast and intended to pay for her own food. His gesture either meant he expected something in return or he was a gentleman. She was inclined to believe the former.

"That wouldn't be proper, Mr. Ackerman. I'll pay my own way." She looked around for Margaret.

"Nonsense. I insist." Ackerman reached out and took Naomi's hand, sending a cold shiver up her skin. "Please consider it a thank you for welcoming me to Tanger."

It took every ounce of self-control not to yank her hand away and rub it on her dress to get rid of the feel of his soft, clammy skin. She was raised better than that, however much her circumstances had changed.

"If I accept a meal from you, folks will talk, and I don't want to be beholden to you, so thank you, but no." Naomi took her hand from his and stepped towards the kitchen.

"Admirable, but unnecessary. I wouldn't expect anything from you." Ackerman smiled, yet it didn't feel genuine. "I'm afraid I must insist."

The one-armed man appeared beside the table. "Why don't you let your boyfriend pay for you, Miss Tucker? After all, you are spending time with him. It's only fair you get paid for your time."

Naomi's temper bubbled up at his insinuations and before she could stop herself, she'd slapped him so hard, her hand stung from the contact. A red mark blossomed on his cheek beneath the muscle working in his jaw.

"That wasn't very nice," he ground out.

"Neither were you." She turned and left the restaurant, sure the entire town would chase her out within days. Why couldn't she just be a happy, sweet girl like Louisa? No, she had to be a hellion and get herself in trouble over and over again.

As Naomi walked down the street berating herself, she belatedly realized she had allowed Ackerman to pay for the meal after all. Stupid girl.

Chapter Six

The night air was thick with the smell of honeysuckle and the song of the cicada. Zeke walked through town doing his nightly rounds, but his mind was on Naomi. At three in the morning, the only two-legged creature about was the sheriff who couldn't keep his mind on his job.

He found himself standing at the back stairs of the saloon, looking up at the corner room. Naomi's room. She'd talked about getting the smallest space with the sloped ceiling and he'd known exactly where she slept. He'd stayed there on occasion when Lucy let him sleep off his frequent binges at Aphrodite's.

The same bed now held the petite body of a saloon girl who'd taken up residence in his head. He'd thought endlessly of what could have happened during her breakfast with that Yankee. He'd avoided the restaurant, the hotel and the saloon all day.

Now here he was outside, his fists clenched so hard, his knuckles popped. Sweat blossomed on his brow as his need for Naomi, to touch her, kiss her, possess her, pulsed through him. He closed his eyes as a throbbing arousal built in his trousers.

The need for whiskey had never been as strong as this. It was as if he was possessed by something or someone. When he started to shake, Zeke groaned like an animal with his leg caught in a trap. After dredging more self-control than he thought he had, he turned and left. Sweat trickled down his back and neck while his dick screamed in protest. A howl rose up inside him, escaping as a moan from deep in his throat.

Anyone passing by might have seen a blond wolf instead of a man.

Naomi sat up in bed, a prickle of emotion sweeping over her. She looked around the small room, peering into the corners and finding nothing. However, the hackles on the back of her neck rose along with every hair on her body.

Zeke.

It was as if she felt him nearby, which was loco, but true nonetheless. She slipped out of bed and padded to the window, the wood floor rough under her feet. With her heart pounding in anticipation, she pushed aside the sheet she'd hung as a temporary curtain.

The darkness below seemed absolute, the only light from the stars in the black velvet sky. The moon hadn't risen yet and every building was asleep in the eerie gloom. The meager light from her candle barely permeated the shadows outside. She looked out for ten minutes, but nothing moved, the only sound the music of the night creatures.

She knew he was out there, somewhere, watching her. With a frustrated sigh, she walked back to bed, blew out the candle and lay down with a sigh.

Within minutes, her restlessness had not abated and she had the insane urge to take off her shimmy. So she did. With her naked on top of the covers, the slight cool breeze ruffled the sheet and slid over her skin. Goose bumps turned into arousal as she let her body take over.

Her nipples hardened into near painful peaks as a throb

began in her lower belly. Of their own volition, one hand landed on a nipple while the other crept down her belly to the nest of curls below.

The first stroke of her finger in the moist folds of her sex made her moan. Tingles spread out from the contact. Her short breaths were the only sound in the room. She pinched her nipple as she stroked her clit.

She began to imagine it wasn't her hands, that she was being aroused by a lover she knew, who knew her. Sensuous, sweet heat began to build in her core. She lifted her knees and spread her legs as far as they'd go. One finger, then two, slid into the part of her that ached for more than she could give herself.

When roughened hands covered hers, Naomi almost screamed. Zeke's scent washed over her and a fresh burst of arousal slammed into her.

"Zeke," she breathed.

"Shhh." He raised her hand to his lips and licked her fingers. "Sweet as honey."

She shivered at the touch of his tongue. Perhaps he was real, but maybe he wasn't. It didn't matter—he was there in her arms, in her bed, and nothing else was important.

If he was a ghost, he was a damn fine one. Calloused hands landed on her knees, rubbing in circles as they went up her thighs, moving closer and closer to that which pulsed and ached with need.

"You have such a pretty pussy." He skimmed the edge of her nether lips, sending a jolt up her body straight to her nipples. "Do you mind if I have a taste?"

Naomi would have laughed if she'd had breath left in her body. Instead, she grabbed his hand and placed it on her mound.

He chuckled. "I guess that's a yes."

She waited in anticipation, her body thrumming with arousal. It seemed to be hours, but was only moments before two fingers ran up and down her wetness. She closed her eyes and absorbed the pleasure. He nudged at her thighs, spreading them wider, and her heated flesh nearly hissed in the cool night air as it was exposed.

The first touch of his tongue felt like a lightning strike. She almost jumped off the bed, bumping him with her hip. He pushed her back down and spoke to her like she was a wild mustang.

"Easy, girl, easy. Just enjoy the ride, little one."

This time at the touch of his mouth on her, she closed her eyes and let herself go. She fell into a whirling pool of pleasurable feelings, all concentrated between her legs, until his hand crept up her stomach to her aching breasts. He cupped one breast as if weighing it, then pinched the nipple just as his teeth closed around her clit. Naomi gasped at the sensation, forcing herself to lie still and revel in the fact a man was pleasuring her.

His tongue swept up and down, licking and lapping at her as two fingers slid into her. Triple points of sweet ecstasy for her to enjoy. Each swipe of his tongue, each pinch and tweak of her nipple, drew her closer and closer to something amazing.

He seemed to know it because he slowed his pace, bringing her back from the edge. Her muscles tightened as he started his assault again. Lick, nip, suck, again and again.

"Now." She could have said please, but her pride always got in the way. Instead she ordered him, and he obeyed.

Zeke latched onto her clit and sucked her as his tongue tickled it. It was extreme, intense and explosive. Her entire body clenched around his fingers as a wave of sheer ecstasy enveloped her. He held her down to the bed, licking and nibbling her, pulling pulse after pulse from her until she thought she'd faint.

He gentled his touch, releasing her nipple and removing his fingers from her convulsing pussy, licking her slowly.

"God, you're amazing." He kissed each thigh in turn while she lay on the bed, a boneless heap of smiling woman.

She heard the rustle of clothes as he undressed in the meager light. By the time he crawled on the bed, the stars behind her lids had faded and she remembered her name.

When his hard body lay atop hers, she came to life as if the most incredible orgasm of her life hadn't just happened. Already she was panting in anticipation, eager to join with him again. Their night in the jail seemed like a million years ago.

Being completely naked with him on her bed was a much different experience, one filled with new sensations and delights. He had deliciously tickling hairs on his legs and chest, which rubbed on her skin, raising goose bumps as he moved against her, settling himself between her legs.

"Mmm, you feel good."

He chuckled against her neck. "Not as good as you do. Damn, woman, I think I died and went to heaven."

His hardened staff pressed against the entrance to her pussy, the mushroom tip teasing her with pleasure to come.

"Put it in." She wiggled against him, trying to pull him inside her. Naomi sounded like a wanton, when Zeke was the only man she'd ever found pleasure with.

"Pushy, ain't you?" He pinned her wrists to the bed and kissed his way down to her breasts. The nipples peaked, aching for his touch. His tongue circled them, keeping her panting for more. By the time he finally closed around the tip, she nearly had an orgasm from the warmth of his mouth, the rasp of his tongue and the nip of his teeth.

Sweet wet heat ran through her like liquid honey. The buzzing deep within her spiraled tighter and tighter as he made his way up to her lips. When his tongue entered her mouth, his cock entered her aching core, mimicking the movement.

Naomi pushed up to meet his thrust as he stretched her, filled her, showed her what it meant when a woman was ready for a man. It was sheer magic to her, a feeling of completeness she hadn't experienced with a man before. He moved in and out in a rhythm designed to make her wild.

She scratched at his back, eager for him to go deeper and harder. Her muscles clenched, needing something else, but she wasn't experienced enough to know what.

"Zeke," she gasped. "I need...God, I don't..."

"I know, little one. I understand." He pushed her knees up, opening her wide. When he landed deep inside her, Naomi found what she needed.

As they rode the waves of pleasure together, she held on with both hands to her soul, but the winds of their passion and yes, love, swept it away to merge with his. It wasn't God or anyone else's name she called as her second peak hit with the force of a twister. It was Zeke's.

The room was silent except for the sound of their breathing. The air was thick with the smell of sex and body heat. Naomi was truly stunned by what happened, and she wanted answers from her two-time lover.

"Why did you come to me?"

He rolled to his side, bracing his head with one hand. In the dim light, she couldn't see the expression on his face. "I couldn't seem to stay away."

She didn't understand his answer. "Did you try to stay away?"

"I'm risking my job being here. I made a promise to the town council to uphold the law and keep away from women and whiskey. You made me break that promise." He picked up a lock of her hair and brought it to his nose.

"I didn't make you do anything." She frowned. "You came to my bed, remember?"

After a beat of silence, he sighed. "I couldn't forget even if I tried."

"I am still mad at you for how you treated me in front of Mr. Ackerman. You were an ass." Naomi sat up, fresh annoyance slipping through her sensual haze.

Zeke sat up too. "I don't like or trust the man. He's up to no good."

She noticed he hadn't apologized. "And?"

"And I'm sorry." He sounded pained. "I— Well— You— Hell, I don't know what I'm saying." Zeke put his head in his hands.

Naomi's anger deflated in an instant, and she was reminded of the bond that had developed during the night at the jail. Not just the sexual one, but the emotional one. Each of them had survived the aftermath of the war in the south, had lost their homes, their families, to be cast adrift.

Now the drifting souls had found each other. She didn't know what it meant, but it frightened her.

Zeke sipped his coffee as he watched Margaret bustle around the restaurant getting it ready for the breakfast crowd. It was early, with the pink shards of the sunrise just fracturing the sky. He hadn't been to bed and counted on the coffee to get him through the day.

His body was well sated after climbing into Naomi's bed the night before. God only knew what possessed him to do it. However, he knew it couldn't happen again. She couldn't become a habit, a mistake that could bring him down.

"Breakfast?" Margaret startled him. He hadn't even heard her approaching.

"Don't think my gut could handle much." He lifted the mug. "This here's all I need, and it's damn good too."

The ghost of a smile flitted across her face. "I'll get you a biscuit to go with it. That's your brother's coffee and it's thicker than mud."

Zeke hadn't known Lee was up or that he could make such good coffee. Wonders never ceased.

The door to the restaurant opened and the bell jingled at the movement. Zeke glanced up to see a fresh-faced young man wearing a minister's collar and a huge smile. He reminded Zeke of Gideon a long time ago, before the war had stolen that youthful look. He even had wavy brown hair like his cousin.

"Good morning, sir. I wondered if the restaurant was open." The drawl of a Midwestern state echoed in the minister's voice.

"Come on in. I'm sure we could scare up some vittles for you." Zeke watched as the young man loped in. He was like a puppy with paws too big for his body. Long, lanky and full of what Zeke could only think of as joy, the kid came in nearly tripping on his own big feet.

"Thank you kindly. I arrived very late last night and I haven't eaten since yesterday's breakfast." He held out his hand. "Gregory Conley."

"Zeke Blackwood. Please sit down and join me."

After shaking his hand, the young man plopped down in the chair at the table. He pointed to the star on Zeke's shirt.

"You are the sheriff in town?"

"Yep, that I am." Zeke watched Margaret out of the corner of his eye as she brought a plate with biscuits on it. She slowed just a moment when she spotted Gregory, but kept walking.

"Good morning, ma'am." Gregory eyed the fluffy biscuits with a hungry gaze.

"Mornin'." She set the plate on the table and nodded to the kid. "You new in town or passing through?"

"Oh, I'm new in town. I want to set up a church here in Tanger. I heard there was no preacher in town and well, here I am." He talked fast enough to put a knot in his tongue.

"We surely need some spiritual guidance." Margaret, to Zeke's surprise, seemed to warm to Gregory immediately. She hadn't spoken much to anyone, yet here she was chatting with the young minister.

"I thought I'd just start by meeting everyone and then worry about where we could hold services. It's beautiful here. I think I've come to the right place." Gregory smiled at Zeke.

Zeke didn't want to, but the boy's enthusiasm coaxed a smile out of his creaky face. "I think you have too."

Lee walked in with coffee in hand, papers tucked under his arm. "You know, Gideon couldn't cipher if you held a gun to his head. These accounts are a fucking mess."

"Gregory, this is my foul-mouthed brother Lee. Lee, this is Gregory Conley, a preacher new in town." Zeke enjoyed the emotions that crossed his brother's face. In the end, Lee set everything down and stuck out his hand to the man.

"Pleased to meet you, Greg."

To Gregory's credit, he didn't miss a beat although Lee's

cursing had put a pink blush to his smooth cheeks. "It's a pleasure to meet you too, Mr. Blackwood."

"Ah, hell, boy, I mean, just call me Lee. I ain't been Mr. Blackwood before and I don't plan on starting now." He grinned at Zeke. "I'll leave that to my big brother. He wears mister better."

"Sit down, fool, and have some breakfast." Zeke pulled the chair out next to him. "Margaret, could you please get some food for them?"

Margaret shot a cold glare at Lee. "I know what he wants. Mr. Conley, what would you like?"

Gregory smiled at her. "Eggs, bacon, biscuits, anything really. Oatmeal is great too."

The preacher seemed to be an honest, open person who didn't set off any of Zeke's inner alarms.

"Be right back then." Margaret swiped Lee's mug and went into the kitchen.

"Did you see that? She took my coffee. Geez, you would have thought I committed a cardinal sin or something," Lee groused.

"Cardinal sins are nothing to joke about." Gregory obviously didn't understand Lee's sense of humor yet.

"What did you do?" Zeke cocked one eyebrow at his brother.

With a dramatic sigh, Lee frowned at the closed door she'd walked through. "I added something to her stew last night."

Zeke burst out laughing at the idea his brother was cowed by a cook angry at him for tampering with her cooking. Gregory smiled, but didn't join in Zeke's humor.

"She's formidable when she wants to be. Who knew adding some parsley would turn her into a vicious witch?"

109

That made Zeke laugh harder, even if Lee threw him a wicked glare.

"If you could see your face," Zeke got out.

"Shut up, Ezekiel, before I put some parsley on you and roast you on the spit." Lee stood, the chair skidding across the floor. His anger was taking over his common sense, yet again.

Zeke put his hand on his brother's, swallowing the rest of his mirth. "I'm sorry, Lee, it's just good to laugh again, you know?"

"Hmph, just not at my expense." He pulled the chair back and sat down heavily. "She's driving me plumb loco."

"Sounds as if you like her. Perhaps we have a first wedding for you, Reverend Conley."

Lee's mouth dropped open. "Excuse me? She hates me, and even if she didn't, there's no way any woman would marry a one-armed man."

Zeke clapped his brother on the back. "Don't put yourself down, brother. You're smart, you've proved that by fixing the books for the restaurant. Whoever buys this place next will be mighty appreciative of that. And you're good-looking and young. She'd be a fool not to want to marry you."

"Just the same, Zeke, I don't think that's ever going to happen." As Margaret walked back out with the pot and two mugs, Lee shut his mouth. Zeke found it astonishing that a woman, any woman, could put Lee on his head. He hadn't been serious about the wedding, but perhaps it wasn't too far out of the realm of possibility.

She thumped down the two clean mugs and poured coffee, then topped off Zeke's. "I've got some fresh eggs cooking. Be out in a jiffy."

Lee stared at the cup in front of him then glanced up at

Zeke. The need that shone in his eyes was there for only a split second, but Zeke saw it anyway. His brother must've fallen for Margaret, or at least had feelings for her. Feelings he obviously didn't want anyone to see or know about. Zeke had been joking, but now it appeared to be serious. Damn, another one of the Devils involved with a woman? Jesus, they were dropping like flies.

"Well, at least she brought me another mug." Lee slurped the brew noisily. The flavor apparently surprised him because he stared at the liquid with suspicion. "This ain't my coffee."

"Hm, perhaps Margaret made a pot that didn't taste like old socks." Zeke sipped the bitter version in his own mug. "I'm guessing she's not fond of your coffee."

Lee swallowed and cleared his throat before he spoke again. "I suppose you're right."

"This coffee is tasty," Gregory offered as he looked back and forth between them. "I've had some that tastes like dirty water mixed with dirt while I was traveling."

Zeke wanted to find out what was going on between Lee and Margaret, but now definitely wasn't the time. He focused on Gregory instead. "Where do you hail from, Preacher?"

"Kansas, near Topeka. Right before my granddaddy died, he told me to find a new place to start over. He taught me to be a man of the cloth, read me the Bible and basically raised me after my mama passed giving birth to me. My father did his best to drink himself into a coffin, and finally succeeded last year." Gregory took a much-needed breath, then continued. "I sold everything we owned and started traveling. I've stayed with folks all over on the way from home to here. When I got to Tanger with a family on their way to Houston, I knew I'd finally got to where I was meant to be."

Zeke swallowed back a chuckle at the boy's ability to talk

faster than anybody he'd ever met. "What makes you think Tanger is where you were meant to be?"

Gregory smiled. "I saw an angel when the sun rose."

This time Lee laughed out loud. "Believe me, kid, there ain't no angels in Tanger."

"Oh, I think there is. A blonde angel in yellow, silhouetted in the sunrise as she walked down the street. She smiled at me and said welcome." Gregory sighed. "I am definitely in the right place."

Zeke had a suspicion he knew exactly who the angel was and she sure as hell wasn't a heavenly creature. God knows what she was doing on the street at sunrise, or perhaps he did know why. It had only been an hour since he'd left her bed. His body still buzzed with the arousal his time with her had only served to make more pronounced, perhaps hers did as well.

He'd tried his damnedest to keep his distance from her, had even walked away, yet he'd found himself by her bed. When he saw her pleasuring herself, his body took over completely. God he could still taste the tang of her nectar on his tongue, not even the bitter coffee could erase her sweet flavor.

"...and if you'll help me, I'd be most appreciative." Gregory looked at him expectantly. Zeke realized he'd been daydreaming about Naomi, for Chrissakes, and had missed what the young man had said.

"What do you think?" Zeke looked at Lee to rescue him.

"I think you spent the night forgetting just what your place in the world is." Lee shook his head. "You can't think but for her, can you?"

"Shut up, Cornelius." He was saved by Margaret when she appeared with three heaping plates of eggs, bacon and grits.

"Hearty meal for you fellas. I know there's plenty of work to be done." Margaret shot another glare at Lee. "Nothing like a good breakfast to get the day started right."

It was the most he'd ever heard Margaret say. She was chatting away that morning as if it were the most natural thing in the world. As if she hadn't spent most every minute quiet as a mouse as she worked at Elmer's restaurant. Zeke had an idea that what Lee felt for the reticent widow might be returned.

"Thanks, Margaret." Zeke didn't want all that food but he wasn't about to turn it down. Food had been too scarce to let any morsel go to waste.

"Thank you kindly, ma'am." Gregory dug in with gusto, almost bringing a smile to Zeke's face.

"You're welcome." With another pointed glare at Lee, Margaret returned to the kitchen.

The restaurant door opened and Matthew Marchison walked in. The man had aged ten years in the last one. His son had been killed in the war, then his wife was shot in the streets of Tanger after committing horrific crimes. The bald-headed, bespectacled man had done his best to prove he wasn't painted by the same brush as his cold-hearted bitch of a wife. He murmured a good morning and sat at a table across the room.

Lee glanced at Zeke, then kept his eyes on his plate. The silence was only broken by Gregory's moans of pleasure. Zeke remembered that feeling well, filling his belly with hot delicious food when it had been a dog's age since he'd felt full. He clapped the kid on the shoulder.

"Maybe you did come to the right town, Greg. I think we needed some young blood." He hoped the preacher kept his distance from the angel. Folks didn't take kindly to their spiritual leader keeping time with a saloon girl.

An idea blossomed in his head and he glanced at Matthew. "Hey, Marchison, do you have a minute?"

He looked up from the mug in front of him. "Of course, Zeke, what is it?"

"I wanted to introduce you to Gregory Conley. He's new to Tanger and a minister." Zeke gestured to Matthew to come over. "I think he needs a friend in town to help him get settled."

For the first time since he'd known the shopkeeper, the older man smiled, which completely transformed his face.

"I'd be pleased to." He stood and walked over to the table, holding out his hand. "Matthew Marchison, young man, I'm happy to help."

Just like that, Zeke had helped two men, and in the process, actually made himself feel good about it. It was a foreign feeling, but one he welcomed.

Chapter Seven

On Saturday, the second fight in the saloon gave Naomi the excuse to see Zeke without feeling guilty about it. Not that she felt guilty, but it had been five days since he'd come to her bed. It seemed so odd that less than two weeks had passed since they'd met. Impossible, really.

This time, fortunately, Naomi hadn't started the fight. She crouched behind the bar with Louisa and Carmen.

"What did you do this time?" Carmen's accusatory glare speared Naomi.

"I didn't do anything. They were fighting over a game of cards. I had nothing to do with it." She peeked over the bar, narrowly missing shards from a glass as it shattered against the wood.

"Ha, a *mujer* like you, I don't believe it." Carmen's dark eyes were sharper than the glass.

"I saw them, she's telling the truth." Louisa put her arms over her head. "We need that handsome sheriff to come in here and stop this."

Before Naomi could tell Louisa to leave the sheriff out of her fantasies, all three of them screamed as a body came flying over the top of the bar. Zeke's booming voice filled the room.

"Two fights in one week? I don't think so. Who the hell

started it this time?" The silence that followed was eerie after the cacophony of the fight. "Well?"

"I believe it was the two gentlemen in the back." Ackerman's nasally tone was unmistakable. Naomi had had no idea he was even in the saloon, or seen what happened. "The one in the blue shirt sporting a gash on his cheek and the one wearing the brown shirt and, ah, what seems to be whiskey in his hair."

A few grumbles met his tattling. Naomi shook her head. The man had no idea how to fit in with the townspeople. She didn't know what his thinking was, but he wouldn't make any friends in town by pointing fingers. Naomi tried to stand, but Louisa grabbed her arm.

"Are you loco? Get back down here."

"The fight's over. The sheriff is here." Naomi straightened.

"He is? Oh my." Louisa pulled down her bodice, nearly exposing her nipples before she stood. Naomi resisted the urge to slap her back down, except she had no claim on him. In fact, it seemed he'd been doing his best to avoid her.

Zeke cleared his throat and put his hands on his hips. "Are you sure about that, Ackerman?"

"Oh, quite sure. You see, I was playing poker with them when the fight began. I'm afraid all the money has been mixed up on the floor. I just wanted to be sure I didn't lose my portion." The dark-haired hotel owner was in the corner by the piano. If Naomi had to guess, she figured he'd been hiding during the ruckus, which didn't surprise her. He seemed like the type to avoid anything involving fists.

"You're worried about your money?" Zeke sounded more than annoyed.

"Why yes, I am. You see, it was only twenty dollars, but it truly was mine. I'd like it back."

116

Naomi didn't know if Ackerman was telling the truth about the money or not, but he should be grateful he hadn't gotten pounded during the fight. The hotel man was an odd fellow.

"Steve and John, you come with me. The two of you are spending the night at the jail." Zeke pointed at Lucy. "You figure out the money situation. Everyone else, you know the toll, give the house a dollar on your way out."

He turned and his gaze locked with Naomi's. Heat whipped between them even though they stood fifteen feet apart. Her pulse began to pound as she came around the bar. Her feet had taken over, bringing her closer to the man who occupied her mind.

Before she could reach him, Louisa pushed past her.

"Oh, Sheriff, I'm so glad you're here. I was so frightened." She pushed her overly large boobs against his arm and fluttered her eyelashes. Naomi wanted to pop her friend's breasts like a balloon.

"I'm sure you were, Louisa. Now you just go back to work and help Lucy clean up, okay?" Zeke patted her arm, dangerously close to the right mountain, and Naomi lost her temper.

"For God's sake, Louisa, stop throwing your tits at him." Naomi clamped a hand over her mouth after the words burst forth.

Louisa looked at her with genuine hurt in her eyes. She let Zeke go and walked towards the stairs. Zeke stared at Naomi from beneath the brim of his black hat. It was too dark to read his expression, but she knew it wasn't good. None of it was. She'd let herself get involved with a man who wouldn't acknowledge he came to her bed, or that she was anything other than a saloon girl.

Her heart was at risk with Zeke if she wasn't careful.

He turned away, breaking the spell between them. "Let's go, boys."

The two men pointed out by Ackerman shuffled towards the sheriff, their bloodied knuckles practically dragging on the floor. Naomi knew just what the jail held for them and wished them good luck. For herself, she just wanted to crawl into a hole in the floor and disappear.

"You didn't have to be such a *puta*, Naomi." Carmen smacked her on the arm. "Louisa is a good girl."

Naomi didn't get angry at the volatile Mexican woman. She was right after all. Naomi had been a bitch to sweet Louisa, and over a man no less. Lucy frowned at her and pointed at the floor.

"Get cleaning, Nammy. We need to get this mess righted so we can start serving drinks again." Lucy turned her back on Naomi, as did everyone else, except Zeke.

He met her gaze one last time before he walked out the door. What she wanted to do was turn around and follow him, but she didn't. Her survival instinct was stronger than the need for Zeke, for now anyway. She'd bide her time and visit the sheriff later.

Zeke's prisoners weren't happy about being placed in a cell together, but they quit squawking when he threatened them with a week in jail instead of one Saturday night. The cell wasn't big, of course, but they could get through being incarcerated in it just the same. Thank God Martin had finished the hinges or Zeke would have a lot more trouble on his hands.

His mind went back to Naomi as he sat at the desk, watching his prisoners ignore each other. She'd looked delicious in a bright blue dress that was too big in the chest, probably belonged to Louisa no doubt. That little one had it in her head

118

she needed to bed the sheriff, but he had no intention of it.

Once upon a time, he would have jumped at the opportunity to be with such a pretty young thing without worry of getting tangled with her heart. Louisa made it very clear she wanted nothing more than bed sport and had propositioned him at least half a dozen times.

Zeke, unfortunately, could not imagine himself with the brunette. She was curvy and round in all the right places, but his body just refused to rise to the occasion, so to speak. Aside from that, the town council was watching him like a hawk. He'd seen Oliver on numerous occasions near the jail, although he had no business on that end of town. Word must have reached the council about his association with Naomi or the whiskey. Either way, he knew his job could be yanked out from under him any moment.

However, his thoughts still circled back to Naomi, all the time. He hadn't been able to shake her image from his memory. It wasn't as if he was inexperienced with women, but he'd been selective in his choice of bedmates. She was nothing more than a saloon girl whose body seemed to be made for passion. Just thinking about her made his trousers tight.

Yet he'd picked bluebonnets earlier and left them on her bed. A romantic, stupid thing to do.

"No, I ain't moving, so just shut up," Steve shouted from the cell.

"Make me." John shoved the other man and suddenly his prisoners were coming to blows in the cell.

Zeke jumped out of his chair, embarrassed to be caught daydreaming about Naomi while his prisoners were fighting. He unlocked the cell door and tried to separate the men. Unfortunately, what he didn't expect was the two of them to turn on him.

His control of the situation was wrenched from him in seconds. Hard blows landed on his face and stomach as the cowboys did their best to beat the hell out of him. Hard knuckles, boots and even teeth hit him from two sides. Zeke in turn tried to do as much damage as he could, but surprise had done him in. He should have been paying more attention.

When one of them punched him in the kidney, Zeke gasped and fell to his knees, pain radiating through his body. One of the men escaped through the open door while the other continued to punch Zeke. He blindly punched the man's legs and knees.

"What the hell is going on here?" Gideon's voice boomed through the shit shack. A grunt, curse and a thud followed. "Where the hell are you going, fool?"

The snick of a gun being cocked echoed through the room even as the cowboy rained punches on his body.

"You might want to stop pounding on the sheriff before I give you a new hole in your head." Gideon rarely sounded cold or deadly, but damned if he didn't this time. Zeke sucked in a grateful breath when the punches ceased.

"We was just playing," John said from above him, lousy son of a bitch.

"You're full of shit. Zeke, you okay?"

Zeke held up one hand while the other pressed into his throbbing kidney. "Will be in a minute," he gasped out.

"You. John, right? Step back into the cell and sit on the corner of the cot." Gideon stepped closer. "Zeke, can you get up?"

"Where's Steve?" Zeke crawled backwards out of the cell.

"He's taking a nap by the door. Don't worry, he won't be moving anytime soon." Gideon took Zeke by the arm and pulled him up. He frowned when he caught sight of Zeke's face. "Jesus, please us."

Zeke leaned against the bars. "That bad, eh? They definitely know how to throw a punch." He cracked one eye to glare at John. "This one is spending the week in here until I can figure out how to get him in prison."

"Prison? What the hell are you talking about?" John started to stand, but Gideon raised his pistol again.

"I suggest you sit your stupid ass back down."

The brawler did as Gideon bade and sat in the corner, grumbling to himself.

"You should definitely charge him with assault. In the meantime, you need to go see the doc to get patched up. Don't worry about these two, I'll keep an eye on them." He softened his expression when he met Zeke's gaze. "You need a deputy and another cell, cousin."

"Yeah, well, since Tanger's barely paying me enough to feed me and I might not be the sheriff in another few weeks time, I don't think they're gonna be ready to spend more money any time soon. You volunteering to be a deputy?" Zeke straightened and winced as a thousand pain points echoed through his back and head.

"For now, yep, I'll be your stand-in. Now go see Doc Barham."

Zeke managed a weak salute. "Aye, Cap'n. On my way."

A ten minute walk took him thirty since Zeke's head kept spinning as he plodded along. He must have gotten one too many hits to his noggin from those cowboys. Thinking about Naomi usually got him in trouble and this time it almost cost him much more than wasted time or energy. By the time he made it to Barham's house, he was sweating buckets and his stomach churned without mercy. When the door appeared in front of him, he barely missed knocking with his head as he fell forward.

Naomi finished cleaning without a peep of protest. She still felt badly about what she'd said to Louisa, especially considering Naomi had no claim on the enigmatic sheriff. He did as he pleased without any ties to any woman, regardless of their intimate relationship.

She put the broom away, said good night to Joe and headed upstairs. It would be a restless night, that was a certainty. Louisa's door was closed and Naomi didn't have the energy to apologize just yet. Morning would be better, after they'd all had some sleep. The sounds of the bedsprings squeaking in Carmen's room told the story of just what was going on in there.

Naomi opened the door to her room and spotted bluebonnets on her bed. They'd obviously been there several hours judging by the condition of the blooms, but the sight of the simple prairie flower made her throat close up. Zeke must have put them there, no one else would have. Her heart leapt with sudden lightness as she caressed the delicate petals.

Her energy renewed, Naomi washed up quickly and put on her clean dress. He had always seemed to like the yellow one so it was a good thing the garment was clean. She brushed her hair, then quietly stepped back out in the hallway. The saloon was eerie in the middle of the night, when all was silent and still.

The minute thump of her shoes on the stairs was the only sound until she reached the bottom and the hiss of a match in the shadows made her jump. Lucy lit a cigarette in the gloom, watching Naomi.

"Where you headed, sugar?"

Lucy knew exactly where Naomi was going, yet she was playing a game anyway. That stuck in Naomi's gut and she had to bite back the snide response that threatened to escape.

"I needed some fresh air." Lying was coming easier to her.

"And the air coming through your window ain't enough?" Lucy sauntered over to the stairs, the cigarette tip glowing amber.

"No, not really." Naomi clutched one bluebonnet in her closed fist, unwilling to allow her boss to ruin the sweet gesture.

"All gussied up in clean clothes. You fixing to go see Zeke?" Lucy wasn't dumb, no matter how people viewed her.

"More than likely." Naomi was tired of being coy and didn't want to have to lie anymore. She started walking towards the door.

"I thought as much. You might as well know he don't plan on marrying, ever, so if you are heading that way, best change your mind." Lucy sounded tired, exhausted really. She took another drag of the cigarette. "He might have changed his mind for Allison, but she's gone."

Naomi stopped in her tracks, her heart pounding against the thin cotton dress. "Who's Allison?"

"Hasn't told you, eh? Typical man." Lucy scoffed as she leaned up against the bar and took another long drag from the cigarette, then spit the tobacco off her tongue. "She was the preacher's daughter. Zeke and his friends came to town to help Tanger get rid of some raiders who were picking off women. He and Allison got on real well, were sparking like young folks. She was caught by some raiders after they killed her daddy. Poor thing had her throat slit right in front of him."

Naomi gasped, she couldn't help it. The memory of seeing her father murdered got mixed up with the picture Lucy painted of the ill-fated Allison. Her stomach clenched so tightly, she tasted bile in the back of her throat. No wonder Zeke was so cold and distant and unwilling to acknowledge any kind of relationship with a woman. He kept himself closed off for good reason. How was it possible Naomi, another preacher's daughter, ended up in his arms?

"What happened to the raiders?"

"Zeke and his boys killed them."

Naomi felt satisfaction course through her even if it meant she was bloodthirsty. Anyone who would kill a preacher and a young woman deserved what they got.

"I just thought I'd warn you. He's not going to do anything other than fuck you." Lucy's coarse language didn't serve to deter Naomi from her course of action.

The bluebonnets were a beacon of hope in the dark world Zeke occupied. He'd gone out of his way to show her something beautiful, to give her a piece of sweetness. Perhaps that meant there was more than a physical connection between them.

"Thanks for the advice, Lucy. I'll keep it in mind." She walked towards the door, the soft petals warm in her hand. "Good night."

Lucy didn't respond, but Naomi could feel the older woman's stare nearly burning a hole in her back. It took only five minutes to reach the jail and by the time she arrived, she knew it had been the right decision. A smile spread across her face in anticipation. What she didn't expect was to find a brown-haired man instead of Zeke.

He looked at her with surprise on his handsome face. "Hello there, miss. Can I help you?"

"Where's Zeke?" she blurted.

"He had a bit of a rough time with his prisoners." He gestured to the two cowboys occupying her cell, this time with the door attached. "I sent him to the doc."

She crossed her arms. "Is he okay?"

"I expect so. Elliott is a good sawbones." He stood and held out his hand. The man was as big as Zeke. Must be one of his friends she'd heard about. "I'm Gideon Blackwood."

"Zeke's brother?" She felt a bit of heat on her cheeks. "I mean, the sheriff's brother?"

"No, ma'am, cousin. His brother's name is Lee. He's blond like Zeke and sports one arm. You might have seen him at the restaurant."

So that had been Zeke's brother the day she'd had breakfast at the restaurant with Ackerman. It might explain why he'd been hostile and downright rude to her—perhaps he didn't like her taking up with his brother. Too bad he couldn't be as friendly as Gideon.

"It's a pleasure to meet you, Mr. Blackwood. Naomi Tucker."

Gideon smiled, his blue eyes crinkling at the corners. "Ah, Miss Tucker. Yes, I've heard your name once or twice."

Naomi wondered in what context her name had been mentioned. "Do you think he's still at the doctor's?"

"Maybe. Either that or he's back at the restaurant. We live above it." He stuck his hands in his pockets and rocked back on his heels.

It was very late for a visit, had to be three o'clock in the morning, yet Naomi knew she was going to find Zeke that night, no matter what. She had to.

"Thank you. I'll be on my way now." She nodded to Gideon and turned towards the door.

"Be careful, Miss Tucker. He might be cold and hard on the outside, but he can be hurt real easy. I don't want to have to remind you of that." Gone was the friendly gentleman and in its place, a fierce protector.

Naomi could not only appreciate the sentiment, but she respected it. One day she hoped someone could do the same for her.

"Don't worry, Mr. Blackwood. I have no intention of hurting Zeke."

Zeke sat on the edge of the bed and held his face in his hands. A dull throb in his head was joined by an ache in his ribs. Those boys had lit into him good. Normally he'd be able to hold his own against two men, but with the small space in the cell, he'd had no room to maneuver. Bastards.

He was more angry than anything and fully intended on charging them with assault. A judge came into town every month, should be easy enough to request he come sooner.

He stretched, wincing as a sharp pain gripped his back. With a groan, he lay on the bed and closed his eyes. Doc Barham had given him a little bottle of laudanum, but Zeke hated to take it since it made him lose control. With his behavior of late, losing control had become a problem. It certainly got him in trouble with the two drunks.

When a small knock sounded at the door, Zeke clenched his jaw.

"What?" he snapped, unwilling to talk to Lee about what happened.

"Zeke?"

Naomi's quiet voice made him sit up too fast. He gasped against the rush of blood through his head. She must've heard him because she opened the door and peeked in.

"Zeke?"

"Yeah, I'm here." Zeke didn't want to admit to himself how glad he was to see her. The petite woman had gotten under his skin in the last two weeks, to the point her very presence actually made him feel better. Damn, he was supposed to be avoiding saloon women, not consorting with them every chance he got.

"Can I come in?"

She shouldn't be alone with him in his bedroom though, no matter if she worked at the saloon or not. He was the sheriff and no doubt the old cronies on the town council would fire him if they knew. Zeke was well aware of all of it, yet it didn't stop him from inviting her in.

"Please."

Not only had he thrown caution under her little feet, but he'd said "please" too. Zeke knew then his plan to keep his distance from Naomi had failed miserably, and he started to shake. The urge to sling back a shot of whiskey roared through him.

"I met Gideon and he told me what happened. I was, well, I was worried." Her confession dropped into the silence of the room.

Zeke, for the first time in his life, was overwhelmed by a woman. The sincerity of her tone and the fact she'd been worried about him made his throat close. Soft comfort and words from women hadn't been prevalent in his life. His mother had been weak and dependent on his father, then him, for everything. Naomi had taken a lifetime's worth of experience and reduced it to dust.

She stepped into the room and closed the door, her rose scent washing over him. He clenched his teeth and swallowed, trying to dislodge the words stuck there.

"Are you okay?"

He sucked in a shaky breath and swung his legs around the side of the bed, then patted the spot next to him. His thirst, pain, embarrassment and discomfort forgotten, he could only see her. In the moonlight, she looked ethereal, like an angel come to visit him. It seemed the preacher had been right in his description of her.

Naomi sat down gently, almost as if she was afraid, and peered at him in the dim light. "Zeke, I—"

He put his hand against her lips, their softness making his fingers tremble. "You shouldn't be here alone with me."

She smiled beneath his hand. "I want to be."

Zeke cupped her face and tried to read what lurked in the hazel depths of her eyes. All he saw were shadows and uncertainties, a common theme in his life the last five years. He knew he shouldn't be with her, but for once he was going to do what his heart told him.

God help him. He was listening to his heart.

"You didn't get hurt in the brawl, did you?" He tried to find a topic to keep his mind, and his body, from focusing on kissing her.

"No, we hid behind the bar." She smiled. "Thank you for coming to stop it again. You seem to be quite good at being a sheriff, for a new one, I mean."

He chuckled at her teasing. "I suppose. It ain't hard, well I guess it is sometimes." He pressed a hand to his aching ribs.

"Are you all right? Gideon told me you were hurt." She covered his hand with hers.

"I'll live." He pulled her hand up and kissed the palm. Zeke felt a shiver snake through her at the touch of his lips.

"I'm not sure what's happening, Zeke." She gazed at the palm of her hand. "Why did I come here?" she sounded as confused as he was.

"Probably for the same reason I came to your bed." Zeke's body began to react to being closer to hers. It wasn't just a sexual reaction, it was something else too. That something else was unidentifiable, and it scared him.

Yet he didn't ask her to leave.

She nodded, her blonde hair sliding over the dress with a soft sound. "I've been fighting for survival for three years, and now it seems I have to fight for something else."

"What's that?"

She met his gaze. "My heart. You knocked me sideways, Sheriff, and I find myself liking it."

Zeke knew exactly what she meant. "I don't want to be responsible for your heart, for anyone's heart. The last year has brought me nothing but misery, and I can't seem to get myself out of the hole I dug for myself. I don't want to subject you to the same hell." His voice had descended into a hoarse whisper full of emotion.

She took his hand, her little fingers wrapping around his in comfort, bringing a lump to his throat.

"I understand. Lucy told me about Allison. I'm so sorry."

The mention of Allison made his stomach clench. Once upon a time, she might have been his wife. Now she was just another ghost in his heart.

"She's gone, and I'm still here. Now you're here too." He squeezed her hand. "I just want to be sure you understand I ain't looking for anything from you."

Zeke sensed she didn't believe a word he said, yet she remained silent. He hadn't wanted a woman getting under his skin, but it was too late for that.

"Kiss me." Her husky command sent a shiver down his

skin.

"Are you sure?" He knew she should leave, get away before their sexual relationship continued, but he couldn't seem to let go of her hand.

"Kiss me." This time her voice was firmer, and he obeyed.

He lowered his head and kissed her, capturing her breath into his mouth, inhaling her essence. It began slowly, but the heat between them flared to life.

Their previous encounters had been fierce matings, full of passion and animal instinct. This time it was gentle—for the first time they were making love.

He began by taking off her dress. The tiny buttons at the front almost did him in, but he persevered and soon they were all undone. As he slid the dress from her shoulders, he kissed the alabaster skin and breathed in her scent.

She rose from the bed like a goddess, letting her dress slip completely off. He was thrilled to realize she wore nothing beneath it. His drawers were the only thing keeping him from embarrassing himself with the rock-hard dick screaming for her.

God she was exquisite.

"Looks like you're pitching a tent there, Sheriff."

He reached for her naked form. "Come here."

"Not until you lie down like a good boy and let me have my way with you." She pushed him back on the bed, and his injuries twinged at the movement.

"I'm all yours." It went against his nature to let anyone take control of him, but he allowed it to happen. Naomi meant more to him than he could even put into words. He wanted to be with her and show her he trusted her.

Standing beside the bed, she looked at him in the

moonlight, her gaze touching him like a caress. The small hairs on his body rose to attention as if she used her hands and not her eyes. Unbelievably, his dick grew even harder.

"Like a banquet all for me." She skimmed her fingers down his chest, scraping at his nipples and sending shards of pure need down his skin.

"Then you'd best get to feasting because the meat is getting overcooked."

She laughed and took his staff in her small hand. "Oh I don't know about that. It feels just perfect to me. Let's release it from this prison though." Naomi shimmied off his drawers in a blink, leaving him naked on his back, and at her mercy.

"I like this." She climbed on the bed, straddling his legs. Her pussy hairs tickled him and he shivered at the feeling.

"Me too." His voice sounded gravelly and thick. "Now ride me, filly."

She tsked at him. "I'm in charge of this round, Sheriff. So just hang on and let me handle the reins."

It wasn't easy, but he unclenched his hands and let her do as she asked. There wasn't a woman alive aside from Naomi he would give control to.

She ran her hands up his thighs, skirting his jumping dick, and up his stomach. When her finger circled his belly button, he hissed, eager to do more than be teased. Yet he held his tongue and throbbed with arousal.

Naomi leaned forward and her beautiful hair covered him even as her mouth closed around a nipple. He closed his eyes and held on for all he was worth. She nibbled and lapped at him as her hair caressed his stomach.

He realized he was holding his breath and sucked in a lungful of air. Damn, she surely did know how to drive him insane.

"Feel good?"

He grunted, not trusting his voice to work properly.

She lay down completely on him and his skin sighed in pleasure. When her mouth found his, he wrapped his arms around her and fused with her. Liquid heat poured through his veins as his tongue twined with hers.

Sweet, dueling tongues rasped together as her pussy teased his cock. Her moisture coated his taut skin, made him nearly snarl for more. He reached down and pulled her knees up, opening her up for him.

"In, sweet one, let me in." He couldn't take one more second without being inside her.

Naomi reached between them and guided his throbbing erection to her. When the head of his dick finally entered her, he couldn't be patient any longer. He thrust up, embedding himself deep in her body. She gasped and tightened around him.

Zeke paused for a moment, trying to stop himself from coming too soon. When he felt his control returning, he pulled at her round little ass.

"Ride me."

She bit at his lip one last time then straightened, her hair like a curtain around her beautiful face.

Her tentative movements told him she'd never done anything like this before, but she got the hang of it quickly. Soon she was sliding up and down on his rod, clenching and unclenching with each thrust. He held onto her hips as his balls grew harder with each upstroke. He reached between them and circled her clit with his thumb, eager to bring to her the pleasure coursing through him.

"Yesss." She spread her legs even wider, bringing him so deeply inside her, he touched her womb.

He felt his orgasm starting near his toes and it traveled up until it landed between his legs. She whispered his name as her sweet pussy fisted around him so hard, he saw stars, bringing his orgasm to its fullest. It swept him away on a river of pure ecstasy and he rode in the current with her.

He pulled her to him, their hearts thundering in tandem against one another. Zeke kissed her forehead and tucked her beneath his chin. Sleep tugged at him but he was still deep within her and wanted to enjoy every second of it.

His body shook with the force of what had just happened between him and Naomi. He thought his heart had hardened beyond recognition after Allison's murder and the war. He'd been mistaken, because it trembled more than anything else on him. Zeke had done the unthinkable.

He'd fallen in love. What the hell was he supposed to do now?

Chapter Eight

Naomi returned to the saloon before the sun rose, a smile on her face and a few muscle twinges attesting to her rigorous night's activities. She was no whore, but going to Zeke, being with him, had been the right thing to do. She understood that and accepted all that came with it.

Being with Zeke for the third time had been dangerous for her heart. He had the ability to turn her world upside-down and sideways. Life, however, was meant for the living. She intended to grab on with both hands and savor every second of sweet happiness she could. The last few years had been filled with so many dark moments, and Tanger was turning out to be the light penetrating that darkness.

The saloon was quiet as a church as she made her way up the stairs. The grin on her face faded when she caught sight of Carmen at the landing waiting for her wearing a sheet and nothing else. Her furious expression told a tale.

"Listen, *puta*, you don't do no business outside this saloon. I don't care how good you think you are. You ain't special and you gotta pay Lucy just like me." Her lips curled back in a sneer as she spoke, spittle gathering in the corners of her lips.

Naomi didn't know what to say. The very idea she was prostituting herself outside the saloon had never even crossed her mind, nor was it something she'd ever do.

"Carmen, I'm not doing any business. I went to see a friend who'd been hurt." Truthful, but not entirely. Her cheeks felt hot with the accusation and the lie by omission.

"Ha, as if I'd believe a *puta* like you." Carmen jabbed a finger into Naomi's chest. The sharp point felt more like a knife than a fingernail. "You just be careful, *bruja*. I'm watching you."

Louisa poked her head out of her room, her sleep-tousled hair resembling a rat's nest. She blinked and looked at them with bleary eyes. "Carmen, why are you yelling at Naomi?"

"She is doing business outside the saloon." Carmen's accusation stung each time she flung it around.

Louisa frowned. "What are you talking about?"

"I see her leave and go down the street so I follow." Carmen shrugged. "She went into the upstairs of the restaurant and stayed. I left and come back here."

"Why did you follow me?" Naomi demanded.

"I want to make sure you're not cheating me. A whore doesn't care whose bed she makes money in." Carmen was excessively blunt.

"I didn't do anything wrong and I didn't cheat you out of anything." Naomi wiped the sweat from her forehead with a shaky hand. "I don't have any customers in any bed." Her voice rose on the last words, anger mixing with fear.

"I believe her, Carmen." Louisa brushed the hair from her face. "I ain't seen her go upstairs with nobody."

"That's because she don't want to share her money with Lucy."

"Is that true?" Lucy sauntered out from the end of the hallway, her eyes cold as brown marbles.

"You know it's not true. I went to him because I wanted to. Check my pockets if you like. I barely have two bits to my name." Naomi turned her pockets inside out.

"Maybe I check under your clothes too." Carmen leaned in close, the smell of onions and malice on her breath.

"You touch me and you'll regret it. There's just so much I can take from anyone." Naomi wasn't about to let anyone touch her, much less a jealous woman bent on making her out to be a cheating whore.

"Nammy knows the rules. She gets caught, she leaves." Lucy turned to go back down the hallway. "Carmen, you need to stop being such a bitch."

Louisa barked out a laugh, then clapped a hand over her mouth. With a wink at Naomi, she disappeared into her room.

Carmen looked very angry, but there wasn't anything Naomi could do or say to convince her she was wrong. The whole fight had turned a beautiful morning into a tense standoff and for that Naomi felt resentment towards her.

"You know, we can have a life outside this saloon. I really was seeing a friend who'd been hurt. What we do together, as adults, is our business alone. I'm sorry you can't see that or accept me as a human being with feelings." Naomi stomped past her, determined to put the incident aside and get some sleep.

Carmen, for once, didn't say another word as she turned and went back to her room, the sheet swishing behind her on the wooden floors.

Naomi swallowed and pressed a hand to her chest to calm her racing heart and to mend the wound left by Carmen's accusations. Naomi slammed her door so hard, her teeth rattled. She didn't care who heard or complained, because it sure as hell made her feel better.

The bed reminded her of who'd shared it with her and Naomi laid down, eager to find his scent even if it was just in her mind. After she woke, she would make Carmen understand she was wrong about Naomi and Zeke. It was not a customer relationship. It was much, much more.

*

Their nightly visits continued for a week. Zeke would come to her one night, then she would go to him the next. Sweet, delicious heat in double doses filled their bedrooms, each joining more intense than the last. He was out of control and he knew it, yet it didn't stop him from going to her bed or welcoming her into his.

Each time they came together, they ended up talking for hours. He'd known there was a common bond between them, but he hadn't known how strong it was. On a hot Wednesday night, a few weeks after they'd met, Naomi told him in a broken whisper about why she'd left North Carolina.

"My father was too old to fight. I was a late-in-life child for my parents, so he stayed behind in my hometown. Vista was just that, a vision of gently rolling hills and beautiful trees. Folks in town knew each other and it was a nice place to live." She sucked in a shaky breath. "You see it sat right near the Virginia border, not too far from the battlefields. Sometimes at night when it was really quiet, you could hear cannons."

Zeke tucked her under his arm and pulled her close. Naomi was clammy and cold, stuck in the past, and he needed to let her tell her story. Although, he didn't want to hear what happened, he listened because it was part of who Naomi was.

"A Yankee troop or whatever they call themselves stumbled into town one Sunday morning. Most folks who were left in town were in church—there wasn't much left to do but pray those days. Food was scarce, supply wagons didn't come through anymore. We were getting a bit desperate, but we still had faith." She let out a long sigh, a warm breath against his chest. "Until that morning anyway. They stuck a broom handle or something like that in the door and set the building on fire."

Zeke couldn't help the tightening of his arm or the curse that sprang from his lips. War had turned men into monsters.

"They stood outside and watched as we tried to get out through the two small windows." Hot tears slid onto his skin as she cried silently for what she'd been through. "I-I tried to help everyone, but we were mostly women and children and the windows were too small for everyone to fit through. My father, the reverend, tried to chop a hole in the door with a chair but it was no use."

She was silent for so long, Zeke grew concerned. He tipped her chin up to look at her. "You survived."

"Only in body, my soul would never be the same. You see, I had to watch my father burn to death right after he threw me through the broken window." A sob escaped from her throat. "He sacrificed himself to save us, and in the end, none of us were saved."

It was what she hadn't said that worried him. Her story was familiar in wartime, and he'd heard similar ones, but the quaking woman in his arms had something else to say. The war had taken more than her father from her. The eerie similarity between Allison and Naomi grew stronger after hearing Naomi's story. How had a man stuck in hell been drawn to women born of men of the cloth?

Zeke didn't ask any more questions because he couldn't. Her pain was deep enough to remind him of the pain he'd buried far inside him.

"I'm sorry, little one." He hugged her close until she stopped shaking, though he didn't think he ever would.

✳

He sat drinking coffee in the restaurant, trying to pretend he'd slept more than a few hours in the last two weeks. When he'd glanced in the mirror this morning, he was surprised to see how shitty he appeared. Dark circles lay under his bloodshot eyes, giving him a haunted look.

Was he haunted? Perhaps by the fever that gripped him whenever he thought of Naomi. Jesus, just thinking of her his pants grew tight as his blood rushed around his body. He was becoming hopelessly entangled with her, and he was afraid it had already passed the point of no return. She was too damaged inside, almost as much as he was. Together they would be a lethal combination.

"You look like shit." Lee sat across from him, biscuit in hand and a frown on his face.

"Thanks, little brother. Don't use such pretty words next time, just give it to me straight." Zeke took a big gulp of scalding coffee.

Gideon clapped him on the shoulder, then sat next to him. "Something, or should I say someone, is keeping you up, Sheriff."

"I think it's that blonde whore from Lucy's." Lee didn't miss much.

"Ain't nobody's business but mine. But I'll tell you right now, don't ever call her a whore." Zeke started to rise, but Gideon's hand kept him down.

"It sure as hell is our business, Zeke. We're not only kin, we're a family, looking out for each other." He glanced at Lee. "Both of us are worried."

That idiot Byron Ackerman strolled into the restaurant as noisily as he did everything else. "Good morning, gentlemen. Sheriff." He threw his nose up in the air like a high-fallutin' woman and went over to an empty table by the window.

Gideon shook his head. "That man doesn't like you, Zeke."

Lee snorted. "That's the gospel truth."

"I don't like him either." Zeke watched the hotel man as Margaret appeared by the table and smiled at him. Not just any smile, but a wide one with a pink tinge to her cheeks. "Holy shit."

"What?" Lee glanced back at Ackerman. "What the hell is she doing?"

"My guess is Mr. Ackerman is looking for a woman to spark with and he's found one." Gideon never shied away from speaking the truth, but hell's bells, they didn't want their Margaret sparking with the likes of an uptight Yankee.

Lee let loose a curse under his breath. "That ass has been here every day for breakfast. Margaret should've told him to leave, but no, she must've been enjoying flirting with him 'cause he kept coming back. Now she's making cow eyes at him." His fist clenched as he stood, the chair's scrape on the floor echoing in the restaurant. A few folks eating breakfast glanced up, but it was Margaret who met his gaze.

She pinched her lips together then raised her chin as if challenging him to say something. Margaret waited a few moments before she turned back to Ackerman, pointedly giving Lee the cold shoulder. He started towards them but Zeke grabbed his arm. It was like stopping granite and it damn well stung Zeke's hand.

"You've got no claim on her, brother."

"He's got no claim on her either, lousy Yankee bastard." His voice shook with fury, a very bad sign.

Zeke glanced at Gideon and without speaking decided on what to do.

"Let's go take a walk, cowboy." Zeke stood and pulled Lee towards the door. "Gid can handle the breakfast orders."

Lee gazed at Zeke. The naked longing in the brown depths of his little brother's eyes was all too familiar. "I know, brother, I know. Come on."

Although not an easy task, Zeke got Lee out of the restaurant and into the sunshine.

"You sweet on Margaret?"

Lee almost stumbled at Zeke's question. "What?"

"You were ready to tear Ackerman to bits back there. Jesus, Lee, it ain't a bad thing, you just need to do something about it if you want her for your own."

Lee walked beside him for a few minutes before he responded. "I didn't plan on liking her, that's for sure. The woman is contrary and mean."

Zeke didn't believe that. "Margaret is quiet, but she's never been mean to me."

Lee snorted. "Then count yourself lucky. She's impossible sometimes and dammit, she treats me like I'm a nuisance."

Zeke sympathized with his brother, but to him, the path was clear. "Tell her how you feel."

Stopping in his tracks, Lee looked absolutely horrified. "What? I can't do that. She'd have me in her apron pocket and only let me out for special occasions."

"Well, that's an image." Zeke swallowed the smile that threatened. "Kicking Ackerman around isn't going to help."

"I know that, but hell, Zeke, I just can't let him take her."

It was worse than Zeke thought. Lee just didn't like Margaret, he *loved* her.

"It seems we're both in the same boat, little brother." Zeke's heart crimped at the thought of Naomi. He had to tell someone, and who better than Lee. "I've got myself tangled up with a woman too."

"I heard tell you were keeping time with somebody. It is that blonde I saw with Ackerman, right? She didn't look much like a woman for a sheriff." Lee could sometimes be so abrasive.

"I don't need you telling me that. As soon as one of those biddies on the town council see us together, I'm gonna get booted out on my ass." Zeke's own desperation came back on him like a wave.

"So stay away from her. She's a whore." Lee sounded so matter-of-fact, it made Zeke's teeth grind together.

"Dammit, she's not a whore. And talk about the pot calling the kettle black. Are you steering clear of Margaret? It ain't that easy. Naomi's like a fever inside me and I can't stop thinking about her." Zeke blew out a shaky breath.

Lee was quiet for a minute, and when he spoke, his voice had a husky quality to it. "Yeah, I think I know what you mean."

They walked in silence for a few minutes, each lost in their own thoughts.

"I guess we're both a couple of pitiful fools, aren't we?" Zeke let loose a chuckle.

"Oh, no, you're definitely more pitiful than me." Lee shook his head.

Grateful for the funning, a reprieve from his chaotic thoughts, Zeke punched his brother in the arm. "Ha, that's a big fat lie. You take the cake of pity with your ugly face."

They continued poking fun at each other until the dark cloud over both of them had blown away. Fortuitous or not, they ran smack into the young minister as he strolled down the street.

"Good morning, friends." His smile was wider than the Mississippi.

"Hey there, Preacher." Zeke nodded towards the church. "Did the town council give the okay for you to take over the souls of Tanger?" Much as Zeke avoided the place of worship, it wasn't fair to the rest of the townsfolk to be without a guiding shepherd.

"Yes, they surely did. It's in good shape, but needs some work, especially whitewashing the walls and such. It appears the roof was redone though." Gregory had no idea the storm of memories he invoked at the mention of the church roof.

The roof, the sun and heat, Allison's smile as she brought him lemonade, and the eagerness Zeke had to please the sweet young woman. It seemed like a lifetime ago he'd worked on the roof with Lee. For the first time since her death, the thought of Allison Delmont did not bring pain. He didn't even want to think of why, since it brought him back to a certain blonde saloon girl.

"Yep, we did that last year." Lee looked at Zeke, apparently probing for how he handled mention of the church. "It was sorely in need of repair, much like the rest of this town."

"The preacher was sickly for a while and his daughter"—Zeke swallowed—"she wasn't much for working outside. Lee and I fixed up the roof. We'd be happy to help with the rest of the building."

One of Lee's eyebrows rose. "We will? I mean, sure we will."

"Thank you, Sheriff, Mr. Blackwood." Gregory patted Zeke's shoulder. "You are both very kind."

Lee harrumphed but Zeke simply returned the gesture.

"I'm hoping to catch sight of the angel again today." Gregory spoke as if seeing an angel were an everyday occurrence.

"Is that so?" Lee sounded skeptical the preacher was seeing anything but his own imaginings.

"Yes, I've seen an angel in the night, walking through the streets of Tanger. I think she's the guardian angel over everyone and I'd like to thank her for all she's done." The minister looked up at the heavens. "God is always around us and she's a gentle reminder for me each time I see her."

"I don't think there's any angels about in Tanger, Preacher." Zeke squared his shoulders, not eager for the preacher to find out exactly who his angel was. A fallen angel was more like it. "Some folks just keep different hours than others. The saloon is open kind of late. Are you sure you just didn't see one of Aphrodite's girls?"

Gregory looked startled. "Perhaps, but I don't think so. I must be on my way now, gentlemen, it was good to see you again."

"Sure thing, Greg." The look on Lee's face told Zeke he thought the young man was loco.

After Gregory walked away, Lee shook his head. "Is he really that young? Were we ever that young?"

Zeke frowned. "Maybe, but I doubt it. He's younger than any soul I've ever met."

"I don't know, Zeke. He's still seeing angels." Lee obviously doubted the minister's sanity.

"I'll take care of it, don't worry." Zeke fully intended on making sure the angel didn't appear on the main streets of Tanger anymore.

It seemed Ackerman was stuck on Margaret and it irked the shit out the Devils, especially Lee and Gideon. Each morning the oily-haired hotelier showed up for breakfast and Margaret was there to greet him. He started bringing her gifts, including a book of poems that made Lee snort so hard he hurt himself. Matthew was making regular appearances in the restaurant too, always polite and smiling at Margaret. However, the gentle shopkeeper didn't worry them. Ackerman did. Zeke was also worried about how many men were suddenly interested in the quiet widow—she might be playing with fire and not know how much she could get burned.

Zeke kept his eye on the hotel man, but he never did anything wrong. In fact, he was kind to everyone and had opened up the hotel for business. Zeke had even seen a few new folks stop at the hotel and eat at the restaurant. Ackerman was actually helping the town rebuild, damn his hide.

"Why can't we just get rid of him?" Lee snapped as he threw himself into the chair angled to watch the lovebirds.

"He ain't done nothing wrong." Zeke rose, his coffee drunk and biscuits eaten. "There's nothing I can do."

"He's going to hurt her." Gideon watched them with true concern in his blue eyes. "Margaret is fragile."

"Fragile, my ass. She's bossy, pushy and stubborn as a mule." Lee's words were caustic but beneath it Zeke heard true affection, even respect.

Richard had started joining them for breakfast, becoming a fixture at Elmer's, much to their delight. He was a kind man, with a common past they shared. "Sounds like you're sweet on her."

Lee frowned at his new friend. "Not hardly. She's a harridan."

"She's hardly got over her husband's death. It's only been three years." Gideon's voice was laced with anger. "Stop treating her as if she's unwanted or unwelcome."

Lee couldn't have looked more surprised. "I don't do that."

"Yes you do, and it's no wonder she's looked elsewhere for a man. You've pushed her away." Gideon stomped into the kitchen, leaving the Blackwood brothers to digest his words.

"I don't do that," Lee repeated then he looked at Zeke and Richard for confirmation.

Zeke shook his head. "I hate to tell you this, Lee, but you do, nearly every day." He gestured to Margaret, currently smiling down at Ackerman. "I don't like him or trust him, but he treats her like a gentleman courting a lady."

It was as if Zeke had slapped his brother. The color drained from Lee's face and Zeke immediately felt bad for being so brutally truthful with him. His brother usually wanted everything straight and honest, but maybe this time he should have tempered it with a bit more tact.

"Jesus, really?" Lee's expression of bewilderment changed to one of trepidation when he looked at Margaret. That man was head over heels in love with her, but wouldn't, or couldn't, tell her.

"You should have told her."

Lee whipped his head around and frowned. "I can't."

"I told you days ago you should've told her, but you didn't want to listen." Zeke put his hand over his brother's. "You need to stop punishing yourself."

"I don't punish myself. I just know my limitations. Ain't no woman in her right mind is marrying a man with one arm. I can't even hug her for God's sake." Lee snatched his hand away and rose, only to run smack into Margaret.

As he steadied himself by grabbing her shoulder, she did the same, with only her left arm instead of both. Anyone else might have grasped for the arm Lee didn't have, but Margaret didn't. That small gesture told Zeke she wasn't as unaware of Lee as she presented. With an embarrassed shuffle, they separated and stared at each other for one pregnant pause.

"Mr. Ackerman has asked me to marry him," she blurted.

Lee punched the table beside him as his face flushed. "You're going to say no."

Zeke wanted to shake some sense into his brother, but the fool was making his own mistakes one right after the other.

"Excuse me?" She stepped away from him and crossed her arms.

"You heard me." Lee shot a wicked glare at Ackerman. "That son of a bitch isn't worthy to spit shine your shoes much less be your husband."

"You have no right." She shook her head. "What makes you think I care what you think?"

"What's going on?" Gideon reappeared in the kitchen doorway as the shouting continued.

"I am marrying Mr. Ackerman."

Gideon frowned. "Are you sure that's what you want?" Apparently she hadn't said yes yet, but Lee's stupidness had pushed her right into the hotel man's arms.

"Hell no it's not what she wants. I'm going to go set that fool straight. He ain't marrying Margaret." Lee tried to get around Margaret and get to Ackerman, but before he could, Gideon put a hand on Lee's chest to stop him.

"Margaret might not be kin by blood, but she's family just

the same. Don't do something you'll regret later." Gideon was right, of course, but it didn't make it easier for Lee to accept.

"Get out of my way." Lee's face flushed.

Gideon looked at Margaret. "You've got choices, you know. Don't throw them away."

"Gideon, I appreciate your concern, but this is my choice." Margaret stepped between them, pushing at Gideon's chest. "I'll tell you the same thing I told your cousin—you have no right."

"I have every right. Ackerman is a shady character and I don't care what he's done for Tanger. I won't, I *can't* let it happen. I meant what I said, you're family and that means it's my job to protect you." Gideon gently moved Margaret aside, but Zeke could see his muscles straining to keep his touch from hurting her. "You're going to have to trust me, Margaret."

"You Rebs think you own this town, but you're wrong." Ackerman must have had enough of being a smiling fool because his tone was as deadly as a Bowie knife. "I have every right to court this woman and marry her if I so choose. You cannot stop me."

He poked Gideon in the chest, and in a blur of movement Gid had the man's hand twisted behind his back until he screeched in agony.

"You're breaking my arm. Ah, dammit, let me go. Sheriff, stop him." Ackerman cried out for help and Zeke couldn't refuse.

One drawback to being the sheriff, he couldn't really select to assist only those folks he personally liked. Gideon was faster, stronger and more capable than Ackerman could ever hope to be. Zeke couldn't let his cousin break the bastard's arm.

"Gid, let him go." Zeke reluctantly walked over only to have Lee block his path.

"Don't you dare stop him."

Zeke pushed his brother aside. "It's my job, so don't get in my way." The look of anger and hurt on Lee's face couldn't deter Zeke from what he had to do.

"I'm telling you to stop right now, Gid." Zeke touched his cousin's arm. "Don't do something you can't take back."

Gideon turned and punched Zeke in the face with his free arm, knocking him back into the table. Coffee flew every which way, scalding his face as he tried to roll free. Margaret was yelling and Lee was shouting right back. Ackerman whined like a piglet with his tail stepped on as Gideon growled and snapped.

It was a strange battle scene and Zeke had a responsibility to put a stop to it, much as he didn't want to. He picked himself up off the floor and straightened his gun belt.

"You, get in the kitchen." He pointed at Margaret. "And stay there until I get this sorted out." He grabbed Lee by the arm. "Sit in the corner and shut up."

The razor sharpness of Zeke's voice must have told them he meant business because they both did as he ordered without another word. By the time Zeke made it to the grappling pair of men, his temper had turned into ice-cold fury. Gideon was behaving like a green boy with no self-control. It was completely unlike him, which worried Zeke, but he had to stop the fight first.

He grabbed hold of Gideon's collar and tugged, even as he kicked him behind the knees, bringing his friend to the floor with Ackerman on top of him. Zeke pulled the hotel man off Gideon and deposited him on a chair. The man barely weighed more than a grown woman, or perhaps it was Zeke's anger fueling his strength. Either way, Gideon lay there looking up at him, with disbelief and hurt in his gaze.

"What the hell are you doing?"

"My job." Zeke held out his hand, which Gideon ignored as he rolled to his feet and started after Ackerman again. "Don't make me arrest you, Gid." He yanked on Gideon's arm and that's when the punches flew.

It started off with a simple argument but turned into a damn saloon brawl in the middle of the restaurant. Gideon hung on like an angry bull, unwilling or unable to back down. In the end, Zeke had his knee in Gideon's back while Ackerman whined through a bloodied nose on the other side of the restaurant.

"Ready to give in?"

"Fuck you." Gideon tried once again to get free.

That was that as far as Zeke was concerned. He pulled rope from his belt and tied his cousin's hands together. The hardest thing he'd had to do as a sheriff was arrest his cousin, but he did it anyway.

"You did what?" Gabby stood in the doorway of the jail and peeked over Zeke's shoulder, her dark eyes showing concern.

"I arrested him. He was beating on Ackerman and wouldn't stop. I thought he would break his arm, Gabby. I had to do something." His ears burned with his cousin's frigid silence even as his stomach churned with the knowledge he'd arrested his best friend.

She opened her mouth, then closed it. "Does Jake know?"

"I have no idea, but Lee knows and he sure as hell ain't happy about it." Zeke wasn't happy about it either, but he had a job to do.

"So why did you ask me to come down?" She kept her voice low so Gideon wouldn't overhear.

"As mayor you are what passes for a judge in things like this. Remember you did it a couple weeks ago for those two fools?" He was still annoyed at the cowboys who'd kicked the crap out of him.

"All I did was send them onto the marshal." She didn't appear to be happy about serving as judge any more than Zeke wanted to arrest Gideon.

"Exactly. You make the decision as to what to do with folks who break the law." He shook his head. "Damned if I know what to do with Gid." He swallowed the guilty lump in his throat. Already Ackerman had been at the jail twice since the incident, demanding Gideon be brought to justice. Pompous windbag even had the audacity to suggest he go to prison for it.

"Then I fine him five dollars and release him." She crossed her arms. "Everyone deserves the opportunity to defend themselves or those they love. From what you told me, he was stepping in for Margaret and his intentions were good even if he did go about it the wrong way."

"Ackerman's gonna raise a fuss." Zeke could set his watch by that idiot.

"Then let him come to the town council and raise a fuss. As mayor, I know decisions can be tough to make, but this one isn't. Gideon is a good citizen of Tanger and his punishment is five dollars." She finally stepped into the jail and let Gideon see her. "Hey there, Gid."

He glanced up from the cot, his jaw set in iron. "Hey, Gabby."

"I'm sorry this happened." She frowned at Zeke. "Let him out already. I'm sure he's good for the fine."

"What fine?" Gideon rose, still refusing to look at Zeke.

"Five dollars for breaking the law." Gabby bit her lip but didn't change her mind as Zeke expected. He thought the job would be too difficult for her, but perhaps being in charge of the mill for three years had given her the smarts to run the town after all.

Gideon snorted a laugh. "That's ridiculous. Ackerman deserved to have his ass beat into next week. I didn't do anything one of the other Devils wouldn't have."

Zeke took a deep breath and stepped towards the cell. "I've never broken a man's arm who couldn't defend himself. You were out of control, Gid, and if you had broken his arm you wouldn't be getting off with a five dollar fine."

Gideon ignored him and waited until the cell door opened. "Gabby, come by later and I'll give you the money." He brushed past them, fury emanating in waves from him.

"He's pretty angry with you." Gabby squeezed Zeke's shoulder. "Are you going to be okay?"

"God only knows the answer to that question. He's had fun fucking my life up lately." He closed his eyes and turned away from her. "Sorry, Gabby."

"It's okay. I'm going to let Jake know what happened." Gabby started to leave the jail, her long black braid swinging against the blue dress she wore. "We'll be home at the mill if you need us."

With that, he was left alone in the jail, guilt gnawing at his guts and confusion reigning in his brain. Life had been much simpler when he was drunk all the time. Sleep, drink, puke and sleep more. Now it seemed they were heading into complicated territory again and Zeke wanted to run like hell.

However, as sheriff of the town, he had to sit and ride out the shit storm, like it or not. He'd just put his friendship with

Gideon at risk because of the job. It had damn well better be worth it.

Chapter Nine

Naomi strolled down the main street in Tanger in the early morning sunshine. It was one of her favorite times of the day and she enjoyed the fresh air, especially after the stale stink in the saloon.

Zeke had come to her bed again the night before and she had welcomed him. Their relationship was an odd one, secret and furtive and that aspect bothered her a lot. He seemed to want to ignore the fact they found heaven in each other's arms each and every time.

As she passed the saloon, Zeke popped out of the doorway and started walking alongside her, continually looking around to see if anyone was watching.

She wanted to punch him for it.

Naomi was already in love with the man, much to her consternation. Although Zeke was trying to ignore their relationship, she knew better and she wasn't about to allow him to throw it away.

Zeke had begun to look haggard, with dark circles under his eyes and a tic in his cheek. The man seemed to be falling apart and she didn't know why.

"You look terrible."

He grimaced. "Thanks, and I feel even worse."

"You're not getting much sleep." She knew the exact reason why half of his nights were spent not sleeping, but what about the other half?

He looked at her from beneath the brim of his hat. "Did you know you're Tanger's guardian angel?"

Naomi thought she hadn't heard him right. "Excuse me?"

"Our new young minister has seen you in your, ah, nighttime escapades through town. He's convinced you're the town's guardian angel." He sounded amused.

Naomi, however, was not. "I am no one's guardian angel. That's ridiculous."

"That's the truth." Zeke frowned. "No saloon girl is an angel of any kind."

That comment stung.

She stopped in her tracks. "Did you come out here to insult or harass me this morning?"

He shook his head. "Neither. I saw you out here and, well, I wanted to walk with the angel."

His voice sounded so weary, defeated even. She didn't know what was happening inside his thick head and he wasn't very forthcoming. Before she could ask him if he wanted to talk down by the lake, they were interrupted.

"Well, good morning, Sheriff Blackwood." Hettie Cranston stood before them in all her tiny glory, wearing a bright blue dress, and a straw hat with a little bird's nest on the side. Her sharp gaze raked them up and down, noting the way Naomi's arm was tucked into Zeke's no doubt.

"Miss Cranston." Zeke tipped his hat.

"Introduce me to your, ah, friend." Hettie raised one brow.

"This is Naomi Tucker, originally from North Carolina, who moved to town a few weeks back. She's walking, well, she likes to take walks in the morning and today I decided to join her." Zeke had chosen his words carefully, making Naomi appear to be something she wasn't. The bastard was trying to hide the fact she worked in the saloon.

Naomi wasn't going to let him.

She held out her hand and shook Hettie's with vigor. "It's a pleasure to meet you, Miss Cranston. I work at Aphrodite's serving drinks, and no, I don't work on my back, just in case you were wondering."

Naomi pulled her arm out of his and turned around to walk back the way she had come. Zeke called her name, but she kept walking. Even if she worked in a saloon, that didn't mean he was allowed to judge her. He had no right to do so, and although she wanted to tell him that, loudly, she didn't. The street was no place for her to vent her anger at the handsome sheriff.

The town council called for a meeting two days after the fight in Elmer's restaurant. In addition to Zeke keeping time with Naomi on the streets of Tanger, Ackerman had caused enough fervor to get the older folks on the council heated up about the "problem with the Blackwoods." Much to Zeke's distress, Jake couldn't change their minds. Gideon still hadn't spoken to Zeke, and Lee barely grunted hello and goodbye.

The day dawned cloudy with a light mist falling, making surfaces slick and putting Zeke in an even worse mood. He felt like a Judas for what he'd done to Gideon, but he knew he had been in the right. The tiff with Naomi in the street had kept them apart those two days and he was grumpy enough to realize he missed her. Perhaps this was the opportunity to cut his ties with the saloon girl. What he needed to do was concentrate on the town council and not on the blonde waif who had sneaked her way into his heart.

Ackerman offered the use of the hotel for the meeting and the council readily agreed. As Zeke walked over, some folks said hello, while others barely nodded.

Margaret was just arriving with Gabby and she met Zeke's gaze. "Good morning, Sheriff."

Gabby smiled. "How are you, Zeke?"

"Things have been worse." He couldn't complain about the argument between he and his friends when they'd already survived hell together. Damn sure he couldn't tell her about Naomi.

"Jake's already here with Lee and Gideon. They had breakfast together." She made a face. "I told them they were being little babies about this whole thing, but they wouldn't listen to me."

"Let's just get this over with." Zeke held the door open, reluctant to enter Ackerman's domain but eager to make peace with his friends. It felt uncomfortable to be at odds with them.

Zeke had not seen the town council as a group since they'd appointed him sheriff and they were just as intimidating with their stares now as they were then. The two old biddies Edith White and Hettie Cranston watched him from their perches on some fancy chairs Ackerman apparently had brought in. Gabby stood with Jake talking quietly to Lee and Gideon while the men on the council watched everything from the corner. Even Richard was there, likely to provide evidence of the fight at Elmer's.

The hotel man stood at the windows, rocking back and forth on his heels with a grin on his oily face. The grin resembled a rabid dog more than a man, but he didn't scare

Zeke. In fact, he had trouble keeping himself from punching the bastard.

Every muscle in his body tensed as if he was entering a battlefield, which, in essence, he was.

"Now that the sheriff is here, we can begin." Hettie liked to order everyone around and damned if they didn't all listen. Each member took a seat in the fancy chairs, looking like they were perching on thrones.

Margaret glanced at Ackerman but didn't make a move to approach him. She did nod in his direction, however, and he looked as if she'd given him a million dollars.

"Mr. Ackerman kindly offered us the use of his hotel for this meeting. The council thanks you for your generosity." Hettie's regal tone made Zeke grit his teeth. "We're here to discuss claims made against the sheriff in particular, as well as his business partners, known as D.H. Enterprises."

"I'd like to know what the claims are." Gideon had moved to the right side of the circle, arms crossed, his tone calm and reasonable.

If only Zeke could find his own calm. His guts nearly boiled with anxiety, anger and frustration. "So would I."

"I'll get to that part, Mr. Blackwood. Please have some patience." Hettie nodded at Edith. "Miss White will read the claims."

Edith stood and straightened her navy blue dress, which Zeke grudgingly admitted was very well made, proving her mettle as the seamstress in Tanger. For some reason, he had the notion of asking her to make a new dress for Naomi, a new green one to bring out the color in her eyes. Her own green frock had been torn the night of the saloon brawl, and damn, she looked mighty fine in green.

Jesus, please us, he shook his head to clear the odd

158

thoughts about Naomi and her wardrobe. There were more important things to focus on.

Edith unfolded a piece of paper. The vellum crispness echoed in the wood paneled room.

"To the Tanger Town Council,

As a new business owner in town, I am dismayed at the power the Blackwoods yield in Tanger. They run the restaurant, the law, as well as the saloon, the mill and practically the town council. I don't feel as though I will have a fair chance to make this wonderful town my home.

The sheriff has been consorting with a saloon girl, flaunting her in town as if she was a societal queen. His brother, Lee, feels it necessary to start fights at will, and their leader, Gideon, wields power over all of them.

I humbly ask the town council to step in and stop these men from taking over the town completely. Close the restaurant, fire the sheriff and take back Tanger.

Sincerely,

Byron Ackerman."

She smiled at Hettie and sat back down, her knees creaking with the movement.

"What the hell does all that mean?" As always, Lee used his best manners.

Zeke was reeling over the accusation of "consorting with a saloon girl", recognizing he'd made some mistakes as sheriff, the first one being Naomi. He shouldn't have gotten involved with her, he knew that. Yet his heart grew pained at the thought of never being with her again. The entire letter made the hairs on the back of his neck stand up and definitely riled his anger.

"It sounds like Mr. Ackerman thinks we hold too much

power in town." Gideon frowned. "What is it you want, Mr. Ackerman?"

"I want to be able to do business in peace and bring wealth to the town." Ackerman smiled at Margaret. "And marry whoever I choose to without being assaulted for it."

No mention of love, just a choice. Margaret was convenient, and available, and she was obviously a very good cook. Ackerman was no fool, but Margaret was for accepting the first marriage proposal thrown her way.

"We haven't prevented you from doing business. In fact, Jake here has sent people your way." Gideon gestured to the redheaded Devil. "I spoke to the folks myself."

"Well, that's true. However, you did assault me two days ago for proposing marriage to Mrs. Summers." He pointed to the yellowing bruise on his eye. "Dr. Barham can attest to the severity of the beating."

Zeke couldn't help it, he snorted so loud, he almost choked. "Beating? Byron, he got two punches in before I pulled him off. That does not qualify as a beating. As a matter of fact, I could have let him beat the ever-loving shit out of you, but didn't. I'd say that's a mighty neighborly gesture."

Oliver Johnston squinted at Byron. "Two punches? Nah, that ain't a beating. I've had worse from a twenty-year-old gelding."

This time Zeke swallowed the snort.

"I was protecting Margaret, seeing as how she's a part of our family now." Gideon shot a sidelong glance at Lee. "My cousin here was about to do the same, but I stepped in instead. Mr. Anderson can attest to the details since he was there."

Zeke heard Margaret gasp, low and fast. She tightened her hands into fists and glanced at Gideon from under her lashes. If Zeke didn't know any better, he'd have guessed their cook had

160

set her cap for their former captain. Not a good situation considering Lee had his heart set on her.

What a complicated mess.

"Ridiculous. What would you need to protect her from?" Byron looked honestly confused. Poor bastard.

Zeke decided to save him from his own stupidity. "Margaret has become part of our family and we protect her as if she was our own. Margaret is beautiful, smart and too good to settle for a man like you, a man who treats her as if she were only worth the food she could make for him."

Gideon looked as surprised as Lee at Zeke's defense of their actions. Jake shook his head while Gabby frowned so hard, her dark eyebrows almost formed one big V. Zeke knew he should have told Gideon he agreed with the principal of what they had tried to do, just not the method. That was, if Gideon had been talking to him since the fight.

"She's been a part of this town for a long time, longer than we've been here. She's Mayor Sheridan's friend and amazingly enough, the cook our restaurant was blessed with. She's important to all of us and it's our God-given right to protect her if we feel she's in danger. If it puts your mind at ease, I arrested Gideon for what he did." Zeke took great pleasure in the flush that spread across Ackerman's face.

"You did what?" Hettie's mouth dropped open while Edith smiled.

"He almost took it too far, so I arrested him for it. Mr. Ackerman has no quibble with D.H. Enterprises or anything we do in town. He's angry because he got his ass whooped, plain and simple. I did my job, now you do yours." Zeke ended his speech by crossing his arms and widening his stance.

Richard nodded. "That's what happened, ladies and gentlemen. It was an argument gone awry and the sheriff ended it before it went too far."

"Well, I hadn't realized the entire story." Hettie fluttered a hand at Mr. Ackerman.

"I fined him five dollars and released him." Gabby stepped out from beside Jake. "I agreed with what the sheriff had done and that was the end of it." She speared the council with a fierce glare. "This entire meeting has turned into a lynching party for the Blackwoods and I, for one, am not going to allow it to happen. They are all law-abiding citizens and good folks."

"Hear-hear," Oliver added.

Gabby turned to Ackerman and he had the good sense to back up. "We're glad to have the hotel open again, and we'd like all our businesspeople to get along and help each other." She whipped around and Hettie jumped, probably slamming her bony butt into the chair. "Perhaps Mrs. Cranston can help you, considering her husband used to own the hotel. I'm sure she can be of invaluable assistance."

"That's a wonderful idea." Edith clapped her hands. No doubt that would keep Hettie out of her hair for a while.

"Now does anyone else have anything to discuss?" Gabby asked.

"Yes, we haven't discussed the sheriff's choice of companions." Hettie cleared her throat and fixed her evil glare on Zeke.

His stomach jumped into his throat. "I'm not sure what you mean."

"Now, Mr. Blackwood, I saw you arm in arm with one of those women from Aphrodite's. You can't deny that. It looked cozy to me." Hettie nodded as the other council members eyeballed him.

"Miss Tucker is employed at the saloon, however she only

serves drinks. She takes walks in the mornings and I happened to take a moment to talk to her about how she was faring. She's new to town and I should think it's my job to make sure all citizens feel safe and welcome." It all came out in a rush, surprising the hell out of Zeke.

"Sounds reasonable to me," Oliver piped up.

Hettie's gaze narrowed. "I would suggest you choose your associations more carefully. We have little more than a week left in the trial period. Any transgressions and we'll consider that trial period over." Hettie could be as frightening as any Yankee soldier.

"Yes, ma'am." He forced the words out although what he wanted to do was tell her to go to hell. But he needed to keep the job, needed the purpose it gave him.

"Then we're finished here, I believe." Gabby nodded to the council. The silence in the room was only broken by Oliver's snickers. "Then this meeting is adjourned." She marched out of the hotel, Jake hot on her heels, his gaze a mixture of love, awe and pride.

Zeke was proud of her too. He and Gabby hadn't gotten along too well when they'd first met, but he'd been wrong about her and her abilities as mayor. She left them all in the dust, eating her words. The town council whispered amongst themselves as they rose to leave.

As Gideon and Lee walked to the door with Richard, they pointedly did not speak to Zeke. It hurt, quite a bit, even though he'd done his best to stop Ackerman's complaints in their tracks. Margaret, however, had no qualms about being polite.

"Thank you, Zeke." She looked down at her folded hands. "I appreciate you all trying to protect me, but I need to make my own decisions."

To Zeke's surprise, she left the hotel without speaking to

Ackerman. He hoped that meant she wasn't going to marry him. God knows she didn't need any more men messing up her life.

As he left the hotel, Hettie nodded at him, which for some odd reason pleased him.

"Have a good day, Sheriff. Be careful who you associate with. The town council won't be as forgiving in the future." She tucked her arm into Edith's and they left together.

Ackerman walked towards him but Zeke was in no mood to talk to the blowhard, so he tipped his hat and skedaddled out of the hotel. The first thought that jumped into his head when he stepped out into the rain was that he wondered what Naomi was doing.

Dammit to hell.

Zeke stared at the amber liquid in the glass. He licked his lips and could almost feel the burn of the whiskey as it slid down his throat. Self-pity roared through him as he realized he sat in the sheriff's office with a drink. Granted it was the middle of the night, but he'd nearly lost his job that day. Yet there he was, an idiot with an almost insurmountable need for liquor.

When he began to shake, he knew he had to get out of there and fast. Ignoring the little voice inside his head reprimanding him, Zeke walked outside and turned left, straight for Aphrodite's.

If he was honest with himself, he wasn't actually going to the saloon, he was headed for Naomi's room. The idea of being with her had beaten back the thirst for whiskey at least temporarily.

No doubt she was mad at him for whatever transgression

he'd committed, as were the Devils, but this time he couldn't stop himself from following through on his impulse. He crept up the back stairs, pausing as he got to her room. Leaning his forehead against the rough wood, he swallowed the misery and fear with effort. Naomi might be forbidden, but he realized she was an important part of what he needed to survive. Perhaps the most important. For now, he wasn't thinking clearly enough to figure out why, so it didn't matter until he could.

He pushed open the door silently and stepped into the room. The blackness of the moonless night hid her blonde hair, but her scent was unmistakable. Zeke couldn't stop himself from climbing into her bed any more than he could stop the sun from rising. He was addicted to her.

When he touched her shoulder, she rolled over, instantly awake. "I'm still angry with you."

Her voice was like a balm to his frazzled soul. God, he needed to be with her. "I'm sorry if I hurt you."

"You don't even know what you said, do you?" She sat up and wrapped her arms around her knees. "You lied to Miss Cranston about me, do you remember?"

He did remember and given his current state of mind, would likely do it again. Good thing Naomi wasn't privy to what the council had discussed earlier that evening. She'd have known he lied again. Life was becoming a series of lies.

"You treat me as if I'm dirty, to be hidden from view of respectable folks. I'm not a whore, Zeke, and I do have feelings." She laughed without humor. "I've spent the last few years surviving, doing what I needed to do to live. Then you come along and my life turns upside down."

Zeke took off his hat and slapped it on his leg. "My life's been inside out for the past five years. I didn't mean to hurt you, Naomi. I'm sorry for that."

She shook her head. "I can hear the sincerity in your voice, but I also hear something else, a part of you hidden from everyone. It's that part I think controls you and what you do. You've judged me and it seems I've come up short."

"I haven't judg—"

"Oh yes you have. Don't bother denying it. You judged me the second we met. Let me tell you something about me, Sheriff Blackwood." She rose from the bed, ethereal in her white nightdress. "The one time in my life I laid on my back for money was to escape from a town called Passman. The bastard mayor had spread enough rumors about me they were ready to lynch me in the morning for stealing." She paused to suck in a breath. "He offered to fuck me in exchange for twenty dollars, enough to get out. I took it, so I guess you're right about me being a whore, doubly so if you include what I've done with you."

Her voice was thick with rage and hurt. He'd had no idea of what she'd done or why, and his assumptions had caused her pain. Before he could apologize or even think about what to do, she walked over to the window, her back to him.

"I think it's best you leave."

Zeke knew it was for the best, but it still hurt like a goddamn knife to the chest. He deserved her censure and her anger. He'd made a mess of another important part of his life, and he couldn't do anything but leave.

He wandered back to his room at the restaurant, unsettled and uneasy. For hours he lay there thinking about how to fix the mess he'd made, what he was going to do about Naomi and how he'd gotten himself so twisted up over a woman. He knew he was in deeper than he'd ever been before. The sun's pink rays painted the walls of his bedroom before he finally gave up.

As he walked down the stairs, he heard Lee and Gideon

talking and laughing in the restaurant. His eyes stung with tears as he realized just how much he missed them. As a lawman, he knew he wouldn't be popular, especially with the drunks, but he thought he'd have his friends at his back.

When he got down to the bottom step, they both turned to look at him. Lee scowled while Gideon looked sad and disappointed. Zeke ached to sit with them and talk, to just be with them, but judging by their expressions, he wasn't welcome.

"No matter what you think, I was doing my job, nothing more. I gotta do something that matters so I can be human again." He choked back a sob. "If you want to hang me for that, then so be it. I wouldn't change what I did. A man's got to hold onto his integrity and honor or there won't be enough to feed the buzzards."

Gideon looked at him as if he'd gone loco, and perhaps he had. Zeke could hardly get a breath in and he had to go *now*. He turned and ran like a coward. Out of the restaurant, ignoring Lee's shout, he kept going.

Zeke found himself on the steps of the saloon, breathing like a bellows. Young Gregory Conley stood on the street, staring openmouthed, yet Lucy opened the door and smiled and Zeke forgot all about the minister.

"Come on in, sugar. You look like you could use a friend."

Zeke swam in a sea of pain and confusion, one made of whiskey and cigars. He vaguely remembered laughter, some bad piano music and at least two bottles of whiskey. At some point, he remembered cutting his hand on a glass, groping Louisa's ass—or was it Carmen's?—and falling asleep at the back table.

After he emptied the contents of his stomach onto his own clothes, the world started to whirl around faster and faster. He saw faces swimming around him, and as hard as he tried to block everything and everyone out, he saw her.

Naomi.

She watched him with tears glistening in her eyes and her hand pressed to her mouth. There was some shouting and then gentle hands picked up him and he knew no more.

Naomi wanted to go back downstairs and punch Lucy. She deliberately gave Zeke too much to drink until he nearly choked on his own vomit. Naomi wondered what set off the binge drinking, but Zeke obviously had a high tolerance for alcohol because he didn't stop until he was halfway through the second bottle of whiskey.

His brown gaze had been so full of pain and self-loathing, it made her heart hiccup just to look at him. There must be a wound deep inside the aloof sheriff that made him want to literally drown himself in alcohol. Of course, she knew he had secrets—everyone did—but his must be poisonous enough to be killing him slowly.

She never expected to see him so incapacitated. He couldn't even stand, much less take care of himself. His hand was bloodied and cut up by something. Fortunately Joe was there to help her get him up the stairs to her bedroom. She thought about getting his brother or cousin to help, but figured he didn't want them to see him in this state.

"Just lay him down on my bed, Joe." Naomi opened the door wide and they stumbled in, nearly dropping him. With more than a few mumbled curses, they made it to the bed and got him on his back. He smelled of whiskey, vomit, sweat and something she thought was desperation.

It was going to be a long night.

"Thanks for your help." She sucked in a much-needed deep breath, then gave Joe a quick kiss on the cheek. "You're a true gentleman."

"Ah, if only you knew, Miss Naomi." He chuckled rustily. "That Zeke is a good man, just lost his way a bit with the hooch. Shouldn't've been drinking in the first place 'cause he hasn't in three months." Joe shook his head. "Crying shame what that devil's brew will do to a man."

Naomi'd had no idea Zeke had a drinking problem or that he hadn't had any in months. Something had set him back on the path to self-destruction and Lucy had helped him along. Naomi didn't know what or why, but she intended on finding out. She agreed with Joe wholeheartedly. Zeke was a good man and he deserved happiness, even if she was angry at him for the way he treated her. She sighed when she saw the mess that was the man who held her soul in his calloused hands.

"You take good care of him, y'hear? I'll fetch some hot water for you to get him cleaned up." With one last baleful glance at Zeke, Joe left the room, closing the door behind him.

Naomi tried to shake off the foreboding that gripped her when she looked down at Zeke. He deserved much more than to be a stumbling drunk. She mentally pinched herself to get moving. In minutes, she'd removed his stained clothing and tucked him under the sheets. No need for modesty, after all, they'd seen every square inch of each other.

A soft knock at the door signaled Joe's return. She opened it only to find Carmen outside the door.

"Look, Carmen, I'm not doing business so find someone else to yell at." She was not in the mood for the Mexican woman's diatribe.

"I don't want to yell at you." Carmen put her hands on her

hips and looked at the floor. "I thought you, well, you know what I thought. But I see how you look at him all night, and then when he was sick, in your eyes I see the truth. You love him."

Naomi opened her mouth to deny it, but she didn't. She recognized the truth in the words even if she couldn't say it out loud.

"I just want to say I'm wrong. Louisa yelled at me and, well, we will take care of the rest of the night without you." Carmen finally met her gaze and Naomi saw a wary acceptance in there.

"I, um, thanks, Carmen. I really appreciate you telling me, and please tell Louisa I said thank you." Naomi felt like the world had tilted the last two hours and didn't know what else to say to the other woman.

"Good night then." Carmen saved Naomi the trouble of talking more by doing her normal thing and leaving abruptly. For once, Naomi was grateful for her co-worker's unusual habits.

Naomi was shutting the door when Joe popped up with a bucket of water, steam rising from the top.

"Here you go, girl." He walked into the room just as Zeke threw the covers off. "Well now, he's gonna catch a chill."

Naomi felt her cheeks heat at the sight of a naked Zeke in her bed. "He's starting to fuss a bit as the whiskey moves through him." She quickly covered him up. "Please put the water here by the bed."

Joe set the basin down, then shook his head as he looked down at Zeke. "Damn, I mean, pardon me. Darn shame, that is. You take care now, y'hear? There's folks who would like to see the sheriff fall down and never get up, if'n you know what I mean."

"Who?" Naomi scowled at her friend as protective urges

flooded through her. Someone wanted Zeke gone as sheriff? From what she'd heard and been told, he was a popular sheriff, bringing order to the town in only a month on the job. Besides that, he and his friends had saved the town from annihilation a year ago. How was it possible someone wanted Zeke dead?

Joe shrugged, his gaze unreadable. "Just whispers I hear in the saloon, nobody in particular. Just be careful." With that, the enigmatic older man left her alone with a drunk, naked Zeke.

A shiver crawled up her spine at his vulnerability, that someone wanted him permanently gone. She trusted Joe and if he told her Zeke was in danger, it was the truth. Naomi cupped his whiskered cheek, the rasp of the stubble on her hands almost as loud as the cacophony through the floor. She expected him to look innocent and sweet in his sleep, but he looked just as dangerous as always.

More so since he now depended on her to get through the next twelve hours.

Naomi grabbed her tattered shimmy from the peg on the wall and tore a piece off to get him cleaned up. She wiped him down, getting most of the muck off him, although the smell of the whiskey wasn't going anywhere soon, even his sweat reeked of it.

She took his clothes and got the worst of the vomit off and hung the clothes up to dry. As she was putting the bucket of water outside the room, Zeke came to life behind her.

"Fucking bitch," he growled from the bed. "Why did you do it? Why?"

There was fury in his tone, but more than that, there was agony. Deep, vicious pain dredged from down in his soul, which she recognized all too well. Naomi closed the door and walked over to the bed, determined to do what she could to help Zeke.

He grabbed her arm when she got close enough, twisting it until she almost screamed in agony. Being on her own for the last few years gave her some tricks though. She pinched the skin between his arm and his chest until he let her go. Rubbing the burning skin, she fell to her knees and looked at the man who was so hurt and angry he lashed out even when unconscious.

She blew out a breath and carefully reached out to brush the blond hair from his forehead. Matted with sweat, the normally vibrant locks were as pitiful as the man who owned them.

Naomi had a lot of time to think as she took care of Zeke, too much time really. It was disturbing to see him reduced to a crawling drunk. He seemed to be so strong and capable, albeit arrogant. Yet she knew the liquor was only a temporary balm to whatever was eating him up inside.

"I'll watch over you." She cupped his cheek. Tomorrow she would deal with Lucy and find out why she deliberately encouraged Zeke to get drunk.

Zeke tried to swallow but it seemed every drop of moisture was gone from his mouth. The taste of whiskey and vomit told him all he needed to know. He'd gone to the saloon and after that, everything was blurry. He tried to take a deep breath, but the pain in his chest stopped it cold. However, he smelled something much more familiar and welcome—Naomi.

As if he'd conjured her from a dream, her soft fingers touched his face, which was currently pressed into a pillow. *Her* pillow. The idea she was taking care of him made his throat close and he started to choke. God knows he never wanted

Naomi to see him like this.

After she rolled him on his side, she rubbed circles on his back until the coughing subsided. She wiped his face and helped him back up onto the pillows in a sitting position. Still, he didn't open his eyes.

"It's okay, Zeke." She continued to dab the cool cloth on his forehead. "Everyone stumbles now and then."

Zeke had vague memories of the night before, most of them bad. Yet through it all, Naomi's presence had been constant. She pressed a tin cup to his lips and the sweetness of the water coated his mouth. He tried to slurp more but she pulled it away.

"Too much and you'll get sick." She squeezed his hand. "Are you even going to look at me?"

Reluctantly, Zeke opened his eyes to slits and knew he shouldn't. Tears blurred his gaze but he saw the earnest love in the hazel depths of her eyes. He expected much less, even recrimination, censure and disgust. Yet what she gave him in return made him look away.

"Zeke, please look at me."

"Why did you help me?" He kept his gaze averted.

"I help everyone who needs it. Many a time I needed some and didn't get it. I'm going to get some warm water to wash you up."

Blessedly, she walked out of the room, leaving Zeke to his own misery. Swimming in the hell of his own making, he curled up in a ball and wept.

He didn't know how long she'd been gone, but he must have fallen asleep. Zeke woke to her pulling the sheets down and the cool air hitting his naked body. He wasn't embarrassed to be nude, she'd been intimate with him too many times now for that, but he wasn't ready for her gasp.

Zeke popped one eye open to find her staring at his body, her hand pressed to her mouth and an expression of pain on her face.

"What? What's wrong?" He sounded as if he'd been gargling rocks.

"Sweet Jesus." She perched on the edge of the bed and reached out a shaking hand. "You have so many scars." Her fingers traced the outline of the pink scar on his left shoulder from a year ago.

"A man ain't a man unless he's got scars." He didn't want her to continue worrying over him. He sure as hell wasn't worth it.

"But you've been hurt so much." She skimmed over the ragged scar from a knife wound.

"I can handle it." He stopped her hand. "Don't worry."

She nodded but he could see her biting that plump lower lip as she dipped a rag in a basin of steaming water. "Let's get you cleaned up properly then."

Even in the surgical tent during the war, he'd never had a nurse or a corpsman give him a good washing. The last time anyone had done it for him, he'd been in short pants and in his mama's care.

Zeke closed his eyes and held back the tears. He was so lost in what could be, should be, but wasn't. With every stroke of the warm cloth, he finally heard what she was trying to tell him, what he refused to listen to.

Without words, she told him she loved him, that she worried for him, that she wanted to take away his pain. Zeke's head pounded right along with his heart as he paid attention to what was in front of him. Naomi had come to mean more to him than anything and he'd ignored everything but her body. He couldn't allow her to throw her heart away on a man like him.

$$*$$

After he fell asleep, Naomi left the saloon and headed to the restaurant. She knocked on the door with a trembling hand. When Gideon opened it, he looked behind her in the predawn light.

"Where is he?"

"In my room at the saloon. He's drunk about two bottles of whiskey near as I can tell and he's suffering for it." She swallowed the lump in her throat before it stole her voice.

"He's a man in so much pain he can't remember a time without it." Gideon's blue gaze locked with hers. "Zeke might seem like a cold man but that's only to keep a lid on what he can't control."

She nodded, recognizing his words as the absolute truth. Naomi had believed the sheriff to be a pushy, bossy hard-ass, but he was so much more than that.

"I want to help him."

Gideon stared at her hard. "You have feelings for him."

Although she hadn't told Zeke yet, she told his best friend. "Yes, I love him and I won't turn away now."

"Good, he'll need as much love as we can give him." He put his hand on her shoulder. "We'll be there in a few minutes. Keep him safe for us until then."

Chapter Ten

Naomi cleaned up the room, then brought the bucket of dirty water downstairs. Her mind kept returning to Zeke and why God had seen fit to match the two of them together. She often wondered if there was a purpose to the way things happened. Perhaps since they'd both had enough misery to last a dozen lifetimes, they were meant to find each together.

When she arrived in Tanger, she wouldn't have predicted falling in love with Zeke or finding a man she could spend her life with. Yet she had, and he was a bigger mess than she. God must have a sense of humor.

It was probably nearly seven already. Her stomach rumbled with hunger but she ignored it. Time enough later for vittles after Zeke was taken care of. Perhaps he might feel up to dinner at Elmer's later—or maybe not. He was still in very rough shape. She wanted to help him, but knew keeping him in her bed wasn't the wisest choice. She was glad she'd gone to tell his friends, but knowing they would come and get him soon made her wish she hadn't.

"Good morning, angel."

Startled, Naomi dropped the bucket on her foot as she whirled to face the speaker. A young man stood there with wavy brown hair and sparkling blue eyes. He was a stranger to her, but she'd seen him in town before. No doubt the minister's collar meant he was the town's new reverend.

"Good morning." She reached down to massage the bump on her foot.

"My apologies if you hurt yourself. I didn't mean to scare you." He held out his hand. "Reverend Gregory Conley."

Embarrassed by her appearance, she briefly shook his hand, looking like death with snarls in her hair and a stained dress. Not to mention she'd been avoiding ministers, church and God since He'd seen fit to take her father and her life away from her.

"Pleased to meet you. I'm Miss Naomi Tucker. I've got to get back inside, Reverend." She grabbed the bucket handle and turned to go back up the steps when his hand on her arm stopped her.

"Please call me Gregory, if you would. I'm new in town and wanted to be sure to meet everyone." His wide smile was so open and innocent, it made her lips twitch. However, she needed to get back to Zeke.

"I'm sorry but I don't have time to talk more today. I appreciate you introducing yourself to me, but I really must go." She started up the stairs. "If you'll excuse me. Good day, Reverend."

Naomi closed the door behind her, ignoring the minister's stutters. She didn't need a sermon, and definitely didn't need a young man meddling in her life no matter how sweet or innocent he was.

Zeke watched the door, at peace for the first time in a long time, as he waited for Naomi to return. She'd been gone only a few minutes, but he already wished she was back. He'd never thought to be a man mooning over a woman, but he was doing it anyway.

When the door opened, he almost smiled, until he caught sight of the paleness of her face and the dark circles under her eyes. After she shut the door behind her and leaned on it, she met his gaze with a tremulous smile. The night caring for him was nearly as hard on her. God only knew why she did it—he didn't deserve it.

"You're awake."

A knock at the door made her jump a country mile. She pressed her finger to her lips to shush him and he understood she didn't want anyone to find him there. Zeke would definitely be fired if they did, considering Hettie would know he'd lied to her.

"Zeke, you in there?" Gideon's voice came through the closed door.

He let out a huge sigh, relieved to know his cousin was on the other side of the door.

Naomi opened the door, blocking the opening with her slim form. "He's still not doing very well."

"It's okay. That's why we're here." Gideon sounded calm.

Lee, on the other hand, wasn't even remotely calm. "You got him drunk, you goddamn whore, now let me in there before I tear your fucking arms off."

Zeke vaulted off the bed, ignoring the lurch in his stomach. "I told you more than once, she is *not* a whore. You'd best never say that again, Lee."

Gideon, Lee and Jake came in, giving Zeke time to absorb the shock of the Devils coming for him. After the tumultuous few weeks and the falling out they'd had, it warmed Zeke's heart to see them protecting him.

"Lee, you owe Naomi an apology. She didn't give me any booze, you idiot."

His brother frowned as he unclenched his fists. "That's not what Lucy told us."

Zeke's stomach dropped to his knees. Lucy had told them Naomi got him drunk? His head pounded with liquor and confusion.

"Lucy lied. Naomi was the one who took care of me and cleaned up my vomit and shit." He glanced at her, at the hurt plainly written on her face.

"So you're cozy with her now, then?" Lee gazed around the room, always ready to believe the worst in people.

Zeke swayed on his feet and Naomi caught him. "Sit down before you fall down." She was bossy when backed into a corner, but in this case he allowed her to walk him to the bed to sit.

Gideon smacked Lee in the arm. "He's still drunk, you idiot. Stop being such an ass."

"Yeah, don't be an ass," Jake chimed in. His blue gaze found Zeke's and he asked without speaking if everything was okay. They'd always shared the responsibility of watching each other's backs and it would likely never change.

"Look, I'm fine. Still a bit drunk, feel like shit on a horse's ass, but thanks to Naomi, I'm alive." He rubbed his hands over his eyes. "I don't know why the hell Lucy lied to you."

Naomi snorted. "I do. She's in love with you, you dolt." She tucked her hair behind her ear. "You can't tell me you didn't notice."

Zeke shifted on the bed, uncomfortable with the topic and unwilling to feel guilty. "I told her I wasn't interested in marrying her."

"What did she say to that?" Gideon looked at him much too intently.

"She said something about she had always hoped something would happen." He shrugged. "I ain't never even kissed her, Gid. I don't know how she got it in her head to snag me for her man."

"Must be your charm." Lee paced the small room like a caged panther.

"Shut up, Lee." Zeke pressed his palms to his temples. "I told you to apologize to Naomi and I meant it."

Lee stopped pacing and stared at his brother. "What for? She's a whore."

All thought flew out of his head as he jumped on his brother and started pounding the piss out of him. Gideon and Jake pulled him away, but not before he'd split Lee's lip and given him a shiner to last at least a week.

Naomi stood in the corner, her hand over her mouth, watching them as if they were the crazy freaks at the circus. He wanted to reassure her the fighting was normal for them, but that might make her think they really were crazy.

Gideon pushed him onto the bed. "We came here to rescue you from yourself, but it seems we were too late." He nodded at Naomi. "I thank you for your help, Miss Tucker, but we'll take him home now."

Jake pointed to the corner of Zeke's lip. "Looks like Lee got a punch in after all."

A twinge of pain radiated from the spot. "Dammit, I'll likely have to explain that to the damn town council too."

"You might want to wait until you're sober," Gideon suggested dryly.

Zeke knew his cousin was right. He was still swimming with whiskey in his veins, and the liquor wasn't about to let go for a while. Naomi stood next to the bed, concern and love evident in her expression.

"Thank you, little one, for everything."

"Take care of yourself, Sheriff." She stepped towards the window without saying goodbye. Perhaps she was feeling the same tightness in his chest that he was. That would be something.

Jake, Gideon and Lee waited for him by the door. The sight of them standing in Naomi's room told him they were still family, no matter what had happened between them. He wanted to say thank you but couldn't. It wasn't easy for him to say on the best of days, much less when he had been drinking.

Instead he nodded at them, a bad idea because his stomach rolled with the movement. Lee was beside him in seconds, his arm around Zeke's waist followed by Jake on the other side. Gideon walked ahead, scouting for anyone who might see the sheriff in such a state.

"Hang on there, big brother. We'll get you home."

Zeke wanted to walk on his own, but he was obviously in no shape to do that just yet. His family was there to help and that's all that mattered. For the first time in days, the pain inside him abated.

It took a bit longer than usual to walk to the restaurant, and by the time they arrived, Zeke was a bit lightheaded. Early Sunday morning and he was half-drunk in the street. Although they wanted to remain unseen, luck was not in their favor.

Gregory Conley strolled down the street, bible in hand and a frown on his normally chipper expression.

"Sheriff, are you hurt?" He headed towards them and Zeke couldn't stop him before he got too close. The young minister wrinkled his nose and stopped dead in his tracks. "What is that smell?"

"Medicine," Lee snapped. "We're bringing him to his bed to get better."

"Better from what? If I didn't know better, I'd think it was whiskey I smelled." Gregory took another loud whiff. "I did see him entering Aphrodite's last evening."

Zeke wanted to find a hole and drop himself in it. As if it wasn't bad enough to be drunk and incoherent in front of Naomi, now the new preacher in town was witness to his stupidity. Just lovely.

"I told you it's medicine. The sheriff needs to get to bed so get out of the way, Conley." Lee didn't cotton to treating men of the cloth like they were better than anyone else.

"Reverend Conley, we appreciate your concern, but we've got it under control." Gideon was always the peacekeeper.

"I'm concerned about the well-being of every citizen of Tanger and that includes the sheriff." Reverend Conley looked older than his probably twenty years. "I must insist on helping. He obviously needs spiritual guidance."

Zeke wanted to dropkick the kid back to Kansas or wherever the hell he'd come from, but he could barely stand up straight.

"I don't want any help. Just find someone else to save."

They made it to the restaurant with Conley dogging their tail. He continued his diatribe about the sins of liquor until Lee practically slammed the door in his face. Gideon shook his head at his cousin.

"What? The idiot wouldn't shut up."

"I realize that, but it wouldn't kill you to be polite to the town's new minister," Gideon admonished.

Lee snorted. "As if I ever wanted to be polite."

"That's the gospel truth." Jake chuckled.

"You are a serious redheaded pain in the ass. Why don't you go home to your Italian wife?" Lee glowered at Jake.

"Make me."

They started up the stairs and Zeke's stomach flipped upside down. He closed his mouth and swallowed back the bile that threatened.

"Hurry," he managed to get out.

"Okay, shut up, both of you, Zeke needs our help," Gideon snapped. "Let's get him upstairs."

Zeke wanted to protest, really he did, but he couldn't. Everything from the previous day and night hit him with the force of a sledgehammer. As soon as Jake and Lee took his arms, blackness threw a cloak over him and then he knew no more.

Chapter Eleven

The first formal Sunday service in a year in the town of Tanger began at ten on a beautiful morning. It was expected that the old Reverend Delmont's followers would take time to warm up to the young reverend. However, the townspeople didn't live up to that expectation. They came to the old church in droves.

The town council led the way, with Hettie Cranston in her faded but serviceable, cranberry-colored dress. On her arm was Byron Ackerman in a spiffy shiny suit with his hair slicked back with pomade. Edith walked with Martin. The big burly blacksmith couldn't have looked more proud. Naomi was surprised to see Margaret walking with Matthew, but glad for it. They were both gentle souls and maybe they'd find happiness together. Even that new banker with the cane arrived in his Sunday best.

Naomi watched it all as if it were a parade. Many folks passed under the saloon as they made their way to the church. Perhaps they were all in need of praying or salvation or whatever it was they were searching for. She had given up on church after her father's death.

It had taught her to stop asking God for help because he didn't listen, any more than anyone else did. She had to rely on herself, not a deity she'd never seen nor heard from. During her incarceration in Tanger's jail, she'd broken down and prayed, not that it had done any good. However, it reinforced her belief in self-reliance.

She couldn't see the front of the church from her perch by the window, but she imagined Conley greeting each of them with his boyish smile. A knock at the door interrupted her thoughts.

"Who is it?"

"It's Louisa. Me, Joe and Carmen are going to go to church to see what the fuss is about." Louisa poked her frizzy head through the open doorway. "Do you want to join us, or are you still entertaining your man?"

"I'm alone." Naomi looked at her friend's earnest expression and wanted to ask what she was excited about.

"We hear the preacher is going to do some good old-fashioned fire-and-brimstone type sermon." Louisa came fully into the room wearing a light blue dress with frayed edges. The garment had obviously served the purpose of a Sunday dress in a previous lifetime.

"Why would you want to hear that?" Naomi couldn't control her distaste. Men of the cloth who threw bolts of fire at ordinary folks just to make them quake in their shoes and throw up their hands in surrender weren't worth the effort to listen to.

"'Cause he's talking about the wages of sin, 'specially whiskey and women." She waggled her eyebrows. "We thought we'd have a little fun and sit in the back."

Not even remotely fun in Naomi's opinion, but if they wanted to go, she wasn't about to stop them.

"I reckoned I'd ask if you want to go with us."

"No thanks." Naomi smiled at Louisa. "Thanks for inviting me though."

Louisa shrugged and waved. "We'll see you later then." As she walked through the door, she stopped. "I told her, but she don't want to come."

Carmen pushed past the sweet brunette. "*Oiga, chica.* They're talking about your *hombre* today." She looked deadly serious. "I hear they want him to stop being sheriff."

The bottom dropped out of Naomi's stomach at Carmen's warning. "How do you know?"

Carmen raised one dark brow. Naomi knew then the Mexican woman told the absolute truth and it scared the hell out of her.

"I'm coming with you."

Naomi didn't know whether to run away or find a corner to get sick in. The dilapidated church was filled nearly to capacity. Every eye in the building turned to look at the contingent from Aphrodite's. Lucy wasn't with them, but nonetheless they were painted with the same brush. Another reason she didn't like church, people were judgmental.

Joe looked dapper in a starched white shirt and brown trousers, while Carmen wore a blue peasant blouse and skirt. Naomi had chosen her only acceptable dress, the yellow one she'd met Zeke in. It seemed fitting that she'd come to a church to relive her own personal nightmare and protect the man she loved. Kind of a fitting way to exorcise her personal demons.

It had been cloudy the day the Yankees burned her father's church down, the day they murdered his congregation. She had tried to forgive and forget, but God had taken everything she loved that day. Most folks would have prayed for help to get through such a trying time. Naomi simply grew a steel spine and moved on.

Gregory Conley stood at the pulpit, reading through his

bible presumably. When he caught sight of them, he smiled in a way that made her skin crawl. The rest of the folks just nodded and turned around, satisfied the preacher had welcomed the tainted souls. Perhaps they hoped he'd save them. Naomi wanted to snort at the thought.

"Good morning, everyone," he began. "I want to thank you all for making my first sermon such a success by coming to the church."

More smiles all through the pews.

"Today's sermon is a timely one. I happened to witness one of our finest members in the community suffering the sins of imbibing too much." His smile vanished as the man started in on a subject that obviously bothered him. "The wages of sin aren't worth the everlasting damnation you'll suffer for enjoying them." He pounded the wooden altar. "We cannot allow this to continue, and for that, my friends, I need your help."

Matthew Marchison seemed to be the only one frowning at the minister. When he glanced at Naomi, she saw the same concern she felt. The shopkeeper had been kind to her and she hoped he wasn't the only one who didn't like the direction the sermon was headed.

Naomi's throat went dry as sand when Gregory's gaze met hers. In the depths of his eyes she saw not only passion for preaching, but fervor as well, reminiscent of her father when he thundered from the pulpit.

"Who was it, preacher man?" came a question.

"An appointed man we all rely on to keep us safe. I don't think I need to say his name, do I? He violated our trust by falling victim to man's oldest vices—liquor and women. We need to help him, and thereby help our town."

Byron Ackerman stood and Naomi's hands clenched into fists. This definitely did not bode well for Zeke.

"I know of whom he speaks. Sheriff Zeke Blackwood has made a mockery of lawmen everywhere. He has embarrassed this town too many times." Murmurs of agreement rippled through the church. "I agree with Reverend Conley, something must be done."

Naomi didn't wait to hear what else Byron or Gregory had to say. She jumped out of the pew and ran from the church, her heart pounding so hard, her ears hurt from the vibrations. She had to warn him, to protect him from small-minded fools like Reverend Conley and whatever frenzy he could whip up in church with the unsuspecting citizens of Tanger. She'd been wrong about him—he wasn't as sweet as he appeared.

The streets were nearly deserted, giving an unreal feel to the morning. She should have been embarrassed by her behavior in running through Tanger, but there was no time to be. A fierce protective urge gripped her and she had to follow through on it.

There was a time in her life when she would have run the opposite direction from conflict or fear, but no more. She had grown up in the last three years, like it or not. Now her man, the one who held her heart, needed her and she'd damn sure be there for him.

She slammed into the restaurant and ran up the stairs, regardless of the astonished looks thrown her way by several folks. Although she was going too fast to see who they were, one of them was probably Zeke's brother. More than likely he'd follow her up the steps, but she didn't care one whit.

She wanted to burst into the room, but knocked on the door instead in a staccato rhythm designed to wake the dead.

"What?" came a groggy, annoyed voice.

"Zeke, can I come in?"

"Naomi?" A thump, a groan and a curse preceded him

opening the door.

Naomi had to stop herself from breaking it down.

He looked out at her with bloodshot eyes and a terrible smell of stale whiskey—definitely a man who had been raked over the coals. She stepped back and covered her mouth. He ran a hand down his whiskered cheeks. She gazed down and realized he was quite naked.

"What is it?"

"You're still drunk and you haven't got a stitch on." How was she going to clear his good name if he resembled the exact sins Gregory spoke of?

"Did you come here to tell me what I already knew? I ain't still drunk, just got a hangover bad enough to kill a buffalo." He opened the door wider and gestured with his hand. "You might as well come in before somebody sees you up here."

"I don't care if they see me or not." She marched into his room, head held high. "You've got to come to church with me."

The last thing she expected was for him to burst out laughing, but that's what he did. Then he moaned and grabbed his forehead.

"Jesus, no laughing, that really hurts." He closed the door and sat down heavily on the edge of the bed. "Why do you want me to go to church? You planning on getting hitched today?"

"Reverend Conley and Byron Ackerman are stirring up the town to lynch you." It wasn't exactly what she wanted to say, but it got his attention.

His face lost all color and his jaw tightened. "Who's lynching me?"

"Well, not actually lynching, but they're talking about your sins, or judging you for what they believe are your sins." She wrung her hands together. "You need to get over there and set them straight before the town council decides to fire you."

He scowled at her. "You mean he's telling about what he saw this morning? What a little shit."

"Zeke, you're missing the point." She knelt in front of him, ignoring his nakedness in favor of saving him from small-minded fools. "Regardless of the drinking binge, and your behavior toward me, I've seen what you can do as a sheriff. You're good at it and I believe Tanger needs you."

He shook his head, the scowl fading. "You came over here to warn me."

"Well, yes, I did. Somebody's got to protect you." Naomi had no idea how to explain to him why she needed to shield him from harm without confessing she loved him. He certainly wasn't ready for that considering he could barely stand or think.

"Believe it or not, I do have friends, little one." He reached out a shaking hand to cup her cheek. "But having a fierce little doe stand by my side is an amazing thing."

Naomi wasn't sure she wanted to be known as a fierce little doe, but the sentiment made her heart gallop. He wasn't the type of man to give compliments lightly, or ever flatter anyone, which meant his words carried more than their weight. He kissed her.

"You deserve better than a broken-down soldier who crawls into the bottom of a whiskey bottle."

"That's my choice to make, not yours. Now let's get you cleaned up and go to church." She tugged at his shoulders, but he didn't budge. "I'm not going to let you lie here and let him win."

Zeke looked up at her, his beautiful brown eyes swimming with agony. "Why shouldn't I let him win? He's right about me."

Naomi had had enough. She spotted a basin of water on the washstand. Before he could realize what she was doing, she threw the water in his face.

"Get up." This time she didn't wait for an answer, she took the pitcher and refilled the washbasin. "I haven't shaved anyone in two years, but I'm sure it will come back to me quick."

He wiped the water off his face and glared at her.

She had wanted him to jump up and fight for himself, but he didn't. So she had to do it for him, come hell or high water. Naomi would wash, shave and dress him. After finding his shaving gear, she set to work. He winced a few times when she scraped the razor across his face, but other than that, he didn't speak or stop her from what she was doing.

After wiping off his face with a towel, she used soap and a rag to wash his face and armpits so he didn't smell quite so badly. Spotting clean clothes on a hook, Naomi grabbed them and dressed Zeke as she would a small child. He simply let her do what she wanted.

It scared the hell out of her because it appeared he'd given up.

She wouldn't allow that to happen.

It took about ten minutes, but she had him somewhat presentable and ushered him down the stairs. They went slowly because he gripped the banister as if it had magical powers to keep him upright. Naomi had a hard time believing he wasn't still drunk because he sure acted like it.

Either way, they made it out to the street and to the church within twenty-five minutes. Fortunately it appeared the congregation was still inside since the town was almost empty of folks. When they arrived in the church, Zeke started to drag his feet.

"Get moving, Ezekiel, you're not backing out now." She

pushed him up the steps and into the church.

The doors banged open and every head turned to face them. Zeke's face flushed red and Naomi straightened her shoulders, not in the least afraid of what would happen. Or at least that's what she told herself as her knees knocked together.

"Sheriff." Gregory frowned, looking a bit startled at Zeke's appearance.

"Morning, Reverend." Zeke glanced around, his thumbs tucked into his waistband. "I hear you folks are talking about me this morning."

He strolled in slowly, as if he didn't have a care in the world or that he was drunk and naked half an hour earlier. The low buzz of conversation followed his progress.

"I came by to see what was going on."

Byron popped up from the front row. "I'll tell you what's going on. You've been flaunting your fornicating and drinking, a poor example for the rest of the town to follow. You're a poor excuse for a sheriff and if the town council won't get rid of you, perhaps we can."

The threat hung in the air, leaving a tang of disbelief and outrage on Naomi's tongue. She stepped towards him, but Zeke grabbed her arm.

"Let me fight my own battle, little one," he whispered.

As Naomi watched, Zeke walked towards the altar and turned to face everyone. They likely saw a big blond man with guns and an attitude, but she saw a man consumed by pain and self-loathing who did his best to survive moment by moment.

"I ain't perfect and probably not the best person to be sheriff." He nodded to Hettie and the rest of the town council.

"Folks gave me a chance to do my best and I guess I didn't do what was expected. I appreciate that chance, but there's no need to talk about getting rid of me. I quit."

To Naomi's horror, he walked out of the church.

Reverend Conley thanked the congregation for coming to church and announced the services were over. Pandemonium reigned as rumors and innuendo flew through the crowd.

She was angry and frustrated with the man who'd crawled into her heart only to step on it on his way to hell. Fury surged through her as she started after him, but the reverend stopped her.

"Miss Tucker." He took her arm. "I am surprised to see you here." He blushed. "I mean, glad to see you attended church. Everyone is welcome."

"Except for the sheriff, right? He's a person too, with feelings. How dare you crucify him in front of these people?" She wanted to tear her arm from his grasp, but in his gaze, she saw an earnestness that had been missing earlier.

"Please listen to me." He took a deep breath and blew it out. "I've only been in town a short time. Mr. Ackerman had told me how the sheriff was drunk all the time or over at Aphrodite's, ah, upstairs. Then this morning when I saw him, well, I came to the conclusion Mr. Ackerman was right. I like Mr. Blackwood, he was kind to me and I didn't mean to hurt him. Please, you must believe me."

"It doesn't matter what you say now because the damage is done." She shifted her anger to the young minister. "You said you liked Zeke, so how could you destroy him like that?"

Red flags of shame appeared on Gregory's face. "That wasn't my intention. I got a little carried away."

"You got a lot carried away. The job was the last thing that mattered to him. Do you understand? He's given up and you gave him permission to do it." Naomi wanted to howl and cry at the naiveté of the minister. Although she and the young man were probably close in age, she felt decades older than him.

"I'll go find him and apologize. Next week I'll do it in front of the congregation." He wrung his hands together. "It was my first sermon and I wanted it to be a powerful one. I-I made an awful mistake."

She didn't have time for his self-recrimination or his apologies. Gregory could speak to his God about that.

"I'm sorry, but I've got to go." Naomi knew where Zeke would be and she had to stop him before he truly jumped straight into hell.

Zeke walked away from the church, ignoring the shouting and the hideous mess he'd left behind. Pain began somewhere near his toes and spread through his body until he could barely breathe through it.

Naomi had been a beacon for him, a light he tried to reach and bask in the glow of. However it hadn't been fated to last. She was a good person, a better person than he could ever hope to be. After all, she had at least tried to save him while he threw himself off the cliff of despair and misery. Now that he'd destroyed his chance at a respectable job in Tanger and his future with Naomi, there was nothing left for him to look forward to. He couldn't stay there, which left him completely alone.

A pitiful man walked towards Aphrodite's and away from the church. The building held so many bad and good memories for him, just being there mixed him up terribly. Allison had represented all that was good in the world after the war, but she'd been taken away from him. Then there was Naomi, a tough, no-nonsense survivor who represented the person he wanted to be.

And God help him, he loved her, enough to let her go and save her from the depths to which he was about to plunge. No doubt Gideon would try to stop him, and perhaps Lee and Jake, but this time no one would be able to stop his descent.

When he arrived at the saloon, it was dark, but he knew Lucy wouldn't care if he helped himself to a drink or two. He'd done it before after all.

The gloom inside the building was only broken by shafts of sunlight sneaking through the slats in the shutters. His boots thunked on the wooden floor as he walked towards the bar. He half expected Joe to come running out with a gun and shoot him, but it didn't happen. That's when he remembered seeing the older man and the rest of the girls at the church.

Lucy appeared on the stairs, as if she'd been waiting for him. By his estimation they were alone in the saloon. The look of naked longing on her face unnerved him, but he didn't run. He stood in place and awaited his fate.

She wore a chocolate-colored dress that complemented her eyes. Lucy was a beautiful, shapely woman, of that there was no doubt, but she wasn't Naomi. That woman might be a wisp of a thing, but she had more strength in her slender form than he did in his entire body, which was likely almost double her size.

Lucy was more like Zeke. Lonely, desperate and willing to do whatever she needed to make the pain go away. In this case, it was Zeke she wanted and he decided to give himself to her. Perhaps that would make Naomi realize what she'd set herself up for.

"Mornin', Zeke." Lucy walked behind the bar, a knowing look on her face. "Thirsty?"

He pretended not to notice that his hands shook or that his

stomach tightened up so hard, bile coated the back of his throat. It was too hard to keep pushing himself to be something he wasn't. For once, Zeke wanted to do things the easy way.

Lucy poured the amber liquid, the good stuff she kept behind the bar, not the rotgut, then pushed the glass towards him. There were at least three shots in the tall glass. The demons inside the glass shrieked at him, taunted him with their jibes, and he listened.

As he lifted the glass to his lips, he closed his eyes. A fierce slap made the glass fly across the room, spraying him with whiskey. A second slap landed on his cheek and he opened his eyes to find a furious Naomi in front of him.

Her chest heaved as emotions swam across her face. Disappointment, anger, love and annoyance. She put her hands on her hips and glared at him.

"You are a fool, Ezekiel Blackwood. You're just going to go ahead and throw away a good life, aren't you? Hardships are plenty in the new south and you've been handed a gift of a job and a second chance on a silver platter." Her face grew flushed as she shouted at him. He hadn't known a lioness lurked behind the petite woman. "Before the war, I had dreams of marrying my beau, Ronald Cooper, but he was killed along with my father. On one day I lost everything I loved."

She poked one sharp finger into his chest. "God knows I hadn't intended on doing any of things I've done over the last three years, but that was what life gave me so I did what I could with it. How dare you think for even a minute that being a lawman with good friends, a home to live in and good health were to be thrown away?"

Naomi took a breath then swung to Lucy. "And you! What kind of friend are you to Zeke? Friends don't give each other whiskey when they're drunkards. You're purposely keeping him pickled and it makes me mad enough to beat you blind."

Lucy stepped back a pace or two. "Zeke is a grown man who makes his own decisions."

"Is that so? Who gave him the whiskey last night and this morning?" Naomi was starting to scare the other woman, judging by the expression on Lucy's face.

"I-I was only protecting my business."

"I don't even know what that means. You know I was really grateful for the job and I still am, but I can't be party to digging Zeke's grave." Naomi swung back to Zeke and he jumped.

"You're a pitiful excuse for a man, Zeke, and unless you walk out of this saloon for good right now, you'll be throwing me away too." She crossed her arms and pinched her lips so hard, they turned white. Her eyes shone with unshed tears and Zeke was sorry he had been the cause of them.

But he couldn't leave the saloon. Not yet.

When he turned back to the bar and gestured to Lucy to pour him another, Naomi's gasp of pain echoed through his body. He couldn't even swallow the lump of regret and agony that had taken up residence in his throat.

Zeke closed his eyes as her footsteps faded. When he opened them, Lucy was scowling at him.

"You love her, don't you?"

"It don't matter if I love her or not, Naomi don't need a drunk husband and I can't be anything else." Zeke took the bottle out of Lucy's hands and walked out of the saloon.

Alone.

Zeke threw a change of clothes and a few other essentials in his saddlebags and left the restaurant without speaking to Gideon or Lee. Right about then, he couldn't talk even if he wanted to. Naomi's loss had robbed him of the ability to speak, much less think.

He shoved a whiskey bottle in the saddlebags as he walked down the street towards the livery. Folks stood in clumps on the street, pointing and whispering as they watched him. No doubt he was adding to their gossiping, as if he wasn't already the main topic.

It didn't matter. None of it mattered. He needed to pick up his horse and go away for a while. He needed to be alone, to think and maybe figure out what he wanted to do with the rest of his life.

Zeke had a feeling he knew what he wanted, but couldn't make himself take a chance and grab it. He'd broken Naomi's heart, and for that he'd never forgive himself, and she'd never forgive him.

Naomi went upstairs to pack, ignoring knocks at the door from Louisa, then Carmen. Her heart was shattered and nothing they said could fix it. She'd been so full of high hopes about Tanger and starting a new life, but everything had been snatched away from her.

The fourth time someone knocked, Naomi snapped. "What? Can't you two just leave me alone?"

When Lucy poked her head in the door, Naomi stopped packing and simply stared at the older woman. "Can I come in?"

Naomi wanted to scream at her, but knew it wouldn't solve anything. "It's your saloon." She turned away, keeping her temper reined in.

Lucy stepped in and closed the door, leaning on it with her head down. "I'm sorry."

Naomi frowned, unsure of what she'd heard. "What did you

say?"

Lucy raised her face and tears steamed down her cheeks. "I'm sorry for what I did. Zeke's a good man and I wanted him for my own." She pushed away from the door and swiped at the tears. "I wanted him from the second I saw him, but all this time he ain't never looked at me like he looked at you. He loves you."

She wanted to believe Lucy, she did, but Zeke had chosen whiskey over her, and that left Naomi alone again. This time with a broken heart and the knowledge of what it felt like to be loved and cherished by someone.

"He didn't love me enough." Naomi shoved the yellow dress into her tattered traveling bag. She wanted to tear it to pieces, but the dress was still the only link to her former life. It had been her favorite Sunday dress, the reminder of who she used to be and what she used to have.

"I just wanted to tell you that and ask you to stay." Lucy swallowed so hard Naomi heard it.

"You want me to stay?"

Lucy looked her in the eye, the tough saloon owner replaced by a regular person. "I know it's hard out there, Naomi, and you're a good person, better than me, that's for sure. Folks like you and, well, I can't let you leave because of what I did."

The rug had been pulled from beneath Naomi's feet in the last day, but this gave her a tiny glimmer of hope. She wasn't sure if she believed Lucy or not, but she wasn't going to throw away her chance to keep a roof over her head.

"What do you say?" Lucy held out her hand.

Naomi stared at the calloused palm of the woman who had given her a job when no one else would. There really wasn't a question in her mind what her answer would be.

199

"Yes, of course." They shook hands and Naomi let out the breath she'd been holding. Life, it seemed, would continue in Tanger with or without Zeke by her side.

Chapter Twelve

The sun scratched at Zeke's closed lids, disturbing his deep slumber. He rolled over, noting sharp pains in his shoulder and side. The stale taste of cheap whiskey coated his tongue, yet the jolt of its flavor made one eye pop open.

A small lizard sat a foot from his face, watching him with beady eyes, startling him. His other eye refused to open and his head was fuzzy from the booze. The ground beneath him was dusty, rocky and unfamiliar.

He blew dust at the lizard, but it merely blinked.

"You know whiskey will kill you."

Nate's voice, in the middle of God knew where, scared him so badly, he scrambled backwards. The rocks cut at his bare skin and he realized somewhere along the way he'd shed his shirt and boots.

Zeke forced himself into a sitting position with a mighty groan, making his head spin. He wiped at his eyes, trying to clear away the drunken haze. It didn't work because Nate was still sitting on a rock, plain as day. He wore a pressed dark brown suit, cream-colored shirt and the shiniest boots Zeke had seen in years. His hair was perfectly groomed and his eyes had no shadows in them.

The fifth Devil had appeared from thin air in the middle of Zeke's binge. Nate was living in Grayton, half a day's ride from

Tanger. Either more time had passed than Zeke was aware of, or he was drunker than he thought.

"Nate?"

Nate smiled, that grin that made women swoon. "Hey, Ezekiel."

Zeke closed his eyes and counted to five, but when he opened them, Nate was still there. He looked as perfect and *whole* as he did before the war. Perhaps it was the way Zeke remembered Nate in his mind.

"Are you really here?" Zeke tried to ignore the urge to find the whiskey bottle he had apparently dropped somewhere.

"Do I look real?" Nate raised one brow.

Zeke shook his head, which proved to be a mistake when his stomach flipped upside down at the movement. "No, you look, well, you look like a dream."

"I'm flattered you think I'm a dream. Aren't you going to ask why I'm here?" He rose and began walking back and forth slowly. Amazingly enough, dust coated his boots with each step. Maybe he was really there and not Zeke's drunken imagining.

"I figure I might be dead or maybe I just drank myself into making up stuff in my head that ain't real." Zeke clutched his stomach, surprised to see blood seeping from numerous scrapes on his chest.

"You're not dead, but you're drunk. Again." Nate shook his head. "I am hard pressed to believe you were that stupid, Zeke. You're the smartest among us."

Zeke didn't like the reminder of his own failings. "Well if you're here to tell me what an ass I am, don't bother." He glanced around, needing to find that damn bottle.

When Nate appeared beside him, Zeke let out a yelp of surprise. "What the hell are you doing, trying to take a year off my life?"

Nate's brown gaze was intense. "You will die out here, alone and drunk. If you don't break your neck, the animals will finish you off. You're throwing your life away, Zeke Blackwood."

Zeke opened his mouth but nothing came out. The image of Nate was right. He'd gone out there to escape, and maybe to die. The charred remains of his heart cried out at the thought. What was he doing? Naomi had been more than right, she'd been justified.

"What should I do?" Zeke reached out for Nate, but he was back on the rock.

"Go home."

"I can't go back to Georgia." Zeke screamed inside and out. "It's gone, everything's fucking gone. How do you expect me to go back?" The image of Briar Creek, of the devastation left of their hometown, tasted like ashes.

"I don't mean Georgia, Zeke." Nate smiled gently. "Tanger is your home now. You and the others have found a place to belong. Now you just have to forgive yourself and begin living again."

Zeke lurched to his feet, sick of the imaginary Nate. He was going to find that goddamn bottle, come hell or high water. "You need to find your way back to Grayton and leave me the hell alone."

This time, Nate laughed. *Laughed!* "I am in Grayton. This me only exists in your head and your heart."

Sweat rolled down Zeke's face as he stumbled forward, ignoring the annoying Nate. The scrubby brush told him he'd gone quite a ways from Tanger, to where the green hills disappeared. The dry, dusty ground appeared to be his own personal hell and Nate the devil in the disguise of a Southern gentleman.

"Allison's death was not your fault," Nate said from the right.

Zeke turned and lunged at his friend, but ended up slamming his shoulder into a rock and almost knocking himself unconscious. He slid to the ground, a primal sob exploding from his throat.

"What Veronica did to you was not your fault. The war was not your fault." Nate wasn't giving up until he turned Zeke inside out. "You're a good man, a good person, and you *must* forgive yourself."

Agony roared through Zeke as every wound he tried to drown was ripped open anew. Once the tears began, he couldn't stop them until he simply had no more left within. His face was hot and gritty, as the salty wetness mixed with the elements of the rawest human emotion.

As the sun set, a solitary figure huddled between two rocks, shirtless and shoeless, hugging his knees while rocking back and forth. Zeke Blackwood had finally hit bottom.

Zeke had been gone a full week when all hell broke loose in Tanger. It was as if the fates were waiting to unleash themselves and cause melee amongst the townsfolk. Three fights at the saloon in one evening ended with Matthew Marchison's beaten body being discovered by the outhouse behind Aphrodite's. They brought him in the saloon and Naomi helped try to stop the bleeding. The man was nearly unrecognizable as the kind, bespectacled older man she knew.

After he was rushed to Doctor Barham's house, Naomi got on her hands and knees to clean up the blood left behind on the floor. The sobering reality of Matthew's condition had finally stopped the fights, but the saloon was a wreck. She dipped the rag in the bucket beside her and continued cleaning the floor. The water had already started to turn a murky red color.

Lucy brought in two fresh buckets of water. "Lord have mercy, you'd think they would get tired of beating the shit out of each other."

Naomi harrumphed. "Men will never tire of using their fists."

She wished Zeke had said goodbye or even explained why he left. Instead she was left with unanswered questions and a saloon full of rowdy cowboys who delighted in making enormous messes.

"I'm going to go check on Matthew at the doc's house. He didn't deserve nothing like that." Lucy stood and surveyed the room, giving Naomi a chance to watch her boss.

In the last seven days, Lucy's hard edges had softened and she was a much less caustic person. Even the mention of Zeke didn't upset her anymore. Naomi was surprised to see genuine concern in Lucy's expression when she spoke of Matthew. Perhaps the dragon lady of Aphrodite's was human after all. They'd come to a peace of sorts between them, a mutual respect for which Naomi was grateful.

She needed as many friends as she could get and fortunately Lucy was becoming one of them. Louisa and Carmen were in the back picking up the broken glasses and cards that littered the floor. Each of them had volunteered to do that rather than clean up blood. For Naomi, it didn't matter one way or the other.

"I'll be back in a while, girls. Joe is in the kitchen and if any of those fools stop by again, send 'em packing. If they don't listen, shoot 'em." With that the older woman left the saloon, shawl in hand.

"Naomi?"

She looked up to see Gregory Conley peeking through the door. The young man had done his best to do some true-blue courting. Truth was, it flattered Naomi to be treated like a genteel lady. Over the last week she realized he was as gentle and innocent as he appeared. His most recent sermon had been about apologies and jumping to conclusions about folks.

He knew she didn't love him, maybe never would, but it didn't stop him. The minister was apparently determined she would be his bride and he didn't give up easily.

"Come on in. We're just cleaning up in here."

He stepped in and his eyes widened when he caught sight of the chaos. It was as if a twister had run through the building and left behind nothing but destruction and broken beer mugs. This time Joe had protected the liquor bottles so at least the damage wasn't as great. Too bad they didn't have a sheriff to make the cowboys pay for what they'd done.

"What happened?"

"A saloon fight." She wanted to roll her eyes sometimes at his naiveté. "It happens in saloons."

"I know that but this...it's beyond my imaginings." He glanced down at the floor beneath her. "Is that blood?"

"Yes, Gregory, it's blood. Someone nearly beat Matthew Marchison to death." She had forgotten the two men had formed a bond weeks earlier when Gregory had first arrived in Tanger. His face blanched at her pronouncement. "I'm sorry, I didn't mean to sound so callous. He's over at the doctor's now getting fixed up. I'm sure he'll be all right."

She was lying, of course. Mr. Marchison was barely breathing when he left and even that sounded like a death rattle. He'd be lucky to survive the night, much less recover completely. However, in her odd relationship with Gregory, he needed to have things tempered, whereas she usually laid everything on the line in black and white.

"I must go see him." Gregory turned to leave, then swung back around and dropped to his knees. He cupped her chin and kissed her lightly on the forehead. "Even on your hands and knees, you're stunningly beautiful. Don't forget to marry me, angel."

Then he was gone, through the doors as if he had wings on his shoes. Naomi sat on her knees wondering how it was she engendered such devotion in one man and such complete disregard in another. God must be punishing her for all her sins, either that or she just had the worst luck in the world.

"How did you get two men, *chica*, and I have none?" Carmen leaned against the broom and scowled at her.

"Yeah, she sure does have them falling all over her, don't she?" Louisa hauled a crate full of broken glass to the bar. "I wish I had her hair. Mine won't stay put for anything."

"I don't want her hair, but aye, I wouldn't mind a piece of either one of those men in her pocket. A blond devil and a brown-haired angel." Carmen waggled her eyebrows. "Or perhaps both at the same time."

Naomi couldn't help it—she blushed at the thought. There was no way Zeke and Gregory would be together with her, and the very idea made her wiggle.

"Don't tease her, Carmen. She's still pretty innocent." Louisa got to the kitchen door with the crate.

Carmen eyed Naomi on the floor. "Oh, she's no innocent, but she doesn't have the experience to go with it."

The Mexican woman was too smart for her own good. Naomi did have quite an education, just not the carnal side of it, or at least not all of it.

"I don't think we have a chance of seeing Zeke again." Naomi swallowed the pain at the thought.

"*Si, pero* the minister is here to stay, I think." She nodded at the door. "He is very much in love with you."

Naomi agreed with Carmen, but didn't want to voice it aloud. There was no chance she'd ever love Gregory in return, but she didn't want to break his heart either. He wasn't going to give up, so she either had to decide to settle for a man who loved her or wait forever for the man she loved.

Regret was a bitter taste on Zeke's tongue, yet he swallowed it anyway. After a hellish night shivering in his own misery, he found himself clear-headed. A fruitless search yielded no sign of his horse or the rest of his clothes, but he did find his boots. Zeke knew what he needed to do, he'd just have to do it bare-chested. The image of Nate stuck in Zeke's head, hounding him as he walked back to Tanger.

The walk took two days, which gave him too much time to think. Or perhaps it was what the imaginary Nate wanted. Zeke's mind kept returning to his biggest regrets.

The job had been a godsend and he'd thrown it away. He'd walked off when challenged, ran like a dog with his tail between his legs. Zeke came to realize his actions had not only been embarrassing but downright stupid.

Then there was Naomi. She loved him, he knew that, yet he treated her badly. Not only that, he'd disappointed her and likely broken her heart. It would take some serious groveling and the devil's own luck to win her back.

When he reached the outskirts of Tanger, he glanced down and almost groaned at his appearance. He couldn't see his face, but it was probably as bad as the rest of him. Dirty, bloody, scraped and pitiful.

No doubt the gossips in town were having a grand old time talking about him and his utter stupidity. Hopefully his return wouldn't cause even more talk, but that was wishful thinking. Naomi had been right—God had given him a second chance and he'd let his fear get in the way. Tanger wasn't perfect, but over the last year the townsfolk had embraced the boys from Briar Creek. Zeke had been dumb enough to push away from that embrace.

Already Hettie Cranston had spotted him as he walked past the hotel. It seemed she'd gotten close to that ass Byron Ackerman and was firmly seated at the registration desk while he ran the hotel. Her mouth dropped open in a big O when she saw him and he saluted and kept walking.

He wanted to stop at Aphrodite's to see Naomi, but knew his first priority was to get cleaned up, and to apologize to his friends. He headed straight for Elmer's. The breakfast crowd had gone and it was too early for dinner, so Zeke knew the restaurant would basically be empty.

However he didn't expect a cloud of smoke from the kitchen. His veins turned to ice as he ran into the building, slamming into the kitchen. Lee and Gideon were by the back door waving the smoke out when he burst in.

"What's on fire?" he shouted, looking around for the source of the smoke.

"Lee's cooking."

"Shut up. I'd like to see you make biscuits."

Zeke held up both hands. "You mean Lee was baking and nearly caught the place on fire?"

"That's about it." Gideon pushed away from the doorframe and looked at Zeke. His eyes widened as his gaze wandered up and down the wreck Zeke had become. "I won't ask what happened to you, but I will admit I was worried about you." Zeke was grateful to have such staunch friends. "You look terrible."

"Where have you been? And what the hell happened to you?" Lee frowned at him, still waving the smoke from in front of his face.

"In the middle of nowhere, thinking. I owe you all an apology, a big one."

Gideon turned to him, seriousness in his gaze. "You don't need to apologize to us. Water under the bridge, cousin. Do you want to talk about why you left?"

Zeke swallowed the lump in his throat at the easy acceptance of his apology. "I need a shave and a bath first. Let's get that done then we can sit and jaw."

"And none too soon either." Lee wrinkled his nose. "You stink, brother."

"Maybe you can boil some water without burning it so I can take a bath." Zeke ducked when a blackened biscuit came flying at him. "Or maybe Margaret should help you."

By the time the tub had been filled the smoke had dissipated from the kitchen and Zeke was able to finally clean himself. Once the dirt and grime were rinsed away, he felt human again. He felt *home* again.

Lee brought him some clean clothes since all of Zeke's were missing or encrusted with dirt. After his bath, he scrubbed his trousers and left them to hang on the line outside. Feeling as if he was a new person, Zeke went in search of Gideon and Lee. He was ready to face whatever Gideon had to say, no matter how bad it was.

Of course, Zeke was wrong. He sure as hell wasn't ready to hear what Gideon told him.

He stared at his cousin, sure he'd heard him wrong. Blood thundered through his ears as he tried to make sense of it. "Say that one more time."

"Margaret is set to marry Byron on Friday morning. That young minister convinced Naomi to marry him next month, and the cowboys have almost destroyed Aphrodite's without the law around to stop them." Gideon fiddled with the tin mug in front of him. "I've tried to help, and so has Jake, but when there's fifty of them and you don't have a badge, ain't nobody gonna listen."

It took Zeke a few moments to find his voice again. "What happened to Matthew Marchison?"

"Somebody beat him almost to death. He's been at the doc's for two days hanging on." Gideon shook his head. "Damn shame too. He's a good man, no matter what his wife did."

Zeke pinched the bridge of his nose and swallowed back the tears that threatened. He'd left nine days earlier and it appeared Tanger had been turned on its head during that short time. He'd thrown away everything he had because of his lack of courage and conviction. It would take hard work and quite possibly a miracle to get it all back.

"I need to get my job back." He looked up at his brother and cousin.

Gideon reached over and squeezed Zeke's shoulder. "I was hoping you'd say that."

Zeke swallowed the rest of the cold coffee in his cup. "Where's Gabby?"

"At the mill more than likely." Gideon jerked his thumb north, towards the mill. "She's been hunting for a new sheriff, but nobody wanted the job."

"Sure as hell I didn't." Lee scowled up at his big brother. "I ain't no second-choice lawman."

Zeke had had no idea Gabby would ask Lee to be sheriff, but it made sense. Other than a missing arm, Lee had the best tracking skills of the Devils, and he was damn good with a gun. Zeke always puzzled everything out before acting, which could be good or bad depending on the situation.

"You could've done it, you big baby. Don't let your lost arm dictate your life." Zeke strapped his gun belt on and squared his shoulders. Time to fight for what was his.

He found Gabby in the office at the mill, her head bent over a ledger book as flour particles floated on the air. Zeke had never quite understood the machinery that made the mill work, but he respected the hell out of Gabby for taking it over when her father was incapacitated. She had proved herself to be smarter and more capable than most men.

It had taken him a while to come to that realization and even longer to let her know about it. The first step had been when she'd stood by his side after Allison had been murdered, ready to hunt down the bastard raiders with him. Gabby had really been the first woman to become his friend.

She glanced up and smiled when she saw him. "You cannot know how glad I am to see you."

To his delight, she hugged him fiercely, a back-cracking one that made him smile. It had been too long since a friend hugged him and he found the experience to be very worthwhile.

"I won't ask what happened, but judging by the circles under your eyes, it wasn't fun." She sat back down and gestured for him to sit on the other side of the desk in the wood-slatted chair by the window.

"I left to figure things out. Then I realized what an ass I'd been and came back. Gideon filled me in on what happened." He shoved away the thought of Naomi marrying the fresh-faced minister. "I want my job back."

She leaned forward on her elbows and studied his face. "The town council might not approve."

"You're the mayor, you can make a decision stick no matter what those old cronies say." He hoped like hell he wouldn't be at odds with the council, but he was determined to be sheriff again.

"If I make you sheriff again, folks are going to look down their noses at you for what you confessed to in church." She shook her head. "It's going to be a long road to earn back what you lost."

Naomi's image flashed through his mind. "More than you know." He cleared his throat. "So what do you say, Mayor? I want to find out who hurt Matthew and put Tanger back to rights."

Gabby reached into her desk drawer and pulled out the sheriff's badge. As she handed it to him, the complete rightness of it hit him square between the eyes. It might have cost him a great deal, but Zeke Blackwood finally knew where he belonged.

"He's back." Lucy sat beside Naomi as she ate a small dinner of ham and biscuits. The food sat like a rock in Naomi's stomach. There was no need to ask who "he" was.

"Since when?" She took off a bird-size bite of biscuit and chewed it, trying desperately not to crush it in her fist.

"This morning. He walked in looking like he'd been wrestling a wild-eyed steer and lost, half-naked and dirty as hell. I heard tell he went straight to Elmer's, then to the mill." Lucy leaned in close. "I also heard Gabby Sheridan made him sheriff again."

Naomi swallowed the biscuit, although considering the tightness of her throat, she was surprised it went down at all. Lucy watched her closely so Naomi kept her shoulders straight and her eyes dry. Later on, she could figure out how she felt. For now, she would act as if Zeke was her past and that's where he belonged.

"I'm engaged to be married, Lucy. Zeke had his chance and he threw it away." She dared her friend to refute the truth.

"Zeke can be a horse's ass, that's for damn sure, but you can't tell me you don't love him. And I sure don't think you should be marrying that preacher. He can't do anything for himself, he's needy and the boy clings to you like a cocklebur." She stood and waggled her finger at Naomi. "Mark my words, you will regret marrying a fool like Gregory Conley."

Lucy left Naomi alone in the kitchen with her thoughts. They whirled around and around until her temples started to pound. She threw the rest of her dinner in the slop bucket and headed outside for a walk. Perhaps fresh air would help her sort everything out.

She walked towards the cottonwood grove at the end of the street, the sun beating down on her uncovered head, giving her a taste of the summer heat. Naomi walked on, heedless of any discomfort.

The truth was, she loved Zeke, but he'd broken her heart. It would take great effort to forgive him for choosing whiskey over her, even if he did come by to convince her. The fact he'd been in town for hours and hadn't come to see her spoke volumes about what his priorities were, and she wasn't one of them. He'd gone straight to get his job back.

His actions drove the nail of pain deeper into her heart. She wished she loved Gregory at least a little, but her traitorous heart beat with a rhythm it hadn't in more than a week.

*

Zeke ran back to the restaurant already feeling better. He had yet to see Naomi, but he wanted to get all the facts before he did. Until he had the rest of his life in order, he couldn't deal with what his heart needed.

Lee was washing dishes when Zeke came in. "Back already?"

"I need you."

His younger brother stopped scrubbing and stared at him. "You need me?"

"I want to find out what happened to Matthew and I need your help." Zeke tucked his hands into his back pockets. "I know I've been a horse's ass the last few weeks. I'm sorry for what I've done and I swear to you, I'm done with whiskey for good."

Lee looked at him with suspicion. "I've heard that before."

"I know and this time I really mean it from the bottom of my pickled heart." Zeke held out his hand to his brother. "Please, Lee, I need you."

It was important he apologize to everyone for his stupid behavior and bad choices, but his brother was the most important. It was Lee who had stuck by him through the worst of everything.

"Fine, but if I even see you near a whiskey bottle I'm going to beat you until you can't see straight." Lee dried his hand on the towel next to the sink. "I'll also be happy to leave these for Gideon." His gleeful smile told Zeke that his brother had forgiven him.

"Let's go. We've got a mystery to solve." Zeke found himself smiling again. It was time to hunt for a potential murderer.

They headed to the doctor's to check on Matthew. Zeke felt alive for the first time since he'd left Naomi's arms. He should have faced what was bothering him instead of running, but what was done was done. Now was the time to help a friend in need.

Doctor Barham was a thirty-five-year-old single man with straight brown hair and glasses. He was friends with Gabby, so even though he was a little odd, the Devils were grateful to him for all he'd done to patch them up since they arrived in Tanger nearly a year earlier.

The doctor opened the door and didn't bother to disguise his surprise. "Zeke, I thought you'd left town." He squinted at the badge. "Are you sheriff again?"

"Yes, Doc, I'm sheriff again and for good. Can we come in?" Zeke kept his impatience hidden.

"Of course, please come in." He opened the door wide and the brothers stepped inside. "I'm afraid Matthew has not been coherent since he was brought in."

"Can you tell what happened to him?" Zeke hated the smell of the doctor's office. Why did it always have to smell like blood? Reminded him too much of a battlefield sometimes.

"He was beaten with something, likely a club or a heavy branch. Someone did a thorough job on him and it appears as though he did his best to cover his head, because he has multiple fractures on his arms, contusions and gashes on nearly every inch of skin, and his face is nearly unrecognizable." Doctor Barham stopped with his hand on the door to the examining room. "I'm afraid I don't hold out much hope for him."

Matthew had survived many things including his son's

death and his wife's horrendous crimes. He was a tough man. However, the creature on the bed hardly resembled the shopkeeper. He was swathed in bandages with only a swollen left eye, the end of a nose and the bottom part of his right ear showing. The slow stain of blood appeared at the base of the bandages, letting Zeke know the man was still bleeding even through all that.

"Jesus, he's still alive?" Lee was his usual blunt self.

"Yes, he's alive, but barely. I don't think he can hear us though." The doctor stepped back into the hallway. "I'll be out here if you need me."

Thankfully, he left the door open. Zeke wasn't squeamish, but nobody liked to be in a sickbed room. He approached Matthew and knelt beside the bed. The only sound in the room was the man's labored, rattling breaths.

"Matthew, can you hear me? It's Zeke Blackwood."

No response from the patient on the bed.

"I'm going to find out who did this to you. I promise you that."

"You can't—" Lee began.

"Yes, I can and I will." Zeke stood. "Nobody gets away with trying to murder someone in my town."

He started towards the door when a moan sounded from the bed. Zeke whipped around and stared at Matthew, then glanced at his brother, who looked as astonished as Zeke felt.

"Matthew?" Zeke went back to the bed and lowered his ear towards the other man's mouth. "I'm here."

"Love her," Matthew whispered.

Zeke frowned. Love her? What did that mean? He should find Naomi and finally tell her how he felt?

"What did he say?" Lee demanded.

"I think he said 'Love her.'" Zeke got to his feet. "Which doesn't make any sense."

"Not now, but maybe if we start looking into what Matthew was doing right before this happened, it might." Lee was smarter than folks gave him credit for. "We need to talk to the preacher."

The last person Zeke wanted to see, but Lee was right. Gregory might know what his friend had been doing.

"Fine, let's go." His stomach was already flopping like a fish, but Zeke headed towards the door again. "We'll be back, Matthew. You keep yourself alive, y'hear?"

The Blackwoods headed towards the church, one with enough enthusiasm for both of them. Zeke didn't look forward to talking to the boy who'd taken his woman after he'd rejected her. He couldn't hide any longer—it was time to be a man.

They arrived at the church and went straight to the rectory house next door. On a Tuesday afternoon, he was more likely to be at home than in the church. Zeke couldn't bring himself to knock so Lee did it for him.

The sheriff waited with his hands fisted and his heart aching, but no one answered. They checked the church and it was empty too. He was grateful but annoyed. His determination to find out what happened to Matthew had hit a wall.

"We need to go to the saloon. The preacher might be there. Besides we really need to look at where it happened."

Lee was right, of course, but didn't know if he was ready to see Naomi.

They walked around behind Aphrodite's, looking around at where Matthew was beaten. He didn't know what they would find, but it was worth a look. Zeke's stomach jumped around, hoping Naomi wouldn't come outside, or perhaps he was hoping she would. He forced himself to concentrate on what he saw.

"What are you doing?"

Zeke whirled around to find Lucy behind him. She scowled at him, then at Lee. In contrast to her normal sexy dresses, she wore a plain navy blue dress with barely any cleavage showing, and for the first time since he'd known her, no face paint.

"Nothing." He was shocked enough by Lucy's change to sound like an idiot.

"Trying to find out who beat the shit out of Marchison." Lee stood in the high grass at the edge of the clearing by the outhouse.

She gestured to his badge. "So you're sheriff again, I hear."

"Yes, ma'am." Zeke cleared his throat and shuffled his feet. "I needed to get my head situated on my shoulders before I came back."

To his surprise, she nodded and her expression softened. "I know exactly what you mean. Have you seen Matthew?" There was genuine concern in her voice.

"Yeah, we did. Damn shame what somebody did to him." Zeke tried to forget who might be in the saloon and focused on interviewing his witness. "What do you remember about that night?"

Lucy looked up and tapped her chin with two fingers. "It was busy for a Sunday. The girls were running their tails off trying to keep up with the drink orders. Joe had to throw out one or two drunks, but those cowpunchers just kept getting rowdier by the minute."

"Anybody in particular causing problems?" Zeke figured one little piece of information might be enough to help them move forward with the investigation.

"No, but that hotel man Ackerman was there playing cards again." She wrinkled her nose. "He's a bit of an ass."

"A bit isn't strong enough." Zeke made no bones about disliking the Yankee. "Did he do anything unusual?"

"Not really. He's been something of a regular since he came to town. Comes in and plays cards, never drinks and never gambles. The other cowboys use him to practice their card skills." She snapped her fingers. "Aha! I remember now. When Matthew came in he had a long face so I asked him what was wrong. He said something about losing the lady he thought he could love."

Love her.

Zeke could taste the clue on his tongue. "Did he say who it was?"

Lucy frowned. "No, just that she'd chosen another man, one who didn't have an ex-wife."

That left only ninety percent of the single men in the county.

"Did he say anything else?"

"No, but I remember him shooting daggers at Ackerman. I ain't never seen Matthew have an unkind word for anyone, so it surprised me to see him do it." Lucy nodded. "After that I lost track of Matthew until Joe came running in to say he'd found the poor man beaten half to death out here." She glanced down at the grass. "Damn shame, that's what it is. He's one of the good ones."

In Lucy's voice, Zeke heard what she did say. Matthew was a good man and she might have wanted him for her very own. Now it appeared he was going to die.

"I'll find out who did this, Lucy. I promise."

"You'd better stop making so many promises, Zeke." Lee

walked up gripping a three-foot-long branch with a dried brown substance on it. "Even if you have your brilliant brother to help you."

Zeke could have done a jig. "Damn, you found it! Let's take a look and see if we can find anything on it that might tell us who swung it."

As he and Lee looked at the branch, the back door opened and closed with a bang. He heard Lucy murmur something then the door closed again.

Zeke nearly jumped out of his skin when Naomi spoke from behind him.

"Hello, Zeke."

Lee glanced at her, then back at Zeke. He stepped back with the wood in his hand. "I'll be over yonder by the cottonwoods."

Zeke waited for the kick on his ass he deserved, but it didn't come. He took a deep breath for courage before turning to face her. Naomi had circles under her haunted eyes and her face looked wan as if she hadn't been sleeping. Even her normally vibrant blonde hair was a dull color.

She was so beautiful it took his breath away.

"Hey there, little one," he managed to get out.

"You're back as sheriff, I see." She pointed at the badge with a trembling hand. "Good thing too. Tanger needs you."

Her voice broke on the last word and he cursed himself six ways to Sunday for being the cause of her pain.

"Look, Naomi," he began, but then stopped to gather his thoughts. "I reckon I owe you an apology every day for the rest of your life for what I did. I was a lousy bastard and I know it. I heard you and the preacher are gonna get hitched." Now it was his turn for his voice to break. "You deserve a man who'll treat you as if you are his heart."

With that, he had to turn away before he really embarrassed himself. As he walked towards Lee, he half expected her to throw rocks at his back, but she didn't. Behind him lay a silence so thick, it was only rivaled by the tears clogging his throat as he left the woman he loved behind.

Naomi wanted to scream and shout at him, but she stopped herself. It would accomplish nothing and likely start more gossip about them. She'd made her decision and Gregory was it. Now if only her heart would stop running like a thoroughbred when she caught sight of Zeke.

Lord have mercy, she truly loved that man.

After a few minutes, she was able to go back into the saloon, but she left her hopes in the dirt behind her.

Chapter Thirteen

They looked the branch over until Zeke thought his eyes would pop out of his head, but he didn't see anything extraordinary about it. Time was slipping away and they had to find something that would point them toward the man who'd nearly killed Matthew.

Lee threw up his hands and walked around the copse of trees. "I can't find nothing, Zeke. Dammit."

"Me either." He reached out with one finger and traced the knot at the end. "It could be from any tree in any yard. Somebody sawed it off to kill Matthew." Inspiration slapped him in the face. "The tree, Lee, the tree. We need to figure out where this branch was cut from."

"You're right. Damn, why didn't I think of that?"

They walked around town for the next two hours looking at every cottonwood. Luck was on their side when they found what they were looking for behind the hotel.

Lee touched the light-colored spot, showing where the branch had been cut. He grinned at Zeke. "I think we found where our murder weapon came from."

"What do you think you're doing?" Byron Ackerman stood in the doorway behind the hotel. "This is private property and you are not welcome here, Mr. Blackwood."

"That's Sheriff Blackwood." Zeke tapped the badge. "I have every right to investigate Matthew Marchison's beating. This tree is where the branch came from used to beat him into a bloody pulp. Do you know anything about it?"

"Of course not. Anyone could have cut that branch off without my knowledge. It's behind the building where I rarely go." He straightened his bright red vest. "Now if you don't mind, you can leave the premises immediately."

Zeke started towards him, intent on kicking the man's ass into next week, when Margaret appeared in the doorway. She rushed forward and threw herself between them.

"Let me speak to them, Byron." She pleaded with her eyes to Zeke and he finally backed away, fists clenched.

"Fine, but then they are to vacate post-haste." His nasally Yankee accent grated on Zeke's ears.

Margaret watched Byron go back into the hotel before she spoke. "He's a good man, Zeke. You might not like him, but he's very good to me."

"Yeah, well, we think he's the one who beat Matthew." Lee held up the branch. "This was the weapon and it came from that tree."

Her mouth dropped open and tears filled her eyes. "No, I won't believe it. It couldn't have gone that far."

Zeke took her arm and led her to the crates behind the building. "Sit and tell me what's going on."

She fidgeted on the crate for a few moments before she threw up her hands. "Matthew started courting me about the same time as Byron. I surely enjoyed the attentions of two men, I mean it was flattering, but Byron asked me to marry him. I talked to Edith about it and she convinced me it would be better to marry him instead of Matthew because he had more money and was more stable."

224

Zeke looked at Lee who appeared surprised as well. "You mean you had two beaus? And we didn't even realize you had one?"

Margaret scowled at them. "You boys can barely see past your own noses to what's in front of you. Look what you did, throwing away a chance with Naomi, and you"—she pointed at Lee—"won't let the world see past your arm that isn't there anymore. You've no call to be judging me."

"We're not judging you, Margaret. I'm sorry we missed what was happening between you and Matthew. I think he's a much better choice for a husband, but you made your decision and that's that. However"—Zeke took a deep breath—"I think your fiancé tried to kill your other beau and I aim to prove it."

"Zeke, you can't be serious. We're getting married in three days. Please, you mustn't think Byron could do anything like that." She sounded as if her heart was breaking, but Zeke was determined to see the investigation through.

"Then I've got three days to find enough evidence to arrest him." He would move mountains to do it too. There was no chance Byron was marrying the woman who'd become a sister to the devils. No chance in hell.

Friday morning dawned overcast and gloomy, with a pressing mugginess in the air. Zeke waited in the shadows in the alley next to the hotel. He only had at most fifteen minutes to search the building while the wedding commenced down the street at the church. Gabby had called in some favors to try to get him a search warrant from the judge she knew in Houston, but he couldn't wait. Zeke needed to find the evidence he'd been lacking. By the time he was done, she'd have the warrant anyway.

Byron walked out of the hotel with a glowing Margaret on his arm. Zeke didn't bother to wait more than ten seconds before he climbed in the window. Time was too precious to wait. He landed in the kitchen and made his way through the empty hotel to the office Byron worked in. Thank God everyone was at the church or surely someone would see him.

The weak sunlight coming through the windows gave him just enough light to search the man's desk. At that point, he knew Ackerman would realize someone had been there so Zeke just upended the drawers and shook everything out. The last drawer seemed shallow for the depth and when he knocked on the side, he realized why. It had a second chamber below.

He grinned in triumph as he looked for the switch to access the secret compartment. Ackerman was guilty as hell. Now he had the evidence to prove it. All he needed was to get the warrant from Gabby and arrest the son of a bitch.

Naomi stood as witness to the wedding at the front of the church. Gregory was all smiles in his minister clothes and he kept winking at her, much to her chagrin. How was it she found herself engaged to such a boy? He still thought life was so rosy and simple. After Margaret's wedding, she was going to have to tell him she couldn't marry him.

The decision to tell him the truth finally gave her room to breathe. She pressed a hand to her chest and felt the lightness that had been lacking since she agreed to marry him. She would apologize to him, but Naomi knew she'd made the right choice.

Edith sat at the piano and plunked out music as Byron and Margaret walked down the aisle together. Margaret had insisted on it, seeing as how this was her second wedding. It didn't feel right to walk down alone since her daddy was gone. As a thirty-year-old woman, she had been down the path before and this time, it was one she wanted to walk with her future husband.

They had just arrived at the front of the church and Gregory opened his mouth to speak when a commotion erupted from the back. Naomi peeked around Margaret to see Zeke stalking down the aisle with what appeared to be something black in one hand and a pair of shoes in the other.

She glanced up at Byron's face and he lost all color. Perhaps Zeke had been right about Byron's involvement with Matthew's beating. Judging by the panic on his face, he was guilty as hell.

"Byron, what's happening?" Margaret clutched the daisies to her chest and swung her gaze between Ackerman and Zeke.

"I don't know, dearest." The hotel man buttoned his jacket and crossed his hands in front of him. Naomi wasn't surprised to see them shaking.

"I've got you, Ackerman." Zeke's voice was so cold, it seemed that icicles should have been shooting from his mouth. He held up the black object. "Riding gloves with dried blood from the beating." Then he held up the shoes. "And your fancy high-heeled shoes covered with mud and spatters of blood from Matthew's body as you beat him nearly to death behind the saloon."

"Where did you get those things? They're not even mine." Perspiration dotted Ackerman's forehead.

Lee appeared behind Zeke with Gideon, Gabby and Jake in tow. They were looking as serious as they possibly could and Naomi realized it was completely true. Byron had beaten Matthew to within an inch of his life. No one had suspected him or even thought to find out who'd done it, until Zeke came back and picked up his badge.

"Oh yes they are. I had a search warrant signed proper-like by Judge Hiram Oaks in Houston and witnessed by our own Mayor Gabrielle Sheridan." His wolfish grin flashed as he patted a paper in his shirt pocket. "You are hereby under arrest for the attempted murder and assault of Matthew Marchison."

Margaret let out a sob and Naomi took hold of her shoulders. "Be strong," she whispered.

"I refuse to cooperate. That evidence was planted. You all know Zeke Blackwood hates me and has done his best to run me out of town since I arrived." Ackerman's accusations were met with a few murmurs of agreement.

"That's a bunch of horse shit and you know it." Lee would obviously never change his ways, even in a church. "He's the one who arrested his best friend and cousin when you got the shit kicked out of you."

Ackerman turned his back on the Blackwoods. "Reverend, please continue with the ceremony. Ignore the hooligans back there."

Naomi had heard enough. She might still be considered new in town but she wasn't about to let the farce continue. She stepped in front of Ackerman and resisted the urge to slap him.

"How dare you?" She pushed at his chest. "These good people deserve better than a man like you. Tanger is a town of good folks and you come here and push your way in, trying to convince us you're going to help the town. How does that work when you almost kill the man who's owned the store for twenty years?"

Zeke watched her with his intense brown gaze and it gave her courage to continue.

"Don't touch me again, whore." Ackerman's heated breath gusted on her cheeks.

"You, Byron Ackerman, deserve to rot in jail with the rest of

228

the rats." She pulled Margaret aside and started for the back door of the church.

A roar of rage preceded footsteps, punches, shouts and screams. Naomi turned around to see Zeke jumping on Ackerman as he reached for her. She fell back into the wall with Margaret as the men grappled at their feet. Chairs and pews flew right along with the punches. Lee and Gideon assisted and soon Ackerman was overcome by the three of them. Jake stood at the ready to assist, with Gabby hovering behind him.

As they carried Ackerman out of the church, Naomi stood with Margaret and held her hand.

"Are you all right?" Gregory walked over to them, visibly shaken and pale as milk.

"We're fine. I knew Zeke would take care of it." Pain flashed across his face, and she wanted to snatch her words back. She took Gregory aside as folks chatted about the drama of Ackerman's apprehension. "You are a good man, Reverend Conley, but I can't marry you. I'm sorry for all this."

He let out a shaky breath and touched her cheek. "I understand what love is, Naomi Tucker, and I saw it on your face when you looked at Zeke, and when he looked at you."

She hoped he was right but she dared not say it out loud. Trapping Gregory in a loveless marriage would have been a cruel thing to do and Naomi was glad she'd stopped herself from committing such a grievous mistake.

"I'm going to bring Margaret back to her house and get her settled. Thank you for understanding." She didn't, couldn't, look back at him to see the pain she'd caused. Instead she took Margaret by the arm and left the church.

Townspeople had gathered outside to talk, goggle and gossip about what had just happened. Maybe someday Zeke might not cause so many tongues to wag, but apparently it wasn't that day. He was larger than life to her, coming in to stop the wedding and save his friend. It was almost the stuff of fairy tales.

And it made her heart thump hard against her ribs.

It was time to confront Zeke and make him see what a mistake he'd made in letting her go.

The last person he expected to see when Zeke walked out of the jail after locking up Ackerman was Naomi. His heart contracted at the sight of her in that yellow dress, like a big spoonful of sunshine just for him. It was a near thing, but he stopped himself before he groveled at her feet.

"Congratulations on your upcoming wedding, Miss Tucker," he managed to get out before tipping his hat and walking away. He had a message to give to Matthew so he walked towards the doc's house.

A she-devil jumped on his back and knocked him off-balance. She hung on like a cockle-burr as he wobbled back and forth, trying to catch hold of her.

"Naomi, what the hell are you doing? Get off me."

She shouted in his ear. "No, not until you stop being such an ass and listen to me, you dumb cracker."

He'd never heard her so angry before. Zeke had come to respect Naomi for her strength, her intelligence and her beauty, but this went beyond all that. He reached around and flipped her so fast, she didn't have a chance to fight him. Soon he had her under him while he straddled her.

"Get off me."

"Not until you stop shouting at me."

"You two need to get married so you can fight in private." Gideon stood over them, his hat pushed back and a grin on his face. "I don't think I've ever seen two people more perfect for each other."

Her beautiful face was flushed and her hazel eyes flashed fire. Anger mixed with what he thought was arousal until he felt more alive than he had in years. How could he ever have thought he could survive without this woman?

"Let me up."

He stood and scooped her up. "I'm done fighting with you for a while." Folks stopped to stare as he walked down the street, this time with Naomi in his arms instead of flung over his shoulder.

"Where are you taking me?"

"Back to your room, little one, so just hush up for five minutes."

Naomi opened her mouth but closed it without speaking. She loped her arms around his neck and hung on. They got to the saloon in record time. When Lucy smiled at him, he knew his friendship with her was still strong.

"Have fun, y'all." Lucy winked at him.

He heard Carmen and Louisa giggling from the back and he ran up the stairs so fast, he could barely remember his feet hitting the wood. They arrived at her door and he set her on her feet. She opened the door and led him into her room as his heart pounded so hard his bones rattled. This was the moment that would determine the rest of his life.

After she closed the door she smiled, and Zeke swallowed with difficulty. "It's about time you came to your senses. I'm yours for good, Ezekiel Blackwood, and I'm afraid there's nothing you can do about it."

He had trouble finding his voice and she seemed to understand that. After swallowing the enormous lump in his throat, he took her hands in his shaking ones.

"I've been a hard-ass most of my life. I never let anyone get away with any shit and I've prided myself on being a straight shooter. But I did you wrong, Naomi." He looked down at their joined hands. "I've disrespected you, treated you as if you were nothing more than a bedmate and left you wondering if I had a heart at all. For that and any pain I've caused you, I'm sorry, honey, so sorry." His voice broke on the last syllable, and she squeezed his fingers.

"Zeke, I—"

"Let me finish." After a moment, he was able to continue, as he worked to keep the tears from falling. "I found a woman I thought I loved in Tanger, but it was just an infatuation. She was murdered and I lost my way for a while. Getting the job as sheriff got me off my knees, but you, Naomi, you"—he raised his gaze to look at her as tears streamed down her cheeks—"you breathed life back into me, made my heart beat again and saved me. God, I don't know how to say all this, it's all jumbled up inside me."

She closed her eyes and swallowed so loudly, he heard the gulp. "I love you, Zeke."

He froze in place, wanting, needing to hear her say it again. Somehow, some way, Zeke and Naomi had found their way through the darkness and into the light of a love that beat within them. He felt it and allowed it to spread through him.

His entire body shook with it and when she opened her eyes again, he was ready.

"I love you, Naomi."

With a sob, she threw her arms around him, and Zeke held her so close, her heart beat in tandem with his.

Tanger had brought him misery, happiness, and everything in between, but now it had brought him something of infinite value. And he intended on holding onto her for the rest of his life, come hell or high water.

Naomi was his and he was hers, and nothing would ever change that.

Zeke was able to extract himself from her arms and sit on the bed. "Sit down, little one. I have some things to tell you."

She perched beside him and gazed at him with those unreadable hazel eyes. He needed her to understand why he did what he did and start their lives without secrets.

"When I left Georgia after the war, I didn't hold out much hope I'd find a new home. It didn't much matter because I had my friends with me and we were together." Zeke took her clammy hand in his. "I can't explain other than to say we're brothers, friends and part of each other. Without them, well, I don't think I'd be here now and not just because of the fighting during the war."

She squeezed his fingers. "I understand. Truth is, I'm a bit envious of how close y'all are. I've never had anyone, except my daddy, that I've been particularly close to."

"They might be fools, but I'm lucky to have them, especially Lee." He took a deep breath before he could continue. "I drank myself into a hole and Lee was the one who pulled me out, inch by inch. Now I think he might have some difficulty with you and me, well, being together."

"Are we together, for good I mean?" She searched his face for a sign. "I wasn't rightly sure we made that decision yet."

Zeke was on uncharted ground, and it was a might shaky beneath his feet. What he said right now could affect the rest of his life with this woman.

"I don't think I've run across anyone like you before. You confounded me, angered me, aroused the hell out of me, and made me become human again." He looked away, unable to meet her gaze as he poured out what was in his heart. What if she said no? "I've never told a woman I love her, not even my mama, and I sure as hell never asked anyone to marry me before."

Her hand tightened so hard on his, her little nails dug into his skin. He didn't know if that was a good sign or not.

"I know we've only known each other a month, but I sure as hell love you as if it's been years. I'm not much of a catch, and a drunk to boot, but I'd be right proud if you'd marry me." The words came out in a rush because if he even remotely hesitated, he'd never have gotten it all out at once. Not that it was the most fancy marriage proposal in the world—he'd sounded like an idiot.

The silence in the room made his pulse echo like a big bass drum in his ears. He had to force himself to raise his gaze to hers. What he saw made his heart miss a beat. Tears streamed down her face as the love of a thousand years shone in her eyes.

She tried to speak, but it came out as a croak. After clearing her throat, she tried again. "What other answer could I possibly give? Yes, yes, yes."

This time when their lips met, it was as if they were sealing a pact. Yes, that was it exactly. He was promising her his heart, and she did the same.

"I can't believe you said yes." He smiled, a genuine grin he felt all the way down to his toes.

"I can't believe you asked."

Naomi floated on a cloud as she counted the blessings in front of her. A man who loved her, who wanted to marry her, and looked at her as if she were precious to him.

"I'm sorry if I embarrassed you before in the street, you know when I jumped on your back." She winced.

He chuckled. "You didn't embarrass me. People can think what they want."

Naomi laughed and kissed his cheek. "You are a tough man, Ezekiel."

"I'm not sure I want you calling me that." He cupped her cheek as his gaze locked with hers. The moment became much more than a tease between them.

"Too bad because I don't plan on stopping." She leaned forward and swiped her tongue across his lips. "I like the way you taste on my mouth."

The slow beat of arousal pulsed low in her belly as she watched his pupils dilate. His thumb grazed her lips.

"Then taste me again, little one."

When his lips touched hers, Naomi opened her heart and let herself go. They had been together many times, but this was different. It was the promise of a future, of love and commitment between them.

Her breasts pressed into his chest, the nipples tightening to near pain. He flipped her around until she sat on his lap, straddling him. With a roguish smile, he started unbuttoning her dress.

Naomi raised one brow and reached for his shirt. He laughed and worked faster. By the time they'd both finished, she didn't care who'd started it or who won. She slipped the dress off her shoulders and bared her aching breasts to him. Zeke immediately latched onto one and used his talented fingers to tease and tantalize the other.

Naomi closed her eyes and leaned her head back, reveling in the pleasure from his mouth. He licked, nibbled and sucked at her, sending bolts of ecstasy straight to her pussy.

She rubbed herself against his already hard staff. His chuckle tickled her skin.

"Want something, little one?"

"You, naked on my bed." She pulled at his hair. "Now."

"I can see our marriage will never be boring." He grasped her by the waist and stood her up, although her knees wobbled. "Let's get the rest of this off."

Soon they were both nude and Naomi crawled onto the bed, spreading her legs and crooking her finger. Zeke stood there in all his glory, his proud staff jutting from a nest of dark blond curls, his scarred body hard and strong.

"Come to me, cowboy."

He smiled then, the most beautiful thing she'd ever seen in her life. It was a true smile, an expression of his love just for her. Naomi's heart slammed against her ribs as tears pricked her eyes.

This, *this* is what she'd been searching for.

When he lay down on her and slid into her slickness, Naomi wrapped her arms around him and held on. Sweet, slow thrusts were all they needed. His mouth found hers and they kissed with the passion of a thousand years.

"Love," she managed to gasp out as his strokes grew deeper and harder.

"Love," he responded.

Then the stars in the sky came to earth and landed all around them. Naomi held onto him as she rode the wave of pure ecstasy and they sealed their union with their bodies, souls and hearts.

Epilogue

Byron Ackerman was charged with attempted murder and hauled off by a Texas Ranger to face charges in Houston, for which the town breathed a sigh of relief. Matthew Marchison was even healing and seemed to be well on the way to a full recovery. Life, it seemed, had found a way to return once again to Tanger.

A grand wedding was planned for two weeks later. Naomi had no idea what to do, but luckily Margaret, Lucy and interestingly enough, Hettie Cranston, were eager to help. Edith made a beautiful bridal gown of yellow and white with intricate lacing she'd designed herself.

Naomi felt like a fairy princess the morning of the wedding as the sun streamed through the windows in Edith's shop. The dress almost sparkled on her.

Lucy, Hettie, Carmen and Louisa all stood in the back of the room, murmuring amongst themselves. Margaret fashioned a crown of daisies for Naomi as Edith made last-minute tucks to the dress.

"Is that really me?" Naomi peered into the mirror.

Everyone laughed and Naomi smiled at her reflection.

"Yes, darlin', it's you. Now let's get this finished before you're late for your own wedding." Lucy could be bossy when she wanted to, that was for certain. She hadn't changed that much.

The ladies filed out of the room after giving Naomi a quick hug. Only Margaret was left, holding out the crown she'd made. The older woman had a sadness lurking behind her eyes, one that had deepened after Byron Ackerman's arrest. The son of a bitch should be shot for what he'd done to the dear woman who had become a friend.

"You look beautiful." Margaret situated the crown on Naomi's head. "The sheriff won't know what hit him."

"Thank you, Margaret, for everything." Naomi clasped her friend's hands. "You've been so amazing to me and I wanted to thank you."

"No reason to thank me. That's what friends are for." Margaret hugged Naomi hard, and she could see tears in her friend's eyes. "Now let's get to the church."

Naomi thought it would be awkward to have Gregory marry them, but he'd insisted. In fact, he'd met a young woman at church the Sunday before and it looked as if the minister had already found someone to capture his heart.

She took a deep breath and entered the church.

Zeke tugged at the collared shirt, silently cursing Gideon for making him wear it. The bolo tie was at least more comfortable than one of those bowtie things Gabby had tried to give him. None of it really mattered though because it was his wedding day and soon Naomi would be his wife.

To his surprise, Gideon, Lee and Jake had fixed up the old carriage house behind the restaurant and made it into a cozy house for him and Naomi. They'd even had Margaret fix it up real nice and Edith had made curtains.

Someday they'd have a proper house, but for now they

would begin their lives together in that little nest. Naomi didn't know about it yet and he couldn't wait to show her.

Gregory stepped up beside him and gazed down the long line of men. "You have a lot of friends."

"I have a family and I thank God for that."

Lee stood beside him, then Gideon who talked with Jake, and then a beaming Nate. They hadn't seen their friend, their fellow Devil, in months, not since his wife Elisa had given birth to their first child. He was the handsome, refined one of the group while his wife was an untamed hellion who wore trousers and cursed like a muleskinner.

Elisa, the redheaded curmudgeon, sat in the pew with the baby in her arms. They'd named him Sean after her papa and he had a shock of red hair to match his mama's.

Zeke's heart was nearly full to bursting as he gazed at his family. They meant the world to him. The only missing piece was his bride. When he saw Margaret walking down the aisle, a small smile on her face, Zeke knew it was time.

She nodded to Gregory and sat beside Elisa, cooing at the baby. Edith plunked out the wedding march and everyone stood waiting for Naomi to appear.

From the shadows of the vestibule, she walked forward, gliding towards him like the angel Gregory had seen. Perhaps she was Zeke's angel. After all she'd breathed life back into his bleak world.

When she got to his side, he looked down into her hazel eyes and saw the love shining up at him. "You ready to get married today?"

"More than anything in the world." She took his arm then smiled. "I love you."

"I love you too, little one." He tucked her under his arm and turned to face the preacher.

"Dearly beloved," Gregory began.

Zeke held onto Naomi as they began their new lives.

The celebration in Tanger that night was genuine, the love between the sheriff and his new bride everlasting. Another son of Briar Creek, Georgia found home.

About the Author

You can't say cowboys without thinking of Beth Williamson. Her love for all things western shines through in her writing. A true Scorpio, she once described her "word" as passion. Read her work and discover for yourself how hot and enticing a cowboy can be.

Born and raised in New York, she holds a B.F.A. in writing from New York University. Currently, Beth lives just outside of Raleigh, North Carolina, with her husband and two sons. She welcomes readers to contact her on her website or by e-mail.

To learn more about Beth Williamson, please visit www.bethwilliamson.com or send an email to Beth at beth@bethwilliamson.com.

Sometimes a journey of the heart is the most dangerous journey of all.

A Desperate Journey
© *2008 Debra Parmley*

Sally Wheeler learned the hard way that men aren't always what they seem. Now she will stop at nothing to track down the bigamist husband who stole her child and abandoned her on their failing Kansas farm. Even if it means traveling with a handsome maverick who could change her mind about men.

Free after spending seven years in prison for a crime he didn't commit, Rob Truman aims to balance the scales of justice on the man who sent him there—Luke Wheeler. His quest doesn't include falling for the one woman who will lead him to his quarry, but Sally's courage in the face of her fear touches his soul.

Through dangerous days and nights on the trail, neither Sally nor Rob can ignore their growing feelings for each other. Yet both are haunted by the poor judgment that, in the past, led them down the wrong road. Love—and trust—are luxuries neither of them can afford.

But as the bullets start flying, love may be all that saves them—and Sally's son.

Available now in ebook and print from Samhain Publishing.

Enjoy the following excerpt from A Desperate Journey...

"Well, damn my eyes if it ain't an angel come to save me," the man roared as he stood with a lurch.

Sally jumped and took a step back.

"Ain't you the purtiest thing," he said with a leer.

She smiled nervously, not wanting to anger him.

Rob chose that moment to enter the store. "Morning. It's about time you were awake. Name's Rob."

"Fletcher, but you can call me Fletch."

"We need to buy passage across the river."

The ferryman's gaze drifted back toward Sally. "Cain't take you across." He shook his head. "Not for another two weeks."

"Why the hell not?"

"Water's running too high." Fletch stepped behind Sally. "That bacon sure does smell good." He peered over her shoulder. "You smell mighty good too."

"That's it." Rob's voice hardened.

Sally heard the cock of a gun and turned.

Rob stood with his gun pressed to Fletcher's head.

"I think you'll be taking us across. You'll be taking us across today." He jerked his head. "Sally, get your things."

"Ye heard the man," Moss argued. "That water is too fast, too high."

"We're going now." His tone brooked no argument.

"Ain't we goin' ter eat first?" Moss persisted.

"Lost my appetite." Rob's jaw clenched and he nudged Fletch with his gun. "Now move."

Sally watched Rob force the ferryman out the door and her hands shook as she gathered their things. "Carolyn, you stay away from those men and do as I tell you."

"Yes, Mama."

Even her bubbly daughter was subdued by the force Rob had brought into the store. And just when she'd begun to relax around him.

But he was no better than Luke. He was just another man who would use force to get what he wanted. And men like that were dangerous.

Sally reached for Carolyn's hand while they silently watched the men load the ferry. Rob stood atop the bank with his hand on his gun as Moss began to coax the mules up the dock and onto the ferry.

"You better pay me double like you said," Fletcher shouted to Rob.

The coolness and steel in Rob's reply made Sally shiver. "You'll get your money when we're on the other side."

"Stupid cowboys," Fletch muttered with a frown. "Water's too high."

Rob's expression did not change, yet Sally knew he'd heard the man.

"Get them mules on up in front, just them two," Fletcher directed Moss, as he squinted against the sun. "Get 'em up on that hitching post."

Moss hitched the first two with a grumble.

"Now them other two in the middle." Fletcher frowned. "And keep them calm. I don't want no animals giving me trouble."

"Don't ye worry none about my mules." Moss hitched the other two. "I know my business good as you know yourn."

Rob led his horse up the ramp next. As Moss took the

reigns from him he said, "I hope like hell you know what you're doing."

Rob merely grunted.

Finally Fletcher called to Sally, "Come on, little lady, you get on over here by me." He held out his hand to her.

Though Rob's eyes narrowed, he said nothing, just continued to stand with his hand on his gun as he watched them.

Sally lifted Carolyn up to Moss and reached for Fletcher's hand. Though he was behaving like a gentleman now, his bloodshot eyes took her in. "That's it," he said as he helped her onto the ferry, his sour-whiskey breath making her wish she could hold her nose. His hand was raspy, rough and strong.

She waited till he turned away to push off from the bank to wipe her hand on her dress.

The ferryman grabbed a pole and gave a shove off the bank.

Moss squinted at him when he turned back around. "I 'spose ye expect me to hep ye."

"One of you has to. I let my men off for two weeks till this river is ready to cross, and they'll be at the nearest saloon till I send for them."

They both glanced at Rob who stood by his horse, his right hand never far from his gun. He'd just displayed how fast he was with it.

"It's gonna be hell to get this ferry back across the river by myself." Fletcher grabbed the rope and began walking hand over hand down the length of the ferry.

Though the ride was smooth at first, Sally eyed the rushing waters into the middle of the river and wondered what would happen when they reached it. From the glances of the men, they were wondering the same thing. This did not reassure her.

Carolyn stood with Sally in the middle where it was most stable. She bounced up and down with excitement.

Sally gripped Carolyn's shoulders. "Stand still."

"Ma'am, you got to control your child," Fletcher said as he continued working the ropes.

Sally looked down at the cold, dark, swiftly flowing water, remembering with a shiver of panic that neither she nor Carolyn could swim.

"Carolyn, sit down."

Her daughter obeyed and Sally looked for something to hold onto. The ferry didn't feel so sturdy as it began to creak and shift with the water becoming steadily rougher. Sally's knees shook as her thoughts ran with the dark and dangerous river. The creaking grew louder as the mules shuffled and shifted their hooves.

The whites of their eyes rolled in fear when the boards of the ferry began to moan and groan. They didn't like this raft any more than she did. She briefly touched the brooch at her neck and reached out to balance herself against a mule.

"I told you this river was too fast," Fletch growled at Rob as the creaking and groaning grew louder and the river shook the ferry.

They were three quarters of the way across and the ropes were straining as Fletcher and Moss strained to pull them across.

Crack!

The rear guide post holding the guide ropes snapped in two.

GREAT
cheap
fun

Discover eBooks!

THE FASTEST WAY TO GET THE HOTTEST NAMES

Get your favorite authors on your favorite reader, long before they're
out in print! Ebooks from Samhain go wherever you go, and work with
whatever you carry—Palm, PDF, Mobi, and more.

Samhain
publishing ltd

CPSIA information can be obtained at www.ICGtesting.com
Printed in the USA
LVOW13s0842060614

388786LV00001B/161/P

INFLUENTIAL
L!VES

JEFF
BEZOS

TECH ENTREPRENEUR AND BUSINESSMAN

Adam Furgang

E **Enslow Publishing**
101 W. 23rd Street
Suite 240
New York, NY 10011
USA

enslow.com

For Gizmo Jones—a dog who gets
his food delivered from Amazon.com

Published in 2019 by Enslow Publishing, LLC.
101 W. 23rd Street, Suite 240, New York, NY 10011

Library of Congress Cataloging-in-Publication Data

Names: Furgang, Adam, author.
Title: Jeff Bezos : tech entrepreneur and businessman / Adam Furgang.
Description: New York : Enslow Publishing, 2019. | Series: Influential lives
| Audience: Grades 7-12. | Includes bibliographical references and index.
Identifiers: LCCN 2018010815| ISBN 9781978503403 (library bound) | ISBN
9781978505155 (paperback)
Subjects: LCSH: Bezos, Jeffrey—Juvenile literature. | Amazon.com
(Firm)—History—Juvenile literature. | Booksellers and
bookselling—United States—Biography—Juvenile literature. |
Businessmen—United States—Biography—Juvenile literature. | Internet
bookstores—United States—History—Juvenile literature. | Electronic
commerce—United States—History—Juvenile literature. | Entrepreneurs.
sears
Classification: LCC Z473.B47 F67 2019 | DDC 381/.4500202854678 [B] —dc23
LC record available at https://lccn.loc.gov/2018010815

Printed in the United States of America

To Our Readers: We have done our best to make sure all websites in this book were active and appropriate when we went to press. However, the author and the publisher have no control over and assume no liability for the material available on those websites or on any websites they may link to. Any comments or suggestions can be sent by e-mail to customerservice@enslow.com.

Contents

Introduction

· · · · · · · · · · · · · · · · · · ·

What does the average person do when he or she needs to buy something? Going to the store is one option, but today, for a majority of people, checking Amazon.com comes to mind. The online store is a growth story about retail and economics, but it all started with the vision of one person—Jeff Bezos. And that vision didn't stop at just a store. Today, products from Amazon.com have changed not only the way we shop but also the way we watch television and run our homes.

In 1994, thirty-year-old Jeff Bezos quit his lucrative job at investment firm D. E. Shaw & Co. in New York City and moved to Seattle with his wife, MacKenzie, to start an online bookstore.[1] At the time, Bezos had not even settled on a name for the company, but he was

Jeff Bezos is the founder and CEO of Amazon.com. The online retailer has an annual revenue of $177.9 billion.

very excited. He had become inspired by a fascinating statistic he had recently read about how internet activity at the time was growing at an astonishing rate of 2,300 percent annually.[2] Bezos chose Seattle, Washington, as the location for his new startup because it was a fast-growing area for technology companies. It also meant that because of a tax loophole, he would not have to charge sales tax to the forty-nine other states.

Amazon.com was started with an initial $10,000 from Bezos's personal savings and a larger $100,000 investment from his parents' retirement money. Bezos's wife, MacKenzie, would later invest personal money, too.[3]

The website launched on July 16, 1995. Some skeptics and analysts felt that large, established book chains such as Barnes & Noble and Borders would keep Amazon.com from succeeding. While the company grew very quickly and had tremendous sales growth, it did not actually make a profit for many years.

Bezos carried on despite a lack of profit. He believed the internet had vast, untapped growth potential. The company's early internal slogan was "Get Big Fast." In the first week of official business, the company had $12,000 in book orders. The following week, it grew to $14,000.[4] After just one full year in business, Amazon.com had 180,000 user accounts.

Bezos took advantage of the quick growth and kept offering more products, such as DVDs and music. Eventually the company partnered with Toys "R" Us to compete in the toy market.

Since its inception, Amazon has grown to be one of the largest retailers in the world. It has branched out with the popular Echo and Kindle products and continues to compete with just about every business, from home entertainment and package delivery to cloud-based computer services, home security, music services, and gaming.

In early 2018, Jeff Bezos was named the richest person ever, surpassing even Bill Gates at the height of his wealth.

CHAPTER ONE

Bezos in His Prime

· · · · · · · · · · · · · · ·

It's hard to believe, but there was a time when there was no internet and no personal computers or mobile devices to browse the internet and buy stuff from any place at any time of day or night. Since the late 1990s, when the internet first became popular, a lot has changed. Today Amazon.com is the world's largest online retailer, with 304 million active accounts as of 2015.[1] As of June 2017, roughly 80 million customers of Amazon are members of its paid service, Amazon Prime.[2]

Amazon.com has not been around forever, though. Like the internet itself, online shopping did not become popular until around the late 1990s. Today you can easily shop from Amazon on your mobile phone and a few days later a box containing your merchandise will appear, delivered right to your door. Believe it or not, one man is responsible for this groundbreaking shopping experience: Jeff Bezos.

Bezos from the Beginning

Jeff Bezos was born Jeffrey Preston Jorgensen on January 12, 1964. Bezos's birth was the result of a short-lived teen marriage. Bezos's mother, Jacklyn Gise, met Ted Jorgenson in high school, and the two began dating. Jorgenson was a unicyclist in a circus and was considered one of Albuquerque, New Mexico's best unicyclists. Ted and Jacklyn fell in love, and she became pregnant when she was just a sixteen-year-old high school sophomore. Jorgenson was eighteen at the time.

They married on July 19, 1963, moved into an apartment, and had their baby, Jeff. Jacklyn's mother watched the baby while Jacklyn finished high school. Ted Jorgenson had a hard time earning a living as a unicyclist, and finances for the two teens were tight. Jorgenson was also abusing alcohol at the time, and this strained the relationship. Jacklyn's dad tried to help with Ted's education and a job opportunity, but Ted never followed through. Jacklyn

After divorcing Bezos's biological father in 1965, Jacklyn Bezos raised Jeff as a single mother for a time before meeting and marrying Miguel Bezos.

eventually took baby Jeff and moved back in with her parents. She filed for divorce from Ted in June of 1965—less than two years after they were married. Ted did not keep up with regular visits or child support and was not in his son's life much.[3]

Jacklyn was working in the Bank of New Mexico's bookkeeping department when she met a Cuban refugee named Miguel Bezos.

After arriving in Miami, Florida, from Cuba when he was just sixteen, Miguel Bezos and his cousin Angel were sent to live in a group home in Delaware. After a year, Bezos moved to New Mexico, enrolled in the University of Albuquerque, and began working at the Bank of New Mexico. It was at the bank that he met Jacklyn, a coworker, when their shifts briefly overlapped. Although he asked Jacklyn out on a date several times and was turned down, Miguel persisted, and they went on their first date, to see *The Sound of Music*. They were married on April 1, 1968.[4] At the time, Jeff was only four years old. Miguel Bezos legally adopted Jeff, and the family lost all contact with Jeff's biological father, Ted. It was not until Jeff was ten years old that he would learn that Miguel, who also goes by Mike, was not his real father. According to an interview with *Wired* magazine, Jeff accepted the news without a problem.

Childhood and Teen Years

Even in his early childhood, Jeff Bezos showed signs of intelligence that was advanced for his age. According to his mother, Jacklyn, Jeff took apart his crib with a

Preston Gise

Jeff Bezos's maternal grandfather, Preston Gise, was a big influence in his grandson's life. He worked as regional manager for the Atomic Energy Commission. He was a very technical man and taught Jeff a lot. From the time Jeff was four years old until he was sixteen, he spent summers with his grandparents on a ranch in Cotulla, Texas. Gise and his grandson would work together on the ranch and do a variety of labor-intensive jobs, such as basic plumbing, windmill repair, grading roads, and tending to cattle. During these summers, Jeff also visited the local library, where he read many science fiction books by Jules Verne, Isaac Asimov, and Robert Heinlein. It was during these summers with his grandfather that made Jeff contemplate the idea of becoming an astronaut when he grew up.

screwdriver at age three because he wanted to sleep in a regular bed.

Jeff attended a Montessori preschool, which teaches using a specific type of hands-on education. Teachers from the school remember Jeff would become very absorbed in his activities. To keep from disturbing his concentration, sometimes the teachers moved Bezos from one activity to the next by picking him up in his chair.[5]

Jeff took a standardized IQ test at age eight and scored well, so his parents enrolled him in the Vanguard Magnet Program at the River Oaks Elementary School in Houston, Texas.[6]

Growing up, Jeff was a big fan of the 1960s television show *Star Trek*. He watched reruns of the show after school and quoted his favorite lines. The space show's forward-thinking ideas, as well as the *Apollo 11* moon landing, would come to have a big influence on Jeff as he got older.[7]

Jeff was also a prolific tinkerer. He worked at constructing a hovercraft from an old vacuum and would frequently booby-trap parts of the house. In an interview Bezos gave to the Academy of Achievement on May 4, 2001, he said,

Turning on Bright Minds

During the early 1970s, an advertising executive named Julie Ray self-published a book about education called *Turning on Bright Minds: A Parent Looks at Gifted Education in Texas*. While researching her book, Ray visited the River Oaks Elementary School and interviewed a twelve-year-old student, "Tim." Tim was not the student's actual name because his parents did not want his real name used. Tim, it turns out, was actually Jeff Bezos. Many years later, author Brad Stone tracked down Ray and interviewed her for a book he was writing about the famous CEO of Amazon.com, Jeff Bezos. Ray said of Bezos, "When I met him as a young boy his ability was obvious, and it was being nurtured and encouraged by the new program. The program also benefited by his responsiveness and enthusiasm for learning. It was a total validation of the concept."[8]

I was constantly booby-trapping the house with various kinds of alarms and some of them were not just audible sounds but actually like physical booby traps. I think I occasionally worried my parents that they were going to open the door one day and have thirty pounds of nails drop on their head or something. Our garage was basically science fair central, and my mom is a saint, because she would drive me to Radio Shack multiple times a day.[9]

Mike Bezos began working as petroleum engineer for Exxon, and the family moved several times during Jeff's childhood—first from Albuquerque to Houston, then for a short time to Pensacola, and then to Miami, both in Florida, where Jeff Bezos attended Miami Palmetto High School.[10]

Bezos grew up watching the sci-fi television show *Star Trek*. For a time, Bezos had briefly considered calling his company Makeitso .com after a command often given by *Star Trek: The Next Generation* captain Jean-Luc Picard.

Teachers and fellow students remember his ambitious nature fondly. According to Cullen Bullock, a Palmetto high school science teacher, "Even when he was in high school, all the teachers who taught him knew Jeff was something special and that he would be going places."[11]

Ursula "Uschi" Werner, a girlfriend of Bezos's from high school, said, "Jeff always wanted to make a lot of money—it wasn't about money itself. It was about what he was going to do with the money, about changing the future."[12]

During the summer Jeff took various jobs. One summer he worked at McDonald's, where he flipped burgers on the grill. In the book *Golden Opportunity: Remarkable Careers That Began at McDonald's*, Bezos told author Cody Teets, "You can learn responsibility in any job, if you take it seriously. You can learn a lot as a teenager working at McDonald's. It's different from what you learn in school. Don't underestimate the value of that!"[13]

> "I was constantly booby-trapping the house with various kinds of alarms."

Jeff did grow tired of his job at McDonald's, however, and it was during high school that he started his first business. It was an educational summer camp, called The Dream Institute, for fourth, fifth, and sixth graders that concentrated on science and reading. DREAM stood for **D**irected **REA**soning **M**ethods, and Bezos charged $600 per person. A total of six kids signed up—two of them

Bezos (behind the camera) and his high school girlfriend Ursula Werner are pictured instructing students during their educational summer camp called the Dream Institute.

were his own brother and sister. Some of the required reading included *The Once and Future King*, *The Lord of the Rings*, *Dune*, *Gulliver's Travels*, and *Treasure Island*.[14]

During his years at Palmetto High School, Jeff attended a Student Science Training Program at the University of Florida, receiving a Silver Knight Award.[15] He was also the high school valedictorian and a National Merit Scholar. Today there is a plaque outside Palmetto's school auditorium honoring notable graduates, which includes Bezos. After being accepted to Princeton University's early admission program, Jeff celebrated the news by taking his girlfriend to New York City.[16] Jeff graduated from high school in 1982 and continued his education at Princeton University, where he hoped to study physics.

CHAPTER TWO

Studying at Princeton University

A round the time Jeff Bezos was in fourth grade, a local company donated a mainframe computer to his school, the River Oaks Elementary School. Personal computers were not yet available at that time, so Bezos and some of his friends had rare, early access to a computer before they became commonplace. They spent many hours on the machine and figured out how to program it.

Bezos reminisced about his time on the computer in an interview he gave on May 4, 2001, to the Academy of Achievement. He explained,

> We had a teletype that was connected by an old acoustic modem. You literally dialed a regular phone and picked up the handset and put it in this little cradle. And nobody— none of the teachers—knew how to operate this computer. Nobody did. But, there was a stack of manuals and me and a couple of other kids stayed after class and learned how to program this thing, and that worked well for maybe about a week.[1]

Soon after learning how the computer worked, Jeff and his friends discovered that the original users of the mainframe computer had programmed a *Star Trek* game into in. From then onward, Jeff and his friends played the *Star Trek* game. This early access to a computer, well before they became commonplace, helped to nurture Bezos's love of computers.

It wasn't until around the time Jeff was in eleventh grade that he had his own computer. He continued to learn and work on the Apple II Plus computer, one of the earliest versions of a personal computer. Jeff carried his interest with computers with him when he entered Princeton University as a freshman in 1982.

The Apple II Plus computer was released in 1978. It was one of the very first personal computers released by computer manufacturer Apple and the first personal computer Jeff Bezos owned.

A Quandary over Physics

In 1982, Jeff Bezos entered Princeton University, in Princeton, New Jersey. Princeton University is one of the United States' eight Ivy League schools; "Ivy League" is a term often used to describe the schools with the highest

Princeton Neuroscience Institute

As Jeff Bezos's wealth grew from the success of Amazon.com, he decided to use some of his money to give back to his alma mater, Princeton University. In 2011, Jeff and MacKenzie Bezos—who is a 1992 graduate of Princeton—donated $15 million to help create a center in the Princeton Neuroscience Institute. The generous donation established the Bezos Center for Neural Circuit Dynamics with the goal to help build knowledge of how the brain works. According to the website, "The Bezos Center for Neural Circuit Dynamics focuses on the development and application of microscopy imaging techniques for measuring neural circuit dynamics in the functioning brain."[2]

Speaking of his donation Bezos said, "We can hope for advancements that lead to understanding deep behaviors, more effective learning methods for young children, and cures for neurological diseases. MacKenzie and I are delighted and excited to support Princeton in their focus on fundamental neuroscience."[3]

Since its creation, the Bezos Center for Neural Circuit Dynamics has supported faculty research in many areas of the brain.

academic standards. Princeton was founded in 1746 and is the fourth oldest university in the United States. Bezos expressed an interest in physics, and the program at Princeton was considered one of the best in the country.

Bezos was also inspired to go to the school because one of the people he admired most, physicist Albert Einstein, had lived and taught there. Decades earlier, Einstein had taken a position at Princeton's Institute for Advanced Study in 1933. He lived and worked in Princeton, New Jersey, for the rest of his life.

During his freshman year at Princeton, Bezos enrolled in the honors physics program. At the end of his freshman year he met with his faculty advisor, who was also the chairman of the physics program. After reviewing Bezos's university application as well as his strong freshman grades, the chairman accepted him as one of the top twenty-five students to the program.[4]

Despite Bezos's good grades in the physics program, he found the subject difficult. He felt that many of the other students were able to grasp and understand the work far more effortlessly than he could. Once he began studying quantum mechanics—a particularly difficult branch of physics that concentrates on the activities inside of atoms—he started to realize that he was struggling to keep up with his peers.

In an interview Bezos gave to the Academy of Achievement on May 4, 2001, he recalled this time, "Things went fairly well until I got to quantum mechanics and there were about 30 people in the class by that point and it was so hard for me. I just remember there was a point in this where I realized I'm never going to be a great physicist."[5]

Bezos has spoken highly of his fellow students, "It was awe-inspiring for me to watch them because in a very easy, almost casual way, they could absorb concepts and solve problems that I would work 12 hours on, and it was a wonderful thing to behold."[6]

> "I just remember there was a point in this where I realized I'm never going to be a great physicist."

Bezos concluded he was not smart enough to be a great physicist. He also knew he did not want to just become a mediocre theoretical physicist. In an interview with the Guardian on February 10, 2001, he said, "Mediocre theoretical physicists make no progress. They spend all their time understanding other people's progress."[7]

Years later Bezos told Princeton University, "My best memory of Princeton is finishing problem sets and partial differential equations. And my worst memory of Princeton is *starting* my problem sets and partial differential equations."[8]

Bezos humbly decided to leave physics as a major and returned to his fascination with computers.[9] Computer science was still a very new field at the time. Bill Gates's software company Microsoft and Steve Jobs's Apple Computers were both founded in the mid-1970s, when the widespread use of the internet was still decades away. Computer science and electrical engineering were still a single department at Princeton

Princeton Commencement Speech

On May 30, 2010, Jeff Bezos returned to his alma mater, Princeton University, and delivered the commencement speech to the graduating class. In his speech, Bezos recalled a somber story from his youth in which he used statistics he had learned about the detriments of smoking to inform his grandmother about the damage her own smoking had done to her life. Thinking he was being clever, he calculated the potential damage of her smoking habit and told her, "At two minutes per puff, you've taken nine years off your life!" Bezos was thinking he might get praised for his calculations. Instead, his grandmother cried and his grandfather told the young Bezos, "Jeff, one day you'll understand that it's harder to be kind than clever."

He used the story to inspire the young graduates to use their intelligence and education to do the right things in life. He asked the audience, "Will you be a cynic, or will you be a builder? Will you be clever at the expense of others, or will you be kind?" He then concluded, "In the end, we are our choices. Build yourself a great story. Thank you and good luck!"[10]

when Jeff entered the programs.[11] He double majored in computer science and electrical engineering. Computer science and electrical engineering eventually split into two separate departments at Princeton in 1985. Once immersed in computers, Bezos found he was very skilled at creating computer software programs, something that would come in handy for him in the years ahead. In

Steve Jobs presenting the Macintosh personal computer in 1984. Personal computers, along with the internet, would help set the stage for Jeff Bezos's idea of selling books online in the early 1990s.

an interview Bezos gave to Achivement.org he said, "I always had a facility with computers. I always got along well with them and they're such extraordinary tools. You can teach them to do things and then they actually do them. It's kind of an incredible tool that we've built here in the 20th Century."[12]

Gaining Valuable Experience

Bezos excelled during his years at Princeton and used his summers to travel as well as to pursue his interest with computers and programming. In 1984, Mike Bezos was temporarily transferred by Exxon to work in the country of Norway. Jeff accompanied his family to the town of Stavanger, Norway, in June of 1984[13] and worked for Exxon as a computer programmer for the summer. He worked on a 4341 IBM Processor computer and developed a computer program with IFPS (Interactive Financial Planning System) software language to calculate oil royalties for Exxon.

> "In the end, we are our choices. Build yourself a great story."

The following summer Bezos lived and worked in San Jose, California—part of the so-called Silicon Valley—and worked at IBM's Santa Teresa Research Center. He added his summer job experience to his resume and wrote that in three days he had "completed a project allocated for four weeks for completion, re-implementing an IBM software productivity tool user interface by writing exec routine to automatically and selectively change the productivity tool."[14]

With excellent grades, Bezos was elected to the Princeton honor societies Phi Beta Kappa and Tau Beta Pi.[15] He was also the president of the Princeton chapter of the Students for the Exploration and Development of Space.

Before graduating he was already in high demand by companies who were at Princeton attempting to recruit the best and the brightest. According to *Wired* magazine, Bezos turned down job offers from three major technology companies.

Founded in 1746, Princeton University is one of the oldest colleges in the United States. In addition to Jeff Bezos, former First Lady Michelle Obama, activist Cornel West, and actress Brooke Shields all attended Princeton University.

Looking back he told Princeton University in an interview, "If I were to go back in time and give myself one piece of advice as an undergraduate it would be 'take pride in your decisions and hard work, but not in your gifts.' Celebrate your gifts, enjoy them, but don't take pride in them. Take pride in your decisions and hard work."[16]

Bezos also had advice for incoming Princeton freshman: "For anybody who is starting their freshman week and they are starting at Princeton I think the advice as to what to focus on is pretty simple which is to figure out—which is not always easy—but try to figure out what you are genuinely interested in and then pursue those things."[17]

Before graduating Princeton all students are required to draft a senior thesis. As part of Bezos's senior thesis he conceptualized and constructed a computer capable of performing complex calculations to help analyze DNA.

In 1986, Jeff Bezos graduated from Princeton University summa cum laude (with greatest honor) with a bachelor of science degree in electrical engineering and computer science.[18] His grade point average for the classes in his department was 4.2, which is nearly an A+ grade. Overall, he graduated from the school with a 3.9 grade point average, which is a nearly perfect record.

To get his first job after graduation, Bezos ultimately answered a full-page advertisement in the university newspaper, the *Daily Princetonian*, which requested Princeton's "best computer science graduates."[19] The ad was run by a financial startup company called Fitel, and the company would give Bezos some of the essential experience he would need to succeed.

CHAPTER THREE

In the Working World

·······················

I In Jeff Bezos's Princeton University yearbook, graduates chose an inspirational quote to represent themselves and what they stood for. Bezos chose a quote from science fiction author Ray Bradbury's dystopian classic, *Fahrenheit 451*. The quote reads, "The Universe says No to us. We in answer fire a broadside of flesh at it and cry Yes!" Judging by the quote he chose, it seems Bezos was not going to sit back idly and let fate determine his future. He moved forward deliberately and purposefully after he graduated from Princeton in 1986. Every step Bezos would take over the next few years would culminate in his internet retail brainchild, Amazon.com.

Fitel and Bankers Trust

Jeff Bezos had briefly considered going out on his own and starting a business right after graduating college. He ultimately decided against that course of action. In an interview he gave to the Academy of Achievement Bezos said,

I toyed with the idea of starting a company and even talked to a couple of friends about starting a company, and ultimately decided that it would be smarter to wait and learn a little bit more about business and the way the world works. You know, one of the things that it's very hard to believe when you're 22 or 23 years old is that you don't already know everything.[1]

> **"The Universe says No to us. We in answer fire a broadside of flesh at it and cry Yes!"**
> —Bezos's Princeton University yearbook quote from Ray Bradbury's novel *Fahrenheit 451*

Instead of joining one of the established technology companies that he had turned down around graduation time, Bezos decided to join a startup so he could learn how companies established themselves and grew into profitable ventures. In May 1986, after answering Fitel's full-page ad in the *Daily Princetonian* requesting Princeton's "best computer science graduates," Bezos moved to New York City and began working at his first full-time job after college. Fitel was started by two professors, Graciella Chichilnisky and Geoffrey Heal, who came from the economics department at Columbia University in New York.

For the late 1980s, the work that was done at Fitel was ahead of its time. The company used a network of computers to link various financial institutions, banks, and brokerage firms. The network's job was to transfer money, stock trades, and data between different institutions all around the world. Eventually, websites like

Personal Computers

Today we can fit a mobile device in our pocket that can allow us to easily research, order, play, or watch just about anything we can think of at the click of a button or simply by the sound of our voice. The earliest electronic computers were nothing like this.

One of the earliest computers was the Electronic Numerical Integrator Analyzer and Computer, or ENIAC. The ENIAC was constructed at the University of Pennsylvania to help the United States military do ballistics calculations during World War II. The computer weighed 30 tons (27 metric tons) and took up almost 2,000 square feet (185 square meters) of building space. The new technology cut down on human calculation times for missile trajectories from twelve hours to just thirty seconds.[2]

But computers still had a long way to go before they could be used for the types of interactions and retail tasks imagined by entrepreneurs such as Jeff Bezos.

E*Trade and TD Ameritrade would make transactions like this commonplace, but at the time this kind of technology was advanced for the world of finance.

Due to his skills as a computer programmer, Bezos was promoted quickly in the company, and in February 1987 he became the associate director of technology and business development. Professor Graciella Chichilnisky had designed a financial computer network called Equinet, and Bezos helped to build and market it.

Bezos began his career using his computer programming skills to help create new ways to trade stocks electronically. Today electronic stock trading and online banking are standard.

. . . .

Through his improvements to computer protocols, which are a set of rules that help different and often incompatible computers communicate over a network, Bezos was able to save Fitel around 30 percent in communication costs. Thousands of trades were sent between different firms and banks. Although this kind of trade is commonplace now, stock traders at the time did not know what to make of the system and could not believe it was real.[3]

Chichilnisky recalled working with Jeff Bezos on Equinet, "The communications protocols were the most challenging. It was damn well engineered because Jeff did it himself. He was one of the best communications engineers I had."[4]

In addition to his computer programming, Bezos managed a group of a dozen programmers and analysts based in New York and London, and he traveled between the two offices on a weekly basis. Bezos's other duties at Fitel included supervising the design and testing of programs, as well as handling important clients like the investment bank Salomon Brothers, one of Fitel's biggest accounts. Bezos also managed customer service departments around the world and was in charge of starting Fitel's new office in Tokyo, Japan.

Only a year after Bezos had started working at Fitel, Chichilnisky left the company to raise her child. Bezos absorbed as much as he could at Fitel, but after another year he left, in April 1988. He moved on to another company, Bankers Trust, that was, as Bezos said, "working at the intersection of computers and finance."[5]

Bezos's job at Bankers Trust was similar to the one he held at Fitel. He managed the engineering department and worked on another communications network called BT World. The software allowed large clients to keep track of the money Bankers Trust handled for companies that gave employees special funds in addition to their regular pay. These other sources of money, called pension funds and profit sharing, could be difficult to calculate because the amounts fluctuate, or change, due to many factors. The new computerized system cut down on the traditional mail that was sent out to clients and allowed for more up-to-the-minute information about the funds.

The Charging Bull statue in Manhattan's Financial District is a symbol of a positive and growing economic market.

•••••••••••••••••••••

As with many new systems, especially ones that relied on new technologies, Bezos had to contend with resistance to changing business practices. Many people were resistant to change and wanted to keep doing things the traditional way. Eventually Bezos persisted and explained away any doubters. His boss at the time, Harvey Hirsch, recalled, "He sees different ways of doing things. He told the naysayers, 'I believe in this new technology and I'm going to show you how it's going to work'—and he did. At the end of the day he proved them all wrong. He has no trouble puncturing someone's balloon if he thinks they're proposing to do something the wrong way or in an inappropriate way."[6]

Ten months after starting at Bankers Trust he became the company's youngest vice president at only twenty-six years old.[8]

Not content to sit still, however, Bezos kept looking for new opportunities to grow. He tried to start his own company in 1990 after meeting a Merrill Lynch

The Internet and the World Wide Web

The internet is an electronic communications network that connects computer networks around the world. During the Cold War with the Soviet Union (approximately 1947–1991), the United States military was worried that an attack could destroy the phone systems in the United States.

In 1962, a scientist named J.C.R. Licklider from Massachusetts Institute of Technology (MIT) proposed a "galactic network" of computers that could communicate with one another. This network would allow government officials to communicate even if the telephone system were destroyed.[7] This predecessor of the internet was known as the Advanced Research Projects Agency Network, or ARPANET.

As newer computer networks sprang up, ARPANET could not communicate with them. To fix the problem, computer scientist Vinton Cerf devised a new computer communications system called transmission-control protocol/internet protocol, or TCP/IP. It allowed different types of computer networks to communicate with one another.[8] TCP/IP is still the foundation of the World Wide Web as well as the modern internet.

investment banker, Halsey Minor. Minor had been developing an ambitious computer network that combined graphics, text, and information. Bezos and Minor almost got funding from Merrill Lynch to begin the company themselves, but in the end the funding did not happen. Bezos moved on and continued looking for something new.

D. E. Shaw & Co.

Bezos distributed his resume to different agencies that try to match companies with the best employees looking for work. He was hoping to find a new job in technology, away from the world of finance. Despite Bezos's strict requests that these agents, called headhunters, help him find something *outside* the world of finance, he was contacted with an opportunity from another financial firm. The headhunter called and said, "I know you said you would kill me if I even proposed the finance thing, but there's this special opportunity that's actually a very unusual financial company."[9] The company, called D. E. Shaw, was a hedge fund, which is a group of investors that can make higher-risk investments than traditional financial groups making trades on Wall Street.

The company was started by David E. Shaw, a former computer science professor at Columbia University. After leaving Columbia, Shaw worked for Morgan Stanley and then left to start his own company with $28 million from investor Donald Sussman. Shaw's company was unique because he used his mathematical skills to write software and formulas that exploited small differences in stock prices around the world. This new software

Conversations with David Shaw sparked ideas in Bezos that served him when he started Amazon.com.

could quickly execute a trade and take advantage of small variations in stock prices faster than traditional methods. This software gave the company an advantage over other firms, and using new and innovative methods was important for the firm's continued success.[10]

In December of 1990, Bezos took a job as vice president of D. E. Shaw and quickly became friendly with David Shaw. Bezos recalled Shaw as "one of those people who has a completely developed left brain and a completely developed right brain. He's artistic, articulate, and analytical. It's just a pleasure to talk to someone like that."[11]

After a few years of working very hard, Bezos became the youngest senior vice president at the firm and managed a twenty-four-person department that researched new markets.[12] He even kept a sleeping bag at his office if he needed to work late and stay the night.[13]

Bezos wound up meeting his future wife at D. E. Shaw. MacKenzie Tuttle graduated from Princeton University in 1992 with an English degree and joined D. E. Shaw as an administrative assistant that same year. She would eventually wind up on Bezos's team, with her office next to his. She liked Bezos and asked him to lunch. In an interview she gave to *Vogue* magazine in 2013, MacKenzie said, "My office was next door to his, and all day long I listened to that fabulous laugh. How could you not fall in love with that laugh?"[14] The two dated for three months before they got engaged. Three months later in 1993, they were married in West Palm Beach, Florida.

> "My office was next door to his, and all day long I listened to that fabulous laugh. How could you not fall in love with that laugh?"
> —MacKenzie Bezos

By 1994, the internet was beginning to spring to life, and D. E. Shaw was already well positioned to take advantage of the financial boom. Shaw realized that Bezos was the right person to help him explore business possibilities on the internet, which he saw as the future. They brainstormed ideas, such as email services and online trading for internet users.

Bezos married MacKenzie Tuttle in 1993 before starting Amazon .com. MacKenzie Bezos was one of Amazon.com's first employees.

Another business idea Shaw and Bezos kicked around was something they called "the everything store"—an online middleman company that sold products from every type of manufacturer imaginable to consumers around the world. The store would be similar to a traditional catalogue-based business, but it would use the internet as its storefront for customers.

These early discussions would eventually become what Bezos later developed into Amazon.com.

CHAPTER FOUR

Venturing Out on His Own

· · · · · · · · · · · · · · · ·

I n February 1994, while still working at D. E. Shaw, Jeff Bezos was reading a monthly newsletter called *Matrix News* about growing possibilities related to the internet, published by writer John Quarterman.[1] The newsletter described the incredible growth of the new World Wide Web and suggested that more and more people would soon be using it as a means for all kinds of communication. One graphic that caught Bezos's eye showed that web activity increased roughly 2,300 percent in a single year.

According to Bezos, "The wake-up call was finding this startling statistic that web usage in the spring of 1994 was growing at 2,300 percent a year. You know, things just don't grow that fast. It's highly unusual, and that started me about thinking, 'What kind of business plan might make sense in the context of that growth?'"[2]

Even though Bezos already had the idea for an "everything store," he felt it was not realistic to start by selling everything in the beginning. He made a list of what he felt he could sell on the internet, such as music, clothing, software, and office supplies. Bezos concluded that books would be the easiest things to start out selling.[3]

On the Road

In the spring of 1994 newly married Jeff and MacKenzie Bezos were living in a nice apartment located in Manhattan's Upper West Side neighborhood. Bezos also had a great job at D. E. Shaw, but he decided to give it all up and risk going out on his own to try and create an online bookstore. MacKenzie was supportive of the

When Bezos first had his idea for Amazon.com, few people used the internet to shop. Malls were popular shopping centers, but today many are struggling because of the success of online retailers.

idea, but not everyone agreed with Bezos's decision. His boss, David Shaw, understood his decision because he too had left Morgan Stanley years earlier to start D. E. Shaw on his own. Still, Shaw did not want to see Bezos leave, and he convinced him to consider his decision for another forty-eight hours before concluding what to do. Bezos's mother, Jackie, also did not want him to leave his great job in New York and suggested that he try to start the new company on the weekends or at night. Bezos told his mother, "No, things are changing fast. I need to move quickly."[4]

Bezos's thoughts on his decision to venture out on his own are quoted in the book *Get Big Fast* by Robert Spector:

> I knew that when I was eighty there was no chance that I would regret having walked away from my 1994 Wall Street bonus in the middle of the year. I wouldn't even have *remembered* that. But I did think there was a chance that I might regret significantly not participating in this thing called the Internet, that I believed passionately in. I also knew that if I tried and failed, I wouldn't regret that. So, once I thought about it that way, it became incredibly easy to make that decision.[5]

After concluding he was going to attempt to start his own online bookstore, Bezos began formulating a plan. The first thing he did was to throw a party at his apartment to watch the last episode of *Star Trek: The Next Generation*—one of his favorite TV shows. Next, Bezos told his friends he was quitting his job at D. E. Shaw. Bezos knew he was going to need help building the bookselling website, so he traveled to Santa Cruz, California, to meet with some skilled programmers recommended to him by a D. E. Shaw coworker. One of the programmers he met over breakfast was named Sheldon Kaphan, nicknamed Shel.

Bezos briefly considered starting the company in Santa Cruz, but he eventually chose the city of Seattle, Washington, for his company for several reasons. First, he knew Washington State had a small population. He learned that as long as his company did not have offices in other larger states he would not need to charge customers in those states sales tax on their book purchases. Bezos wanted to take advantage of this technicality to help put his new online bookstore in a good position and make it a favorable choice for customers. He also chose Seattle because it was a technology hub. Other technology companies were already in place there, and he would be able to find many skilled and experienced workers to work for him. Last, he had a close friend, Nicholas Hanauer, who already lived in Seattle.[6]

> "I knew that when I was eighty there was no chance that I would regret having walked away from my 1994 Wall Street bonus."

The Bezoses were still not exactly sure where in Seattle they'd be moving, so when the movers asked Bezos where to deliver all their belongings, he replied that they should just start driving the moving truck west and he would notify them in a few days exactly where the final destination would be. Jeff and MacKenzie then flew to Texas and borrowed a car from Bezos's parents. Then they drove northwest toward Washington. Bezos soon called the movers and told them to deliver his possessions to his friend Hanauer's house. With their belongings already sitting in Seattle, MacKenzie drove while her husband worked out an early business model on his laptop.

After Jeff and MacKenzie had been in Seattle for a few days, they moved into a ranch house in the city of Bellevue, located across Lake Washington, a short distance from Seattle. The house had a garage, which

Earliest Financing

Starting a company requires money for supplies, employee salaries, and other various expenses. In the very beginning, Bezos backed Amazon.com with $10,000 of his own money. In 1995, Bezos's parents invested $100,000 in personal savings to help their son start his company. Bezos informed his parents it was a risk and that there was a 70 percent chance they could lose their money.[7]

In other attempts to obtain startup money, Bezos took out $84,000 in bank loans over the next sixteen months.[8] Sheldon Kaphan, the company's first official employee, was required to invest $5,000 when he was hired. His investment in the company paid off. By the year 1999, Sheldon Kaphan had become the CTO of the company and had an estimated net worth of $236.9 million.[9]

suited Bezos. It brought to mind other businesses and technology startup companies such as Apple, Google, and Hewlett-Packard, which all started in garages.

Bezos wanted to learn more about selling books, so in the fall of 1994 he attended a bookselling course in Portland, Oregon. He was the only person taking the course who said he wanted to start an online bookstore.[10]

Once Bezos decided to sell books online he had to secure financing, research the industry, and take some risks before Amazon.com would become an online retail site.

Early Company Names

Amazon.com was not the first name Jeff Bezos had chosen for his internet bookstore. Cadabra Inc. was the first name officially registered in 1994. One of the earlier names that Bezos liked a lot was MakeItSo. com. "Make it so" was a command that *Star Trek*'s Captain Picard often said. Other names such as Awake. com, Browse.com, Bookmall.com, and Aard.com were all briefly considered. Jeff and MacKenzie also liked the name Relentless.com and even went so far as to register the name. Today you can still type Relentless. com into a web browser and you will be taken to Amazon.com's home page.[11]

Around the same time, Bezos also convinced his programmer friend Sheldon Kaphan to move to Seattle and help him build his online bookstore.[12]

Basements and Cafes

The first name Bezos had in mind for his online bookstore was Cadabra Inc., a name he registered on July 5, 1994. The name was short for the word "abracadabra," which magicians typically exclaim aloud before revealing the result of their magic tricks. However, "Cadabra" was often misunderstood as the word "cadaver," so Bezos decided that he'd need to come up with a better name. In August of 1994, Bezos posted a help wanted ad online stating that he was looking for skilled programmers. At the end of his post he added a quote by computer scientist Alan Kay: "It's easier to invent the future than to predict it."[13]

Bezos wanted a company name that started with the letter A so it would appear atop any alphabetical list. Many other names were considered, but ultimately, Bezos chose Amazon. Bezos chose the name Amazon because it is one of the world's longest and largest rivers, which runs through the largest rain forest in the world, the Amazon. On November 1, 1994, the name Amazon.com was registered.[14] On February 9, 1995, the company was officially renamed Amazon.com. At the time, many other internet companies did not use "dot-com" as part of their name. Bezos did not want the company to simply be called Amazon and insisted it be named Amazon.com. It was the first internet company to be marketed and branded that way.[15]

> "It's easier to invent the future than to predict it."
> —Alan Kay

At the time it first started, Amazon.com had only four employees: Jeff and MacKenzie Bezos, Sheldon Kaphan, and another programmer named Paul Davis. Davis was originally from England and worked in the computer science and engineering department at the University of Washington before helping to start Amazon.com in Bezos's garage. While Bezos, Kaphan, and Davis worked on computer programming, MacKenzie did all of the other tasks. She acted as an administrative assistant, accountant, and purchaser of the site's merchandise.

Although Amazon.com began as an online bookstore, Bezos always intended to sell much more. His early concept for Amazon was an "everything store," where a customer could buy anything.

MacKenzie wound up doing the accounting for Amazon until 1996, when an actual accountant was hired.[16]

Before Amazon.com could officially launch, the website needed to be created from scratch. Other online bookstores already existed, but Bezos and his small team were convinced they could do a better job. All of the work took more than a year of programming. To make things easier on themselves they used freely available open source software languages called C and Pearl.

The company was also quickly outgrowing its garage space. The computer servers needed to run the company used so much power in the house that Jeff and MacKenzie could not run a vacuum or hair dryer without blowing a fuse.[17]

Sometimes when the small group needed to have meetings with other people and the cramped garage would not suffice, they would meet at a café inside a local Barnes & Noble to discuss the future of Amazon.com. Years later, Bezos would often recall the irony of meeting in locations like that in those early days because in the long run they would end up being the largest competitor of bookstores such as Barnes & Noble.

Despite the fast growth, Bezos wanted even more. He wanted Amazon.com to eventually sell "everything" and had ambitions of it becoming a technology company. But for the time being, the company would need to get its footing just selling books better than the few other online competitors. Before the website was even finished, and before a single book could be sold, Amazon.com would need to move out of the small garage and into a larger location in downtown Seattle.

CHAPTER FIVE

Early Ideas and Growth

• • • • • • • • • • • • • • • • • • •

By the spring of 1995, Jeff Bezos and his few Amazon.com employees outgrew the garage of his rented house and moved to a small office in downtown Seattle. The first company warehouse was a 200-square-foot (18.5-square-meter) section in the basement of their office building. Jeff and MacKenzie also moved from Bellevue into the city of Seattle. Around the same time, the beta version of Amazon.com was launched and shared with family and friends so it could be tested before its official launch. A friend placed the first Amazon.com order on April 3, 1995. Amazon.com officially went live to the world on July 6, 1995. Neither of the major brick-and-mortar bookstores at that time, Barnes & Noble and Borders, had websites.

Bumpy Startup

When Amazon.com first launched in 1995, success was not a foregone conclusion. When initial orders started coming in, the few people working with Bezos struggled

It took a while for brick-and-mortar bookstores to expand into the online market. Barnes & Noble did not start its online bookstore until 1997.

•••••••••••••••••••••

to ship all the merchandise. In the first week, there were $12,000 in orders, but they only managed to ship $864 in books. In the second week, $14,000 in orders came in, but they shipped only $7,000 in books. The orders and initial sales were promising, but without a fast and efficient shipping plan in place, the new company struggled to keep up with orders.

A week after the launch, Bezos was approached by the website Yahoo.com, which was extremely popular at the time. Yahoo! asked Bezos if Amazon.com would like to be featured on Yahoo!'s home page. Bezos agreed that the potential for publicity could not be turned down. As a result of the exposure, sales continued to increase, and within one month of launching, Amazon.com had sold books to forty-five different countries and all fifty states.

User-Generated Reviews

Today people post online reviews of products all the time. We often look at customer reviews before purchasing a product. But this was not always the way things were. Jeff Bezos felt customer satisfaction was the most important key to Amazon.com's success and that user reviews of books could help people decide more easily what to buy and what to avoid. At the time, critics thought the practice would be more harmful to the retailers than helpful because it could make shoppers decide *not* to buy a book. Others felt the opportunity to leave bad reviews could promote negativity and offensive comments. To avoid this problem, Bezos himself often monitored the reviews to check for offensive or rude comments. But the idea was well received by customers, and they appreciated the opportunity to read others' feedback. Now, online customer reviews are so commonplace they are expected.

Like all of the earliest websites, the first Amazon.com home page was extremely simple and mostly text based.[1] At the time, internet connections were notoriously slow and connections were made by dial-up modems attached to landline phone connections. As a result, visual graphics or photos slowed down loading times even further.

Many people used to jokingly call the World Wide Web the "World Wide Wait" because of slow internet connections.[2] In order to streamline connection times the only graphic on the Amazon.com home page was a stylized marbled blue *A* logo with a river snaking through it. Underneath the logo it read, "Amazon.com Earth's Biggest Bookstore." The website also advertised "One million titles, consistently low prices." The majority of the website, however, was text based with text links.

Paul Davis programmed the computers so that every time a sale came in, a beep would sound. Initially the beep was fun when there were only a handful of sales a day, and hearing it encouraged the staff. As sales increased, so did the frequency of the beeps. They quickly became an annoyance and were replaced by an onscreen system that could be used at any time to see up-to-the minute sales figures.[3]

Soon after being featured on Yahoo!, the relatively new web browser Netscape added Amazon.com to its "What's New" webpage and sales increased again from the additional publicity.[4] Bezos's early idea of having the company name start with the letter A helped too, since it typically appeared atop any list of new and popular websites. Within the first two months, sales were $20,000 a week.[5]

The early plan for selling books on Amazon.com was much different than it is today. Customers would make online orders for books, and in turn, the employees would order the books from one of the two large wholesale book distributers: Ingram or Baker & Taylor. Amazon. com did not have a warehouse or store any inventory, at least not initially.

Soon the site's early ordering system ran into a snag because the book distributors were designed for large sales to bookstores. They required Amazon.com to place a ten-book minimum for any orders it made. According to Bezos, he found a clever solution to get around the book distributors' order requirement of a ten-book minimum. "Their systems were programed in such a

When Amazon.com first launched, high-speed Internet access did not yet exist for home use. To allow the website to load quickly, the website had to be mostly text based, with few images or graphics.

way that you didn't have to *receive* ten books, you only had to *order* ten books," Bezos said. "So, we found an obscure book about lichens that they had in their system but was out of stock. We began ordering the one book we wanted and nine copies of the lichen book. They would ship out the book we needed and said, 'Sorry, but we're out of the lichen book.'"[6]

Once orders came in from the distributors, they had to be shipped out to the Amazon.com customers who ordered them. No one was initially hired to pack books at the new online store. Bezos, Kaphan, and the few other employees would pack book orders in the building's basement after work, often staying late into the night.[7] Jeff

Early Investors

Many people became wealthy for taking a risk on Amazon.com and investing in the company early on. According to a CNBC article from 2017, "If you had invested in Amazon early on, when it first debuted on the Nasdaq in 1997, you could be worth a lot of money today, too. In fact, if you bought $1,000 in stock even 10 years later, in 2007, your investment would be worth $12,398 as of October 31 of this year."[8]

Billionaire Warren Buffett, the chief executive officer of Berkshire Hathaway, did not invest in Amazon early on. Buffett was quoted as saying, "I was too dumb to realize. I did not think [Bezos] could succeed on the scale he has." Buffett also praised Bezos calling him, "the most remarkable business person of our age."[9]

or MacKenzie typically drove the boxed orders directly to the post office or a UPS shipping office the following day.

For the first few weeks, everyone struggled on their hands and knees packing book orders into boxes on the floor.

> **"I was too dumb to realize. I did not think [Bezos] could succeed on the scale he has."**
> **— Warren Buffett**

Soon, a new part-time employee, Nicholas Lovejoy, who had worked with Bezos at D. E. Shaw before moving to Seattle to teach math, had a solution. Since the new Amazon.com offices were located across the street from a Home Depot, Lovejoy and Bezos looked at large desks in hopes of solving the company's packing problem. Bezos noticed how expensive desks were and realized that the doors on sale at Home Depot were much cheaper and about the size they needed for packing. So, they decided to buy a door and construct legs for it to turn it into a table.[10]

Bezos then asked another employee, Laurel Canan, to help out. Canan was also a carpenter, and he constructed tables out of doors for the rest of the company, including Bezos's office desk. Canan later took over the operations of the Amazon.com warehouse as the company grew, and the "desk door" became a symbol of the company's problem solving and ingenuity. Bezos's original desk door was eventually auctioned off in 1999 for $30,100 (to Bezos's mom, Jacklyn) to raise money for the World Wildlife Fund to help the Amazon River.[11]

Early Growth

To compete with the few existing online bookstores as well as top brick-and-mortar booksellers Barnes & Noble and Borders, Amazon.com offered discounts of 40 percent off the list price of bestseller books and 10 percent off the price of all other books. As a result, the company was not making a profit on its sales. It was hoping that attracting customers with its discounts would eventually give it enough business so it could make a profit.

Another plan to compete with other booksellers was to pass another savings along to the customer. Because of state laws, customers who made online purchases outside the state of Washington would not have to pay sales tax on their items. In the mid-1990s, shopping online was not the common or trusted transaction it can be today. But Bezos felt confident that early adopters— people who like to try new technology and gadgets first—could help Amazon.com grow quickly early on by taking advantage of these shopping perks.[12]

Despite its fast growth in sales, Amazon.com still lost money. In 1994, the company lost $52,000. By the end of 1995, the loss for the year was $303,000.[13] Despite all of Bezos's personal and extended family investments, the company was running out of money. In order to keep his fast-growing yet fledgling company afloat, Bezos needed to raise money from new investors. Convincing people to invest in an online bookstore was not easy. Many investors hardly knew what the internet was back in 1995. Bezos's friend Nick Hanauer helped set up meetings for Bezos to try to raise capital from local investors.

Warren Buffett regrets not investing in Amazon.com early on. Eventually Bezos would surpass Buffett's net worth and become the richest person in the world.

Hanauer explained that "Jeff was the *only* thing we had to sell. Nobody knew what the internet was and being in the book business on the internet in 1995 just didn't sound like that big of an idea. It was sort of an amusing idea at the time. But people don't want to invest in amusing ideas."[14]

Ultimately, Bezos met with around sixty different people looking for small investments with the hope of raising $1 million overall.[15] Bezos felt the company should be valued at $6 million but eventually compromised with one investor, Eric Dillon, and agreed to $5 million. Hanauer wrote the first check and helped Bezos secure $981,000 overall from about twenty different investors.[16] The money was needed to keep the company operating as it continued to grow.

Amazon.com continued to grow in popularity, and by the end of 1995, the website was visited by 2,200 users a day. In early 1996, Bezos decided that the company would need an even larger space, and plans were made to move again.

CHAPTER SIX

From Books to Everything

· · · · · · · · · · · · · · · · ·

As Amazon.com was succeeding in the mid- to late 1990s, Jeff Bezos kept his long-term vision in mind. He had always envisioned an online retail company that sold everything. Early employees Paul Davis and Nicholas Lovejoy both remembered Bezos's early, often-grandiose, ideas. Davis recalled Bezos saying he wanted to build "the next Sears,"[1] a reference to the department store that became popular for its mail catalog sales rather than its in-store shopping.

Lovejoy, who enjoyed kayaking back when he first worked at Amazon.com, remembered Bezos saying that he saw a day when Amazon did more than just sell books about kayaks and kayaking, but also sold actual kayaks and everything related to kayaking—including reservations for a kayaking trip! Bezos's early view of a true "everything store" was always in the back of his mind, and as Amazon expanded, so did his plans.[2] Today it is possible to order a kayak from Amazon and have it shipped directly to your home.

Get Big Fast, Faster, Fastest

In early 1996, Amazon.com was growing at a rate of 30 to 40 percent a month[3] and was projected to earn $5 million by the end of the year.[4] Because of the fast growth,

Amazon.com Sued for "Earth's Biggest" Claim

The competition between online book sales and traditional store book sales became more intense in the late 1990s when Barnes & Noble actually *sued* Amazon. com. In May 1997, the book retailer giant filed a lawsuit that alleged that Amazon.com was falsely advertising itself as "the World's Largest Bookstore." The bookseller claimed that the online bookstore was only a "book broker" because it sold its books on the Internet. A dispute about who had a greater selection of books was also brought up in the lawsuit.[5]

After a counterclaim, the two companies came to an agreement. In October 1997, Barnes & Noble and Amazon.com settled their disputes out of court. According to an article in the *New York Times*, "The rival booksellers said that neither party admitted wrongdoing of any kind, and neither paid damages. The companies said they 'simply decided that they would rather compete in the marketplace than in the courtroom.'"[6]

Amazon had also already outgrown its first building. In March 1996 the company left its first official location in downtown Seattle and moved a few blocks away into a much larger, 17,000-square-foot (1,580 sq m) building with two floors.[7] Bezos predicted they would only last at the new location for about six to ten months. In reality, they lasted at the new location for only five months.[8]

As growth increased, Bezos liked to say, "Get Big Fast," and that became the unofficial company motto. At the first company picnic in 1996, Bezos gave out T-shirts printed with the phrase "Get Big Fast" to everyone.[9] Despite the lack of profits in the early years, Bezos recognized that Amazon needed to grow and capture as much of the new online market as quickly as possible. His hope was that once his company had a large customer base, the profits would eventually follow.

On May 16, 1996, Bezos and his company were featured on the cover of the *Wall Street Journal*. The article was titled, "Wall Street Whiz Finds Niche Selling Books on the Internet." The article introduced Bezos and Amazon.com to many people for the first time. The article described the site as "an underground sensation for thousands of book-lovers around the world, who spend hours perusing its vast electronic library, reading other customers' amusing on-line reviews—and ordering piles of books."[10]

The article served as free publicity for the site, which had not spent any advertising money to promote itself in any other way. After the article ran in the *Wall Street Journal,* a new fresh batch of customers flocked to the site, and growth for the company continued to increase

Like Steve Jobs of Apple and Bill Gates of Microsoft, Jeff Bezos eventually became a world-famous CEO. In 1996, Bezos appeared on the cover of the *Wall Street Journal*.

quickly. By September 2016, the *New York Times* ran an article about Amazon.com. The interviewer asked Bezos if he was worried about competition from traditional bookstores. Bezos's response showed the confidence he had in the way the internet and home computer use would change retail in the coming years: "I'm actually more worried about two guys in a garage than Barnes & Noble," he said. "It's a totally different business, and the chains are going to have a lot of unlearning to do."[11]

> "I'm actually more worried about two guys in a garage than Barnes & Noble. It's a totally different business, and the chains are going to have a lot of unlearning to do."

Neither of the major brick-and-mortar bookstores, Barnes & Noble or Borders, even had websites in 1996. In early 1997, Barnes & Noble started selling books online exclusively through America Online Inc. (AOL). At the time, AOL had more than eight million subscribers. Barnes & Noble launched its own official website, barnesandnoble.com, later that same year. Despite having not yet made a profit, Amazon.com had sales of $147.8 million by 1997 and was gobbling up customers from the much larger established book chains.

With Amazon.com's continuing growth and increased sales, Bezos and his team started courting a new round of investors, this time venture capitalist companies. But a major investment came from an unsolicited phone call from Ramanan Raghavendran, who worked as a senior associate for the private equity firm General Atlantic Partners. Raghavendran called Bezos directly after reading about Amazon.com, and soon his company offered a small but sizeable investment and estimated Amazon's value at around $10 million.

Rather than accept the General Atlantic offer, Bezos and his team decided to carefully wait for an even larger offer. The strategy of waiting proved to be a good one. Soon another venture capital firm, Kleiner Perkins

In Amazon.com's early days, the busy Christmas season became a crisis. Employees often had to sleep over in the warehouse to ensure all the orders were shipped out in time.

Caufield and Byers, was hoping to invest in Amazon. com, too. With the competing interest from more than one firm, estimates of Amazon.com's value rose. Bezos finally chose to accept an investment offer of $8 million from Kleiner, who valued Amazon.com at $60 million. This gave Kleiner 13 percent ownership of Amazon.com.

The "Save Santa" Incident

As the holiday season approached in 1998, Amazon. com was receiving many orders but was having trouble keeping up with shipments. The situation quickly became an emergency and all employees had to stay late or overnight to help pack as many orders as possible. The frantic effort to ship everything out before the holidays became known as "Save Santa." Some employees had their friends and family help and often slept at Amazon.com or in their own cars overnight.

Despite Bezos's efforts to put measures in place to ensure the crisis would never happen again, the 1999 holiday season saw a rush of orders and Save Santa had to be implemented once more. Many employees took two-week shifts and were put up in nearby hotels by Amazon.com so they did not need to commute back home when it came time to sleep.[13]

The holiday crunch time taught the online retailer a lesson. For the 2017 holiday season, Amazon.com hired as many as 120,000 seasonal workers in 33 states at its fulfillment centers, sorting centers, and customer service sites to keep up with holiday orders.[14]

Amazon.com employee James Marcus wrote a memoir in 2004, called *Amazonia*, about his time at Amazon.com. Markus recalled the influx of investment money and said, "The cash from Kleiner Perkins hit the place like a dose of entrepreneurial steroids, making Jeff more determined than ever."[12] After the $8 million investment from Kleiner came innovation and expansion, and a push from Bezos to establish Amazon.com as one of the great internet companies of all time.

The Road from Books to Everything

As more book orders came in, work increased, and Amazon.com moved yet again to a 93,000-square-foot (8,640 sq m) space in Seattle. The ranks of employees swelled to almost 150.[15] Attempts were made to implement new innovative features with the hope of personalizing each user's experience upon visiting the website. One new feature, called Bookmatch, required users to rank a few dozen books. Based off the rankings, Bookmatch would then recommend new books that a customer might enjoy. The system did not work well because users did not always want to rate books. Bezos suggested an easier system in which new books were suggested based on what a customer had already purchased. The new feature, based off Bezos's suggestion, was called Similarities. The Similarities feature wound up replacing Bookmatch and helped to increase sales by accurately suggesting what customers might be interested in purchasing.

Bezos was very passionate about personalizing Amazon.com for the customer. He believed that new technology could produce data to help Amazon understand each customer in a personal way that had never been done before. In a 1998 speech to the Commonwealth Club of California, Bezos said, "Great merchants have never had the opportunity to understand their consumers in a truly individualized way . . . ecommerce is going to make that possible!"[16]

"It would literally be the stupidest decision any management team could make to make Amazon.com profitable right now."

By the beginning of 1997, Bezos began thinking about taking Amazon.com public—the status a company has when its stock is offered to anyone to purchase at a predetermined starting price per share.[17] When asked about Amazon.com's lack of profitability, Bezos told the *New York Times*, "We are not profitable. We could be. It would be the easiest thing in the world to be profitable. It would also be the dumbest." He explained that any profit the company might make right now should be spent on further improvements. "We are taking what might be profits and reinvesting them in the future of the business. It would literally be the stupidest decision any management team could make to make Amazon.com profitable right now."[18]

More investors were sought out, and many often asked if Amazon.com had plans to expand and start selling more than just books. Although Bezos did intend to eventually create a store that sold "everything," he did not let potential investors in on these plans, and he continued selling just books.[19]

Just less than two months before the company went public on the stock exchange, an article in the *Wall Street Journal* revealed that the company did intend to expand into areas other than books. Other financial information revealed to the public at the time showed the company's massive climb in sales from year to year. These factors made the company appealing to potential investors, even

Amazon.com became a publicly traded company on May 15, 1997. The stock was priced at $18 a share, but within one week the shares were trading below the initial $18 selling price.

though the company had not yet made a profit. That meant that investors had a chance to become part of that profit if the company did indeed expand as it intended and increase sales as it had been doing year after year.

This excitement over investments in websites such as Amazon.com in the late 1990s became known as the "dot-com bubble." The public invested a lot of money in the stock market based on the idea that the technology market would continue to grow. The initial public offering, or IPO, of Amazon.com was part of that big dot-com bubble.

The Amazon.com stock became available to the public for purchase on May 15, 1997. Before trading started, the stock was priced at $18 a share, well above the initial $13 that was first estimated for the filing with the Securities and Exchange Commission. According to the *Wall Street Journal*, "Instead of raising about $37 million in the IPO, the company ended up grossing $54 million." By the end of the first day of trading, the share price had increased to $23.50.[20]

The exuberance over Amazon.com did not last long, however. Only one week after the company's IPO, its shares were trading below the initial $18 share price. Even though the drop in price was not unusual, it did signal a coming downturn for internet companies that had been valued well above their actual worth.

CHAPTER SEVEN

The Dot-com Bust

● ●

Use of the internet grew quickly between the years 1995 and 2001, and so did excitement and speculation over the moneymaking potential of new online companies like Amazon.com. As excitement grew, investors and everyday consumers placed lots of money in the stock market to support and become part of internet company gains. As the stock market as a whole gained value, this period of growth became known as the "new economy." With the hope of making money quickly, many investors ignored traditional calculations often used to make a smart stock purchase. Typically, a company's stock share price is related to how much money the company earns. Many internet companies had not yet shown profits, but they were still growing quickly as a result of large investments.

The hype, false excitement, and often grandiose publicity that surrounded many internet startup companies, while also ignoring the reality that many were still unprofitable, became known as the dot-com bubble. By 1999, the dot-com bubble began to collapse. As investments dried up and companies were still not profitable, many ran out of money and went bankrupt. Investors referred to failed dot-com companies as "dot-bombs."

Amazon.com had to weather this period of time, along with countless other internet companies. Many of the calculated decisions made by Bezos, along with luck and good timing, would help Amazon.com through this difficult period. Eventually Amazon.com became one of the great internet success stories of all time. Back then, however, there was much uncertainty.

During the dot-com bubble many internet companies were overvalued when they entered the public stock market. The "bust" of the dot-com bubble caused the stock market to crash in 2000.

War of Words

As soon as Amazon.com went public on May 15, 1997, Jeff Bezos, his parents, and his siblings all became millionaires.[1] Because Bezos already had 9.88 million shares of Amazon.com stock from before the company went public, his shares became worth $177.8 million overnight.[2] Bezos owned 42 percent of the company, and his extended family owned another 10 percent. Altogether, the Bezos family had 52 percent of the voting power in Amazon.com going forward.

Early investors of Amazon.com also saw their bets on Bezos's online bookstore pay off. Despite the stock dipping below the initial IPO of $18 a share briefly, it did eventually climb in value.

Many people thought Amazon.com would fail against the retail strength of Barnes & Noble. *Fortune* magazine published a story on September 29, 1997, titled, "Why Barnes & Noble May Crush Amazon." The article stated that "All one needs, it would seem, is a Website to present the face that greets customers and takes their orders. Other parties handle the capital-intensive aspects of stocking inventory." Steven Riggio, chief operating officer of Barnes & Noble, was quoted as saying, "There was a mystique about how difficult it was to get started on the Web, but it's quickly fading."[3]

Customer Service

Despite competition with Barnes & Noble and its online store, Amazon.com continued to grow. It concentrated heavily on customer service and won over many loyal customers with Bezos's insistence on extra attention

As early investors in their son's company, Mike and Jackie Bezos became millionaires as soon as Amazon.com went public. Today, Jeff Bezos still holds the majority of the company's stock.

to detail. One costumer, Patricia Seybold, recalled receiving a package from Amazon.com. The softcover book she ordered was not in stock, so the hardcover version of the book had been delivered to her instead at no extra charge with a handwritten note explaining the issue.[4] Bezos continued to preach his "customer-centric" philosophy to the media and acted as showman every step of the way.

In 1997, Bezos traveled all the way to Japan to hand-deliver a book order to Amazon's one-millionth customer.[5] Just two years later in 1999, Bezos traveled to Boston, Massachusetts, to hand-deliver a set of golf clubs to Amazon.com's ten-millionth customer.[6]

By the end of 1997, Amazon.com had more than a million and a half active accounts and nearly $150 million in revenue. By this time, Bezos felt it was important to shift his efforts toward the company's internal dynamics and operation. According to Bezos, "We've basically gotten past the point where 70 to 80 percent of the risk was external and where we needed a huge amount of luck to get to where we are now. Now, all we need is a clear, consistent vision and the ability to execute on it very, very well at high speed."[7]

By the beginning of 1998, marketing executive Mark Breier informed Bezos of a survey that was done to inquire about people's book-buying habits. The survey revealed that many people did not buy books at all, making their chances of ever using Amazon.com slimmer than they had hoped. Rather than get upset by the news, Bezos was inspired and excited. He instructed Breier to form a "SWAT team" of new employees and begin researching which products were not readily available in physical stores that also could be easily shipped to customers. The list of possible new product categories included music, DVDs, and software.

> **"We've basically gotten past the point where 70 to 80 percent of the risk was external and where we needed a huge amount of luck to get to where we are now."**

Nisqually Earthquake

On Wednesday, February 28, 2001, employees at Amazon.com were holding a meeting in their Seattle office when the building started to shake. Objects fell to the floor, and sprinklers turned on, causing the employees to hide under their desks. It was a strong earthquake, measuring 6.9 out of 10 on the Richter scale.

During the quake, many of Bezos's *Star Trek* collectables fell to the floor. One employee, Tom Killalea, bravely retrieved his laptop off his desk and checked that the company website was still up and running.

After a long 45 seconds the earthquake ceased and everyone evacuated to the street. Bezos playfully left the building with one of his collectables—a hard hat shaped like a ten-gallon cowboy hat.

To reward Tom Killalea for his selfless deed during the Nisqually earthquake, Bezos gave him a "Just Do It" Award. Bezos gives out the awards periodically to employees who take initiative and do something to help the company. Northwestern University basketball player Dan Kreft supplied Bezos with his used sneakers, which were periodically given out as the prize for receiving a Just Do It Award.

Music became Amazon.com's first deviation away from just selling books, and soon after came movies—the most popular formats at the time being VHS tapes and DVDs. Eventually, Amazon would start selling tools, video games, and computer software. The online retailer once known as "Earth's Largest Bookstore" suddenly became "Amazon.com Books, Music and More."[8] The *more* in its slogan was an understatement.

The Everything Store or Bust

In order to expand Amazon.com so the company could sell more than just books, Bezos needed to raise more money. In May 1998, Amazon raised over $300 million by offering junk bonds, which are a type of high-risk debt that companies sell to raise money quickly.[9] In February 1999, Bezos raised a staggering $1.25 billion selling more bonds. At the time this was the largest bond offering of its kind. Overall, between 1998 and the year 2000, Amazon raised $2.2 billion from investors.[10]

With the large amounts of investment money Bezos raised, Amazon.com expanded by building new distribution warehouses, or distribution centers as another large competitor, Walmart, called them. A new Amazon.com distribution center was built in Fernley, Nevada, and existing warehouses were also acquired in Georgia, Kentucky, and Kansas.[11]

Bezos then went on a shopping spree and acquired many smaller companies. In August 1998, Amazon.com announced that it had purchased the Junglee Corporation, which allowed people to comparison shop on the internet for a variety of goods and fit nicely into

Bezos's idea of Amazon.com eventually becoming a true "everything store."

At the same time, Amazon announced the purchase of a company called Planet All, which ran a large internet e-mail address service. Planet All had 1.5 million members, and Amazon.com was hoping they would soon become new customers.[12]

With 3.1 million customers, Amazon had grown to become the most successful internet company at that point. Its sales for the first half of 1998 were $203 million—almost five times more than sales had been the previous year. Amazon.com's losses were still growing,

As Amazon.com grew in size, large fulfillment centers were built to handle orders. This 1,000,000-square foot (92,903 square meter) Amazon.com fulfillment center is located in Patterson, California.

too, although not as fast as they had been.[13] Bezos's wealth was also growing, and he was then worth $2.5 billion because of the value of the Amazon.com stock he held.

With all eyes on Amazon.com's incredible growth, Bezos told the *New York Times,* "We're at an inflection point where we are now looking at a broader range of products. Our focus has always been to help people find and discover things they want to buy."[14]

Bezos did not stop with the purchase of Planet All and the Junglee Corporation. During this period, Amazon. com purchased a film database called IMDB.com, a

1-Click Patent

New features were added to Amazon.com, such as the sales ranking of books and an innovative new feature called 1-Click. 1-Click would allow existing Amazon.com shoppers who had previously entered their payment information and shipping address to click one button to make purchases. Amazon.com trademarked 1-Click and would eventually sue Barnes & Noble in 1999 for infringement when it used a similar tool. Amazon won the lawsuit, and as a result Barnes & Noble had to remove its similar service from its website. Other companies like Apple would eventually license the trademarked feature from Amazon.com if they wished to use it on their website. Today 1-Click is a common fixture on Amazon.com and makes it very easy to shop without many steps to buy things.[15]

British internet bookseller called BookPages, a German internet bookseller called Telebuch, exchange.com, and a data-collection company called Alexa Internet. Bezos also invested in other dot-com companies such as Drugstore.com, Pets.com, Gear.com, Wineshopper. com, Greenlight.com, Homegrocer.com, and a delivery company called kozmo.com. Many of these companies did not survive after the dot-com bubble burst in the year 2000.

In 1999 Bezos started Amazon Auctions in an attempt to compete with the profitable internet auction company eBay. Amazon Auctions eventually became zShops. Over time these services evolved on Amazon. com so anyone could sell merchandise on the Amazon. com website.

After Amazon.com's success selling music and DVDs, Bezos chose toys and electronics at the start of 1999 as new markets for the company to expand into. In order to ensure Amazon.com had enough toys stocked for the holidays that year, $120 million was spent. After the holidays that year, Amazon had $50 million worth of unsold toys, and many were donated to Toys for Tots.[16]

Because the company was still not profitable, investors became cautious and started to sell their Amazon.com stock. Because of this activity, the company's stock price tumbled. In May 1999, the financial magazine *Barron's* reported,

> Just over a month ago, the stock market was indicating that Amazon was worth a remarkable $36 billion and that Bezos' own stake was worth $13 billion. But since early May, a lot of investors have been learning that a

good story does not always make a good stock. From an April high of 221 1/4, Amazon shares have been sliced nearly in half, to 118 3/4, cutting the company's worth to about $19 billion and reducing Bezos' fortune to $7 billion. The stock could fall a lot further.[17]

Because Amazon.com was still not profitable, it needed more money from investors to keep afloat. Just one month before the stock market crashed on March 11, 2000, Amazon.com secured $672 million from bond sales to investors in Europe. The dot-com bubble had burst, but Amazon.com had narrowly escaped the fate of many internet startups that were bought by other companies or went bankrupt. The Amazon.com mantra of "Get Big Fast" was replaced by "Get Our House in Order."

CHAPTER EIGHT

Boom After the Bust

••••••••••••••

After the dot-com bubble burst and the company's stock price fell, Amazon.com had to do some restructuring. In early 2001, an announcement was made that 15 percent of Amazon.com's workers would be laid off.[1] Many people who had just been hired lost their jobs as the restructuring took place.

Amazon.com briefly raised prices on some of the categories of goods to help earn more money. However, Bezos quickly rethought this decision after he met with Jim Sinegal, the founder and CEO of Costco. The men met in a Starbucks in the spring of 2001, and Sinegal explained to Bezos that he prized customer loyalty above everything else. Sinegal's words about customer loyalty resonated with Bezos, and in July 2001, Amazon.com rethought the brief price increases it had implemented only a few months earlier. Across all categories, it reduced prices on books, videos, and music by 20 to 30 percent.

During a quarterly conference call, Bezos told analysts, "There are two kinds of retailers: there are those

Costco cofounder Jim Sinegal explained to Bezos how he prized customer loyalty above everything else. Bezos took the words to heart and applied them to Amazon.com.

folks who work to figure how to charge more, and there are companies that work to figure out how to charge less, and we are going to be the second, full-stop." Bezos wanted Amazon.com to have "everyday low prices."

Growth and Innovation

By the year 2000, Amazon.com had achieved Bezos's goal of becoming a true "everything store." The myriad of product categories had expanded beyond just books and included toys, kitchen items, electronics, DVDs, videos, music, makeup, cameras, health supplies, video games, software, furniture, and even cars. The increase in categories was partially fueled by third-party sellers.

After false starts and hoping that Amazon Auctions and zShops could compete with eBay, a used book service, called Marketplace, launched on Amazon.com in November 2000. Unlike previous efforts to host small sellers, Marketplace would direct users to used copies of a book right alongside new copies of a book. Even if the customers did not make a purchase, Amazon.com collected a small commission on every sale a third-party seller might make. This innovative feature was not well received at first by publishers, and it caused friction for years. Bezos ignored the protests and only wanted more choices for Amazon.com customers, which he felt helped increase Amazon.com's overall customer base.

Another idea that helped increase customer loyalty to Amazon.com was free shipping. During the holiday seasons of 2000 and 2001, any customer who spent $100 or more was given free shipping on their order. This promotion had the effect of making people spend more than they had originally intended so they could take advantage of the free shipping. As a result, Amazon.com sales increased. By January 2002, the concept of free shipping became permanent and was named Free Super Saving Shipping. Customers who wanted free shipping would have to wait a few extra days for their orders to arrive, but they felt it was worth it to get the free perk. As time went on, the price threshold for free shipping lowered to $49, and eventually to $25. This concept would eventually become known as Amazon Prime, a paid membership program offered to any Amazon.com customer.

Another innovation that aided Amazon.com customers was called P13N. This was an abbreviation for the 13-letters between the *P* and *N* in the word "personalization." By 2001, the P13N technology began suggesting products to Amazon.com customers not just based on what they purchased but also based on what they were looking at.

Third-party sellers, new personalization innovations, and consistently low prices all paid off, even if only slightly. By January 2002, Amazon.com had its first profitable quarter, in which it earned $5 million. With the good news came a jump in Amazon.com's stock price as investors returned.

The pace of growth, expansion, innovations, and announcements at Amazon.com began to steadily increase. In 2000, Amazon launched Amazon.co.jp (Japan). The same year, third-party Amazon.com

Amazon Prime started as a free shipping service for frequent customers who spent $100 or more. In a 2018 letter to shareholders, Bezos revealed that the subscription service had more than 100 million members.

Marketplace launched as well as Free Super Saver Shipping for orders over $100. By October, the Camera & Photo Store launched, and in August, Amazon.com announced an alliance with Toys "R" Us and launched Amazon.fr (France). By May, Martha Stewart and Jeff Bezos posed together to announce the launch of the Amazon.com Kitchen Store.

The year 2001 also saw more innovations and announcements. In October, a free service called Look Inside the Book was launched, allowing customers to browse several pages of a book online just like they might if they were inside a physical bookstore.[2] Publishers were allowed to participate in the free service if they chose.

Alliances with home retailer Target and the bookstore Borders were both announced in 2001.[3] Amazon.com helped the retailers enter into online sales, and the partnerships helped to boost Amazon.com's selection of products. The partnerships with Toys "R" Us, Target, and Borders would eventually end, but they were helpful for Amazon.com at the time.

Despite the partnerships with Amazon.com, many brick-and-mortar retailers still struggled or failed in the coming years. Borders filed for bankruptcy protection in February 2011. No offers to buy the failing book retailer came, and by July 2011 it liquidated its remaining 399 stores and closed for good. Toys "R" Us accumulated a large debt of $5 billion and filed for bankruptcy protection on September 17, 2017.[4]

Amazon Prime

Bezos did not want Amazon.com to be only a store for purchasing physical merchandise on the internet. He also wanted Amazon.com to be a technology company that continually innovated to stay ahead of the competition.

Because of the success of Free Super Savings Shipping in February 2004, Amazon.com launched an annual membership free shipping service called Amazon Prime. The service provided free nationwide two-day shipping for an unlimited number of orders for customers who paid a $79 annual fee. For customers who ordered a lot from Amazon.com throughout the year, the service added additional savings to their shipping. Amazon Prime also guaranteed two-day delivery so customers would know when to expect boxes at their doors. For

The Tale of Two Alexas

Alexa, what's the weather going to be like today? The Amazon Echo is one of the most popular home devices on the market today. The intelligent personal assistant, however, is not the only "Alexa" that Amazon.com owns. On October 2005, Amazon.com launched Alexa Web Information Service on the Amazon Web Services website.[5] The company, Alexa Internet, was founded in 1996 and purchased by Amazon.com in 1999 for $250 million.[6] Alexa Internet, which is a subsidiary of Amazon.com, follows websites people visit and then offers suggestions about other Internet sites they might enjoy seeing. The company was named after the ancient Egyptian library of Alexandria."[7]

> "There's a good chance you're already one of them, but if you're not—please be responsible—join Prime."

loyal customers, Amazon Prime became another reason to shop exclusively through the website and not elsewhere on the internet. Since its inception, Amazon Prime has added many benefits to customers who pay the annual fee and join the service. According to Amazon.com, "Members receive benefits which include FREE fast shipping for eligible purchases, streaming of movies, TV shows and music, exclusive shopping deals and selection, unlimited reading, and more."[8]

By December 2017, Amazon.com announced that Amazon Prime same-day delivery and free one-day shipping would be available in more than eight thousand cities. Today Amazon Prime subscribers get access to Amazon.com's streaming cloud-based services, including Prime Video, Prime Music, and more. As the benefits included in the service increased so did the cost of joining.

In a 2016 letter to Amazon.com shareholders, Jeff Bezos mentioned Amazon Prime: "Prime has become an all-you-can-eat, physical-digital hybrid that members love. There's a good chance you're already one of them, but if you're not—please be responsible—join Prime," Bezos said.[9]

Although Amazon.com keeps its exact number of Prime subscribers a secret, in its filing with the Securities and Exchange Commission in early 2017, Amazon listed retail subscription services and said those services generated $6.4 billion in revenue in 2016. Guggenheim Securities analyst Robert Drbul estimated that Amazon.com has 65 million Prime members and as many as 80 million members globally.[10]

Amazon Vine

In 2007, Amazon.com launched yet another new program: Amazon Vine, "The Exclusive Club of Influential Amazon Voices." The program allows customers with many favorable reviews that customers found helpful to review products free of charge. Twice a month, Vine reviewers are given a list of products to choose from and then write reviews based on their honest opinion.

According to the Amazon.com Vine page, "Amazon Vine invites the most trusted reviewers on Amazon to post opinions about new and pre-release items to help their fellow customers make informed purchase decisions. Amazon invites customers to become Vine Voices based on their reviewer rank, which is a reflection of the quality and helpfulness of their reviews as judged by other Amazon customers. Amazon provides Vine members with free products that have been submitted to the program by participating vendors. Vine reviews are the independent opinions of the Vine Voices. The vendor cannot influence, modify or edit the reviews. Amazon does not modify or edit Vine reviews, as long as they comply with our posting guidelines. A Vine review is identified with the green stripe Customer review from the Amazon Vine Program."

Amazon Web Services

Another technology service launched by Amazon.com that became very important to the company was Amazon Web Services, or AWS. Launched in July 2002, Amazon Web Services started internally but quickly grew to offer its services to anyone who wanted to use them. According to Amazon.com, "Amazon Web Services (AWS) is a secure cloud services platform, offering compute power, database storage, content delivery and other functionality to help businesses scale and grow." [11]

Today, many other internet companies and government agencies use AWS, including Netflix, General Electric, the Central Intelligence Agency (CIA), and NASA. [12] This service allows companies to pay to run computer services without needing to buy computers and build systems themselves. One aspect of AWS is the Elastic Compute Cloud, or EC2. This service allows customers to pay only for exactly how much computing power they use. [13] Netflix, for example, is able to stream films directly to customers with these Amazon.com services.

Today AWS helps to generate a large portion of Amazon.com's profits. In 2012, Morgan Stanley estimated that AWS earned Amazon.com $2.2 billion, and in 2017 Amazon.com reported AWS revenue of $4.58 billion. According to Amazon.com, AWS is used by over 1,000,000 active users. [14] In 2017, AWS added 722 new features to the service. According to Bezos,

> Many characterized AWS as a bold—and unusual—bet when we started. 'What does this have to do with selling books?' We could have stuck to the knitting. I'm glad we didn't. Or did we? Maybe the knitting has

Jeff Bezos introduced the first Kindle e-reader at a 2007 news conference. Just like a real book, the wireless tablet can be read in direct sunlight with little to no glare.

• •

as much to do with our approach as the arena. AWS is customer obsessed, inventive and experimental, long-term oriented, and cares deeply about operational excellence.[15]

As Amazon.com grew, Jeff Bezos pushed the company's technology-based services more and more. In the coming years, Amazon.com would develop and release more technology and would even begin selling its own products. One product—the Kindle—would turn the publishing industry on its head.

CHAPTER NINE

Amazon Grows and Grows

• • • • • • • • • • • • • • • •

In 2004, Jeff Bezos started a secret experimental department of Amazon.com called Lab126. Bezos put Gregg Zehr in charge of the operation. Prior to working for Amazon, Zehr was the vice president of hardware engineering at Palm Computing.[1] Bezos wanted to develop an e-reader, or electronic book, to compete against Apple. The designers and engineers at Lab126 worked for nearly two years on what would eventually become known as the Kindle e-reader. According to Amazon.com, "Lab126 is an inventive San Francisco Bay Area research and development company that designs and engineers high-profile consumer electronic devices. We engineer devices like Fire tablets, Kindle e-readers, Amazon Fire TV, and Amazon Echo."[2]

Kindle E-Reader

On November 19, 2007, Amazon.com announced the Kindle e-reader—a handheld electronic device from

Rufus and the Dogs of Amazon

In the early days at Amazon.com, employees Eric and Susan Benson worked such long hours that they brought their dog Rufus to work with them. When Amazon.com moved to a new location in 1996, the new landlord allowed the Bensons to bring their corgi to work every day. Eventually, an Amazon.com building would be named after Rufus, who died in 2009.

Today at Amazon.com, many employees are still allowed to bring their dogs to work, and there is a page dedicated to the dogs of many Amazon.com employees. The webpage even lists "Rufus's Recommended Reading" and some facts about the first of the Amazon.com dogs.

which books, newspapers, and magazines could be read. The device was so popular that it famously sold out on Amazon.com within the first few hours of its release and was unavailable for months. The first Kindle device had a black-and-white six-inch e-Ink display, which imitates printed books and can be viewed in direct sunlight with little to no glare.

The first Kindle was not a touchscreen device, so there was a full keyboard as well as navigation buttons. The unit had 250 MB of internal memory and could be expanded to hold more with the addition of an SD memory card. It sold for $399 and offered users access to as many as ninety thousand books when it was first released.

During the Kindle launch event in New York City Bezos said, "We forget that this is a technology...but books are a technology. And the process for making them is a very sophisticated technology."[3]

Bezos did not want users to worry about having to pay extra to connect the Kindle to the internet, so a free internet connection was provided by Sprint to every Kindle owner. During the launch event, Bezos boasted about the Kindle's free internet access. "Everybody knows that using these wireless cell networks there's a data plan, a contract, a monthly bill. But we didn't like that, either. So we built Amazon Whispernet. It's built on top of Sprint's EV-DO network. There's no data plan, no contract, no bill. We pay for all of that behind the scenes so you can just read."[4] Kindle owners could buy books directly from Amazon.com on the device and download them to read.

The Amazon Echo is a voice-controlled home assistant speaker that was first launched in 2014. Echo owners can ask it to play music, answer questions, provide reminders, and much more.

An experimental browser included within the software allowed Kindle users to browse the internet, too. "If you were to print Wikipedia you'd need two miles of shelves. You can access Wikipedia from this device, so you have not only a dictionary but the world's greatest encyclopedia,"[5] Bezos said at the Kindle launch event.

Improvements were made to the Kindle throughout the years, and on November 15, 2011, Amazon.com released the Kindle Fire, a color tablet that could run apps and play games. The Fire was meant to compete with other tablets on the market, such as the Apple iPad. *Forbes* magazine estimated that about 43.7 million Kindles had been sold in total by the end of 2013.[6]

Alexa and the Amazon Echo

More technological innovations kept coming for Amazon.com, and in November 2014 the company announced another device from its secretive Lab126—a smart speaker called the Amazon Echo. The Amazon Echo device is always on and connected to the internet. The device also connects to smartphones via Bluetooth and plays music, researches information from the internet, does math calculations, and plays simple games.

Since its release to the general public in 2015, Amazon has released several updated versions of the Echo: the 2nd Generation Echo, the Echo Dot, and the Echo Plus. Video versions of the Echo, Echo Show, and the Echo Spot, were released in 2017 and 2018. The Echo Show and Echo Spot are both color touchscreen devices with cameras that allow users to place two-way video calls to one another.

Blue Origin

In the year 2000, Jeff Bezos secretly fulfilled a childhood dream and started a space exploration company called Blue Origin LLC. Bezos's goals are to make space travel common, but first he had to create advances so it is cheaper. Traditional rocket technology does not reuse rockets. Bezos's dream was to advance technology so that rockets could be launched into space and then come back to Earth and land safely for reuse. "One day, all rockets will have landing gear," Bezos said.[7]

Bezos privately funded his space company with around $500 million.[8] NASA also invested $3.7 million in 2010 and $22 million in 2011.[9] After more than a decade of development and rocket tests, Blue Origin finally made history. On November 24, 2015, Blue Origin's *New Shepard* space vehicle successfully flew to space and reached an altitude of 329,839 feet (100,535 m). The *New Shepard* space vehicle then returned safely to Earth and made a successful vertical landing back at the launch site in west Texas. The *New Shepard* space vehicle was named in honor of Alan Shepard, the first American in space.

Blue Origin is in direct competition with Elon Musk's space company, SpaceX, which announced it plans to take average citizens—not trained astronauts—on trips into space.

According to Amazon.com, "Echo is designed around your voice and is hands-free and always on—ask it for information, music, news, and weather from across the room and get results or answers instantly. Alexa is the brain behind Amazon Echo—since Alexa is built in the cloud and leverages AWS, it is always getting smarter and adding more functionality."[10]

Although the Amazon Echo with Alexa is perhaps the most well-known smart speaker and virtual assistant, it was not the first. Many other companies ventured into producing their own smart speaker assistants. Apple had already introduced its virtual assistant, Siri, in 2011. Siri was not part of a device but an app that ran on Apple's mobile devices' iOS operating system. In 2013, before

In 2013, it was announced that Bezos would buy the struggling *Washington Post* newspaper for $250 million. By 2017, the newspaper was declared profitable and had plans to hire dozens of new journalists.

Bezos had even started his secretive Lab126, Google had been busy working on its own voice-activated device. Google released a smart speaker, Google Home, in 2016. In 2018, Apple released a high-end Siri-enabled smart speaker called the HomePod to compete with Amazon's personal assistants.

> **"I didn't know anything about the newspaper business, but I did know something about the Internet."**

News and Food

While Jeff Bezos was busy running Amazon.com he also found time to accomplish a lot of other things, too. On October 1, 2013, Bezos finalized his purchase of the *Washington Post* for $250 million.

In an interview with Business Insider, Bezos said, "I didn't know anything about the newspaper business, but I did know something about the internet...That, combined with the financial runway that I can provide, is the reason why I bought *The Post*."[11]

By 2015, Bezos had helped to turn around the struggling 140-year-old newspaper. In October 2015 for the first time ever, the *Washington Post* received more visitors to its website than those visiting the *New York Times*. By 2018, the *Washington Post* reported profits for two consecutive years in a row.

When people were still digesting the idea of Bezos's purchase of the *Washington Post,* it was announced that Amazon.com would purchase the grocery store

On August 28, 2017, Amazon.com bought the upscale grocery chain Whole Foods Market for $13.7 billion. This sign in a California store helped announce the deal to customers.

• • • • • • • • • • • • • • • • • • • •

chain Whole Foods Market, Inc. for $13.7 billion.[12] Just before the deal was finalized on August 28, 2017, Amazon announced in a press release that "the two companies will together pursue the vision of making Whole Foods Market's high-quality, natural and organic food affordable for everyone. As a down payment on that vision, Whole Foods Market will offer lower prices starting Monday on a selection of best-selling grocery staples across its stores, with more to come."[13]

In early 2018, Amazon.com announced that Amazon Prime subscribers in Austin, Cincinnati, Dallas, and Virginia could get groceries delivered from Whole Foods for free within two hours of placing an order. It also announced Whole Foods labels would be sold through the Amazon.com website.[14]

The purchase of Whole Foods even benefitted Amazon.com customers waiting for delivery or return of packages. Amazon.com placed its self-service kiosks, called Amazon Lockers, in select Whole Foods markets to allow customers to easily pick up or return items shipped between them and Amazon.com.

On November 3, 2015, Amazon.com did something unusual. It opened its very first brick-and-mortar physical bookstore. The 7,400-square-foot (687 sq m) store is located in Seattle's University Village shopping center. The selection of books, which are all displayed with the cover facing outward, is based off Amazon.com user reviews.

On the first day, the store filled with customers in fifteen minutes, and a long line formed outside. Amazon Kindle e-readers were on display for people to try.

By 2017, Amazon.com opened its tenth bookstore, located in downtown Bellevue, Washington. Other Amazon.com bookstores were opened in San Diego, California, and Portland, Oregon. Other locations are already being planned in the San Francisco Bay Area, New York, Massachusetts, Chicago, and New Jersey.[15]

CHAPTER TEN

Amazon
and Beyond

· · · · · · · · · · · · · · · · · · · ·

Early in Amazon.com's history Jeff Bezos knew he wanted his company to sell "everything" and become the next "Sears" by allowing customers to shop from their own homes. Bezos succeeded with Amazon.com, but with the rise of internet shopping, traditional stores like Sears have not survived well. In April 2016, Sears Holdings announced the closing of dozens of its corporate-owned retail stores, including Kmart stores, which it owns. The one-time giant in the industry announced losses in the hundreds of millions of dollars, for several years in a row.[1] Sears Holdings reported a loss of $580 million for the fourth quarter in 2015, after a loss of $159 million in the same quarter in 2014.

Bezos's dream of succeeding online has overtaken and broken up the traditional retail market, changing the way people shop and the way companies operate.

Bezos founded Blue Origin LLC, a space exploration company, in 2000. In 2018 he told *Business Insider*, "I believe and I get increasing conviction with every passing year, that Blue Origin, the space company, is the most important work that I'm doing."

E-Commerce and the Death of Retail

As more and more people continue to shop online at Amazon.com for better prices and the convenience of having purchases delivered right to their door, the financial damage to traditional brick-and-mortar stores continues to mount.

Large stores like Sears and Macy's are called anchor stores at malls. These larger stores attract customers who then walk the malls and shop elsewhere at smaller stores. The smaller stores' lease agreements are often tied to the existence of the larger stores. When a large store like Macy's leaves a mall, smaller stores can break their lease agreements and attempt to pay a cheaper rent. The

Ten-Thousand-Year Clock

In 1995, inventor Danny Hillis had the idea to build a clock that would keep time for ten thousand years. He called it the Clock of the Long Now, to help people think critically about how our actions today affect the future. The clock is being constructed to tick just one time every year, for approximately ten thousand years.

After hearing about the project and meeting with Hillis, Bezos invested $42 million of his personal wealth to help back the project.[2]

On February 20, 2018, Bezos tweeted, "Installation has begun—500 ft tall, all mechanical, powered by day/night thermal cycles, synchronized at solar noon, a symbol for long-term thinking—the #10000YearClock is coming together thx to the genius of Danny Hillis, Zander Rose & the whole Clock team! Enjoy the video."

loss of a large store translates into fewer shoppers. This downward spiral creates empty stores, with less revenue for mall owners.[3] According to Credit Suisse analysts, more than 8,600 mall stores closed in 2017. The report also predicted that as many as 25 percent of all shopping malls in the United States would close in the coming years.

According to the *Chicago Tribune* many malls across the country today are repurposing old spaces for "housing, hotels, offices, fitness centers or even trampoline parks."[4]

Recently Amazon.com has made small but significant steps into the physical market. It has already

After competing with traditional book retailers for nearly a decade online, Amazon.com opened several physical bookstores across the country, including this one in New York City.

opened twelve physical bookstores, with more planned in the coming years. On January 22, 2018, Amazon.com opened its first experimental grocery store, Amazon Go, in Seattle. The futuristic store has no checkout lines and relies on sensors to see what customers leave with. Customers need to have their credit card on file with Amazon Go and are then billed for what they take.[5]

Drones

In the coming years Amazon.com plans to start delivering packages to customers with autonomous flying drones. In 2013, Jeff Bezos appeared on *60 Minutes* and explained to correspondent Charlie Rose how drones could deliver packages to people. "If you go back in time 18 years, I was driving the packages to the post office myself, and we were very primitive," said Bezos.[6] After the show, Bezos revealed a secret octocopter Amazon.com drone that can fly and deliver a package in as little as thirty

The World's Richest Person

On January 8, 2018, Jeff Bezos was declared the richest person in the world. According to the Bloomberg Billionaires Index, Bezos's net worth reached $105.1 billion. The reason for his staggering wealth has a lot to do with the number of shares he owns in his company. The news of Bezos's great success reflected back onto the company, making the stock rise even more. About a month after being declared the richest person in the world, Bezos's worth jumped another $20 billion.[7]

> **"If you go back in time 18 years, I was driving the packages to the post office myself, and we were very primitive."**

minutes. At the time, Bezos estimated it would be another four to five years before deliveries could start.[8] Today Amazon Prime Air has a webpage on the Amazon.com website. It reads, "We're excited about Prime Air—a delivery system from Amazon designed to safely get packages to customers in 30 minutes or less using unmanned aerial vehicles, also called drones. Prime Air has great potential to enhance the services we

Amazon Prime Air delivered its first package via drone in Cambridge, England, in 2016. Prime Air uses drones to deliver packages to customers in thirty minutes or less.

already provide to millions of customers by providing rapid parcel delivery that will also increase the overall safety and efficiency of the transportation system."

Amazon.com drones can fly at 60 miles (96 km) an hour and take a 20-mile (32-km) round-trip flight from a fulfillment center to a package drop-off point and the return flight back. Drone delivery packages can weigh up to 5 pounds (2.2 kilograms). After a delivery, the drone returns for a new battery and sets off on a new flight.[9]

Changing the World

The influence that Jeff Bezos has had on our world cannot be overestimated. He has single-handedly changed the way we shop, read books, and organize our lives. As a brainy kid and a Wall Street whiz, Bezos might have been destined for obvious success by most standards. But it is his ability to take risks, to trust his instincts, to work hard, and to always be searching for the next territory to explore that has set him apart.

Bezos is changing our world one venture at a time. For now it's e-commerce, groceries, media, and aerospace. Bezos has famously said that he has built his businesses on finding the things that *don't* change. By innovating and improving many of the basic pieces of our daily lives—books, TV, groceries—Bezos has guaranteed longevity for his brand. Only time will tell where his focus will be in the future, but it seems safe to say that we can look forward to many exciting, life-changing innovations from Jeff Bezos in the decades to come.

Chronology

1964 January 12, Jeffrey Preston Jorgensen is born to Jacklyn Gise and Ted Jorgenson.

1968 April 1, Jacklyn Gise marries Miguel Bezos, who adopts Jeff.

1982 Bezos enters Princeton University.

1986 Graduates from Princeton University with highest honors and a degree in electrical engineering and computer science.

1987 In February, becomes associate director of technology and business development at startup company Fitel.

1988 Begins working at Bankers Trust and becomes the company's youngest vice president.

1990 Takes a job as vice president at financial company D. E. Shaw.

1993 Marries MacKenzie Tuttle in West Palm Beach, Florida.

1994 Jeff and MacKenzie Bezos move to Seattle, Washington, and start Amazon.com.

1995 Amazon.com moves out of the Bezos's garage and into a small office in downtown Seattle.

1995 Amazon.com makes its second move to a larger office and operates at a loss despite good sales.

1996 Inventor and scientist Danny Hillis establishes the Long Now Foundation, which would later be invested in by Bezos so Hillis could begin work on the ten-thousand-year clock project.

1998 Bezos decides to sell more than just books at Amazon.com, expanding into music and movies.

2000 Bezos starts space-exploration company called Blue Origin.

2000 Amazon.com partners with Toys "R" Us to sell toys.

2001 Amazon.com partners with Target and Borders.

2007 November 19, Amazon.com announces Kindle e-reader.

2007 Amazon.com launches Vine program for customer reviews.

2011 Amazon.com starts Amazon Locker, a pickup and drop-off service for Amazon.com customers.

2013 Amazon.com purchases the *Washington Post* newspaper.

2013 Bezos announces that Amazon.com is developing a plan to use drones to deliver packages in the future.

2014 In November, Amazon.com announces the Echo, the in-home talking digital assistant that uses Alexa.

2015 Amazon.com opens its first physical bookstore.

2017 Amazon.com buys Whole Foods Market.

2017 Toys "R" Us files for bankruptcy protection.

2018 Amazon.com opens first experimental grocery store, Amazon Go, in Seattle.

2018 The *Washington Post* reports profits two consecutive years in a row.

2018 Amazon.com announces that Prime subscribers in some cities can get Whole Foods groceries delivered for free within two hours of placing order.

Chapter Notes

Introduction

1. "Jeff Bezos," Biography.com, https://www.biography.com/people/jeff-bezos-9542209.

2. Brad Stone, *The Everything Store: Jeff Bezos and the Age of Amazon* (New York: Little Brown and Company, 2013), p. 25.

3. Stone, pp. 32–33.

4. Stone, p. 39.

Chapter 1: Bezos in His Prime

1. "Annual Number of Worldwide Active Amazon Customer Accounts from 1997 to 2015 (in Millions)," statista.com, https://www.statista.com/statistics/237810/number-of-active-amazon-customer-accounts-worldwide.

2. Shep Hyken, "Sixty-Four Percent of U.S. Households Have Amazon Prime," Forbes.com, June 17, 2017, https://www.forbes.com/sites/shephyken/2017/06/17/sixty-four-percent-of-u-s-households-have-amazon-prime/#62a637a44586.

3. Brad Stone, *The Everything Store: Jeff Bezos and the Age of Amazon* (New York: Little Brown and Company, 2013), p. 142.

4. Rand Duren, "Jeff Bezos: At Amazon.com, He's the Mouth That Roared," *Dallas Morning News*, August 8, 1999, https://www.dallasnews.com/arts/arts/1999/08/08/jeff-bezos-at-amazon.com-he-s-the-mouth-that-roared.

5. Stone, p. 145.

6. Mike Tenney, "Amazon.com Founder to Celebrate 75th Anniversary of River Oaks Elementary," *Houston Chronicle*, January 28, 2004, http://www.chron.com/neighborhood/bellaire/news/article/Amazon-com-founder-to-celebrate-75th-anniversary-9772095.php.

7. Stone, p. 147.

8. Stone, pp. 3–4.

9. "Jeff Bezos Interview," Academy of Achievement, May 4, 2001, https://web.archive.org/web/20131005111700/http://www.achievement.org/autodoc/page/bez0int-2.

10. Luisa Yanez, "Jeff Bezos: A Rocket Launched from Miami's Palmetto High," *Miami Herald,* August 5, 2013, http://www.miamiherald.com/news/local/community/miami-dade/article1953866.html.

11. Ibid.

12. Ibid.

13. Cody Teets, *Golden Opportunity: Remarkable Careers That Began at McDonald's* (Kennebunkport, ME: Cider Mill, 2012).

14. Chip Bayers, "The Inner Bezos," Wired.com, March 1, 1999, https://www.wired.com/1999/03/bezos-3/.

15. Colin Dodds, "Jeff Bezos: Early Life and Education," Investopedia.com, https://www.investopedia.com/

university/jeff-bezos-biography/jeff-bezos-early-life-and-education.asp.

16. Mark Leibovich, "Child Prodigy, Online Pioneer," Washingtonpost.com, September 3, 2000, https://www.washingtonpost.com/archive/politics/2000/09/03/child-prodigy-online-pioneer/2ab207dc-d13a-4204-8949-493686e43415/?utm_term=.107b20dc3012.

Chapter 2: Studying at Princeton University

1. "Jeff Bezos Interview," Academy of Achievement, May 4, 2001, https://web.archive.org/web/20131005111700/http://www.achievement.org/autodoc/page/bez0int-2.

2. "Bezos Center for Neural Circuit Dynamics," Princeton University, http://pni.princeton.edu/centers/bezos-center-neural-circuit-dynamics.

3. "Jeff and MacKenzie Bezos Donate $15 Million to Create Center in Princeton Neuroscience Institute," Princeton University, December 13, 2011, http://giving.princeton.edu/news/2011/12/jeff-and-mackenzie-bezos-donate-15-million-create-center-princeton-neuroscience.

4. Bernard Ryan, *Jeff Bezos: Business Executive and Founder of Amazon.com* (New York: Ferguson, 2005).

5. "Jeff Bezos Interview," Academy of Achievement, May 4, 2001, https://web.archive.org/web/20130728160328/http://www.achievement.org:80/autodoc/page/bez0int-2.

6. Ibid.

7. Andrew Smith, "Brought to Book," *Guardian*, February 10, 2001, https://www.theguardian.com/books/2001/feb/11/computingandthenet.technology.

8. "Jeff Bezos: Engineering After Princeton," Youtube.com, https://www.youtube.com/watch?v=TYwhIO-OXTs.

9. "Jeff Bezos Biography: Success Story of Amazon Founder and CEO," astrumpeople.com, https://astrumpeople.com/jeff-bezos-biography/#Education.

10. "2010 Baccalaureate Remarks," Princeton University, May 30, 2010, https://www.princeton.edu/news/2010/05/30/2010-baccalaureate-remarks.

11. "Jeff Bezos Biography: Success Story of Amazon Founder and CEO," astrumpeople.com.

12. "Jeffrey P. Bezos on Passion," Academy of Achievement, achievement.org, http://www.achievement.org/video/bez0-pas-008.

13. "Jeff Bezos," preceden.com, https://www.preceden.com/timelines/32998-jeff-bezos.

14. Robert Spector, *Amazon.com: Get Big Fast: Inside the Revolutionary Business Model that Changed the World* (New York: HarperCollins, 2002), p. 372, Kindle.

15. "Jeff Bezos: Biography," thefamouspeople.com, https://www.thefamouspeople.com/profiles/jeff-bezos-4868.php.

16. "Jeff Bezos: Engineering after Princeton," Youtube.com.

17. Ibid.

18. "Jeff Bezos: Biography," thefamouspeople.com.

19. Chip Bayers, "The Inner Bezos," wired.com, March 1, 1999, https://www.wired.com/1999/03/bezos-3/.

Chapter 3: In the Working World

1. "Jeffrey P. Bezos on Preparation," Academy of Achievement, http://www.achievement.org/video/bez0-prp-009/.

2. History.com staff, "Invention of the PC," History.com, 2011, https://www.history.com/topics/inventions/invention-of-the-pc.

3. Richard L. Brandt, *One Click: Jeff Bezos and the Rise of Amazon.com* (New York: Portfolio, 2012), p. 34.

4. Ibid.

5. Ibid.

6. Brandt, p. 36.

7. History.com staff, "The Invention of the Internet," History.com.

8. Kevin Featherly, "ARPANET," Encyclopedia Britannica, May 11, 2016, https://www.britannica.com/topic/ARPANET.

9. Chip Bayers, "The Inner Bezos," wired.com, March 1, 1999, https://www.wired.com/1999/03/bezos-3/.

10. Brad Stone, *The Everything Store: Jeff Bezos and the Age of Amazon* (New York: Little Brown and Company, 2013), pp. 17–18.

11. Bayers, "The Inner Bezos."

12. Robert Spector, *Amazon.com: Get Big Fast: Inside the Revolutionary Business Model that Changed the World* (New York: HarperCollins, 2002), p. 505, Kindle.

13. Stone, p. 21.

14. Rebecca Johnson, "MacKenzie Bezos: Writer, Mother of Four, and High-profile Wife," Vogue.com, February 20, 2013, https://www.vogue.com/article/a-novel-perspective-mackenzie-bezos.

Chapter 4: Venturing Out on His Own

1. "Matrix News Extracts 1991–1994," http://www.quarterman.com/pictures/1991–1994–mn/.

2. Tom Robinson, *Jeff Bezos: Amazon.com Architect* (Edina, MN: Essential Library, 2009).

3. Brad Stone, *The Everything Store: Jeff Bezos and the Age of Amazon* (New York: Little Brown and Company, 2013), pp. 25.

4. Robert Spector, *Amazon.com: Get Big Fast: Inside the Revolutionary Business Model that Changed the World* (New York: HarperCollins, 2002), p. 694, Kindle.

5. Ibid.

6. Spector, p. 733.

7. Stone, p. 32.

8. Ibid.

9. Ibid.

10. Spector, p. 872.

11. Stone, pp. 28, 30.

12. Craig Cannon, "Employee #1: Amazon," Y Combinator, https://blog.ycombinator.com/employee-1-amazon/.

13. Stone, pp. 30–31.

14. Ibid, pp. 35.

15. Spector, p. 769.

16. Spector, p. 943.

17. Avery Hartmans, "15 Fascinating Facts You Probably Didn't Know About Amazon," *Business Insider,* April 9, 2017, http://www.businessinsider.com/jeff-bezos-amazon-history-facts-2017-4/#in-the-early-days-of-amazon-a-bell-would-ring-in-the-office-every-time-someone-made-a-purchase-and-everyone-would-gather-around-to-see-if-they-knew-the-customer-2.

Chapter 5: Early Ideas and Growth

1. Anne Quito, "This Is What Amazon's Homepage Looked Like When It Launched 21 Years Ago This Month," *Quartz*, July 18, 2016, https://qz.com/734985/this-is-what-amazons-homepage-looked-like-when-it-launched-21-years-ago-this-month/.

2. Robert Spector, *Amazon.com: Get Big Fast: Inside the Revolutionary Business Model that Changed the World* (New York: HarperCollins, 2002), p. 1157, Kindle.

3. Spector, p. 1320.

4. Spector, p. 1351.

5. Aurelia Jackson, *Amazon: How Jeff Bezos Built the World's Largest Online Store* (Broomall, PA: Mason Crest, 2014).

6. Brad Stone, *The Everything Store: Jeff Bezos and the Age of Amazon* (New York: Little Brown and Company, 2013), p. 37.

7. Stone, p. 38.

8. Shawn M. Carter, "If You Invested $1,000 in Amazon 10 Years Ago, Here's How Much You'd Have Now," cnbc.com, November 28, 2017, https://www.cnbc.com/2017/11/28/if-you-put-1000-in-amazon-10-years-ago-heres-what-youd-have-now.html.

9. Ibid.

10. Neal Karlinsky, "How a Door Became a Desk and a Symbol of Amazon," Blog.aboutamazon.com, January 17, 2018, https://blog.aboutamazon.com/working-at-amazon/how-a-door-became-a-desk-and-a-symbol-of-amazon.

11. Spector, pp. 1457–1458.

12. Spector, p. 1339.

13. "Amazon.com Sued for 'Earth's Biggest' Claim, *Seattle Times*, May 13, 1997, http://community.seattletimes.nwsource.com/archive/?date=19970513&slug=2538869.

14. Spector, p. 1369.

15. Spector, p. 1554.

16. Ibid.

Chapter 6: From Books to Everything

1. Brad Stone, *The Everything Store: Jeff Bezos and the Age of Amazon* (New York: Little Brown and Company, 2013), p. 44.

2. Robert Spector, *Amazon.com: Get Big Fast: Inside the Revolutionary Business Model that Changed the* World (New York: HarperCollins, 2002), p. 1627, Kindle.

3. Stone, p. 46.

4. Spector, p. 1664.

5. Patrick M. Reilly, "Barnes & Noble Sues Amazon Over Rival's Book-Selling Claims," *Wall Street Journal*, May 13, 1997, https://www.wsj.com/articles/SB863470993368690000.

6. Dow Jones, "Two Booksellers Settle Lawsuits," *New York Times*, October 22, 1997, https://www.nytimes.com/1997/10/22/business/two-booksellers-settle-lawsuits.html.

7. Spector, p. 1653.

8. Spector, p. 1664.

9. Spector, p. 1699.

10. G. Bruce Knecht, "Wall Street Whiz Finds Niche Selling Books on the Internet," *Wall Street Journal*, May 16, 1996, https://www.wsj.com/articles/SB832204437381952500.

11. Doreen Carvajal, "Titles, Titles Everywhere but Not a Page to Turn," *New York Times*, September 2, 1996, http://www.nytimes.com/1996/09/02/business/titles-titles-everywhere-but-not-a-page-to-turn.html.

12. Stone, p. 94.

13. Chris Isidore, "Amazon Wants to Hire 120,000 U.S. Workers for the Holidays," CNN, October 12, 2017, http://money.cnn.com/2017/10/12/technology/amazon-holiday-help/index.html.

14. Stone, p. 49.

15. Stone, p. 50.

16. "Pop-up Shops: Why We Still Need Them," *Retail This Week*, November 20, 2014, http://www.

retailthisweek.com/pop-up-shops-why-we-still-need-them/

17. Stone, p. 57.

18. Seth Schiesel, "Payoff Still Elusive in Internet Gold Rush," *New York Times*, January 2, 1997, http://www.nytimes.com/1997/01/02/business/payoff-still-elusive-in-internet-gold-rush.html.

19. Stone, p. 57.

20. "Investors Offer Amazon.com A Warm First-Day Reception," *Wall Street Journal*, May 16, 1997, https://www.wsj.com/articles/SB863709881148258500?mod=searchresults&page=1&pos=10.

Chapter 7: The Dot-com Bust

1. Paul R. LaMonica, "$1,000 in Amazon 20 Years Ago Is Now Worth $638,000," money.cnn.com, May 15, 2017, http://money.cnn.com/2017/05/15/investing/amazon-ipo-20-year-anniversary/index.html.

2. Robert Spector, *Amazon.com: Get Big Fast: Inside the Revolutionary Business Model that Changed the World* (New York: HarperCollins, 2002), p. 2838, Kindle.

3. Randall E. Stross, "Why Barnes & Noble May Crush Amazon Selling Books Online Was a Neat Concept. The Nation's Leading Bookstore Is Turning It into a Cutthroat Business. What's a Poor Startup to Do?," *Fortune*, September 29, 1997, http://archive.fortune.com/magazines/fortune/fortune_archive/1997/09/29/232065/index.htm.

4. Spector, p. 2635.

5. Spector, p. 2908.

6. Spector, p. 2647.

7. Spector, p. 2908.

8. Brad Stone, *The Everything Store: Jeff Bezos and the Age of Amazon* (New York: Little Brown and Company, 2013), p. 66.

9. Stone, p. 73

10. Stone, pp. 67–68.

11. Stone, p. 73.

12. Saul Hansell, "Amazon.com Is Expanding Beyond Books," *New York Times*, August 5, 1998, http://www.nytimes.com/1998/08/05/business/amazoncom-is-expanding-beyond-books.html.

13. Ibid.

14. Ibid.

15. "Amazon's Patent on One-Click Payments to Expire," *Business Insider*, January 5, 2017, http://www.businessinsider.com/amazons-patent-on-one-click-payments-to-expire-2017-1.

16. Stone, p. 85.

17. Jacqueline Doherty, "Amazon.bomb," *Barron's*, May 31, 1999, https://www.barrons.com/articles/SB927932262753284707.

Chapter 8: Boom After the Bust

1. Brad Stone, *The Everything Store: Jeff Bezos and the Age of Amazon* (New York: Little Brown and Company, 2013), p. 120.

2. "Look Inside the Book Program," Amazon. com, https://www.amazon.com/gp/feature. html?docId=1001119971.

3. Nick Wingfield, "Amazon.com, Target Plan Online Sales Partnership," *Wall Street Journal*, September 11, 2001, https://www.wsj.com/articles/ SB1000177752821017751.

4. Lauren Gensler, "Toys 'R' Us Files for Bankruptcy, but Will Keep Stores Open," *Forbes*, September 19, 2017, https://www.forbes.com/ sites/laurengensler/2017/09/19/toys-r-us-bankruptcy/#643d7b1c574a.

5. "History and Timeline," Amazon.com, http://phx. corporate-ir.net/phoenix.zhtml?c=176060&p=irol-corporatetimeline.

6. Jon Christian, "The Two Alexas," *The Outline*, October 6, 2017, https://theoutline.com/post/2377/why-does-amazon-have-two-completely-different-products-called-alexa?zd=2&zi=usml5n5z.

7. "Amazon Prime," amazon.com, https://www.amazon. com/p/feature/zh395rdnqt6b8ea.

8. Ryan Mac, "Jeff Bezos Calls Amazon 'Best Place in the World to Fail' in Shareholder Letter," *Forbes*, April 5, 2016, https://www.forbes.com/sites/ ryanmac/2016/04/05/jeff-bezos-calls-amazon-best-place-in-the-world-to-fail-in-shareholder-letter/#6acf0a9e7bc5.

9. Krystina Gustafson, "Amazon Hints at One of Its Best-Kept Secrets: How Many Prime Members It Has," cnbc.com, February 17, 2017. https://www.cnbc.

com/2017/02/17/amazon-hints-at-its-big-secret-how-many-prime-members-it-has.html.

10. "The Exec Behind Amazon's Alexa: Full Transcript of Fortune's Interview," *Fortune*, July 14, 2016, http://fortune.com/2016/07/14/amazon-alexa-david-limp-transcript/.

11. "History and Timeline," phx.corporate-ir.net. http://phx.corporate-ir.net/phoenix.zhtml?c=176060&p=irol-corporatetimeline.

12. Stone, p. 211.

13. Richard L. Brandt, *One Click: Jeff Bezos and the Rise of Amazon*.com (New York: Portfolio, 2012), p. 179.

14. Benjamin Wootton, "Who's Using Amazon's Web Services?" *Contino*, January 26, 2017, https://www.contino.io/insights/whos-using-aws.

15. Liam Tung, "Jeff Bezos: AWS Is a $10bn Business Made Possible by Failing Frequently," *ZDNet*, April 6, 2016, http://www.zdnet.com/article/jeff-bezos-aws-is-a-10bn-business-made-possible-by-failing-frequently/.

Chapter 9: Amazon Grows and Grows

1. Jillian D'Onfro, "Here's What Amazon Did for the Head of Its Kindle Lab on His Tenth Anniversary with the Company," *Business Insider*, December 23, 2014, http://www.businessinsider.com/amazon-gregg-zehr-lab126-2014-12.

2. "We Are Amazon Lab 126," Lab126, https://www.lab126.com/.

3. Jillian D'Onfro, "Here's What Amazon Did for the Head of Its Kindle Lab on His Tenth Anniversary with the Company."

4. Ryan Block, "Live from the Amazon Kindle Launch Event," engadget.com, November 19, 2007, https://www.engadget.com/2007/11/19/live-from-the-amazon-kindle-launch-event/.

5. Ibid.

6. Trefis Team, "Estimating Kindle E-book Sales for Amazon," *Forbes*, April 2, 2014, https://www.forbes.com/sites/greatspeculations/2014/04/02/estimating-kindle-e-book-sales-for-amazon/#979faca23c65.

7. "Amazon Echo Now Available to All Customers," Amazon.com, June 23, 2015, http://phx.corporate-ir.net/phoenix.zhtml?c=176060&p=irol-newsArticle&ID=2061798.

8. Jeff Foust, "Bezos Investment in Blue Origin Exceeds $500 Million," *Space News*, July 18, 2014, http://spacenews.com/41299bezos-investment-in-blue-origin-exceeds-500-million/.

9. Charles Fishman, "Is Jeff Bezos' Blue Origin the Future of Space Exploration?" Smithsonian.com, December 2016, https://www.smithsonianmag.com/innovation/rocketeer-jeff-bezos-winner-smithsonians-technology-ingenuity-award-180961119/.

10. "Commercial Crew Program: Launch America," NASA, https://www.nasa.gov/content/commercial-crew-program-the-essentials/.

11. Eugene Kim, "Amazon CEO Jeff Bezos Signed the $250 Million Washington Post Deal with No Due Diligence," *Business Insider*, March 24, 2016,

http://www.businessinsider.com/amazon-ceo-jeff-bezos-bought-washington-post-with-no-due-diligence-2016-3.

12. Nick Turner, Selina Wang, and Spencer Soper, "Amazon to Acquire Whole Foods for $13.7 Billion," Bloomberg.com, June 16, 2017, https://www.bloomberg.com/news/articles/2017-06-16/amazon-to-acquire-whole-foods-in-13-7-billion-bet-on-groceries.

13. Ibid.

14. Jordan Valinsky, "Amazon Prime Members Can Get Free Two-Hour Delivery from Whole Foods," CNN Money, February 8, 2018, http://money.cnn.com/2018/02/08/news/companies/amazon-whole-foods-delivery/index.html.

15. Jillian Stampher, "Amazon to Open 10th Brick-and-Mortar Bookstore, Second in Seattle Region, Later This Year," Geek Wire, March 8, 2017, https://www.geekwire.com/2017/amazon-open-10th-brick-mortar-bookstore-second-seattle-region-later-year/.

Chapter 10: Amazon and Beyond

1. Chris Woodyard, "78 Sears, Kmart Stores to Close; See the List," *USAToday*, April 22, 2016, https://www.usatoday.com/story/money/business/2016/04/21/sears-close-78-more-kmart-and-sears-stores/83357662/.

2. Brad Stone, *The Everything Store: Jeff Bezos and the Age of Amazon*. (New York: Little Brown and Company, 2013), p. 63.

3. Laura Sanicola, "America's Malls Are Rotting Away," CNN Money, December 12, 2017, http://money.cnn.com/2017/12/12/news/companies/mall-closing/index.html.

4. Lauren Zumbach, "Fighting for Their lives, Malls Reinvent Themselves for the Experiential Set," *Chicago Tribune*, June 9, 2017, http://www.chicagotribune.com/business/ct-struggling-mall-redevelopments-0611-biz-20170609-story.html.

5. Jeffrey Dastin, "Amazon's Automated Grocery Store of the Future Opens Monday," Reuters, January 21, 2018, https://www.reuters.com/article/us-amazon-com-store/amazons-automated-grocery-store-of-the-future-opens-monday-idUSKBN1FA0RL.

6. "Amazon's Jeff Bezos Looks to the Future," CBSnews.com, December 1, 2013, https://www.cbsnews.com/news/amazons-jeff-bezos-looks-to-the-future/.

7. "Bloomberg Billionaires Index," Bloomberg.com, March 11, 2018, https://www.bloomberg.com/billionaires/.

8. "Amazon Unveils Futuristic Plan: Delivery by Drone." CBSnews.com, December 1, 2013, https://www.cbsnews.com/news/amazon-unveils-futuristic-plan-delivery-by-drone/.

9. Steven Levy, "Amazon Is Dead Serious About Delivering Your Goodies by Drone," Wired.com, March 31, 2017, https://www.wired.com/2017/03/amazon-is-dead-serious-about-delivering-your-goodies-by-drone/.

Glossary

ballistics The study of the effects of bullets or other firearms.

bankruptcy The state of having no funds to repay debts.

book broker A company that buys and sells books for others.

brick-and-mortar Term used to refer to physical stores, as opposed to online stores.

capital Money or other wealth for investing in or starting a company.

Chapter 11 Protection from creditors that allows a bankrupt company or individual to reorganize.

computer protocol A set of rules that helps different and often incompatible computers communicate over a network.

headhunter A person who identifies possible candidates for jobs.

hedge fund A group of investors that can make investments that are at a higher risk than those made by traditional financial groups.

IPO Initial public offering, or a company's first entry into the stock exchange.

junk bond A high-risk borrowing of money used to gain money quickly.

modem A device that allows transmission of information between computers using landlines.

patent Legal right for a company to sell or own an invention or idea for a period of time.

profitable Having a financial gain over and above the expenses put out.

quantum mechanics Branch of physics that concentrates on the activities inside of atoms.

startup A newly established business.

trademark Symbol, word, or words legally registering a company.

Further Reading

Books

Brandt, Richard L. *One Click: Jeff Bezos and the Rise of Amazon.com.* New York: Portfolio, 2012.

Spector, Robert. *Amazon.com: Get Big Fast: Inside the Revolutionary Business Model That Changed the World.* New York: HarperCollins, 2002.

Stone, Brad. *The Everything Store: Jeff Bezos and the Age of Amazon.* New York: Little Brown and Company, 2013.

Strand, Jennifer. *Jeff Bezos.* Minneapolis, MN: ABDO Publishing, 2016.

Websites

Biz Kids

http://bizkids.com
A website dedicated to students who are interested in business and entrepreneurism.

Lemonade Day

https://lemonadeday.org
A website that offers advice to young people who want to start a business.

Index

126